MW01641713

We Meet After Dark

Stephanie Courtland

Stoneveil Publishing

For my children: Camron & Courtney.

and for Mom. Our blood is forever.

Chapter One

Love was a lie. Sadie Daniels believed that more than anything. As she lay on her bed flipping through channels, she stopped for a moment on a romantic comedy starring Sandra Bullock. Sadie wondered if she would ever see love as more than a sham. Her roommate and best friend, Hayden, adored these types of films. “Love and laughs,” she’d say. “How can anyone not like that?”

For Sadie, it was quite simple. She hated rom-coms because they were unrealistic. No matter how screwed up the circumstances, there was always a happy ending. Life wasn’t made for happy endings – not from where Sadie stood. It wasn’t even a boy who first broke Sadie’s heart and left her in a place of perpetual doubt; the disappointment of romantic relationships would come later. The first person to shatter her belief in unconditional love had been her older sister, Sarah. A woman she’d never even met.

Three weeks after Sadie’s birth, her twenty-year-old sister disappeared. Their parents never said what led Sarah to leave their house on that cold November night. Later, when Sadie was fifteen, she sneaked into Sarah’s bedroom, an unchanged time capsule with posters peeling from the wall and vintage clothes hanging in the closet. Rummaging through her sister’s dresser, she found a small box, and inside was a letter. That was when Sadie discovered the truth of why Sarah left.

Sarah was afraid she would never live up to the expectations of her parents or the world she inhabited. She had written: *"What if, when the end comes, I have nothing to show for the life I lived? My existence is inevitable, but if I'm to keep going, I have to do that somewhere else. Please tell Sadie I love her, and I will always be thinking of her. I pray she never knows the world that I do."*

Sarah was selfish; Sadie believed that wholeheartedly. When Sarah moved forward alone, she never stopped to think about what she was leaving behind. Sadie grew up lost in her sister's shadow, even when Sarah wasn't there to cast it. Her parents pretended Sadie was enough, but it amounted to a quiet, polite indifference. So, when Sadie left for college and then later moved to Brave Beach with Hayden, they didn't seem to mind.

Sadie closed her eyes and listened to the rain fall hard on the one-story beach house. It tapped a steady beat that made her yawn. While she might have been unlucky in love, Sadie had won the real estate lottery when Hayden's father offered them his grandmother's beach house—a weathered cottage nestled along the Washington coastline. Hayden was named after her great-grandmother, and it seemed a fitting tribute that she now slept in her namesake's bedroom.

Of course, Hayden hadn't been her grandmother's real name. Back in the day, she was an actress, part of the tail-end of the silent film era. According to her modern-day IMDB page, Hayden Parker was born Alma Vásquez De León in 1911. She died only twenty-seven years later during an influenza outbreak. The girls hung a picture of her in the living room, a studio portrait in rich black and white. Hayden resembled her great-grandmother; she had the same thick black hair and sun-kissed skin, with a dash of freckles across the bridge of her nose. When she smiled, two deep dimples appeared on her cheeks.

Sadie met Hayden in college. Hayden was the proverbial party girl, and Sadie the shy wallflower out on her own for the first time. It was a stereotypical pairing, but their ability to see the humor in the absurdity of life made them inseparable. They both dropped out during their sophomore year and moved to the beach house. They found jobs and managed to pay their bills, helped by the fact that Hayden's father didn't ask much in the way of rent.

Sadie fished under the covers for the remote and turned off the television. At the foot of her bed was a fat black cat she named Shadow. You couldn't really call him her cat; he was feral. He roamed the beach or climbed the cliffs near the ocean, and no matter how much she tried to tame him, Shadow never stayed put. She had found him on the porch that evening hiding from the rain, so she scooped him up and let him spend the night.

She tapped her fingers against the bed, and Shadow looked up with bright green eyes. "Come here, you," she murmured. The cat yawned and stretched before making his way up the mattress to the pillow beside hers. "Goodnight, Shadow." She closed her eyes and started counting backwards from ten. She was asleep before she reached four.

Sadie awoke the next morning to the shrill beep of the alarm clock. She rolled over and quickly silenced the intrusion. Shadow was still curled beside her, looking like a furry black pillow. Sadie walked to the window and looked through the slats in the blinds. She took a deep breath, marveling at the waves rushing the sand. There was no sign of the rain from the night before, only salty air and warm sunshine.

As she stepped out into the hall, the aroma of her friend's cooking made her smile. Hayden was in the kitchen dancing around the stove, singing into a spatula. When she noticed Sadie take a mug out of the cabinet, she turned the music down.

"You're just in time for breakfast," Hayden said, beaming. "I've got quesitos in the oven and eggs in the pan."

Hayden had grown up on quesitos, a Puerto Rican puff pastry filled with sweet cream cheese and glazed with honey. Her mother made them every weekend; now Hayden did the same.

Sadie filled her mug to the brim with coffee. "This smells fantastic."

"You working today?" Hayden asked. She tried to flip her egg and frowned as the yellow yolk started spreading across the skillet. "Shit," she muttered, before turning the fried eggs into a scramble.

"Yeah, double shift tonight. I'll be off by eleven."

Hayden shook her head. "That's bullshit. You have no business working all those hours. When is Rick going to hire more staff?"

"Well, Leah has a big test tomorrow, so I told Rick I would take her shift so she could study. And he's hired more people for the day shift. It's just been hard finding people to work the bar at night."

"That's the problem with this town," Hayden said as she piled the eggs onto two paper plates. "Too many bars, too many tourists, and never enough locals to fill the slots."

They carried their breakfasts to the living room and sat on the shaggy carpet. They hadn't been able to afford a dining set when they moved in, so the living room became their eating quarters. The habit stuck; even after they purchased a small table and chairs, they still preferred the floor and the coffee table.

"You look like shit, mama," Hayden said, her mouth full of eggs. "You get wasted while I was out last night?"

"I hate to disappoint you, but no. I guess I haven't been sleeping great lately."

"Well," Hayden said, pointing her fork at Sadie to emphasize her point. "You know what that's about, don't you?"

Sadie sighed. "Don't say it, Hay."

"But it's true! I saw it on YouTube. It's a scientific fact that everything bad in life comes from a lack of sex."

Sadie sat back, her palms resting on the floor. "I don't think my sleepiness is coming from not getting laid. If anything, you'd think I'd have more time to actually sleep."

"How long has it been since you got some?" A sly smile spread across Hayden's face. She leaned forward, waiting.

"Okay, so it's been a while. I'm busy."

"I'm busy, too, girl. And I can promise you that I don't let a week go by without taking care of business. At the very least, you should be taking care of yourself. Orgasms lead to a longer life."

Sadie laughed softly. "Did you see that on YouTube, too?"

"Nope. I saw that on TikTok."

They laughed together for a few seconds before Sadie's expression faded. "There's just no one I'm interested in," she said, looking down at her plate. Maybe Hayden was right. It had been four months since her breakup with Kevin Bryan, and since then, she had thrown herself into work just to avoid the process of learning to live without him. She lifted her eyes and shrugged. "I miss him."

"Sweetie, it's time to let go. Kevin was a Grade-A asshole, and we both know it. Maybe you should think about going back to school or something."

"Oh, I'm sure that would make my parents ecstatic. There's no way they'd beam with pride over a daughter who manages a bar."

"Who cares if they're happy? You're the one who has to be happy. Besides, it's not just a bar. You guys have live bands and rare liquor. It's a cool job."

"Rick does know his liquor," Sadie admitted. "It's a cool job to me, but does it make me happy?"

"I don't think a job is supposed to make you happy unless you're a Kardashian."

Sadie shook her head with a smile and finished her coffee. "I was happy with Kevin."

"No, you were not. You pretended to be happy with Kevin, and when you couldn't pretend anymore, you stopped."

"Why can't I be happy without a guy? I live on the beach and wake up to the ocean. I'm twenty-four years old, and I feel like I'll never know what I want to be when I grow up."

"You mean, when you *actually* grow up?"

There was a pause before both girls started to laugh. "You're a goober," Sadie said with a wink.

"It's all part of my charm. Listen, why don't we hang out after your shift? Some band is playing on the pier; it could be fun."

"Yeah, that sounds really good, actually." Sadie forced a smile. She was going to have fun even if it killed her.

The duties of managing a bar were not easy, despite what her parents thought. Rick's Place was one of the most popular venues in Brave Beach, mostly because the owner put so much effort into local talent. Rick had opened the bar in the late 90s, and when Sadie moved to town, he gave her a job despite her lack of experience. There was something fatherly about him that appealed to her. He was different from her own father; Rick seemed proud of her no matter the size of her accomplishment. Alphabetizing the inventory could elicit praise for hours.

It was just after 9 p.m. on Tuesday when Rick came through the back doors. Sadie was sitting behind the bar reading a book. Since it was a slow night, she set the book down and immediately started preparing an Old Fashioned – his favorite.

"Hello, Peanut!"

Rick was shorter than her father, with a full head of brown hair sprinkled with gray and tied back into a tiny ponytail. He wore glasses that slipped down the bridge of his nose every few minutes. She and her co-worker, Leah, often made a game out of counting how many times a shift he had to push them back up.

He walked behind the bar and gave her a gentle pat on the head. "How are we doing tonight?"

"Not bad. Just a regular Tuesday."

"Here, I brought you a snack." Rick set a white paper bag on the counter. Inside were a salted pretzel and a chocolate chip cookie from Blazing Bakery.

"That was nice of you." She tore the pretzel in half and offered it to him.

"Oh, no thank you, Sadie. I'm trying to watch my figure." He laughed and gave his stomach a pat.

She frowned playfully. "Come on, you know you want some."

Rick couldn't say no and popped the piece into his mouth. "Yes, just what I needed."

Sadie was about to ask about the week's shipments, but the sound of a revving engine and squealing tires forced them toward the front window. A silver BMW convertible pulled into a parking space. Sadie had seen the car before and the young men inside it. Most nights they stayed near the pier, but sometimes they drove down the strip slowly, looking for something. She felt Rick's hand on her shoulder.

"Stay here," he told her. "I'll handle this."

"Do you know them?"

"They've been in here before," he said, his lips pursed. "I told them not to come back."

"Why?"

Rick looked at her with concern. "Those boys do nothing to benefit Brave Beach. I've never seen any of them working a real job. No, they just drive the strip talking to women and starting fights. Trust me, Peanut. I want this place to stay safe. Those boys are bad news."

The front door opened, and the brass bell chimed. Sadie took the man in, his warm brown skin, the fitted leather jacket, and the red Converse. His black hair was cut tight against his scalp with razor-clean edges. Handsome and tall with broad shoulders, he reminded Sadie of a rapper Hayden listened to.

"What are you doing here?" Rick asked, his voice hushed.

"Looking for a drink," the man said.

Rick crossed his arms. "I believe we had this discussion. There are plenty of bars on the strip; you're welcome in all of those but mine."

The man's gaze fell on Sadie. She pretended to read her book, but her eyes drifted.

"Come with me," Rick barked. He turned back to Sadie. "I'll be just a minute. Oscar and I need to have a conversation."

Sadie watched as they left. How did Rick know his name? She returned her attention to her book and was so lost in thought she didn't notice one of the other passengers enter and sidle up to the bar. A tap on the wood made her jump.

"Excuse me, can I get some help?"

She set her book down. "Sorry. What can I get you?"

"Surprise me. Just make me something most people never order."

Sadie thought for a second. "Okay, I'll make you a Sazerac. Ever had one?"

He smiled. "Can't say that I have. I'm betting Dylan has, though. He's somewhat of a connoisseur when it comes to booze." He pointed over his shoulder to a man leaning against the BMW, smoking. "That's him."

Sadie nodded as she reached for the rye whiskey and bitters. She grabbed a chilled glass and rinsed it with a spray of absinthe, the herbal scent filling the air. As she reached into the stock cabinet for sugar cubes, she felt his eyes on her. When she turned around, he was flipping through her book.

"This any good?" he asked.

She finished the drink and set it aside while he thumbed through the pages. For a moment, she took him in. The dark brown hair that flopped around his eyes, the army-green gaze that sparkled under the lights. Tattoos peaked from under his collar, and on his right forearm was a broken heart. If he was a threat, she didn't feel it.

"You want my opinion on Poe?"

"Yeah, I do. I vaguely remember him from high school, but I couldn't tell you the name of one thing he wrote." He leaned into the bar, bringing himself closer.

"Well, for a compilation, this is a pretty good one."

"What's your favorite?"

She thought for a few seconds. "The Raven," she finally said.

"Do you know where I could buy this?"

"Online," she laughed. "Or the bookstore on the far end of the strip."

"Well, thank you, Sadie."

"How do you know my name?"

He pointed to the embroidery on her work shirt. "I'm assuming that's you."

She tried to hold back a smile. If she didn't know better, she'd say he was flirting and she was flirting back. It felt strange, but the butterflies in her stomach felt good.

"Are you going to try that drink or not?"

"I was just about to," he said, raising the glass. But before he could taste it, Oscar returned, looking annoyed.

"Tony! Let's get out of here."

She looked from Oscar back to the man. "So, your name is Tony?"

"Yep, that's me. And it looks like my ride is ready to jet. Rain check?"

"Of course," Sadie said. "I'm not going to forget how to make it."

"Tony!" Oscar called.

"See you around, Miss Sadie."

Tony followed Oscar out, stopping to smile at Rick before glancing back at her. Just as he stepped over the threshold, Rick caught him by the arm. "Are you going to pay for that drink?"

Tony smirked and pulled a few bills from his wallet, shoving them into Rick's hand. "The extra is her tip," he grinned. Rick let him go with a shove, and Tony went out the door laughing.

Sadie watched as the car sped out of the lot.

"Sadie Daniels," Rick said, shaking his head.

"What?"

"What did I say about those boys?"

She laughed. "Rick, come on. Tattoos and a smart mouth don't make someone a villain. They're no different than the bands you hire."

"Maybe," he said. "You're a grown girl, Sadie. I'm not your father. But I'm pretty sure your parents wouldn't want you messing with a boy like that."

She flinched at the thought of her parents. They were probably sitting across from one another at the dinner table right now, the only sound the scrape of utensils. Even though Sadie held Sarah responsible for her childhood, she still heaped the blame on her parents for the cold silence that followed.

"It wasn't like that, Rick," she said, ready to end the conversation. "You have nothing to worry about."

"Good." He put a hand on her shoulder. "Because I do worry about you, kiddo. You're like a daughter to me."

A few hours later, while counting the till, Sadie was still thinking about Tony. He sparked her interest. She hadn't even looked at a guy since Kevin, so the fact that a stranger had captured her attention this quickly had to mean something.

"We did pretty well this evening," Rick said as they stepped outside and he locked the door. "Especially for a weekday. I may have to give you a raise."

"You already do too much for me, Rick."

He let out a hearty laugh. "You know, Sadie, you're the first woman I ever met who turned down more money."

She smiled. "Well, if you give me a raise, you have to give one to Leah, too."

He walked her to her car. "That was my plan all along."

Chapter Two

It was midnight, the point where night becomes its darkest. Oscar, Dylan, and Tony drove to the other side of the strip and to one of their favorite bars. There was something about walking into a crowded space and feeling everyone's eyes on you that never got old. As the three of them stood near the entrance, Oscar immediately focused on a brunette sitting alone at the bar.

"See something you like?" Dylan asked, an unlit cigarette dangling from between his lips.

"I do indeed." Oscar smirked. The girl noticed them now, and when Oscar smiled at her, a pink blush spread across her cheeks. She turned away from him quickly.

Dylan swiped a glass off the tray of a passing cocktail server. He downed it in one long gulp, then handed the empty glass back to her with a wink. She giggled with amusement and headed back toward the bar for a replacement. They were regulars here, and that gave them a lot of room to do as they pleased.

"We'll wait in the car," said Tony. "Just don't take too long."

"Do I ever? I'll see you in ten."

Christy could still feel the man watching her, but when she glanced over her shoulder, he was gone. Then the smell of coriander and lavender entered the space, and when she looked to her left, he was sitting on the stool beside her. He was tailored and well put together, wearing a gold chain with a diamond-encrusted letter *O* hanging off it.

"Hey," he said with a soft smile. "Can I get you a drink?"

For a moment it felt like her voice was trapped inside her throat, pushing and fighting to get out. Up close and under the neon lights, his eyes seemed to sparkle in a way that was unnaturally beautiful. He tilted his head to the side and held her stare.

"Yes, I would love one." She heard the words but couldn't remember forming them in her head prior.

"Hey, boss." He motioned for the bartender and pointed at her beer. "Two of these."

Christy shifted nervously in her seat. "Thanks for the beer."

He reached into the pocket of his jacket and removed a worn leather wallet. "You're very welcome," he told her, tossing a twenty onto the bar. "I'm Oscar."

She shook his hand when he offered it. "Christy."

"Where are your friends?"

"At home, I guess." She looked down at her drink. "They were tired, so they left."

"And you're not tired, are you?"

"Actually," Christy said, "I'm not even a little bit. But I think it's time I take their cue and head home."

He kept his eyes on her face, the sweet smile still spread across his lips. "You shouldn't be driving," he told her. "May I give you a lift home?"

Christy laughed. "This feels like a PSA for why you should never get in cars with strangers."

"Everyone's a stranger until they're not." He put his hand over his heart. "I promise, I only want to see you get home safe."

"And I appreciate that, Oscar, but I lied. The truth is I don't want to go home. See, my grandma died today, and if I go home that's all I'm going home to. A bunch of grief and relatives, you know how it is."

Oscar nodded. "I do know that feeling. So, how about you come hang out with me and my friends, and you won't have to feel anything but good."

Christy felt her muscles clench. Her eyes were totally focused on his, on the way his lashes curled just a little. His words didn't just reach her ears; they felt like a warm weight settling in her mind, numbing her will to say no. If she didn't look away soon, something was going to happen, maybe something bad, but she couldn't look away.

"Okay," she said softly. She held his hand as he led her through the crowd and outside, where his friends were already waiting in the backseat.

"Christy, this is Tony and Dylan."

They both waved. Oscar opened the passenger side door and gestured to the seat. She hesitated and bit softly into her bottom lip. It wasn't a smart thing she was doing. Everything about this whole excursion was the start to many a *Dateline* episode.

"Where are we going?" she asked.

"Just for a ride," Oscar told her. "To a place where there is no grief and no grumpy relatives."

Once again, the suggestion felt as if it were vibrating inside her head, urging her to let go of everything and trust him. Trust them. Suddenly she was sitting with her seat belt fastened, and the car was heading down the strip toward the beach.

They drove away from the center of town with Christy clutching the door grip as Oscar increased speed. She closed her eyes when the top came down and the wind ripped through the car, carrying the sharp, cold scent of the rising tide. It seemed like only a few minutes had passed when they hit the gravel road that stretched out next to the sand. The car slowed, and Christy watched as the lights from town disappeared, until the car came to a stop on an empty stretch of beach with no one else around.

She knew this part of Brave Beach only because it was on the news a lot for closures due to rip tides. A group of yellow barricades had been set up to block the rest of the road, and several signs were erected warning people not to swim.

"Now that was a ride!" Dylan said and threw open his car door. He whooped and hollered as he did somersaults across the dunes.

"Ignore him," Tony said behind her. "He's an idiot. But he's our idiot, so..." Christy could see the flicker of a flame and then the smoke of a cigarette as he walked casually towards the water.

"You okay?" Oscar asked.

"I'm fine," she said.

"Come down to the beach with me. I want to show you something."

She got out of the car and held his hand as they walked through the sand. Her heels were slowing her down, so she took them off and let them dangle from her fingers. A steady fog rose from the surface of the water, rolling along toward the lights in the distance.

"So," she said. "How do you three know each other?"

"Ah, well, that's a complicated answer."

"It's a simple question," she said.

"But it's not," he told her. He gave her hand a squeeze. "They're my brothers."

"Oh." Her eyes lit up with understanding. "That's not complicated at all. I mean, I'm sure being adopted has its complications, but they're still your brothers. Blood isn't everything."

He laughed a little and shook his head. "How presumptuous of you. Because I'm Black, you just assume our bond isn't blood?"

Christy swallowed hard. The alcohol was causing her mouth to dig a hole, and she just kept sinking deeper into it. How was it that in the span of two minutes she had already offended him more than once? The chilly water reached her toes now, helping to sober her up. She needed to get home. Oscar's eyes weren't so warm and inviting now, and her insulting his brothers was probably why.

"I'm sorry, really. I'm drunk and not thinking clearly. It's time for me to go home."

"Why?"

"It's late, and I don't want my family to worry about me."

Oscar looked out over the water and sighed. "That's a shame. I wanted you to meet my father."

Christy felt something in the air shift, and goosebumps popped up over her arms. It was quiet; the only sounds were the soft lapping of water and the gentle whoosh of the wind. Then another sound joined the chorus. She heard footsteps on the wet sand behind her and spun around. Tony and Dylan were standing there with crooked grins, and their eyes were gleaming in a way that seemed abnormal.

She turned back to Oscar. "Your father? Who's your father?"

A voice behind her said, "I am."

There was someone else standing in front of Tony and Dylan. It was like he materialized out of nothing. Christy froze, her mind racing. He looked like a boy, no older than his late teens. There was no way he was their father, it had to be some kind of sick joke. He had dark, straight hair, short on the sides, longer on top, and wet with ocean spray. Dressed in a white button-up shirt with an open collar, sleeves rolled to his elbows and tucked into black slacks, he looked like a prep school student from old money. He was gangly and pale, but the way he stood there, grinning knowingly at her, said he was much stronger than he appeared.

"Look," she said sternly, trying to hide the shake in her voice. "I get it. You guys get a kick out of messing with people, and that's fine with me. Is this going to end up on YouTube or something?"

"I'm Alex," the boy said. "And you're incredibly beautiful. My son has excellent taste."

Christy's heart was pounding now. This was the "something bad" she had thought about back at the bar. Why did she leave with them? "I don't care what your name is," she said, her voice trembling. "I just want to get my things out of the car and go home."

Alex looked from Tony to Dylan and then back to her and Oscar. "There was never any intention to take you home, Christy. Certainly, you're catching on to that by now."

Oscar was standing so close behind her that she could feel his breath on her neck. She winced when his hands gripped her shoulders. "Please," she said with tears in her eyes. "Let me leave."

"Of course." Alex smiled and swept his arm out as a gesture of compliance. "It's only fair we give you a head start."

Christy wanted to scream. It was all she could hear inside her head, but nothing was coming out of her mouth. Alex was still smiling, and she realized just how young he really looked with his dimples and inquisitive eyes. Something about that smile was different now. It was his teeth, his incisors. They were growing longer right in front of her eyes. The scream that crawled out of her pierced the night and echoed against the darkness. Somewhere above her, a seagull cawed.

They were laughing at her now, and when Dylan threw his head back with a maniacal cackle, she saw that it wasn't just the boy who was changing. They all were. Their glowing amber eyes stared right through her, daring her to run. Christy screamed louder and took off past them, glancing back only once to see how far ahead she was. They were still where she left them, their shadows silhouetted beneath the moonlight. She kept running, tripping more than once. The screams never stopped. She hoped they would attract some passerby or a police officer out on his nightly patrol.

Laughter came barreling from behind her. She turned around, and what she saw could not be real. Yet there they were, the four of them gliding toward her, arms outstretched and mouths open wide. Their eyes burned bright as they rode the shadows closer to her. Christy could feel the pressure of their speed in her ears. Her toe snagged a piece of driftwood and she plunged toward the sand. She attempted to soften the impact, but the force of her fall was too much. Her wrists snapped under the tension, sending hot pain throughout her body.

They were on her in an instant. She saw them only in a blur of color. Underneath their laughter, she could hear the sounds of her flesh tearing and the crack of their teeth against her bones. Christy managed one last scream before Alex plunged his teeth into the hollow of her throat. Before her eyes closed, embraced by the darkness, Christy had one final thought. Monsters were real.

"How was work?" Hayden asked as Sadie walked through the front door sometime after 1 A.M.

"It was interesting," she answered cryptically.

After she left the bar, Sadie spent the entire drive home thinking about the boys in the silver BMW, Tony in particular. Rick was never one to pass judgment, so it didn't make sense to her why he was so staunch against the three men. Sadie saw nothing unnerving about Tony. It was the opposite, in fact. Everything about him, right down to the eerie calmness in his eyes, felt the opposite of threatening.

"Interesting how?" Hayden asked as she handed Sadie the box of pizza she'd been consuming.

Sadie shook her head and sidestepped the sofa before entering the kitchen. She loved Alfonso's Pizza but not the heartburn that came with it. She settled on a peanut butter sandwich and ignored her friend's question altogether. She wasn't sure she was ready to let Hayden in on everything that happened that night. Besides, there really wasn't anything to tell. She went back into the living room and pretended not to see the puzzled expression on her friend's face.

"So? Spill it. What interesting thing happened at work?"

"It was nothing, really." She said with a shrug and sat next to Hayden on the couch. "These guys came into the bar, and Rick flipped his lid."

"Why? They do something wrong?"

"Not that I'm aware of."

"Sadie, we have to throw you back into the dating pool. If this is the most interesting thing happening to you on the daily, I'm deeply concerned."

"Sure. Because, as you've already reminded me a million times, I just need to get laid and everything in my life will be perfect."

"I said you need to go on a damn date. If sex is the conclusion to that date, then all the better."

"I realize this is hard for you to believe, Hay, but I don't even miss dating. Or sex, for that matter."

Hayden put her hand over her heart and feigned shock and repulsion. "Blasphemy! If you're not missing sex, that's because Kevin wasn't doing it right."

Sadie couldn't help but laugh. "I guess that's fair."

"Well, were your mystery men at least cute?"

"They were okay. One of them came and ordered a drink, but then Rick made them leave and more or less forbade me from ever talking to them again."

"Rick ain't your Daddy, Sadie. Personally, I think this is huge. You haven't even looked at anyone since the evil one."

"His name is Kevin."

"I prefer the evil one. It's more fitting." She leaned closer to Sadie with a smile stretching ear to ear. "Tell me about him. When you say cute, are we talking roses and wine or cuffs and spankings?"

"You're ridiculous, but I love you," Sadie laughed. "I don't really know how to characterize him. I guess he was cute in that bad boy kind of way."

Hayden clapped her hands together excitedly. "You mean this future possible Mr. Right isn't some uptight prick with a trust fund like Kevin?"

"How would I know? It was a six-minute conversation. Oddly enough, about Edgar Allan Poe. And before you suggest we take my day off tomorrow to stalk the strip looking for these guys, I'm not doing that."

"You're zero fun sometimes."

"I can live with that. Besides, Rick was pissed about them being there, so I doubt any of them are coming back unless they want a trespassing charge."

"Fine," Hayden said and turned her attention to the television. Then she quickly turned it off and looked over at Sadie. "I'm sorry, okay? I'm being me again, and I know sometimes 'me' can be very annoying."

"You don't have to be sorry. I realize that I'm not as exciting and outgoing as I used to be."

"That's not my point, Sadie. It's not about being exciting. I love you like you're my sister. I just don't want to see you thinking you somehow deserve not to be happy. I think it's important that you remember you deserve happiness. I'm just afraid you're not going to find it at the bar working, coming home, and repeating that every day."

Sadie smiled softly. "You're my best friend in the world. You make me happy."

"Ditto," Hayden responded with a wink.

Sadie stayed up late that night. She sat on the porch and listened to the waves crash against the shore and thought about happiness, specifically if she was lacking it. There was so much she gave up when Kevin gave up on her. Hayden was right; it had been too many months of Sadie punishing herself for crimes someone else committed. It was time to pick herself up and dive back into life with the excitement she previously had. She swore that tomorrow she would do just that.

Dylan pushed the door open with the toe of his boot. The house was vacant, and the smell of decay hung heavy on the air. He smiled at the young man standing beside him. Any hesitation the kid may have felt disappeared as he grew hungrier for the fix Dylan promised him. His name was Sean, and they'd met outside a bar while Dylan hunted for that night's first course.

The moment he saw the boy, he knew it was an easy meal. A college kid who realized too late that good grades weren't as easy to come by outside of high school. Mommy and Daddy's money was useful in procuring the pharmaceuticals needed to study into the early morning and still be up for class. He would make a nice dinner with a satisfying aftertaste. Money tasted like sugar when it flowed through the red-blooded veins of an all-American teenager.

"What are we doing in here?" Sean asked.

"I'm not doing a buy out in the open, man. It's too risky. Anyway, my stash is in here."

Dylan closed the door behind him and moved through the darkness with ease. His eyes could see everything just as clearly as if all the lights were on. Sean followed behind him, jumping a little with every creak of the boards under his feet. Dylan snickered to himself and then paused when he saw the three shadowed figures standing in the corner. The boy next to him was blind to them, and his hesitation was steadily growing.

Dylan could hear Sean's heart pounding and knew the others could as well. The smell of the kid's perspiration began to mix with the musty air. The others were growing more eager with anticipation. They loved blood, but they loved the hunt almost as much. Oscar was the first to step forward, and the sound of his footsteps made Sean stop moving.

"What was that?" he asked, a nervous tilt in his voice. He took a step backward toward the door.

"Oh, those are my friends," Dylan said.

"Are they buying too?"

"They're here for something else," he laughed.

Sean started to breathe harder as the rest of the boys emerged from the shadows, amber eyes glittering against the dark. Dylan moved so fast that Sean only felt the disturbance in the air for a second before a hand clamped hard over his mouth. He chuckled as Sean kicked his legs out in front of him and struggled to escape.

"Who wants first bite?" Dylan asked.

Alex stepped forward. "I do."

He sneered as he walked closer to them and let his eyes find Sean's. The boy stopped fighting Dylan's grip and went limp in his arms. Alex reached for him, one ice-cold hand cupping the side of Sean's face. They could all sense his fear. It was more alive than he was, a breathing, pulsing entity that called to each one of them. Alex stared deep into Sean's eyes. The kid understood what was happening, and somehow knew that if he would let them, they could make it a painless leap from this life to the next. Sean could hear Alex's voice in his head, calming him with its smooth timber.

We're here to drink from you, Sean. There's no need to scream or cry. Pain isn't a necessary factor in transactions like these. If you let us, it might be enjoyable for you. Do you want that?

Sean could hear the wind outside beating against the house. The tides were coming in. He shivered, wishing that he spent the last hours of his life enjoying the beauty of the ocean and the freedom of the surf, not hunting down Adderall so he could ace his history exam.

You can still have the beauty and the freedom. You can own it for all eternity. All you have to do is give in.

Sean closed his eyes, not wanting this dilapidated shack to be the last thing he ever saw. The vampires were breathing heavily, and Sean could feel Dylan's warm breath on his neck and taste Alex's on his lips. He sensed movement around him and felt Dylan's arms let go. They were circling him, each one laughing softly under their breath. This was exciting for them, watching Sean tremble, watching him give in to the seductive promise of their power. The breathing grew louder and louder, until they were growling. He opened one eye to see them encircling him, faster until he was watching a tornado of color.

There was a blast of air in his face as Alex flew at him. The sudden sensation of falling was cut off by the sharp pain that burned through his neck. He tried to speak, to tell them his full name so they might remember him, but it was impossible. Alex pushed Sean away and sent him careening towards Oscar. He held him tightly by the arms, his strong hands crushing the bones. More pain bolted through Sean as Oscar dug his fangs into the flesh just beneath his collarbone.

Some part of him, maybe it was his spirit, was listening to Alex's voice as it sang a lullaby in his head. Oscar let him go, and he fell back onto the floor with a smack. Only now, the hard ground was soft like a pile of feathers. Alex was right. If he just listened to the voice everything was peaceful. Tony and Dylan took up a space on either side of him. Tony sunk his fangs into the fleshy side of Sean's stomach, while Dylan devoured one side of his chest. As his body delivered those last few ounces of his blood, he heard Alex tell him to go. It was then that these dark angels taught him how to fly.

Chapter Three

Sadie's start to appreciating and living life again hadn't been as exciting as she'd hoped. Rick asked her to come in to work because he had a date and Leah was sick. She could have said no; she could have told him that she and Hayden had plans to hang out in town and find Sadie's missing happiness. In the end, she agreed to work the night shift. Hayden complained, once again, about Rick needing more hired help.

The sky was a milky blue as dusk settled over Brave Beach. Sadie passed the movie theater and inhaled the scent of popcorn that mingled with the salty ocean air. She didn't mind working alone. In fact, she appreciated it. It could have been worse; Sunday nights weren't busy, and she'd be able to sit behind the bar and read. Will, the day bartender, was already packed and ready to go when she arrived. He handed her a note from Rick with specific instructions: do not allow the boys driving the silver Beemer into the bar under any circumstances.

The first hour passed with only a few patrons popping in for a beer or margarita before leaving to find someplace more exciting. Sadie chewed on a toothpick while reading Poe. These were stories she had read a hundred times before, but they never got old. Between the pages, she thought a lot about her relationship with Kevin, trying to remember what exactly she missed.

The reality was that seven months of being his girlfriend had amounted to almost nothing. Sure, there were some good times in the beginning, but that all changed when she found him sucking face with some woman outside C.J.'s Bar and Grill. He'd thought she was in Pineview visiting her parents. He didn't even have an excuse for his indiscretion; he just chalked it up to them growing apart.

Sadie's blood boiled every time she thought about it. The look on his face when he said he was ready to move on. The way he told all his buddies she was a virgin when they met, which wasn't true, and the most boring lay he ever experienced. Then came the phone calls to the bar, strangers asking if Kevin's sloppy seconds were available. So much time had passed, and it was forgotten by many, but Sadie was still hurting and furious.

Without thinking, she threw the book across the bar. It landed with a thud in front of the door just as it was opening.

"And you told me this was a good read," Tony said. He bent down and picked up the book. "Should I rethink your recommendation before I buy it?"

Sadie's eyes went wide, and her face heated with embarrassment. "Hi," she said, feeling even more awkward as she took a step toward him, momentarily forgetting she was trapped behind the bar.

He gave a little chuckle, then stepped up to the counter where he gently set down her book. "So? Is my rain check still available?"

Sadie's brows wrinkled briefly before she remembered the Sazerac he never got to drink. "Absolutely," she said, hoping she didn't look disappointed that he hadn't come for something else. She made his drink and set it in front of him. "That's $8.50."

"Damn, Rick's drinks are expensive." He reached into his back pocket. "What's in this thing?"

"Rick orders the best ingredients."

Tony eyed the drink for a moment, then lifted it to her in a silent toast. He took a sip and closed his eyes, sucking in a sharp breath of air. "I like that. I can imagine you only need one of these to have a good time."

"I'm a heavy pourer," she said.

"Well, I never complain about cute bartenders with a heavy hand." Tony blushed just a little. "I did come back for the drink, which is delicious, by the way. But I also came to see if you would like to have dinner with me. You could tell me more about the stories in that book."

While Sadie had daydreamed about Tony coming back to ask her out, she didn't actually think it was a possibility. That was something just for her imagination to work through. Now that he was here and asking, she didn't know what to say.

"I... I don't know if that's a good idea."

Tony's smile disappeared. "Wow. That wasn't the answer I was hoping for."

Sadie couldn't help but laugh. "It's the Rick thing. I'm not even supposed to let you in here."

"Good ol' Rick." Tony shook his head. "I wouldn't want you to get in trouble. So how about I come back when you're off work and ask again when you're outside the bar?"

"I don't know if it works that way." She looked away briefly and then back to his face.

He was staring at her intently. His brows creased together as if he were concentrating on something very important. Their eyes locked, and for a full minute, a strange, heavy silence fell between them. It felt as though a physical pressure were pushing against her mind, a soft, insistent weight. She broke the stare, blinking the sensation away. When she looked up again, Tony was still watching her, biting into his bottom lip.

"Tony?"

His face softened. "Yeah?"

"Are you okay?"

He looked confused by the question. "Sure I am. Are you?"

"You just looked like something was wrong. I really hope I haven't offended you."

He laughed and leaned into the bar. "How could you offend me? I'm the stranger who shows up and asks you out on a date. I understand."

"Can I ask you a question?"

His smile lessened, pulling up the left corner of his lips into a devilish smirk. "Go ahead, ask me."

"Why doesn't Rick want you guys in here?"

"The truth is, I think Rick's problem is more with our brother Alex than with us. But as usual, we are the company we keep, right? If Rick has a problem with Alex, that problem is ours too."

"You have a brother?"

"My friends are like my brothers."

Sadie nodded. "I get that. My best friend is like a sister." She leaned her elbows onto the bar top. "But what's his problem with Alex?"

"Rick and Alex..." Tony paused, his head tilting slightly. "Shit," he muttered under his breath.

"What's wrong?"

Just as she asked, Sadie's eyes shifted to the front window. She saw Rick's Jeep in the parking lot, and then Rick himself approaching the entrance. She froze, waiting as the brass bell formally announced his arrival.

Rick looked at the two of them, his expression becoming an odd mix of surprise and fury. "It's last call, Sadie," he said curtly. "The bar is closed. Now get the hell out of here, young man."

Tony was smirking, but he lifted his hands in the air as if to surrender. "I was just leaving." He looked at Sadie, and the smirk became a soft smile. It was so sincere that Sadie felt her body warm under its impact. "If you change your mind, come find me."

She watched him walk past Rick, staring the older man down for half a second before finally exiting. Through the window, she saw Tony light a cigarette, look to his left and right, and start walking away. That feeling she had when she woke up that morning—of finding her happiness—filled her. She liked Tony and she wanted to know more about him. No one, not even Rick, would deny her the chance to break away from the ghosts of her past.

She grabbed the Poe book and hurried out from behind the bar. Rick made no move to stop her; he just stared in skepticism.

"Sadie, he's no good," he said when she stopped next to him.

"I have to find that out for myself, Rick." She held his eyes, knowing that while she didn't need his permission, she still wanted it. Over the last year he had become like a father to her. She needed to know that, while he may not approve of Tony, he was willing to accept him for her sake.

He inhaled deeply, then nodded at the door. "Go," he told her.

Sadie shoved the door open and stepped out onto the sidewalk. Tony was almost to the edge of the block when she called out to him. He turned over his shoulder to see her running his way. She was out of breath when she reached him.

"I'm sorry," she said, then let her shoulders slump. She had no idea what she was doing.

"You keep apologizing to me," he said, "when you have nothing to be sorry for. I shouldn't have bothered you here. I didn't mean to get you into trouble with Rick."

Sadie shook her head. "Don't worry about Rick. I can handle him. It's just... if you really wanted to see me, outside of the bar I mean, I think I would like that."

Tony shoved his hands into his jacket pockets. "I'd like that, too."

"This is kind of new for me. I ended something a few months ago, and it's weird to jump back into this whole dating thing."

"It doesn't have to be weird with me," he said. "Look, why don't I meet you here tomorrow night around nine? We'll have fun. You can get to know me, realize I'm an okay guy, and then maybe you'll let me see you again after. Sound good?" He lifted one eyebrow as he waited for her to answer.

"It sounds great, actually." And it did. "Here," she said, handing him the book. "I've read this a thousand times. You can borrow it; test it out, so to speak."

He took the book from her and tucked it under his arm. "Thank you." He pointed toward the bar. "You should get back to work. I'll see you tomorrow, Miss Sadie." He tipped his head toward her, then turned and walked away.

She watched him go. When he was lost in the shadows and she couldn't see him anymore, she dropped her head back and exhaled. She liked this feeling. It wasn't until that moment that she realized how much she had missed it.

Tony walked down to the darkest part of the beach. When he was sure no one was around, he began his ascent into the sky. He rose through the cool air until the pier was just a cluster of distant lights, then headed toward the cliffs.

Their house was hidden in the forests above the rocks, an old Victorian-era mansion that still held the grace and grandeur of its time. The white paint was chipped and flaking. Vines and ivy wound around the porch columns, but inside it was still clean, and the wood shone in the candlelight.

He landed a few feet from the pathway and saw Dylan sitting on the porch smoking a joint. Even if he hadn't seen his brother, Tony still would have known the others were gone. They were connected, all of them; each would feel when the others were close. Dylan looked up as Tony approached and offered the joint, which he refused.

"Did you get what you were after?" he asked with a sly grin.

"Sort of," Tony said, sitting down next to him. "I decided to give it some more time."

He lied only because he didn't want to tell the truth. His mind was reeling with questions. He had pushed at Sadie with everything he had, digging into her mind with his power, and yet she had still denied him the invitation he was after. There was only one mortal he had ever known who could do that, and she was long gone.

"Right," Dylan said with a mocking tilt of his head. "Now, why don't you tell me what really happened?"

"Rick showed up."

"Shit. How'd that turn out?"

Tony shrugged. "He just told me to get lost. She followed me, though."

"Dude, you're leaving something out. I can feel it."

Tony glared at Dylan, then finally relented. "Fine, if you must know. She resisted me. I used every ounce of persuasion I could, and she still resisted."

Dylan's eyes went wide. "That's impossible," he huffed. "Mortals can't resist us."

"Apparently, they can."

Dylan sucked hard on the joint, holding the smoke in deep before tossing the dying ember into the grass. He was the youngest in terms of immortal years, and he was still developing his powers. Yet, even as green as he was, he had never met a human who could deny his charms. The mere idea that this girl had resisted a vampire as old as Tony made everything feel out of shape, like sitting in a bubble that was about to burst. Seriousness washed over him, which was strange; Dylan was almost always the familiar class clown.

"You need to tell Alex."

"No," Tony said firmly.

Alex. Tony loved and hated him at the same time. Theirs was a relationship that existed on a very delicate balance. It was Alex who had sired Tony and brought him into his dark, enchanting world. He held power over all of them, and it was infuriating on many levels. Tony wanted the strength to say "no" just once.

What would happen to Sadie if Alex learned what took place in the bar? Tony wasn't sure if he would kill her or turn her. Either way, he wasn't ready to let her go just yet. He was more intrigued by her than ever. No, it was best if Alex knew nothing about Sadie until Tony got the answers he wanted.

"You can't keep this from him," Dylan said. "He'll find out eventually anyway."

"I'll deal with it when he does."

Dylan pulled his knees to his chest. "Maybe you didn't use as much persuasion as you thought."

"I used everything I had, Dylan. I felt her soul flinch, but she pushed me out without much of a fight. She's different."

"Have you ever known a human to do that before?"

Tony let his eyes move to the army of trees and watched the leaves dance with the wind. He could hear the surf crashing against the rocks at the bottom of the cliff with thunderous rage. The ocean and the earth were at war with one another. That's what Alex was to Tony.

Deep down, there was a part of him that recalled his life before the darkness. If he concentrated hard enough, he could remember the sunshine and how its warm rays felt caressing his skin. He tried not to dwell on memories for too long, though.

"I haven't," he finally answered.

There was a pause before Dylan said, "Alex has, though, hasn't he?"

Tony nodded.

"Who was it?"

Tony looked away. That was Alex's story to tell. Then, as if the mere thought of their sire was a summoning, he and Dylan turned their attention to the sky. Seconds later, Alex and Oscar emerged from the clouds. Their feet hit the ground with a thump that sent dust billowing around their ankles.

"Did you two have fun tonight?" Alex asked. A splatter of dried blood was still visible on his chin.

Dylan nodded. "I had a quick bite to eat, then came back here to see if I could add to the feng shui of our lovely abode."

"Really?" Alex asked. "And what did you find?"

"Come see."

Oscar and Dylan stepped into the house together. Alex was almost to the door when he turned back to Tony. "Are you coming?"

Tony nodded and got to his feet. Before they stepped through the threshold, Alex threw his arm around Tony's shoulder. "You went to Rick's," he said. It was a statement, not a question. "So? How did it go with her?"

"Who?"

Alex laughed deeply. "The pretty brunette that works behind the bar, Tony. I knew you were hungry for her. That's why Oscar and I stayed in the background tonight. My question is, why didn't you kill her when you had the chance?"

"I'm not ready," was Tony's simple but honest answer. He stepped past Alex and into the house, ready to be done with the conversation.

"In here," Dylan called from the parlor.

Leaning up against the fireplace was an enormous painting of a raven perched on the branch of a dying tree. Alex approached the painting slowly, taking in every brush stroke. He tilted his head this way and that with intrigue.

"And the Raven, never flitting, still is sitting, still is sitting—on the pallid bust of Pallas just above my chamber door." He looked up at Dylan. "I like it. Very much."

Dylan gave a cheeky grin, obviously happy that Alex was pleased with him. "What was that you said? A song?"

"It's a poem," Tony remarked. "By Edgar Allan Poe."

Alex turned to face him, hands in the pockets of his black pants. "I didn't realize you were a fan."

Tony held up the book Sadie had given him an hour earlier. "And here you thought you knew everything about me."

Oscar could feel the tension and stepped forward. "We have a few hours before dawn. Have you eaten, T?"

Tony nodded. "Had a snack earlier, but I could eat again. She was a vegetarian and didn't satisfy."

"All right then, let's go see what's on the menu tonight in town."

"No," Alex interceded. "You and Dylan go out for a while. Tony and I have plans of our own."

Tony furrowed his brows in confusion as Alex looked at him with knowing eyes. Oscar didn't question Alex's demands. He had nothing but respect for his sire and did whatever Alex asked of him. He nodded toward Dylan, and the two left the house without a word.

When they were alone, Alex turned to Tony. "I thought you would want some time to talk."

Tony felt a swell of anger that quickly shifted to bubbling excitement. This was his nature: to want the things Alex wanted, to seek his advice. "I want her," he said. "But Rick is going to be a problem."

"No, he's not." Alex smiled and clapped his hand on Tony's shoulder. "I'll take care of the old man. You just keep seasoning up your future dish. Enjoy yourself."

Tony smiled. "Oh, I plan to."

CHAPTER FOUR

Sadie was sitting behind the bar, her leg bouncing with growing anxiety. It was almost eight, and Tony would be there any moment. Rick had taken the night off and Leah agreed to cover Sadie's shift. The numbers on the digital wall clock were red and mocking. Sadie turned her eyes back to the window, nervously chewing her bottom lip. A splash of light filled a parking space, but it was a small, black Toyota, not the silver Beemer. She frowned.

"You have a big date tonight, huh?" Leah asked. She sidled up to Sadie and plucked a lemon wedge out of the tray to add to her water.

"Yep, and I'm really fucking nervous."

Leah patted Sadie on the back. "You'll be fine."

"This feels so weird, it's embarrassing. I'm shaking like it's the first day of school or something."

"You're going to give Rick a heart attack, you know. I think that's why he didn't come in tonight. He didn't want to watch you ride off with lover boy."

"I need this," said Sadie. "Rick is just going to have to trust me."

"I don't think it's you he doesn't trust. But for what it's worth, I'm happy for you. It's time to get back in the game, girl."

"You and Hayden keep saying that, but I'm not sure I even know how to play anymore."

"It's like riding a bike. Or riding a guy. Either way, you're going to be amazing at it." She winked and bumped Sadie's hip with her own.

"It's a first date, Leah. The only thing I'm going to be riding is in the passenger seat of his car."

"We'll see," Leah said in a sing-song voice.

A new rush of patrons came through the doors. It was a welcome savior from the conversation Sadie didn't want to have, but her relief vanished when she noticed a familiar face among them. *Oh, God,* she thought. *Not tonight.* Kevin sauntered up to the bar with a smile. His blonde hair was gelled in carefully cultivated spikes. He tossed his car keys into the air and caught them in his other hand. "Hey Leah, long time no see."

"What the hell are you doing here?" Sadie hissed, her previous nervousness quickly replaced with boiling anger.

"I came to see you. We need to talk." He reached for her hand, but Sadie snatched it away before he could touch her.

"I haven't seen you in six months," she reminded him. "What could you possibly have to tell me now?"

Leah stepped forward. "Get out, Kevin. She's not interested."

Sadie appreciated Leah's need to play backup. Leah had witnessed all those times Sadie came into the bar with mascara tracks down her cheeks. But Sadie was not that girl anymore, and she wanted him to know it. "Kevin, go outside. I'll be there in a sec."

He gave Leah a victorious grin and strolled out the door, the smell of too much cologne lingering behind him.

"You're not really going out there," Leah asked with wide, disbelieving eyes.

Sadie wiped her sweaty palms on her jeans and let out a sigh. "I'm going out there." She raised a finger, silencing Leah's protest. "Only so I can tell him what I didn't get to before. The dickhead never gave me a chance to say my part."

Leah looked skeptical but nodded. "All right, but if you need me, just holler."

"Thanks."

Sadie moved from behind the bar and went outside to find Kevin leaning up against the stucco walls of the strip mall, waiting for her. With another deep breath of courage, she stomped toward him.

"Are you insane? You can't just pop in here whenever you're feeling confessional."

"I made a mistake, Sadie. I miss you."

"How can you miss me? You dumped me and never called again!" Her jaw clenched tight. "No," she told him, eyes narrowed. "I don't want to hear your shit. Go away, Kevin. Leah was right. I'm not interested."

The look of surprise on his face was a wonderful sight, and Sadie felt strangely superior in that moment. She turned her back on him and started toward the bar with pride, straightening her spine. She was nearing the door when she felt someone grab her arm and pull hard. Kevin spun her around, gripping both her arms in his hands.

"You think you're something special now? You were lucky to have me, Sadie. Lucky I even came back here to give you another shot. Now, you owe me a talk."

She tried to pull away, but his grip tightened. "Ouch! Kevin, you're hurting me."

The sound of her name being called was what finally made Kevin let go, giving her a push that made her stumble backward. Tony was there almost immediately, looking her over and helping her get steady on her feet. He looked at Kevin and then back at her.

"You okay?" he asked.

"Yes," she said, her voice shaking a little. "I'm fine. Let's just go."

Tony gave Kevin a considering look, but Sadie tugged on the sleeve of his jacket to bring his attention back to her. "Yeah, okay," he breathed hard. "My car is parked over here." He put his arm around her, and they started to walk away.

"Go ahead!" Kevin called out to them. "I've already tapped that! And she's a lousy lay anyway."

Sadie felt Tony's arm slip away from her. He was already stalking toward Kevin, and she nearly had to run to catch up with him. "Stop, Tony, please. He's not worth it."

He looked at her, his chest rising and falling with concentrated effort to contain his fury. She held his eyes with a silent plea. She didn't know Tony well enough to know what kind of temper he had, but she knew Kevin was a hothead who never wanted to look like the weaker person. Even if Tony could kick his ass, she didn't want him getting arrested for fighting her dipshit ex-boyfriend.

Tony seemed to get a hold of himself and then looked at Kevin. "Stay away from her," he warned.

Kevin looked Tony up and down, eyes scanning the myriad of tattoos. "So, this is your type now?"

Sadie gripped Tony's arm tighter. "Get out of here, Kevin. Go!"

Instead of leaving, Kevin took a step towards them. He was a good inch or two taller than Tony, and that gave him the belief he was stronger, more powerful. "You fucking my girlfriend, asshole?"

At first, Tony was taken aback; he hadn't been approached by someone actively looking for a fight in a long time. Seeing this rich mama's boy trying to bully him was priceless. It was just a shame the others weren't there to see it, too. He felt his lips curl into a smile. He was already planning big things for Kevin.

"She's not your girlfriend," he stated calmly.

Kevin laughed and leaned into Tony so they were at eye level. "If you don't want my sloppy seconds, you'll have to fuck her in the ass."

Another barrel of laughter came out of Kevin's mouth, and Sadie knew she couldn't hold Tony back forever. She was right. Before she or Kevin could register what happened, Tony's fist connected with Kevin's abdomen. His face paled as he crouched forward, coughing and sputtering as Tony delivered another blow to his kidney. Then Tony grabbed a fistful of blonde hair and pulled Kevin's head back so that he was looking deep into a pair of glittering amber eyes. Kevin flinched, unsure whether what he was seeing was real or a hallucination brought on by the shock of pain.

Tony placed his mouth next to Kevin's ear and released a low, menacing laugh. As Kevin tried to pull away, Tony kept him in place with little effort. "I'm not going to sugarcoat this for you, Kevie. You come near Sadie again and I'll rip your fucking throat out." He said the words low so that Sadie couldn't hear, but Kevin's face registered the terror. "I might do it anyway, just for fun. Sleep with your light on."

He let go of Kevin's hair with a shove. Kevin collapsed to his knees, tears and snot mixing on his face while he gasped in broken breaths.

Tony took Sadie's hand and walked her briskly away from the scene as more people gathered around the crying man. She looked back once to see Kevin waving people away, clearly embarrassed, and then he stumbled into the crowd. When they got to Tony's car, she let go of his hand.

"Why did you do that?" she asked, not angry but concerned. "What if he reports you?"

"He won't report me," said Tony. "He's going to go home and change his pants. Then he'll think twice about ever bothering you or anyone else again."

"You shouldn't have done that."

"He shouldn't have said those things," Tony said simply. "I was going to walk away, but he couldn't let it go."

She could see regret on his face, as if he were afraid he had crossed a line with her he couldn't come back from. Sadie didn't want him to feel bad; she wasn't angry. She just didn't want him to find trouble. She didn't want Kevin to take away her fresh start. "Thank you," she finally said, "for sticking up for me."

"I'm sorry that happened. Not the best start to our first date."

She looked down at her feet and shrugged. "No, I guess it isn't."

"Let me take you home," he said. "And tomorrow night, I'll pick you up here at the same time, and we'll try again."

Part of Sadie was disappointed, but the other part of her was relieved. If they went on their date now, it would consist of awkward conversation that would keep circling back to Tony apologizing and Sadie feeling guilty.

"Okay," she smiled. "I think that's a good idea."

He drove her back to the beach house and walked her to the door. Sadie was glad to see Hayden wasn't home.

"How did you manage to snag this place?" Tony asked, admiring the view of the ocean just beyond her front steps.

"Hayden's grandmother owned it." She took the keys out of her purse. "So, I'll see you tomorrow?"

Tony nodded and took a step closer to her. "You bet." He took another step until he was right next to her. "Goodnight, Miss Sadie."

He closed his eyes, and by instinct, she did the same. Their lips touched, and she felt every bad thing that had happened that evening disappear. Without giving it any more thought, she wrapped her arms around his neck and felt his fingers tangle in her hair. His tongue slipped between her lips, and Sadie's whole body shivered pleasantly. She wanted this guy. And she wanted him now.

"Wait," she said, pulling back and placing her hands on his chest. They were both breathing heavily, Tony smiling like a Cheshire cat.

"Did I do something wrong?"

"No," she laughed. "I just think we should slow down."

"You're probably right."

"I'm sorry," Sadie said, feeling the need to explain. "I'm just not sure..."

Tony put his finger against her lips, silencing her. "You're doing it again."

"Doing what?"

"Apologizing when you shouldn't. I'll see you tomorrow."

He leaned down and kissed the corner of her mouth before walking back to his car. Sadie stood there and watched him go, her fingers subconsciously touching her lips. Tony gave her one last smile before he peeled out of the drive and drove away.

Tomorrow could not come soon enough.

Kevin was thankful his parents' house was away from the center of town. Their little suburban estate on the hill was surrounded by nothing but Ponderosa Pines and manicured gardens. In the distance, the lights of Brave Beach twinkled against the darkness.

He was also thankful his parents were on vacation in San Francisco and wouldn't be there to see the piss stain on his new jeans. He couldn't get those eyes out of his head, only half-convinced the four beers he downed before going to the bar were to blame. The other half knew those eyes were real, and not human.

Kevin walked through the front door and shut it as quietly as he could. He stood there in the dark for a moment, waiting to make sure his sister, Kristen, was asleep. He flipped on the light and started to undo his belt buckle, anxious to get his pants in the wash and himself into a shower. He had his pants unzipped when a voice emerged from the kitchen to his right, and Kristen came walking out with a Coke in hand and a confused expression on her face.

"What are you doing?"

"Nothing," Kevin snapped as he tried to cover the crotch of his jeans with his hands. "Go to bed!"

"Did you piss your pants?" Kristen asked, squinting to get a better look. "Oh my god! You did! You pissed your pants." She doubled over in hysterical laughter.

"Shut up, Kristen!" He marched toward her and held his fisted hands at his side.

When Kristen got a good look at his face, she stopped laughing. "What happened to you?"

"What do you mean? I had some beers and pissed myself. Big fucking deal."

She shook her head. "You've been crying."

Kevin turned away and wiped his cheeks. "Just go to bed, Kristen."

"I take it the talk with your ex didn't go well."

"Fuck that bitch," Kevin spat. "She can keep that freak. What the fuck do I care?"

But deep down, he did care. Yes, he had been an asshole when they were together, and he was certainly an asshole to her tonight. It was possible that being an asshole was his most defining personality trait, but that didn't change the fact that he spent the whole drive home feeling she was in trouble. Those eyes were haunting him.

"I need to call her," he said to himself. "I've got to warn her."

As the last syllable fell off his tongue, there was a sudden, hard knock on the front door. He jumped back in surprise and looked down at his watch. It was after midnight. Kristen moved up behind him.

"Who is that?" she asked, her voice soft.

"I don't know," he whispered back. Then his mind flashed on the image of those eyes and his heart started racing. "Go upstairs," he told her, trying to keep his voice as quiet as possible. "In your room and lock the door."

Another hard bang was followed by one on the back patio doors. Then came a rhythmic tapping on the windows—*click, click, click*—and a chorus of laughter that chilled the air. Kristen was crying and Kevin put a finger to his lips, his eyes warning her to hush. She put a hand over her mouth to stifle the sobs. Kevin pointed to the stairs.

"Go to your room and call the cops."

She nodded and ran up the stairs, stopping abruptly at the landing when she realized the knocking and tapping had ceased. The laughter was gone. Suddenly the lights went out, and the house was plunged into darkness.

"Kevin!" she called, her hands gripping the railing hard.

"It's just a fuse," he answered. "We're okay. I'll go out to the garage and flip the switch."

"Who was that? Do you still want me to call the cops?"

"Yeah, call the cops. I think they left, but... tell them to hurry."

She heard the garage door open and close. Still scared, but relieved that whoever had been outside was now gone, Kristen hurried into her room and locked the door behind her. When she flipped her light switch, nothing happened. She bumped into her dresser while trying to find her cell in the dark. A breeze from the open window made the curtains flap gently, and for a moment Kristen thought she saw a shadow standing in the corner by her bed. She rubbed her eyes, and the shadow was gone.

The moonlight through the window reflected off the face of her cell phone on the bed. Kristen bent forward and suddenly froze. Someone was whispering her name. Her initial thought was that Kevin had come upstairs without her knowing, an idea she knew was impossible as soon as it took root. It wasn't her brother. A noise to her left made her pivot, and this time it wasn't a shadow; it was a person. He was illuminated by a halo of moonlight that shone like a spotlight through the curtains. He was young; he looked like the kids she went to school with.

"Hello, Kristen," he said, his voice hypnotic.

Kristen wanted to scream for her brother. She felt his name on her lips, but it wouldn't form shape enough to leave her throat. Her eyes were glued to the person speaking to her, his eyes burning like orange flames against the shadows.

We won't hurt you, sugar. She heard his voice, but only in her head. His lips stayed stretched in a grin. *Come closer to me so I can look into those beautiful eyes.*

Kristen started to cry. Her hand was still open, mid-reach for the phone. The lifesaver buzzed with a text notification, and Kristen wondered if she would ever be able to answer it. She willed herself to step away from the boy with the burning eyes, but she took a step toward him instead.

Good girl. Then something broke, like a rubber band snapping against skin, and the spell was shattered. Kristen screamed so loud her throat burned. She would have kept screaming, too, but something stole the sound. It was a moment before she realized it was the young man who had taken her voice. He was standing directly in front of her now, blood staining his wicked grin. A heavy heat enveloped her. Her right hand reached up and touched the open chasm in her throat.

I'm dying, she thought. And then she collapsed onto the floor.

Kevin stood in the doorway before gaining enough courage to step inside the dark garage. He felt around for the flashlight that was kept on a hook by the door. He turned it on with a trembling hand and scanned the room. He saw his father's cherry red Porsche, various tools, and workout equipment. He didn't see any glowing eyes, and that gave him the push he needed to hurry over to the fuse box.

Kevin's eyes narrowed in confusion as he saw that each tab was in the right position. The lights should be working. If it wasn't the fuse box, did that mean something was wrong with the electric grid? Maybe it was a blackout. It wouldn't be the first time Brave Beach lost power due to the ACs on the strip, but this was September and the day had been mild. He went over all the possibilities in his mind and walked back into the house.

He looked outside the window next to the front door and saw the lights were still on in town. He wondered if Kristen had called the cops and if they were on their way. He'd call Sadie as soon as he was done with them. He didn't know what he would say or if she would even listen. The feeling in his gut was cold and stale every time he thought about what happened outside Rick's Place.

He turned, and the flashlight fell from his hand, hitting the tile floor with a clank. "I'll be damned," he stuttered, and fear set his bladder loose for a second time that night. Sadie's boyfriend was standing in front of him with his lips twisted into a garish grin. But all Kevin could focus on were those eyes.

"Scared?" Tony asked.

Kevin lunged toward the monster, not giving himself time to think. He was reaching for Tony when his hands were suddenly grabbing air. Kevin stumbled forward off the step that led into the formal living room and grunted when he hit the sofa hard.

"Where are you?" he shouted. He got to his feet quickly and scanned the darkness. He was turning in slow circles, his hands balled into fists, warm urine running down his leg. "What are you?"

"Me?" Tony's voice came from somewhere above Kevin. He looked up in time to see a fist smashing into his face.

Kevin stumbled backward, clutching his nose as his hands filled with blood. Laughter was now on the opposite side of the room. Sadie's boyfriend raised his brows, delighting in Kevin's confusion and fear.

"I'm death," Tony said.

"Where's Sadie?" Kevin asked. "What did you do to her?"

"Nothing yet," said Tony. "Killing her now, before I've had a chance to have any fun? That seems kind of cruel."

"Don't you touch her!" Kevin screamed and started turning in blind circles as Tony's laughter drifted from one corner of the room to another.

"It's not Sadie you should really be worried about right now," Tony told him just as he appeared next to the staircase.

His words were followed by a loud thump. Kevin ran for the entryway and skidded to a stop as he saw his sister's broken body lying at the foot of the stairs. A beam of light from the fallen flashlight was shining on her wide-open eyes and bloody face.

"Kristen!" Kevin ran toward her and suddenly found himself face down on the floor, his sneakers having slid in his sister's blood as red rivers spread across the white tile.

"Ah, shit," Dylan cackled from upstairs. "Did you see that?"

"I certainly saw it," said Alex, emerging from the darkness to stand beside Tony.

Kevin was pressing his hand against the gaping hole in his sister's throat. He was alternating between screaming and crying hysterically. Dylan vaulted himself over the top railing of the staircase and landed with graceful ease in front of Kevin, his sneakers splashing in the mess.

"Could you shut the fuck up, please?" Dylan asked with feigned politeness. "You scream like a bitch."

Kevin looked up into Dylan's face and was once again met with the horror of those amber orbs. "You killed my sister," he gurgled as blood poured from his broken teeth and torn lip.

"She was delicious," Dylan said. He smacked his lips and ran a hand over his stomach, then cackled directly into Kevin's horrified face.

Oscar chose to walk down the stairs, wiping Kristen's blood from his lips with one of the shirts he'd taken from her room. "It's getting late. We need to go."

"Sa... Sadie..." Kevin stuttered.

Tony stepped forward, curious about what Kevin would say. "What about her?"

Kevin's voice was shaking as his whole body trembled. The four vampires slowly surrounded him, but he found Tony's eyes among them. "Don't hurt her," he pleaded. "She's a good person."

"Of course she is. That's exactly why she'll taste so good," said Tony. Then he crouched down and looked his prey straight in the eye. He pulled in his shift so that he was wearing the boyish mask that Kevin had seen earlier that evening. The normalcy of his appearance made the other monsters with him much more terrifying.

"You took her innocence, but I'm going to take her life. How poetic is that?"

Tony's words hit Kevin with finality. He looked over at his sister's body and reached for her hand. He was an asshole; he always had been. Now, in these final moments of his life, he realized that was the legacy he was leaving behind. He was to blame for Sadie falling into the arms of a devil. He was the reason Kristen was dead.

"I'm sorry," he whispered.

Tony lifted his booted heel and drove it into Kevin's back with a force that seemed to shake the room. The sound of his own spine cracking echoed loudly in Kevin's ears, but he was relieved the pain was short-lived.

Tony's eyes glowed once more, and he relished the moment his fangs ripped into Kevin's neck, tearing away pieces of flesh in a frenzy that made the others' hunger rise again. They all joined in on the final feast. Kevin listened to the wet, suckling sounds they made as they took his life.

"I'm sorry," he thought to himself as his vision started to tunnel. "I'm sorry."

Chapter Five

Alex walked alone down the strip, watching couples holding hands and tourists ducking into the specialty shops by the pier. The others were at the house, enjoying takeout. It wasn't often they brought meals home, the cleanup usually wasn't worth the effort, but tonight his boys had stumbled on a group of drunken fraternity members looking for a place to party. With just a little push of encouragement, the humans had followed the Beemer back to the cliffs.

Alex had stayed for a quick meal, then left the boys to their own devices. He had too much on his mind and needed solitude to sort through it. The night was cool, not unlike the one years ago when he met the only girl he had ever truly wanted. He stood in front of the pier and let himself fall into the memory of her – of all he had lost when she denied him.

He saw her that night sitting alone under a streetlamp next to the pier entrance. There was something about her, though at first he couldn't define what it was. The tips of her fingers were covered in a fine sheet of charcoal from the hours she spent sketching tourists for ten dollars a portrait. She was staring at the circling lights of the Ferris wheel when he tapped her gently on the shoulder.

"I'm sorry to interrupt you," he said, "but you're the girl who does portraits, right?"

She nodded. "During the day."

"That's a shame." He shrugged. "I can only make it out here after dark."

"You can't come after school?"

The question elicited a smile. "Unfortunately, no."

"After-school job?" she asked.

He laughed. "Do I really look that young? How old do you think I am?"

"Sixteen?"

"Ouch." He put his hand over his heart. "Felt that one. I'm nineteen," he continued, spinning the web. "Between college classes and a job, after dark is the only time I have for anything else."

"Well, I'm sure your parents appreciate your hard work," she offered.

He looked down at his feet. "I'm sure they would, but they aren't here anymore, so..." He let the words hang in the air for a moment before looking back at her with practiced, sad eyes. "I'm sorry to bother you. Have a good night."

He tipped his head and turned to walk away. He had planned to use his gift of persuasion, but he didn't have to.

"Wait," Sarah called out. "Did you want your portrait done?"

Alex smiled to himself. Guilt was a powerful tool, and he had known exactly how to feed her the story of his "lost" parents. His youthfulness was his greatest attribute; no one ever saw him as a threat until it was too late.

He nodded. "If you think you have the time. I would pay you extra, of course."

That was the clincher. Even someone as carefree as she wouldn't turn down extra cash. She motioned to a bench. "Have a seat."

"Do you think we could do this somewhere with fewer people?" He was still smiling, but there was a tightness to it now. He needed her alone. He prepared to push her mind in the direction he wanted when, once again, the invitation came freely.

She glanced back at the beach. A few fires were scattered around the sand, most of them abandoned in favor of the bars on the strip. The dying embers, along with a bright full moon, would provide enough light for a sketch.

"All right," she agreed. "We can go down to the beach."

"Thank you."

He let her take the lead. They shared small talk as they descended the steep stairs onto the sand. He asked how long she had lived in Brave Beach and she told him five years. He spun a story about his studies at the community college, hoping to transfer to a big university to become a doctor.

"That's admirable," she told him. "I get queasy at the sight of blood."

He laughed under his breath but said nothing. After walking for a while, Sarah noticed a bonfire that was still burning. She was so lost in the easy banter that she didn't realize how far they were from the pier.

"Have a seat," she said, pointing to a spot on the sand. "This shouldn't take too long."

"Please, take your time. I'm in no hurry."

Sarah sat opposite him with her legs crossed. She pulled the battered sketchpad from her bag along with three slim charcoal pencils. Drawing in a deep breath, she made the first line on the paper. Every few seconds she would look up to take in his features. They were delicate and yet hard at the same time. He looked young, but there was something about his eyes that felt like looking into a sea of well-lived years. The dichotomy was fascinating, and Sarah found herself putting more detail into this moonlight sketch than she had in a long time.

"What's your name?" he asked.

"Sarah," she said softly. "What's yours?"

"Alex. So, what do you do around here for fun?"

"What do you mean?"

"With your friends," he said. "What do you and your friends do to kill the time?"

She looked up, and he saw the loneliness in her eyes. "I don't really have any friends," she said stiffly. "And I'm okay with that."

"Everyone needs friends."

She snickered and went back to the sketch. "I used to think that. Then one day you realize you don't need anyone but yourself."

Sarah, look at me.

"Huh?" she asked, looking up. It took her a second to realize he hadn't actually spoken. She apologized, remarking on how tired she must be.

Alex had sent the persuasion into her mind half a dozen times, but she brushed it off like it was nothing. Now, even as he screamed it into her head, she just kept staring at the sketchpad. He placed his elbows on his knees and leaned forward.

I said, look at me.

"We're just about done." She kept her eyes on the paper.

Alex sat back, his mind racing with wonder. He focused harder than he ever had before, trying to dig into her psyche.

Come here, Sarah. Come to me.

No response. Her hand continued to fly across the page in zigzagged swoops. He could hear her heart beating; the blood pumping through her was a song. She was special. She couldn't hear him in her head. It was as if she were deaf to his suggestion, and he had never met a mortal capable of such a thing.

"Would you like to have a drink with me after you're finished?" he asked.

Sarah stopped and looked up. He was leering at her, his eyes shimmering in the orange light of the flames. She felt a strange prickle of nervousness in her belly. "What?"

"A drink?" he repeated.

"You can't buy a drink," she reminded him. "And I'm not supplying a minor."

"This is true," he smiled sharply. "But we could go back to my house and open a bottle of my mother's favorite merlot. You can tell me about yourself, about your gift." He pointed at the drawing.

"Better not," she replied.

"Why?"

"I'm a little old for you, kiddo. Besides, it's late and..." She paused, her eyes narrowing. "I thought you said your parents were gone?"

"Excuse me?"

"On the pier, you said your parents were gone. Just now you said we could open a bottle of your mother's wine."

"Well, aren't we intuitive," he smirked. He avoided the question and pointed at her lap. "All finished?"

"Yes." With a quick flourish, she ripped the paper from the pad and handed it to him.

Alex took it and smiled at the amazing likeness. He inhaled slowly before looking back at her. She was waiting for him to pay, but her uneasiness was growing. She was ready to bolt.

"Does twenty sound fair?" he asked.

"More than fair." She held out her hand impatiently.

He reached into his pocket and took out a handful of crumpled bills. "More than twenty," he said, "but well worth it."

Sarah snatched the money and stuffed it into her bag without counting it. Alex continued to watch her. His excitement grew at the prospect of bringing her into the pack. Her heart rate increased with agitation; each thump seemed to scream at him to take her life and see what she would do with the gift he gave in return.

"Thank you. I hope you like it."

She hurriedly got to her feet just as the last of the flames were swept away by the tide. The night felt too dark now, the stars and moon hiding behind purple clouds.

"Sarah, I really wish you would come spend some time with me," Alex said. He stood up, blocking her path.

"I told you no. Why do you want to hang out with me when you should be with friends your own age?"

"I want to give you something," he said.

"What?"

"Immortality," Alex smiled. "Come with me and you'll never be alone again."

"No," she spat, not even seeming to register the absurdity of the words. "I don't want anything from you." She reached into her bag and shoved the money back toward him. "I don't even want your money."

His face was hidden in shadow as the clouds stole the moon's light. Somewhere behind her, she could hear soft, distant laughter. When Alex stepped toward her, his eyes were glowing. She stumbled back, squinting to see him. Then he smiled and ran his tongue across his teeth – teeth that were sharp and wet with saliva as he grew hungrier.

Tears welled in her eyes. The horror of what he was finally settled over her. Whispered voices grew louder in the dark.

"I don't want that," she choked out.

Alex lifted a brow. "You'd rather die? You would give up the gift I'm offering in exchange for death?"

She suddenly bolted, veering to the left to get past him. He was too quick. One second she was running toward the safety of the pier, and the next he had her in his arms, a hand clamped over her mouth. He held her against his chest with a strength she couldn't fathom. She could feel the tips of his fangs scraping her skin as he spoke.

"Last chance, Sarah. Take my gift, or take my death."

Her thoughts were an incoherent, jumbled mess. In the chaos of her mind, she saw her baby sister, Sadie, in her crib at home, sleeping peacefully, unaware of the monsters in the world. If Sarah accepted his gift, she would become one of them. She could never go home. She would be a monster lurking over her own sister's cradle. That couldn't happen. She wouldn't let it.

"Fuck you," she growled against his palm.

The words were muddled, but Alex heard them. He tossed her down into the sand like she was nothing. Before she could move, he was on top of her, pushing her face into the sand until it filled her mouth and she was choking.

"You're a stupid bitch, Sarah."

He sank his teeth into the back of her neck. He sucked hard, then tore the skin apart. Sarah could feel herself fading. Alex stopped just long enough to flip her over so she could look into his nightmarish eyes. He laughed low, then dropped back down, his teeth piercing the vein in her throat.

Her blood was everything. It was sweet and thick, with a sizzle of something that tickled his throat. The more he drank, the more he felt alive. He found her hands above her head and laced his fingers with hers. He wished she had taken the offer. He wondered what she might have been like as one of them. He continued to drink until the last shudder of life passed through her.

Alex fell out of the memory with a growl. Tony's conquest was everything Alex had been searching for since sweet Sarah denied him. They wouldn't miss out again. He wouldn't allow it.

Chapter Six

"You've done a wonderful job here, Sadie. It's very impressive."

Rick stood back from the display of posters she had arranged in the front window. They were promoting a local band he was quite fond of. Many of the bars and clubs up and down the west coast had been vying to host a concert for Pan, but somehow Rick had won the honor of hosting their record release.

"It's not a big deal, Rick. It's just posters."

"Peanut, you need to give yourself more credit than that. You've done more than hang posters, and you know it. If not for all your calls to Pan's manager, we wouldn't be putting posters up at all. Now, where should we go to celebrate?"

"Celebrate?"

"Yes. I thought we could close early and I could take you and Leah out for dinner. My little way of saying thank you for all the hard work you've done." He looked toward the window. "Besides, it's going to rain tonight. The strip will be dead."

She dropped her eyes to the floor. "That's really nice of you, Rick, but I sort of already have plans tonight."

"Oh?"

"Yeah, a date."

"Oh." The word sounded sharp, forced. "With that boy from the other night?"

Sadie nodded and was about to say more when Leah came out of the back storeroom.

"Hey, we should close up now. They say a storm is coming in tonight, and I don't know about you two, but I sure as hell don't want to be here when it starts raining. I gotta walk home."

Rick ran a hand over the back of his head. "I suppose we could."

"Thank you, Rick! I'll go clock out." Leah skipped toward the back of the bar.

"I don't mind staying with you," Rick said, his tone shifting back to something more paternal.

"No, you should take Leah to that dinner. I know she'd love it."

He gave a curt nod and pursed his lips together. "Very well, then." He turned away from her and went back to his office without saying another word.

Sadie wished there was a way to convince Rick she wasn't making a mistake. This would be their second date, or technically their first if you factored in how much Kevin had screwed up the last one. She didn't know how to explain how she felt, not even to herself. There was just something about Tony that was so different from anyone else. He was a mystery she wanted to solve.

Ten minutes later, Sadie followed Rick and Leah outside. He locked up the bar and hesitated when a rumble of thunder preceded the first fat raindrops that pelted the parking lot. "Are we ready?" he asked.

"Absolutely," said Leah. "I'm starving. Good luck on your date tonight, call me later and tell me all about it."

"I will."

"I wish you'd come with us," Rick said, though there was little enthusiasm in his voice.

"Next time," was all she could think to say.

The look on his face was appraising, as though he wasn't sure about his next move. Then he said, "Goodnight, Sadie."

"Goodnight."

Her eyes followed Rick and Leah as they climbed into his Range Rover. She watched them with a feeling of sadness. If only she could get Rick to understand. It made sense that his dislike of Tony came from whatever issues he had with this Alex person, but why couldn't he trust her to make her own decisions?

She waited under the awning. Tony said he would be there by nine. Thirty minutes later, he was a no-show. Another thirty minutes passed, and Sadie felt the tears sting her eyes when she finally accepted he wasn't coming. She had expected to be riding with him, so she had left her car at home. She chose to walk rather than call Rick back.

She made her way along the sidewalk that lined the beach, the rain coming down hard and soaking her clothes straight through. It was only a mile walk to her house, but it seemed longer. The cold soon turned her sadness to fury. How could she have been so stupid? The excitement of being with someone again had swept her up in an illusion that was dangerous. Rick was right; she was just too stubborn to listen.

When she reached the house, she could no longer feel her feet. The rain blurred her vision, which was why she didn't see him standing on her front porch at first. Tony was leaning against the house, his hair a mess of wet fringe that shimmered under the porch light.

"What are you doing here?" she asked, her voice shaking despite her attempts to sound angry.

Tony took a step towards her. "I'm sorry. Something came up and I, I'm just sorry."

Sadie sighed and shook her head. She was experiencing déjà vu. Kevin had showed up on her porch many times saying exactly the same thing. "Whatever," she mumbled. "If you'll excuse me, I have to get warm." She moved past him and had her key in the lock when she felt his hand on her shoulder.

"Come on, Sadie. I'm sorry, I mean it. Let's just start over."

She couldn't help but laugh. The sound was bitter and drenched in sarcasm. "Start what over? You left me to walk home in the rain. I think it's safe to say I won't be starting anything with you."

Tony dropped his hand but blocked her way to the door. "I made a mistake. You don't make those?"

She had made them all the time when she was with Kevin. One mistake after another, and she had suffered for all of them. Sadie would not be that girl again, so desperate for affection that she lowered herself to this level.

"I make mistakes, but I learn from them. You're not going to be my next mistake." There was a quick flash of something in Tony's eyes. It happened so fast, Sadie wasn't sure she didn't imagine it. The action caused her to take a step back from him. "You should go."

"This is bullshit," Tony said, his eyes narrowed. "I'm not like that asshole you dated before."

"Maybe not," she said, dropping her eyes. "But I think it's what's best for me." She took a deep breath and looked at him again. "It was too early for me to go out with you anyway. I'm not ready."

"So that's it?"

She nodded. It had only been a week since she met him, but she could already feel the ache of his absence. It only reassured her that this was the right thing to do. If she felt this strongly after one failed date, any real relationship would destroy her when it ended.

She didn't want to say goodbye, so she simply side-stepped him, turned the lock, and went inside. With her back to the door, she let the tears fall. Kevin had broken her heart, and she had put too much faith in Tony to be the one to fix it. This was her fault for believing it could be different.

Deep in the corners of her mind, she could almost hear Tony's voice. *Open the door, Sadie. Give me one more chance.* She went into the kitchen and took the bottle of vodka out of the freezer. After three quick shots, she couldn't hear him anymore.

The only sound in Tony's ears was the wind as it whipped around him, slamming him in the face with rain. He was standing on the pier, eyeing Sadie's house in the distance. His stomach growled with hunger. As he gripped the wooden railing, he knew that he was no longer going to deny himself what he really wanted. Her blood.

So what if she could resist his call? What difference did it really make if he couldn't play inside her head like his own personal toy box? Her blood called him more than any other before.

As he dropped down off the pier into the sand, Tony knew what he was going to do. He would go in through the window her roommate left open at the back of the house, the one by the washer and dryer that was never checked. Then he would walk down the hall to Sadie's room and drink from her like the life spring she was.

Lightning forked in the sky, filling the air with electricity. He sprinted across the beach and willed himself to take flight. Minutes later, he landed on her roof. He could hear the slow, steady hum of her breathing. She was asleep now, drunk and unaware. He was almost glad she had refused his apology. If she'd accepted it, he wouldn't be hunting her now.

He tilted his head up to the black sky and closed his eyes. The hunger was gnawing away inside him, begging to be released. He couldn't wait anymore.

"You know, if you kill her now, you'll never know why she can resist us."

Tony was startled by the sound of Alex's voice and turned to find his pack standing behind him. He was so lost to his hunger he hadn't even sensed them there. Damn this girl and the way she had weakened him. Then his eyes shifted to Dylan with an accusing glare. Obviously, he had told Alex what Tony confided.

"Don't blame him," Alex said. "I know about her because I have tried to call to her myself."

Tony slowly stood and shook his head. "Why? You knew she was mine."

"I had to check my hunch. It's not like you to let someone go, especially when I could feel how hungry you were for her." He reached out and placed his hand on Tony's shoulder. "I forgive you for keeping it from me."

Tony shrugged Alex's hand away. He was angry that they had shown up when he was about to indulge in what was rightfully his. He had claimed Sadie fair and square.

"I don't care why she can resist us," Tony spat. "She's just a human. She's just blood."

Alex's lips bent into a smile. He turned to Oscar and Dylan and gave them a nod. Seconds later they were gone, disappearing into the inky night sky. "She's a lot more than that, Tony, and you know it. Have you ever known a human who could resist us before?"

"That artist," said Tony, his jaw set tight. "The one you killed."

Alex shrugged. "A mistake I wish I could take back. The only thing I've ever done in my immortal life I regret."

Tony was boring his gaze into Alex while his chest heaved with angry breaths. They both heard a car coming toward the house and dropped to their stomachs. The roommate staggered up to the porch, clearly drunk. It took her several tries to unlock the door, and when she did, she stepped inside without relocking it.

"Mmmm," Alex cooed. "I like that one. Maybe we can keep her, too."

After Hayden went inside, Alex and Tony stood up once more, the rain hiding them on the flat roof.

"What are you talking about?" asked Tony. "We're not keeping anyone. I'll tell you what, you like that one so much, then you can have her while I take Sadie. I'm done playing this fucking game. I'm hungry."

He prepared to drop down from the roof when he felt a sharp, painful pull at the back of his head. Alex was holding him by the hair, yanking Tony back into his chest.

"She's not on the menu anymore," Alex hissed, then let him go with a shove. He laughed deeply as Tony rubbed the back of his head.

"What the fuck is wrong with you? Since when do you decide who I kill and who I don't?"

"It's not up to me, Tony. This isn't my call."

"Rick." It was a statement, not a question.

Alex gave Tony a long, considering look. He tipped his head toward the empty stretch of beach and took off. Tony followed, his stomach aching, his nature still demanding Sadie's payment of blood. When they landed on the sand, her house was far behind them.

Alex began to explain. "Why do you think she works in that bar? I hope you haven't been so blinded by wanting her that you don't have enough common sense to know she's off limits."

"He let me take her out," said Tony, confused.

"He knew his little princess would like you." There was a hint of disgust in Alex's voice. "Don't you get it? You were the bait, Tony."

"He wants to turn her," Tony said. "Why?"

"The same reason I wanted to turn that artist all those years ago. To see what our blood will do to her. And he cares about her. I don't know why, but I suppose sons aren't enough anymore. Rick wants a daughter."

"No," Tony replied, a feeling of heated anger building in him. "I'm not going to play Mr. Nice Guy anymore just so Rick can have Sadie."

"You think you have a choice? Rick holds the cards, Tony. My blood is his blood. You're his childe as much as you're mine."

Tony turned away and ran his hands through his hair. This wasn't how it was supposed to be. Damn him for not killing her when he had the chance.

"She's through with me," Tony said. "You heard her. It's already done."

"I know you." Alex's eyes remained trained on the sea. "You enjoy playing Mr. Nice Guy. And think about what you're being offered here, Tony. You have the chance to get what you were denied a century ago."

"Stop, please." Tony's voice was tinged with painful pleading. "Don't talk about that."

Alex turned to him with a snarl. "Look at you! Getting sentimental in your old age? A hundred years, and you're still not over that girl. Well now is your opportunity to have what Mary Ann refused you."

"Sadie isn't her," Tony said.

"But she could be. Are you going to try and convince me that some part of you doesn't want her? That you don't want to be her teacher like I was yours?" He gripped Tony by the shoulders. "Mary Ann made her choice, and you made yours. If you won't bring Sadie to us, I will. Is that what you want?"

"No," Tony snapped. If Sadie was to be like them, if she was to be a part of this world, then he wanted to be the one to guide her.

Alex smiled. "Then tomorrow you go and patch things up with her."

"And if she still doesn't want anything to do with me?"

Alex's attention returned to the water. "Then there are other ways to get what we want."

Thunder roared above them, and the rain picked up in intensity. As they lifted into the air, Tony took another look at the beach house. She slept soundly, unaware that she was a pawn on their chessboard. She had no idea about the choice she would soon have to make.

Chapter Seven

It was a dream, and Sadie somehow knew that. She stood and watched everything unfold, a silent spectator to what was playing out in front of her. The house around her was magnificent with its polished wood and marble floors. Her eyes found the well-dressed man by the bar, and suddenly she wasn't watching with her own eyes anymore; now she saw everything with his.

Tony stood next to the bar in the parlor, sipping aged Scotch that burned pleasantly down his throat. He heard the rustle of Mary Ann's skirt and turned to her with a smile. She was dressed in black, her mourning attire. She walked across the room, and he lifted his glass in salute. He was wearing the long wool coat his father had gifted him before he left Italy for this new land. Under the coat was a fitted vest of green silk that Mary Ann herself had made. He reached his hand out to her and relished the way she breathed deeply and closed her eyes when his lips met her cheek with a gentle kiss.

"My love," he whispered in her ear. "I was so afraid you would not come back to me."

"I did not want to," she said. "How can you love me, Anthony? How can you love me when your love belongs to another now?"

He sighed and removed his hat. Thick black hair tickled his brow. "None of that is true, love. My want is not for him, but what he can give us."

She pulled her hand away from him and wiped at the tears he realized were falling down her cheeks.

"I came to say goodbye. That is all." She held his gaze and for a moment, even he was not sure she would do what came next. "Farewell."

She never looked back as she strode across the parlor and out the front door. He hurried after her and was met with a gust of cold air when he stepped onto the dew-covered expanse of the front lawn. His feet carried him across the grass, down the sloping hill toward the cliffs overlooking the ocean below. Moments later he was nearing her, his breath labored.

"I know you are not evil," she told him as he slowed his steps. "But evil follows you. Whatever is left of the man I love will soon be devoured by the demon within. It has been courting you for months, and now you wish me to marry that darkness as well."

"Mary Ann!" he shouted, only a few feet from her now. "Don't walk away from me. Please, come with me."

"Is that what you really want?" she asked incredulously. "To never feel the beauty of time as it fades or know what the peaceful dance of death is like? This is your want, Anthony?"

"Who wants death?" he asked, holding his arms out with exasperation. "Who would choose the withered effects of age and the end of life when they can have youth and life eternal?" He took a step toward her and let his eyes penetrate her own. "I trust him, Mary Ann. All I ask is that you trust him too."

"He drinks the blood of living people," she said sharply. "He is a monster, and you will become like him."

Tony looked hurt and then angry. He closed the distance between them and reached out to grab her by the arms before she could take any more steps away from him. His grip was so tight bruises were already forming. "You promised yourself to me. You are my wife!"

She tried to pull away from him, but his fingers dug into her skin. "I promised you my life, Anthony. My life until death parted us." She shook her head, watching as a fiery tawny hue mingled with his green eyes. "You live on this earth no longer."

"I am not like him," Tony said.

Mary Ann brushed his cheek with her fingertips. "But you want to be."

He let her go with a shove as the awareness of what she was saying settled over him. "I want you," he told her with teary eyes. "For always."

"Not like this."

"Why?" he screamed. "If you love me, then you love all of me!"

She took a step backward. The strength of the wind increased as she moved closer to the cliff's edge. "I will always love the man you once were." Her voice broke with tears as she took another step back, and then another.

"What are you doing, Mary Ann?"

"Better to leave this world," she told him softly, "than to walk it without you."

"Stop," Tony bellowed. "Come back to me, love. Please, come back to me."

"Will you choose me?" she asked. "Will you grow old with me?"

He shook his head, his eyes wide with shock. "Don't do this! Come, be with me as you promised. For always."

"My love will never be enough to stop you from what he is. I see him," she said. "There in the shadows, grinning, knowing he has won. I love you so much it hurts; it always has. The idea of spending forever in servitude to eternal hunger, taking the lives of innocents... my darling, it is too terrible. I must go before you drag me to hell with you."

She blew an invisible kiss, an invisible goodbye. Mary Ann, his beloved, took the last step that sent her careening over the edge of the cliff. Her body thudded over rocks, bones snapping so loud it echoed through the hills.

"Mary Ann! Mary Ann!"

He called to the corpse that could not hear him anymore. In the end, she lived up to her vow. She stayed till death parted them.

When Sadie opened her eyes, the dream was still fresh. She rolled over on her side and stared her alarm clock down, hating the cheerful bright numbers that announced her wake-up call. It was going to be a bad day; she knew that much. Clearly Tony was still hanging out deep in her subconscious. She also had to face Rick at work and explain being stood up to Hayden.

As she brushed her teeth, she continued to fume over what happened the night before. She was pissed that he left her standing there in the rain, alone and humiliated. Rick was right about Tony not being a good guy. He was just like Kevin if you really broke it down. Maybe it was genetic, and deep inside all men were jerks. Perhaps being born with a penis automatically predisposed you to the asshole gene.

She went into the kitchen and found Hayden holding a freshly brewed cup of coffee in one hand and a plate of pancakes in the other. She took one look at Sadie and immediately set the food on the counter.

"Tell me what happened."

Sadie reached for the abandoned cup of coffee. "Nothing happened," she shrugged. "He ghosted me at the bar, and I had to walk home in the rain. When I got here, he was waiting on the porch. Said he had something come up and would I give him a second chance."

"Are you?" Hayden asked.

"I thought about it, but I don't think so."

"But you were so excited about him."

Sadie headed to the living room and Hayden followed. "My subconscious decided for me. I had some weird dream about him last night."

"What kind of dream? Was it a sexy one?"

"Try suicide and blood-sucking monsters."

"Yikes," Hayden said with a little laugh. "Well, at least you know you're not a pushover anymore."

"I guess there is a bright side."

"Of course there is. And some other hot babe will come along. There's plenty of fish in the sea and blah blah blah." She gave Sadie's knee a pat then went back into the kitchen to clean up the celebratory breakfast.

Sadie wasn't so sure there would be another guy. She'd been burned too much in too short a time. "Work is going to suck," Sadie said as she helped Hayden with the dishes. "I really don't want to see that 'I told you so' look on Rick's face."

"So, don't tell him. It's none of his business anyway."

Sadie handed her a plate. "But he was right."

"And? I was right about Kevin, but you didn't listen to me either."

"Thanks," Sadie mumbled, then splashed a bit of sudsy water in Hayden's direction.

Hayden giggled and then turned to face Sadie with thoughtful eyes. "Look, you gave it a shot, and I'm proud of you. Dicks come and dicks go," she waved her hand dismissively. "You just have to get back up, dust yourself off, and move forward."

Sadie pulled her in for a hug. "Thanks, Hay."

"That's what I'm here for."

Sadie spent the rest of the day walking the beach and did everything she could to not think about Tony. When that failed, she reminded herself that she just needed a few days to wallow in self-pity. Maybe in some ways, Tony had been good for her. She realized now that she didn't want to go back to being the sad, broken person she was before he walked into the bar. It was time to love herself in all the ways she had depended on others to love her before.

The forecast for the night was clear, so Sadie chose to walk to work. Leah was the only one there, scheduled to leave when Rick came in at ten. Before Leah could ask how the date went, Sadie raised a hand. "I don't want to talk about it."

Leah nodded then offered to watch the bar while Sadie did inventory in the back. It was a sweet gesture. This way she wouldn't have to put on a happy face for patrons. She could bury herself beneath boxes of booze and be invisible.

She had just started on her fourth box when she heard the door to the back room open. She looked over her shoulder and saw Rick standing there.

"How are you doing back here, Peanut?"

"Okay, I guess." She dug into the box and held up a vanilla-flavored bottle of whiskey. "Rick, why do you keep ordering these? No one ever asks for flavored liquor."

"You know, Peanut, an extended menu brings in more people. Flavor will always be in style."

She set the bottle aside. "You're the boss."

“There’s someone here for you.”

She looked up, a little surprised. She figured it was probably Hayden stopping in to make sure she wasn't crying to the regulars. “Tell her I’m fine, and I’ll be home after close.”

“It’s not Hayden.”

Rick held the door open a little wider, and she could see Tony standing next to the bar swirling the straw in his drink. She bit hard into her lip. She had not expected to see him again so soon. Finally, she returned her attention to the boxes.

“Tell him to go. I don’t want to see him.”

Rick cleared his throat. “Sadie, I think you should come out here and tell him that yourself.”

She looked up at him in shock. “Rick, please.”

“You have to do this for yourself, Peanut. You’ll thank me one day.”

She dropped the clipboard on the floor and got up with a huff. “Yeah, right,” she mumbled. Rick placed a hand on her shoulder as she passed, a way of reassuring her.

“I’ll be in my office if you need me.”

“I won’t,” she told him, then made her way toward the bar.

Besides Tony, there were just a few people congregating around the pool tables. He looked up from his drink and smiled as she approached. She didn’t return the gesture.

“What do you want?” she asked, hands on her hips.

“I can see you’re still pissed.”

She opened her mouth to speak but was cut off by a sudden sneeze. She glared at him. “I have a cold. Thanks to my little jaunt through the rain.”

He absentmindedly strummed his fingers against the bar top. “Scientifically speaking you can’t catch a cold from being in the cold. It’s a virus and...”

"Thank you for that medical diagnosis," she cut him off.

"I'm sorry, okay. I'm nervous. Will you please let me try and explain?"

She lifted her brow and crossed her arms over her chest as he inched a little closer.

"I was late, and I'm sorry. By the time I got here, you were gone, and I didn't know what to do but go wait for you at your house. I had been up late the night before and overslept. I should have just been honest with you about that."

"Seriously, that's it?"

"I could make up a better excuse, but I won't."

Sadie glanced back at Rick's office. His door was open, and she could see him sitting at his desk.

"What do you want, Tony?"

"I want you to give me a second chance."

She was quiet for an agonizingly long minute. "And I want to." His face broke apart with a smile as he reached for her. She held up her hand and took a step away. "But I can't."

A crease formed between his brows. The whole honesty shit was supposed to be enough. "I don't understand why you're so pissed about this. It was an honest mistake, Sadie. Jesus, you act like I was fucking someone else or just had something better to do."

"Who you fuck is none of my business." She could sense his cool composure faltering. Kevin was that way, too.

"I didn't mean it like that."

He put his fingers to his temples, breathed deeply, and then let the full weight of his gaze land on her. He tried again to get into her head, to penetrate all those wispy layers of thought. *One more chance, Sadie. Just one more.*

"Look, it's not even just because you were late," she said, his persuasion still completely absent in her mind. "I'm not ready. I have to have time for me. And I like you, Tony, I really do. But I'm just in a place right now where I have to come first."

"I'm not asking you to marry me, Sadie. I'm asking you to go on a date."

"That's fair, but my answer is still no."

The irritation in him lit like a brush fire. Rick's eyes were boring in on him, and it was only fueling his anger. "Fine," he said, hands up in the air as he backed up towards the door. "I'll leave, but I'll be back."

"Excuse me?"

"I'm not giving up on you, Miss Sadie," he winked. "Not by a long shot."

Tony drove down to the beach where Alex and the others were waiting for him. He approached the three with a pronounced frown. Dylan chuckled and sucked hard on the joint pinched between his fingers. "Somebody looks unhappy," he said, handing the rest of his smoke to Oscar.

Alex had his back to all of them, his grey eyes set on the waves. He didn't turn around but spoke in that calm way that often drove Tony crazy. "So, I take it things didn't go well."

Tony gritted his teeth. "No, they didn't. I told you she wasn't going to give me another shot." He narrowed his eyes and turned to Dylan. "This is your fault, you little shit! If you hadn't needed help dumping that fat guy, I wouldn't have been late to the bar in the first place."

Dylan's mouth fell open. "Fuck you, Tony."

This elicited a growl from Tony whose eyes immediately began to smolder. He took a step towards Dylan before Oscar moved between them.

"Boys, boys," Alex snickered and turned to face them. "Play nice for Daddy."

Oscar, always the solid voice of reason, said, "You're going about this the wrong way."

"Oh yeah," Tony huffed. "Enlighten me, Casanova."

"Girls and their best friends are unbreakable. Get the friend on your side. She'll convince this girl to give you another go."

"That's an excellent idea," chimed in Alex.

Tony wasn't sold. "How? I'm sure she played the whole 'he made me walk home in the rain' record until it was broken. No way is she going to help me out."

Alex crossed his arms. "All she needs is a little push in the right direction. Just because we can't get inside Sadie's head doesn't mean that luscious meal she lives with is off limits." He put his arm around Tony. "I think I know just what we need to get you back in her good graces."

Sadie was worn out by the time she got home. Shadow was on the porch, so she let him follow her inside. With Hayden still at work, Sadie would have the alone time she wanted. She took a beer out of the fridge and escaped to her bedroom.

She was asleep before the cap to the beer was even off and woke up the next morning with the bottle still in her hand. The sound of loud music coming from the living room signaled that Hayden was up and at 'em. Sadie moved down the hallway with a yawn but was surprised when she saw Hayden standing on a footstool hanging crepe paper from the ceiling fan.

"Hey!" Hayden beamed. "You're up." She hopped down and grabbed a notepad. "I've been trying to remember all night if you're a vodka girl or tequila."

"What are you doing?"

"I'm decorating, obviously. We're having a belated birthday party for you."

Sadie's eyes grew wide. "No, no we are not. My birthday was two months ago."

"I'm aware of that, Sadie. Which is why I used such a big word like belated."

She winked before going into the kitchen. Red plastic cups had been stacked alongside paper plates with the words HAPPY BIRTHDAY printed on them in bright bold letters.

"Hayden, this is a sweet gesture, but I don't want a party, belated or otherwise."

"Honey, if anybody in the world ever needed a party, it's you."

"This is insane," Sadie said. "I don't need a party. What I need is a spa day."

Hayden sighed and reached for Sadie's hand. "Mami, I know this has been a rough few months. I really do. But you have got to start living a little before you wither up and die an old cat lady."

"A party isn't going to make things magically perfect again," Sadie insisted.

"When has anything ever been perfect? Face it, girl, you need to let loose. Tonight, we're celebrating your birthday." She pointed the tip of her pen at Sadie. "Which brings me back to the question of vodka or tequila?"

Sadie looked down at the balloons. Maybe Hayden was right. Maybe she did need to just be free for once.

"Vodka," she said and then looked at Hayden with a smile. "And tequila."

Hayden squealed and pulled Sadie into a hug. "You don't have to worry about anything. I've got it all under control."

"I have to work tonight," Sadie reminded her.

Hayden shook her head. "Nope, I already took care of that. Rick is closing the bar early so he can come."

"You invited Rick?"

"Well yeah," Hayden chuckled. "I had to improvise on the guest list a little."

Sadie tore open the package of balloons. "What do you mean?"

"Well, we don't know that many people. So, I took the initiative and decided tonight we would make new friends."

She tossed Sadie her phone where the Brave Beach Facebook community page was pulled up. A graphic announced a birthday bash that was open to everyone, BYOB.

"You posted this on Facebook?"

"Yes, I did. So, it's too late to back out now."

Sadie glanced around their small living room. "Where the hell are we supposed to fit everyone in Brave Beach?"

"We live on the beach. We'll just have the party out there." She stood up and clapped her hands together. "I'm going to pick up the liquor. You work on those balloons." When she was at the door, she called out to Sadie. "Happy birthday, girl."

With one last wink, she was gone, and Sadie was left to blow up the balloons for a party she wasn't even sure she wanted.

Chapter Eight

The beach was lined with cars as far as Sadie could see, which wasn't all that far since her vision had blurred somewhat from three tequila shots. Most of the guests respected the DO NOT ENTER sign taped to the front door, but Sadie did have to throw a couple out of Hayden's bedroom. She recognized faces from the bar and some who worked with Hayden, but she didn't actually know anyone there. The party was raging, everyone was drinking and wishing her a happy birthday, yet Sadie still felt alone.

"Having fun?" Hayden asked as she stumbled up the porch steps and threw her arm around Sadie's shoulder. The smell of alcohol on her breath was overwhelming.

Sadie took the drink out of Hayden's hand. "Maybe you should slow down."

"Why? I'm not driving anywhere." Hayden snatched the cup back and downed the rest. When it was empty, she tossed it to the ground and laid her head on Sadie's shoulder. "Are you having any fun at all?"

"Yes," Sadie lied. She looked over the sea of bodies in front of the house. "Have you seen Rick?"

Hayden hiccupped and shook her head. "Nope, but I'm sure he'll be here."

Sadie heard someone in the crowd say, "Yo, Oscar! Over here." She looked through the current of people and saw Oscar, Tony, and Dylan heading toward the house.

"You invited them?" she asked, turning to Hayden with hurt eyes. "Why?"

"To be fair, I told you I invited everyone in town."

"And I told you that Tony ditched me the other night. What the hell, Hayden?"

Hayden shook her head, her watery eyes blinking fast as she tried to think of the right words. Someone shouted her name, and both girls looked to see Oscar making his way towards them with three shadows behind him.

"There you are," he smiled and pulled Hayden down off the porch to kiss her cheek. "Sorry we're late." He looked over at Sadie and said, "Happy birthday. Alex has the gift."

The mention of his name had Sadie looking for the elusive Alex she had heard so much about. When a young man, surely not old enough to buy the bottle of wine in his hand, approached her, she couldn't hide her surprise.

"I don't think we've ever met," he said. "I'm Alex."

Still stunned by his age, it took her a second to realize he was holding the bottle out to her. She took it and then shook his hand out of politeness but said nothing else. Tony's eyes met hers, and she flushed with remembrance. Realizing her silence was earning her a pleading stare from Hayden, she finally cleared her throat.

"Nice to meet you. And thank you for the wine."

"Thank you for having us," Alex said. He looked around at all the people. "You must be a popular girl."

"Hardly," said Sadie, not meaning to sound as annoyed as she did. "I'm going to take this inside. Thanks again."

She went into the house quickly. Once the door was closed, she fought back tears that turned into sharp sobs. She had to rush into the kitchenette, lean over the sink, and turn on the faucet. The sobbing wasn't helped by the handfuls of water she scooped into her mouth. They pushed out of her throat with force until, mercifully, her breathing started to even out.

How could Hayden invite them after everything, and why didn't she tell Sadie she knew Oscar? The party outside continued, and Sadie forced herself to isolate the droning of music to help regain focus. Without putting much thought into it, she opened the bottle of wine and tipped her head back, gulping the drink until light red streaks poured from the corners of her mouth. When the bottle was nearly empty, she put it on the counter and fought the urge to give it all back. The room was spinning unpleasantly.

"Sadie, are you okay?"

She lifted her eyes and saw Tony standing by the front door. She hadn't even heard him come in. "Am I okay?" she asked, giggling at the absurdity of the question. "My best friend has apparently been seeing Oscar and then invited you all here just to hurt me. And then you show up with Rick's arch nemesis that turns out to be a kid! A kid who will probably get me popped for contributing to a minor. So, no, I am not okay."

"Don't be mad at Hayden," he said softly and took a step forward. "Oscar can be charming, and she didn't want you to say no to the party. And I know he looks like a kid, but Alex isn't... he's fine here."

"Charming, huh?" she scoffed. "I guess you all take after each other. You charmed me, too."

"I'm sorry, Sadie. I never meant to hurt you."

"Yeah, well, no one ever means to hurt someone, do they? It's just one of those parts of life. It doesn't matter." She shrugged and took a step, her drunken mind forgetting the one stair that led back into the living room. She careened forward, and Tony caught her before she hit the floor.

"Shit, girl, how much have you had to drink?"

"A lot," she conceded and let him lead her to the sofa. He sat down beside her, and she dropped her head back into the cushions, willing the room to quit spinning. After a few minutes, she evened out. She opened her eyes and turned them on Tony. "Why are you here?"

He reached into his jacket pocket and offered her his closed fist. "Oscar said I should get you flowers, but I thought this was more you."

She stared at his hand but made no move toward it. "What is it?"

"Open your hand and find out."

Sadie offered her flat palm, and he dropped a silver chain and pendant into her hand. She lifted it up for examination. The pendant was oval-shaped, and engraved on one side was the symbol of a cross with a large circle making out the top of a crossed T. A red stone had been placed there, and it glittered against the filtered moonlight coming in through the window.

"I can't take this," she finally said. "It's too much."

"You have to take it," he said sweetly. "It's got your initials on it."

She turned the pendant over and sure enough, her initials had been engraved in big loopy letters. S. D. No one had ever done anything like this for her before. Not even Kevin.

"You didn't have to do this," she said. "It's not even my real birthday."

"That doesn't matter." Tony slowly reached his hand toward her face, and when she did not pull away, he let his fingers caress her cheek. "Give me another chance," he pleaded. "Just one more shot."

She was still looking down at the pendant but slowly lifted her eyes to his face. She believed everything he just said to her, and she wanted a second chance as much as he did. Not knowing what to say, she smiled softly and nodded her head.

"Yeah?" His smile was wide.

"I mean, why not?"

"Can I put it on you?"

Sadie handed him the necklace and leaned into him, pulling her long hair away from her neck. She could feel Tony's breath on her skin as he reached around her to do the clasp. His cheek brushed hers, and she felt the rhythm of her heart increase. He sat back and touched the pendant with admiration.

"It looks great," he said. "Do you like it?"

She touched the pendant, tracing the grooves of the cross. "I love it. What does it mean?"

"It's an ankh. It means eternal life." He leaned in as she continued to eye the pendant, the red stone reflecting light in her eyes. When she looked at him again, he was so close she could taste his breath.

"So, is this what you wanted?" she asked.

He ran his fingers gently through her hair. "You want it too," he said. "Don't you?" His voice was soft, gentle. It made goosebumps erupt all over her body. He licked his lips, and with his eyes still latched to hers, he leaned forward until their lips brushed. "Don't you?" he asked again.

"Yes," she managed.

He offered her a sweet smile before he pressed his lips against hers. Like before, the kiss started off as simple pressure. Soon though, she opened her mouth, inviting him to take the kiss further. His tongue slipped into the warm cavern of her mouth. He tasted like a dream, like the ocean and the fine mist of early morning. He lit her entire body on fire. His hands went to the back of her neck, holding her to him. She turned her body so she could straddle him, her hands clutching the side of his face.

"We should, we should slow down," he said, feeling his body responding in a way that was more than sexual. Her arousal was pumping the blood through her with a pulsing beat that rang heavily in his ears.

She giggled against his lips. "Isn't that my line?"

She kissed him again and ground her body into his. She felt the hard line of his erection and moaned into his mouth. Tony's hands gripped her hips, moving back and forth, knowing they should stop but wanting nothing to come between them. He wrapped his arms around her waist and moved her away so that she fell back onto the sofa and he could be on top. His lips drew into a smirk as he took off his jacket. She was breathing hard, her hands guided by alcohol and arousal toward the button of his jeans.

"Hold up," he said, glancing behind him at the front door. "What if someone walks in?"

Her whole body was aching with desire. She had not been with anyone since Kevin, and she was ashamed of how much she wanted this now. "Let's go to my room," she said. When she started to sit up, Tony put his hand on her chest to hold her back.

Her heart milled against his palm, and he was fully aware of the danger. He might not be able to stop himself if the hunger took over. "You're drunk, Sadie," he told her softly before leaning down to gently nip at her lips. "I don't want you to do something you might regret."

She looked confused and shook her head. "Quit being such a choir boy, Tony." She wrapped her arms around his neck and pulled him back to her. "I want this," she breathed. "I want you."

"You can't take it back," he reminded her as he brushed the hair from her eyes. "Things will change."

He meant those words with all the definitions attached. Sex for humans was not the same as it was for him. He remembered what it was like with Mary Ann, how sex brought them together. Now, sex was just a prelude to the feed. If he couldn't have her blood, then he should be allowed to have her body. He kissed her harder and slid his pelvis between her legs. His hand crept up her bare thigh, beneath the short black skirt she wore at Hayden's insistence. Tony licked at her neck, loving the salty taste of her skin, and it was his turn to moan when she lifted her hips to meet him.

"Are you sure?" he asked, still giving her the chance to save herself.

She nodded her head. He dipped his fingers between her legs for a moment before they moved upward, his fingers brushing the edge of her panties. Then the front door opened.

"Sadie? Peanut, are you okay in here?" It was Rick, his concerned voice only a few feet behind them.

Her eyes went wide, and Tony's jaw tensed with frustration. She held her finger to her lips, pleading with her stare for him to stay quiet. Rick flipped the switch and took another step into the house. He released a shocked gasp when he saw Tony and Sadie trying to disentangle themselves.

"Oh... I..." Rick was clearly as embarrassed as they were. "I... I'll just... be outside."

Rick eyed Tony, who was trying to put his jacket back on and button his jeans at the same time. Sadie was pushing her skirt back down her hips. Rick's voice had an edge of disappointment, and when he walked outside, he slammed the door hard behind him.

"Oh my god," Sadie groaned and leaned against the sofa. "This is so embarrassing."

"Who cares about him?" asked Tony. He reached down and took her hand, then helped her up. His arms wrapped around her waist, and he started walking her toward the hallway. "Which room is yours?"

"I care," she told him and wiggled out of his arms. "He's been good to me."

Tony leaned back into the wall. He crossed his arms over his chest, and the two of them looked at one another in silence. "Go," he finally said with a nod towards the door. "I'll wait here."

"I'm sorry..."

"There you go again," he interrupted. "Always apologizing for someone else's misstep. Just go on. I promise I'm not leaving."

Sadie gave him a grateful smile, then hurried out the front door. Tony inhaled sharply. He smashed his fist into the wall with a quick punch. "Fucking Rick," he mumbled as he walked toward the room he already knew was hers.

Sadie fought through the crowd looking for Rick. She heard Hayden call her name and saw her very drunk friend being carried into the house by Oscar as Dylan and Alex followed. "Shit," she cursed. She knew she needed to check on Hayden, but first, she needed to see Rick. She finally landed on him about to get into his Rover. She ran towards him and called out, "Rick! Wait!"

He turned to her and adjusted his glasses. Both their faces were pink as Sadie leaned against his car trying to catch her breath. He said, "Peanut, you should get back to your party."

"No," she shook her head. "It's not even my birthday!"

"I'm not your father. You don't have to explain anything to me. I should have knocked."

She leaned forward, hands on her knees. "I don't know what the hell I'm doing," she sighed.

"You're living," Rick assured. "You're a young woman, and you've spent the last two years hanging out with an old man in a bar. All you're doing now is making up for that."

"Is that what I'm doing?"

"I think so. If my opinion still means anything to you, I think you should give this boy a chance. It's obvious he likes you very much." He touched the pendant around her neck. "I think you were right, Sadie. My problem was with his tattooed skin, not the person underneath it."

"And Alex," she said, remembering Rick's apparent hatred of him. "He's a kid, Rick. What could he have done to make you hate him so much?"

Rick shifted uncomfortably. "He's not a child. And whatever problems I have with Alex, I can assure you I won't let those deter me from giving you and this Tony your chance."

"But..."

"Now, go back to your party." He cut her off and reached into the Rover, pulling out a small box wrapped in shiny pink paper. "I know it's not your birthday, so just consider this a thank you. I know you love Poe. When I saw this, well, I just had to snag it."

Sadie carefully removed the wrapping. Inside was a silver charm. It was a raven. She smiled with appreciation. "You're the best, Rick. It's beautiful."

"You're very welcome. Should look quite stunning next to the ankh around your neck." He kissed the top of her head. "Goodnight, Peanut."

Sadie watched him go then headed back to the house. Most of the partygoers were dispersing. When she stepped inside, Dylan, Oscar, and Alex were sitting on her sofa.

"Where's Hayden?" she asked.

"Asleep," Alex answered. He nudged Oscar and Dylan then stood up and stopped in front of Sadie. "Oscar got her all tucked in tight. She's going to have a hell of a hangover in the morning."

"It wouldn't be the first," she shrugged. "Thank you for taking care of her."

Oscar nodded, wished her happy birthday again, and went out the door. Dylan followed. Alex smiled gently. "Isn't it strange how we never really appreciate this day, that of our birth? It marks every second that our feet shift across the soil, but we never give the day the admiration it deserves." Then he took her hand and gave it a chaste kiss before leaving, too.

"Weird kid," she mumbled then locked the front door.

After a quick check on Hayden, Sadie walked to her bedroom. It was dark, the only light coming from the glow of her alarm clock. She looked around but saw no sign of Tony.

"Hello?"

He didn't answer. She hurried to the window and pulled back the curtains. The party was over, leaving only discarded cups and popped balloons. The sound of shuffled footsteps emerged behind her. Tony came to a stop behind her, and Sadie's eyes shut tight as his hands slid up her arms and smoothed over her hair.

"You still want me?" he whispered.

The deep tone of his voice sent shivers up her spine. She let out a breath and said, "I want you."

She did want him, but a part of her was still unsure. She didn't want to get hurt again, especially by him.

He turned her around and cupped her face. "You can trust me."

"Can I?"

He held her stare, and for a moment he wanted to bolt. This wasn't ever going to be love. She would see through him, and after she drank Rick's blood, she would know the monster he really was. Tony had no desire to love this girl; he wanted to feed from her. There was an order on him though, and Sadie was a prize Rick wasn't going to lose.

"Yes, you can." He pulled her body against his.

"I do," she breathed. "I trust you, Tony."

He had to stop her talking. If she kept speaking about trust with that doe-eyed innocence, he would never be able to stop himself from tasting her. He leaned his face into hers, then bypassed her lips to kiss the sensitive spot just below her ear.

His hands moved under her shirt and traced circles across her belly. Sadie clutched his jacket tight. Her head fell back as his mouth explored her collarbone, his tongue sweeping delicately along her skin. Tony felt a tremor move through her body.

He moved the kiss back to her lips. Tony pushed her into the wall, holding her there with his body while he removed his jacket. He pulled the t-shirt over his head and let it fall. She reached for his chest and traced her fingers over the skin. Tony bit his lip, trying like hell to hold back his hunger for her blood and instead embrace the desire for her body.

These moments of passion usually ended in death. It was just the nature of what he was. He would provide pleasure in exchange for life, but with Sadie that was not an option. She moved her fingertips down his abdomen, awestruck as his muscles constricted. Tony knew he had won the game. Sadie was ready to surrender.

She smiled sweetly, then wound her arms around his neck. She kissed him with a tenderness that became more demanding. He braced his hands on the wall and rolled his hips against her, blinded by the desire to own her.

Sadie stepped away, inhaled a breath, then tugged her shirt over her head. She sat on the edge of the bed and watched as he undid his jeans. When they were both free, he knelt in front of her. His fingers traced a line down the front of her chest.

"Are you scared?" he asked.

"No," she answered.

He grinned. She was scared and he knew it; he could feel it in her heart. Tony leaned forward and she went back onto the mattress, welcoming him into her arms. The feel of her warm skin against his cold flesh made her body arch into him. He focused on the vein in her neck, blue and beautiful, stretched against her skin.

Tony felt the ache in his gums, his fangs beginning to descend as his body fought nature. She moved beneath him, ankles crossing above his waist. Her hands raked lightly against his back, urging him to keep going.

He pushed slowly inside her, gritting his teeth as the warmth enveloped him. Sadie let out a sigh and moaned softly. Tony could feel himself shifting, the points of his fangs breaking through his gums. What would she do if she opened her eyes and saw him this way? It would be over then. He would kill her. Rick and Alex would be left with disappointment again.

He dropped his head into the crook of her neck, holding her close. Tony was so close to her skin that he could smell her blood. The aroma was richer than any he had ever consumed before. He wanted to taste her. Sadie tried to move his face to hers, to kiss him, but he began to lick at her neck as a distraction.

Blood. Blood. Blood. The smell was in her sweat and in her heated breath. His mouth opened, his eyes zeroing in on the blue line in her throat. *Do it!* His body was demanding it. Tony brought the tip of his fangs in contact with her skin and felt her body go stiff. There was just a nick, but it was enough that the smell of her blood filled the air and his mouth watered. He was ready to gorge himself on the fragility lying beneath him.

"Tony," she whispered as her orgasm approached.

He lifted his head to look at her. Tony wanted to be looking in those blue eyes when he drained life from them. But her eyes were closed, and her head was tilted back as she moaned his name. Something snapped in him. The control was reclaimed. His fangs rescinded and his eyes simmered back to green. He felt her body tighten around him, and he kissed her hard as they climaxed together.

Tony stayed on top of her, panting in her ear as he listened to her heartbeat slow. He was so close to taking her life, and now, as she looked up with a dreamy gaze, he was glad he hadn't. She smiled at him, her cheeks flushed, and then she let out a laugh of exhilaration.

"I'm sorry," she said, putting a hand over her mouth. She turned her head away, embarrassed.

Tony moved to her side. "What?"

"It's nothing," she said.

He took her wrists and pulled them away, then cupped her chin. "Don't do that, Sadie. Tell me."

"It's just, I never... you know. At least not with another person."

He lifted his brow. "Never? Not even with other guys?"

She looked at the ceiling. "There haven't been a lot of other guys," she admitted. She rolled over onto her side to face him. "Pretty lame, huh?"

He ran a fingertip along her cheek. "Not even a little. I'm glad it was with me."

He really meant it. The idea he was the only person to ever give her that pleasure made him swell with pride. His eyes moved to the clock. It was nearing morning.

"Shit," he said. "I had no idea it was so late." He still had to feed before sunrise. "I better get going." He kissed her again then rolled away.

"You can stay," she offered. "Hayden will be sleeping until tomorrow afternoon."

"Wish I could, but I have to be somewhere early. Believe me, if I could stay I would." He leaned across the bed and kissed her cheek. "Will I see you tonight?"

She nodded. "I get off at ten."

He kissed her briefly. "Then I'll be there at ten. Don't get up," he said as she reached for her shirt. "I can show myself out."

Tony opened her door and stopped, looking back one more time. She had curled into a ball beneath the sheets. He knew she was worried about him leaving right after sex, but there was no time to sweet talk her now. He wanted to say something to her. A line so convincing it would leave her no room to doubt. Then Rick could give her his blood and it would be over. Instead, he left without saying a word.

CHAPTER NINE

Tony arrived back at the house two hours before sunrise. As he stepped through the front door into the darkness, he hoped like hell his brothers were in their rooms preparing to sleep. He needed the time alone. He made a mistake, and there was no way to change it.

Sure, he accomplished bringing Sadie back to his side, but he risked killing her by allowing them to get so close. Tony turned the corner and walked into the parlor where he found Alex sitting in a straight back chair sipping a glass of wine. Alex had been a refuge many times in Tony's immortal life, but now he was looking for ways to escape these moments alone with him. He didn't want to discuss the plan and the reality of what would soon happen.

Before he regained control, he almost took Sadie's blood, and his hunger for it was overwhelming. He wasn't sure he'd be able to stop himself next time. He was a killer who never had to cradle that part of himself before. Now, he was being used as a lure so Rick and Alex could have what they wanted. Tony despised them for it. There weren't supposed to be any rules and regulations in their shadowy existence, just the freedom to indulge with reckless abandonment.

His human life had come to an end just as the twentieth century was blooming. Most of his childhood was spent wishing he was someone else. A rigid upbringing coupled with the stiff and unbending rules of society had nearly driven him over the edge. That was when he left the only life he knew in Venice and moved to America. He met his charming Mary Ann soon after. She was welcome relief when she stumbled into him one sunny afternoon on a cobbled street in New York City. A year later, Alex came along and offered him the chance to live in a world that would sever Tony's ties to the purist dictatorship that was society.

He would never regret meeting Alex or becoming his childe. There were moments when his memories would claw at the grave of recollection and Mary Ann's face would fill his mind. He once loved her with every fiber a human man could. There was no room in his now un-beating heart for that kind of love to ever exist again. Tony knew he should never have marked Sadie and chosen her that night, but once he did, he should have killed her. Now, it was too late.

Alex took a long sip of his wine then fixed his eyes on Tony. "I take it things went well on your end," he said with a knowing leer.

"I guess you could say that."

"I can smell her on you," Alex chuckled. He looked down at his glass. "Is she still alive?"

"Of course she's still alive," Tony huffed. "I can't kill her, remember?"

"Those are the rules. But I still had to ask. I can't think of a single woman, or man for that matter, who has ever had the pleasure of your company and didn't end up a broken pile of flesh underneath you."

"I didn't mean for it to happen," Tony said and stepped into the parlor fully. "I tried to convince her it was a bad idea, but it happened anyway."

"What stopped you? Even miles away I could feel your shift, feel your hunger."

"I don't know. I guess I just have better control now."

"Or," Alex said, pointing a finger at Tony, "you really are hoping she will be a replacement for Mary Ann."

"Shut up," Tony hissed. "I didn't kill her because Rick would have my head on a fucking plate if I killed his little Peanut."

Alex tilted his head back and laughed deeply. "Why do you try to lie to me? You could have killed Sadie that first night, but you didn't. You let her live. Why?" When Tony didn't answer, Alex continued. "I'll tell you why, sweet brother. Because you want what Mary Ann stole from you when she threw herself off that cliff. You never wanted to enter this life without her, and you've been sulking ever since."

"That's bullshit, Alex. This is getting out of control. Do you ever stop to think what will happen when she finds out what Rick has been doing? That we set her up from the word go."

"It won't matter," said Alex before swallowing the rest of his wine. "She won't care."

"Won't care?" Tony released a sarcastic chuckle. "You really don't know as much as you think you do."

"I don't know much? I've walked this earth for over a hundred and fifty years." He stood from his chair and glared hard. "You ungrateful little fuck! There isn't an emotion a human being possesses that I haven't studied and devoured. If Mary Ann had loved you, Tony, she would have come into my arms like a good girl. And you would still have her now."

The words swept over Tony. The accusation that Mary Ann had not loved him enough to be with him forever was unforgivable. Not because it was a lie but because he knew it was the truth.

"Fuck you!" Tony yelled and angrily charged toward Alex like he was possessed.

His sire moved quickly and had Tony by the throat and up against the wall before Tony could register the action. Alex had never raised a hand to him before that moment. They were closer than close, bonded by blood. Tony was the first vampire Alex sired, and they were together for more than eighty years before Oscar came along. It was the rage Tony felt, the memories surfacing under all the years of blood and death that were making him challenge Alex now.

"I cherish you, Tony," Alex said through gritted teeth as his hand squeezed Tony's neck tighter. "I thought you had moved past those pesky leftover human emotions, but I guess I was wrong. We're killers. That is what we are and what we will always be. There is no room for anything else."

"Then let me kill her," Tony choked out. "Stop making me play this game."

Alex's grip loosened some. "This is the game you were made to play. That face is a trap for anyone who trusts it. It was a lie even before I turned you. Do you remember how I found you? You were fucking a whore in an alley while Mary Ann was giving birth to your dead baby in the next building. You were never what she thought you were. You were born to be this beautiful fiend, Tony. It's all you'll ever be." He released him, and Tony slumped down to the floor.

"Don't talk about that," he pleaded, his head dropping forward as a hundred plus years of death zoomed past him until he could see himself standing over Mary Ann's bed watching her hold the waxy corpse of his dead son in her arms. If vampires were soulless, heartless creatures, then why did it hurt so much to remember?

Alex crouched down next to him and caressed his cheek before letting his childe fall into his arms. "She's dust," he reminded Tony. "But Sadie is strong. She hungers for life like you hunger for death. When she turns, she will be an addition to this pack we could only have ever dreamed of. Her power, whatever it is, could be ours too."

Tony looked at him puzzled. He wiped the tears off his cheeks and asked, "What do you mean?"

Alex took Tony's hand and helped him to his feet. "Rick is a fool. He wants a daughter to coddle and protect. I don't want that bitch flying beside us. No, I want her power. I felt it in that artist's blood. There was something there that would have made her a vampire we can never be, until now. When Sadie turns, her blood will ignite, and when it does, we will be there to take it."

"We can't kill her once she's turned. We don't kill our own, you taught me that."

Alex sighed and went back to the bar to pour another glass of wine. "No, we can't kill her, but we can drink from her and leave her here while we go on about our lives. We'll never really let her be a vampire in anything but name only. We'll feed her, keep her alive, and then she'll just stay here, a source of new power just for us."

"But Rick?"

"I don't have all the kinks worked out just yet," Alex said with a dismissive wave. "But Rick loves me, I know that much. I was his first, and Sadie, she's just a curiosity. He can drink from her, too." He finished his wine and set the empty glass on the bar. "It's late. The sun is coming."

Alex lifted into the air, bypassing the stairs and going up to the attic where he slumbered. Tony could only stand there, even as the heat from the rising morning was reaching its fingers in through the cracks. The game had changed in a way he never imagined.

Sadie opened her eyes and felt the heaviness of the night before lingering. Her mouth was dry, and all she could think about was water.

She rolled out of bed and dressed in a pair of boxers and a T-shirt. There would be time to shower and make herself feel human again before work, but first, she needed water and then some coffee. As she opened her door, Hayden was stumbling out of her room. She looked at Sadie with a forced smile.

"Do you feel as bad as I do?"

Sadie's face showed a mock grimace. "Probably not."

Hayden sighed and, with a yawn, went into the living room. The picture window's curtains were drawn, and outside they could both see various party debris scattered in the sand. "We need to get that cleaned up. At least we had a good party, right?"

"It was certainly one to remember," said Sadie. She poured each a cup of coffee and met Hayden on the sofa. "You could have told me you knew Tony and his friends."

"I wish I had. To be honest, I met them the night before, and I really wanted you to have your party. If I'd told you, you would have said no."

"Probably," Sadie agreed.

"Oscar seems sweet, don't you think?"

"As long as he's sweet to you, that's all I care about."

"Thanks, Sadie."

They clinked their mugs together. Then Sadie swung the conversation back to the previous evening. "Don't you think it's a little weird, though, that they hang out with a kid? I mean, Tony referred to Alex as his brother but never actually specified that he was."

Hayden thought about it for a moment and said, "It's definitely weird, but, I don't know. It's like when you're talking to him you forget how young he is. Maybe he is Tony's brother or that other one. I think his name is Dylan."

"What could he have done though to make Rick hate him so much?"

"Maybe he used a fake ID or swiped something from the bar."

"I guess that makes sense. I'll ask him when I see him."

"Are you still mad at me for inviting them?"

"No," Sadie smiled. "I'm glad they came."

Hayden's lips parted into a knowing smirk. "Sadie Daniels, did you and Tony make up?"

Color flushed Sadie's cheeks. "You could say that."

"What was it like?"

"It was amazing, Hay. I like this guy. I really do."

Hayden placed her hand on Sadie's knee and gave it a little pat. "I'm glad, mama. You deserve it."

"What about you? Do you think there's something there between you and Oscar?"

Hayden shrugged. "I don't know, maybe. He asked me to meet him tonight. We could double."

"That might be fun."

"Well," Hayden said, stretching her arms above her head with another yawn. "I'll meet you at the bar when you get off." She offered a weak smile and then disappeared down the hall.

Sadie realized she would be cleaning the mess up on her own. As she was outside filling trash bags, she took a moment to really appreciate where she lived. Even something as mundane as cleaning up empty Solo cups was made better by the sound of the surf and the smell of the sea.

There was a pleasant ache throughout her body which drew her mind back to Tony and the night before. Under the warm sun, she could still feel his cool fingers as they explored her. She always had such rigid rules about sex and relationships, which was why Kevin was only the second man she slept with. It took him three months of wooing her and convincing her that he cared before she gave in. It wasn't until they broke up that she found out he had been screwing women left and right the whole time they were together.

It felt different with Tony, and she couldn't deny that there was a sort of comfortable relief in his arms. She trusted him, and she wanted this to work. And didn't he want that too? It was going to work because that's what she wanted. It was long overdue, but Sadie felt she just might be back on track to finding herself again. Tony may not last. In the grand scheme, it was possible he, too, would become an ex she reflected upon only with lessons he taught her. She smiled to herself. That would be enough.

It was a busier than usual Sunday night at the bar. Sadie was still nursing her hangover with bottled water and a double dose of Advil. She was counting out her till when Tony walked in and met her at the bar.

"Hey, beautiful. You just about ready?"

"Three minutes," she told him. Although not usually one for public displays of affection, when he leaned into the counter for a kiss, she was more than willing to give it to him. "I'll meet you outside."

Sadie stuffed the contents of her register into a money bag and placed it in the safe under the bar. It would go into Rick's office by the time the bar closed. "Bye, Leah," she called out as she grabbed her purse and headed for the door.

"Sadie, wait!" When Sadie turned back Leah was holding the receiver of the bar's phone. "It's for you. It's Hayden. She said she's been trying you on your cell."

Sadie pulled her phone from her back pocket and saw the dozen or so missed calls. "Okay, just a sec." She walked up to the window and tapped on the glass. Tony and Oscar turned to look at her, and she held up a finger indicating she would be just a moment longer. Back at the bar, she picked up the phone, her voice laced with just a hint of annoyance. "Hay, where are you? Tony and Oscar are already here."

There was a second of silence followed by a hard sob. "Sadie, you have to come home. Come home now!"

"What are you talking about?"

"Please!" she shrieked. "Come home!"

Sadie glanced behind her to see Tony looking anxious and maybe bored. "Hayden, calm down. Tell me what's wrong."

"I can't," she whispered. "They might be able to hear me somehow."

Convinced that Hayden had taken something with a friend after work, Sadie asked, "What did you take?"

"Are you even listening to me? Just get home!"

Hayden was slipping into hysterics, screaming things into the phone that made no sense. She told Sadie again that it was an emergency and getting home was the only priority. Then she hung up, and Sadie was holding the phone to her ear listening to a dial tone. She replaced the receiver and walked as calmly as she could outside.

Tony was leaning against his car. "You ready?"

She gave him her best apologetic smile. "I can't," she told him gently. In her peripheral vision she could see Oscar staring at them.

"Why not?" Tony looked confused. "Is something wrong?"

"It's just a work thing," she said with a roll of her eyes. "Something is off with the money, and I'm the only one who can fix it. Rick won't be in until tomorrow evening, so I have to get it done."

"You can't just come in early?"

She shook her head and placed her hands on his hips, looking up at him with doe eyed innocence and hoped to hell it was working. "No, it's going to take me forever as it is." She leaned forward and kissed him sweetly. "Can I make it up to you tomorrow? Maybe take you to lunch."

"I'm not really a lunch kind of guy."

"Then dinner? My treat."

Tony glanced at Oscar and then back at her. "Sure thing. We can do that."

"Thanks," she said. "I'm really sorry."

"That's my girl," Tony smiled. "Always apologizing for things that aren't her fault."

"I'll see you tomorrow." She kissed him again before opening the door to go back inside.

"Where's your friend?" Oscar called out. "She didn't meet me like she said she would."

She took a breath and prepared her lie, then turned to him with a frown. "Yeah, I'm pretty sure she's still puking from last night. She should have called you."

Oscar's lips formed half a smile. "Well, tell her I'll be seeing her soon."

The boys were already peeling out of the parking lot when she had one foot back inside the bar. That was when it suddenly hit her. She didn't even know where Tony lived or what he did for work. The idea that she slept with someone whose house she had never been to and whose last name she didn't even know hit her like a punch in the gut. Before she could really marinate on the thought, Leah was calling her name again. She had the phone in her hand.

"It's Hayden again, and she sounds pretty fucked up."

Sadie gave a long sigh. "Tell her I'm on my way."

Sadie had just pulled into the driveway and cut the engine when her car door flew open and Hayden dragged her out and up the porch steps. She shoved Sadie inside then locked the door, engaging the chain with shaky hands.

"Go make sure the bedroom windows are locked," Hayden ordered. "I'll go do the back door."

Sadie took a breath and set her keys on the accent table. As gently as she could, she approached her friend with outstretched hands. "Hay, I want you to come sit down here and tell me what you took."

"What I took?" she asked dumbfounded. "I didn't take anything! I saw them, Sadie. I saw them!" She breathed out her next words, and they were broken syllables as she trembled. "I saw them on Old Rock Road."

This wasn't the first time Hayden had experimented with friends, and it went badly. Sadie liked to drink, and she liked to smoke weed sometimes, but hallucinogens scared her.

"You saw who, Hay?"

Hayden leaned against the back of the sofa for support. "Tony, Oscar... all of them."

She took ten minutes to relay everything she said she saw. She told Sadie that she was driving down Old Rock Road when she had to slam on the brakes to avoid hitting the four of them. But they weren't alone. On the road with them were two bodies. One of which they were still attacking. When she was finished, Sadie was staring at her disbelievingly.

"It's the drugs, Hayden. None of that happened. There were no bodies in the middle of the road and no monsters eating them."

Hayden was trembling, her eyes wide and her hands clutched together like she was praying. Yes, it seemed impossible, and she knew it might take some time to get Sadie to really hear her, but impossible things were sometimes real, and she knew what she saw.

"I didn't take any drugs."

Sadie took a deep breath then reached into her purse and pulled out her cell phone. She calmly scrolled through her contacts.

"What are you doing, Sadie? You're not calling him, are you?"

"I'm calling your aunt," said Sadie gently. "I'm going to tell her to come over and be with you until you're off whatever it is you're on."

Hayden moved quickly and tried to snatch the phone out of Sadie's hand. "Why? Jesus, Sadie did you hear anything I just told you? I looked right into Tony's eyes. It was him only, it wasn't." She dropped to her knees in front of the sofa and took both Sadie's hands in hers. "They were killing this girl right in the middle of the road."

Sadie tried to push her away, but she only clung to her tighter, pink nails digging half moons into Sadie's hand. "Hayden, it's okay. I'm not going to leave you here; I just can't take care of you by myself when you're like this. Please, calm down."

"I'm trying to help you! We have to leave. We have to get the fuck out of here tonight!" She wrapped her fingers around Sadie's wrist and pulled hard.

There was no choice but to give Hayden a hard shove that knocked her back into the coffee table. "What is wrong with you, Hay?" Sadie started looking for the aunt's phone number again.

Hayden looked at the indentions her nails had left on Sadie's arm and then at her fingers poised to make the call. "Don't call her, Sadie."

Sadie stood up and teetered on uneasy feet for a moment. Then Hayden swung at her, and the phone slipped from her hand and hit the floor. Sadie saw red. "That's it, I'm leaving," said Sadie as her concern shifted to anger. She snatched her phone off the floor and moved toward the front door. She grabbed her purse and was about to open the door when she paused and glanced back. "Oscar was asking about you. You ditched us to get high?"

"You saw them?" Hayden asked, wide eyes wet with tears. "Oh, God, they could be out there right now. He's going to kill you."

The only person Sadie was afraid of at that moment was her best friend. She would leave, call Hayden's aunt, apologize for not being able to handle it herself, and then she'd find Tony. Suddenly Hayden released a banshee like shriek and ran at Sadie, knocking her into the door and trying to wrestle the keys out of her hands.

"Get off me!" Sadie screamed and pushed back into Hayden with everything she could.

Hayden stumbled back into the sofa, and Sadie unlatched the door with lightning speed. Hayden was sobbing, screaming again that Tony was going to kill her. With shaking hands, Sadie turned the keys in the ignition and peeled out of the driveway. She glimpsed Hayden in the rearview mirror, running at the car, pleading with Sadie to stop. She slammed her foot onto the gas and drove away from the house, barely able to see the road through her tears.

Hayden's aunt never answered, and despite driving around town until early morning, she saw no sign of Tony or the others. She couldn't go home and face Hayden yet, she was still too angry with her. She would wait and hope that sobriety and reason would be enough to repair the damage. In the meantime, she had to go somewhere, and she didn't want to be alone. There was only one place for her to go. She drove onto the highway and headed toward Pineview and the family she left behind.

Chapter Ten

It was afternoon when Sadie crossed the city limits into Pineview. Her head was pounding, and she felt dizzy from her hours without sleep and food. She spent the drive worrying about Hayden. They fought before, little quarrels about whose turn it was to empty the dishwasher or missing razors and toothpaste. This wasn't like anything they had experienced before. Sadie could feel rising unease as she flashed back on the look of terror in Hayden's eyes.

Then her thoughts would drift to Tony. How was it that she managed to get close enough to allow him in her bed and never even asked his last name? It was preposterous, but she did it. Would knowing where he lived and worked or his last name have changed how she felt about him now? Maybe, no matter how improbable it seemed, she never asked him because it didn't seem important at the time. Perhaps, he really was different. Or she was stupid and still trapped in a people pleasing conundrum, and only therapy would liberate her. She supposed both could be possible.

Her parents' house was on Chester Street where all the houses were one of three different floor plans in varying shades. Her father repainted the house every few years and as she pulled into the empty driveway, she was shocked to find the exterior painted a bright robin's egg blue.

"Barf," she whispered to herself.

She arrived at a time when she knew she would be alone. Her parents would both be at work, and Sadie was glad about that. She didn't go there because she needed her parents' help or advice. She just needed some time in familiarity. They hadn't put up much of a fuss when she left Pineview for Brave Beach, and Sadie believed her departure might have been a kind of relief for them.

She could remember little from her childhood that involved her father. He worked nights as a grocery store manager back then. Now, he supervised a deli. It wasn't until she left home permanently that he switched to a less demanding job with a day shift. When she was a kid, her father would sleep all day and was heading off to work by the time she got home from school. In many respects, he was a stranger to her. There were times he would look at her and say, "You're like looking at her ghost." Then he would walk into the kitchen to get another beer out of the fridge.

She used her key to gain entry to the house and, as the familiar sights and smells hit her, she found she was glad to be there. It smelled like chocolate chip cookies and cinnamon candles. The house was immaculate; the carpet so clean you could still smell shampoo clinging to the fibers. It threw her back to that time growing up when she felt like the only person living in the house. Her parents worked, bought groceries, and did day to day things that everyone else did, but they were never truly living.

Sadie walked through the family room and tried not to look at Sarah's picture on the mantle. She went straight for the stairs and took them two at a time until she reached the second story. Her old bedroom was to the right, and she knew anything she hadn't taken with her was probably still there. Her parents' bedroom was at the end of the hall, Sarah's room on the left. As a little girl, Sadie spent hours atop Sarah's bed, clutching a pillow to her chest and inhaling the scent left behind. As an adolescent, Sadie's longing for Sarah turned into anger. She was angry that Sarah left her there to be raised by two zombies and never once came back. After she found the letter in her sister's closet, the anger morphed into hate.

Sadie's hands were trembling when she finally reached the faded yellow door of Sarah's bedroom. Everything was just as it was the day Sarah left. An old flannel robe hung on a hook next to the door, and posters of Green Day and Leonardo DiCaprio were still tacked to the wall. Sarah's artwork and supplies littered the surface of a desk in the corner. It felt like walking into a dream. A thin sheet of dust glittered against the light that came in through the blinds.

Sadie closed the door behind her and walked directly to the bed. She knelt down, reached into the dark abyss under the frame and felt around until her fingers brushed the hard edges of a photo album. It was covered in a thick layer of dust and the corpses of tiny bugs in repose. She used the edge of the blanket to wipe away the debris of years in hiding and slowly opened it up. The very first photo was of Sarah holding a newborn Sadie. She smiled wide into the camera, and underneath the picture Sarah had written *Proud Big Sis*.

She could see the similarity between them, and it made her stomach hurt. There was a sharp stab of sadness as the reminder that Sarah was still out there, missing everything, hit her so hard she burst into tears. It never made sense that she could feel so strongly for someone she didn't remember, and yet, staring down at her sister's face behind the plastic cover hurt more than anything ever had.

Sadie turned the page. It was Sarah's graduation photo, identical to the one downstairs on the mantle. She wiped her eyes and sniffed back the next wave of tears. Her eyes focused on the necklace hanging around Sarah's neck. It dipped low, the edge of the photo nearly cutting off the silver pendant that hung from a thin chain. Sadie lifted the plastic and plucked the picture from the sticky backing. She squinted, trying to make out the detail.

She got to her feet, left Sarah's bedroom, and went straight to her own. Sadie opened the dresser drawers, absently tossing items of clothing to the floor until she found the antique magnifying glass her grandmother gave her. She put Sarah's photo down on the dresser and scrutinized it behind a magnified eye. Her heartbeat sped up as she realized the pendant on Sarah's necklace was an ankh, with a red stone in the center.

Sadie dropped the magnifying glass and took a step back. She touched the necklace hanging around her own neck. It wasn't possible, not at all. Without thinking she snatched Sarah's picture off the dresser and began to tear it until there were only pieces fluttering around her feet. She had no idea how long she'd been standing there staring down at the shredded remains of Sarah's face when the sound of the front door slamming broke her from the daze.

"Sadie?" her mother called from the bottom of the stairs. "You up there?"

She wiped her eyes and tucked the pendant back into her shirt. "Yeah, Mom. I'll be right down."

She knelt on the cream colored carpet and began scooping up the tattered picture then dumped the pieces in one of the drawers. It took her several deep breaths and mental preparation before she felt steady enough to head downstairs. She found her mother in the kitchen, sitting at the table sipping a cup of coffee and reading the paper.

"You could have called," her mother said without looking up from the page. "I would have put something out for dinner."

"I can't stay," said Sadie. "I have work."

Her mother finally looked up. "So, things are going okay for you then?"

"They're going really good."

"I read about that Kevin and his sister. Were you two still dating?"

Sadie's brows furrowed. "What did you read about Kevin and Kristen?"

"They don't have newspapers and TV stations on the beach?" her mother scoffed. "Do you and your housemate ever watch anything productive or is it all murder shows and reality TV?"

"I don't watch TV at all, Mom. When I'm not working, I'm at home sleeping."

"Well, I hate to be the one to break it to you," her mother said, though her tone didn't reflect the sentiment. She folded the newspaper in half and tossed it to her daughter. Sadie picked it up and began to read.

SIBLINGS STILL MISSING AFTER HOME INVASION

Janice Bryan, 48 of Brave Beach, is refusing to believe that her children, 24 year old Kevin and 16 year old Kristen, are dead. The two were reported missing by their parents, who found their home ransacked and their children gone after returning from a vacation in northern California. Bryan and her husband Larry, 55, say their children would not have left the home voluntarily.

"Kevin was still living with us because he planned to go back to college. There is no way he would have just taken off. He loved his little sister, and I know that he did everything he could to protect her," Mr. Bryan said through his attorney.

Police say that some valuables had been taken and the house was in disarray. Blood evidence found at the scene strongly suggests that a violent struggle took place. The Bryans claim their children had no enemies and were well liked by the community.

They are not the first missing persons from Brave Beach and its surrounding areas, but are, in fact, part of a disturbing trend of people disappearing and never being seen again. While police will not say that a serial killer might be prowling our city streets, residents of this beachside community are investing in home protection and warning others to do the same.

Police Chief Carl Newcomb told reporters, "This is still a missing persons case. We are a community that hosts many tourists; there is no conclusive way to say whether these crimes are the work of a local citizen or a passerby."

The Bryan family is offering a $75,000 reward for any information leading to the whereabouts of Kevin and Kristen Bryan. If you have any information, you are asked to contact the Brave Beach Police Department or the FBI.

Sadie's head felt like a bubble, floating on her shoulders weightlessly. She slumped into one of the dining room chairs and put her head in her hands. How had she not known this? Why hadn't Hayden told her, or even the police? Then she vaguely remembered that two officers came into the bar one evening and talked to Rick. Were they asking about Kevin? It hit her then that she had been so wrapped in Tony and new beginnings that she shut out the rest of the world.

"Sadie?"

She looked up in a daze. "What?"

"Were you still dating?"

"No," Sadie said, trying to find her voice. "We broke up a while ago."

"Well how was I supposed to know," her mother huffed. "You don't even call anymore."

Sadie kept staring at the pictures of Kevin and Kristen on the page. Her heart hurt. Sure, Kevin had been a colossal prick the last time she saw him, but that did not mean she wanted something bad to happen to him. She pushed the paper away and forced herself to focus on what she found upstairs.

"Mom?"

"What?"

"That necklace Sarah is wearing in her graduation picture. Where did she get it?"

Her mother's brows knitted together as if trying to place the object her daughter was describing. Finally, she released a little laugh and said, "You mean that crazy cross? She had that made at the beach one year. She bugged your dad to get it for her, said she saw it in a book about Egypt. It meant eternal life or some such nonsense. She loved that silly thing."

If it was made on the beach, then surely it could have been one of hundreds, maybe thousands, sold at the vendor stands that peppered the pier. "Did it have anything else on it? I don't know, like maybe her name?"

"Where are all these questions coming from, Sadie?"

"I'm just curious."

Her mother took a long sip of her coffee and nodded. "Your Daddy had her initials engraved on it. He thought it was a waste of money, but he wanted to make his little girl happy." She gave a sigh and rubbed at her temples, like just talking about her lost daughter was igniting physical pain to accompany the emotional. "I know your sister loved it. Never once saw her take it off."

Sadie was on the verge of tears again. She could feel the pendant against her skin, hiding beneath the white and black top she was wearing. It was possible Tony had bought the necklace at a pawn shop. Maybe, just maybe, those people would remember the girl who sold it to them. It was possible Sarah had been in Brave Beach all that time.

"I gotta go," Sadie mumbled, standing up quickly and nearly knocking the chair over in her haste.

Her mother looked worried. "Sadie Marie, you tell me what's going on right now."

"Nothing, I promise. It's just been a rough few days and I'm tired."

"Well, you look awful," her mother said very matter of fact. "Why don't you spend the night? You can see your Daddy when he gets home."

"I can't," said Sadie, already turning to head for the front door. "I'll call soon."

She hurried out to her car, hands shaking so badly it took several attempts before she had the keys in the ignition. She saw her mother standing in the doorway, waving her hands at Sadie, but there was no time to stop. Even Kevin and Kristen's bizarre disappearances were forgotten. She had to see Tony and find out exactly where he got the necklace.

The strip was clogged with afternoon shoppers, and despite walking for an hour and checking all the spots she knew Tony and his friends frequented, she never saw him. The sinking feeling hit her again that she knew nothing about him, couldn't even drive to his house. She walked in a semi daze through the people taking photos of their children in front of the Ferris wheel, the clouds of cigarette smoke, and laughing teenagers. Afternoon sunlight filtered through the clouds in bright patches that made the ocean glimmer in the distance.

Sadie found an empty bench near the bookstore and sat down, her feet aching. Her eyes kept darting around, hoping that Tony would drive up at any moment. She fixed her eyes on a young couple with their small son. They each had a hand and would lift him off the ground in unison, smiling as his infectious giggle filled the air. The sight had her smiling, too. Would she ever have that?

Her fingers went for the pendant, clutching it tight as though it might vanish and take its secrets with it. She knew in her heart this was her sister's necklace. And after all this time, fate had somehow delivered it to her. Tony had the answer to a question that was burning Sadie up from the inside. Sure, she wanted to see him, get his last name, maybe even let him take her back to his place, but more than anything she wanted to find out the origin of his gift.

"Excuse me," a male voice broke her from her thoughts. "Are you Sadie?"

She lifted her head and shielded her eyes from the glaring sun. A man with curly brown hair and a goatee was standing in front of her. He was wearing a tie-dyed shirt and tight black pants; several necklaces hung around his neck with shiny rocks dangling from black twine. He had dark makeup smeared around his eyes, and his nails were painted with each color of the rainbow.

"Yes, I'm Sadie."

"Fabulous, you look exactly like she described you."

Sadie raised her brow. "Like who described me?"

The man laughed a little and slapped his hands against his thighs. "I'm sorry," he said. "I'm Tanner, and Hayden is my friend. She really needs to talk to you."

"Well, I'll be sure to give her a call."

"Oh, no need for that, honey. She's here." He pointed to his right, but Hayden wasn't there.

"She's where?"

"In my store, silly."

She looked in the direction again and realized he was pointing at the metaphysical store that had only opened a few months before. If this man was Hayden's friend, she had never mentioned him. Still, the only thing more important than finding out about the necklace was fixing things with Hayden.

"Is she all right?"

"All right is a spectrum, sweetie. She's somewhere on it."

"Okay, lead the way."

As they walked to the store Tanner engaged her with light conversation. "I hope my shop does as well as other places around here."

"It should," she told him. "So, this store is yours?"

"Mmmhmm," he said with a grin. "I started with tarot on the pier, and then I just manifested this reality."

He opened the door for her, and she was immediately overcome with the aroma of incense and sage. There were crystals and other rocks displayed on cherry wood shelves as well as books and glass jars filled with herbs. In the corner at the back was a long tapestry with an All-Seeing Eye and zodiac symbols stitched into the fabric. She could see light under the edge of the tapestry and realized there was a room behind it.

Tanner locked the shop door and flipped the OPEN sign to CLOSED. Sadie took a step away from him, wondering if she had just walked into a psycho's trap. When he saw her wide eyes, he giggled and playfully slapped her shoulder.

"Oh, honey, you don't have anything to worry about. Hayden? Your friend is here."

Hayden emerged from the hidden room chewing on her fingers. Her hair was a mess, and mascara tracks crisscrossed her cheeks. When she saw Sadie, she ran to her and grabbed her into a fierce hug.

"Let's go to the back," said Tanner, and he stepped past them and disappeared into the room Hayden just vacated.

Hayden clutched Sadie's hand so tight it hurt. She said nothing but guided Sadie back behind the tapestry. The room was filled with ornate pillows and silk scarves covering lamps. A circular table with cards spread across the surface took up the center with four elegantly carved chairs around it. Sadie kept her eyes on Tanner, wondering why he was in the room for a conversation that was supposed to be between the two of them.

"This is my friend, Tanner," Hayden said, her voice hoarse and tired.

"You never mentioned him before," said Sadie softly. She didn't want to make him feel bad.

"He's a new friend."

"Like a last night friend," Tanner clarified. "She came in here just before I was closing up, and well, here we are."

Sadie waited for Hayden to say something, but she didn't. Sadie felt like if she did not start talking, they would just stand there staring at one another uncomfortably forever.

"Hay, I'm not mad at you. And we can have this heart to heart back at the house, okay?"

"Sadie, I need you to listen to us. It's very important, and I need you to know that I love you so much."

Puzzled, Sadie looked from Hayden to Tanner. "Why does this feel like some weird intervention?"

Tanner pointed at one of the chairs. "This is going to be one of those 'you might need to be sitting down' type conversations."

"I'm okay to stand," said Sadie, a little less sweetly than she had before.

"Fair enough," he smiled. "Well, Hayden, why don't you just tell her what we talked about?"

Hayden exhaled slowly then turned to Sadie. Tears were already spilling down her cheeks, and she swallowed her words twice before finally pushing them through her lips. "I'm sorry if I hurt you last night, Sadie. When you left... I was so afraid I would never see you again. I thought they would get you."

"Are you still high?" Sadie tried to ask the question with concern, but the anger she had felt at Hayden the night before was resurfacing.

"I wasn't high last night. I swear to God, I saw them. They saw me."

"Hayden, what you saw wasn't real."

"With all due respect," Tanner gently broke in. "This is very real, my dear, and you are in a lot of danger."

"Excuse me? What do you even know about any of this besides the story of someone you didn't even know until last night?"

Tanner stepped forward. "Look around you, weird shit is like my calling card. All the things this world tells you aren't real, aren't possible, well I know they are."

Sadie took a deep breath. "Listen, I can appreciate your beliefs, and hell, who am I to say magic isn't real and you don't have some crystal ball that tells the future? However, my boyfriend, if you could even call him that, is not a serial killer."

"You're right," said Tanner. "He's so much worse than that."

"Nothing is worse than a serial killer," she said. "It's literally the worst thing you could be."

"In terms of humanity, absolutely," he said. "But we're not talking about humans. We're talking about vampires."

Sadie's jaw clenched. All the anger and annoyance combined with the worry about her sister and the necklace took whatever calmness she usually maintained and ripped it to shreds.

"Okay, that's it. I'm done. Hayden, I know the house is technically yours, so I'll leave if you need me to. Take the time to get yourself together. But I'm not doing this with you. I can't do this with you."

Hayden held onto Sadie's arm tighter. "Please, believe me. Why would I make this up?"

"I don't know!" Sadie said exasperated. "I've been spending all night trying to understand this, and now something's come up about my family. On top of all that, apparently Kevin and his sister fucking disappeared, and nobody bothered to tell me."

"I just found out about Kevin, Sadie. I swear. No one around here is really talking about it, which is weird by itself but... now that I've seen who Tony is, I think he did something to Kevin."

"You're unbelievable. I love you, but I just can't handle this right now."

"This is not an easy thing to hear," Tanner said, his voice calm and the timber soothing. "She's not trying to hurt you. This isn't a desire to keep you from your truest self; this is about her loving you and you being a possible feast for your boyfriend and his pack."

"Pack?"

"Pack, coven, blood-sucking bad boys club. I mean these are just words, but they all mean the same thing."

"Wait," Hayden suddenly said, her eyes wide with realization. "Maybe he doesn't want to kill her. I mean, he didn't kill her when they were doing it."

Sadie's mouth fell open. "Do you mind? You know what, that's it. I'm out of here."

"Wait," Tanner stepped forward. "You've had sex with this vampire?"

Sadie narrowed her eyes. "I am not going to discuss my sex life with someone I've never met and my bestie who suddenly believes in vampires. Do you two not hear yourselves?"

She turned on her heel to burst through the tapestry and finish her mission for the day when Hayden stepped in front of her to block Sadie's exit. Then Sadie laughed. Not because she found any of this funny; but if she didn't laugh, she was going to cry. And she would, not, cry.

"Just listen to me," Hayden pleaded softly. "Hear me out and then you can leave, and I won't ever mention it again. In fact, I will go stay with my aunt, and you can have the house until we figure this all out."

"Say it. Whatever you have to say, and let's be done with this please."

Hayden nodded softly. "I want you to know that no matter what you say to me, no matter how mad you get, I'm not mad at you. I pushed you into getting involved with Tony, and I'm sorry. I was a little jealous, I'll admit. And then one day they all came into the restaurant, and Oscar seemed so into me, and I thought, well this is great. Now, me and Sadie can do all these fun things together in these new relationships." She took a deep breath and tried to steady the shake in her voice. "I saw them on Old Rock Road. I saw them killing... eating this girl right in front of me. When they saw me, when they looked at me with those eyes I... I couldn't believe it. I wanted to pretend none of it happened. But it did happen, Sadie. And I'm scared for you." She passed Sadie and took the books that Tanner had been holding. "We've always been taught that these things are fairy tales, and then I saw it with my own two eyes, and I can't pretend like I didn't."

She handed the books to Sadie, who stared at them like they might bite her. Eventually, she took them from Hayden's hands. "What do you want me to do with these?"

"Read them," Tanner said. "There's a lot of good information in those about lore and how to protect yourself from them."

"Aren't you the expert?" she asked, voice dripping with sarcasm.

He didn't take offense. "Not about this. I've researched them through books and stories my grandfather told me. I met a woman in New Orleans once who taught me how to make something she said could protect me from them." He reached into his pocket and pulled out a little jar filled with water, herbs, and dirt. "Take it."

"Okay," she said and put the jar and books into her purse. "Are we done?"

Tanner pressed his hands together like he was praying and said, "If you are sleeping with this guy and he hasn't even tried to taste your blood, it's possible he has no intention of killing you at all."

"Oh, good," she responded with as much sarcastic sting as she could muster. "Now that that's all cleared up, I'll just be going. Hayden, when you come back to reality, I'll still be here. I'll always be here."

She had her hand on the tapestry when Tanner quickly said. "He wants to turn you."

Sadie looked back at him over her shoulder. "Turn me?"

"That's the only reason to keep you as his companion. I mean, vampires aren't the romantic Dracula that Bram Stoker told us about. They're vicious and cruel, and they don't have feelings. So yes, I think he wants to turn you into one of them."

She allowed the full weight of her glare to land on both of them. "Well, let's hope that's not the case because if I do become a vampire the first thing I'm going to do is come back here. Goodbye."

She pushed roughly past Hayden and was out the door and onto the street with angry tears flooding her face. She heard Hayden calling out to her and only stopped walking to keep a scene from happening. "Why are you doing this to me?" Sadie asked, hurt and confused. "Why now?"

"I'm sorry. I know this sounds crazy, that I sound crazy. Just promise me that if Tony ever tries to hurt you, you'll take that jar and smash it in his fucking face."

Sadie couldn't argue the lunacy anymore. So, she just nodded and bowed her head. Hayden grabbed her before she could pull away and held her tight. "Hayden, please stop this," she said, giving in to the emotions overtaking her and returning the hug with full force. "Let me take you to a doctor or something. Let me help you."

"Just promise," Hayden said softly. "You'll throw it in his face." She gave Sadie a quick kiss on the cheek before she let go and ran back toward the store.

Sadie stood there, the sun setting behind her, and the floodgates let loose. She couldn't believe any of this had happened. Kevin and Kristen missing, Hayden losing her mind, Sarah's necklace ending up around her neck. It was all too much. She went to her car, and as soon as the door was closed, her crying turned to heaving sobs. She needed someone who could help her, who would do anything to make it all better. Right then, she needed a father. She needed a pair of strong arms to hold her and swear that the big bad world and all its craziness wasn't going to swallow her whole. Right now, she needed Rick.

Chapter Eleven

Rick lived on the edge of town in an area that was well known for its affluent residents and catered to their need for privacy. Sadie had never been to Rick's house but had written the address down so many times on invoice forms she knew it by heart. The house was a mile from its nearest neighbor and perched atop a cliff that overlooked the calming blue waters below. There was a long walkway leading up to the single story ranch home with a row of white lilies bordering the lawn. She glanced at the clock. It was after nine.

Sadie stepped out of her car and shivered as a cool breeze kissed the exposed skin on her arms. There were no more tears, but her eyes felt raw from crying. She was nearing the front door when she heard music coming from inside the house. *Blue in Green* by Miles Davis. Rick played it at the bar on slow nights, and tonight it was accompanied by his booming laugh. Sadie pressed her finger against the doorbell and waited. Rick was still laughing when he opened the door and stopped abruptly as soon as he saw her standing there with red rimmed eyes and tear tracks on her cheeks.

"Sadie, what are you doing here?"

"I'm sorry I didn't call," she started. "I just didn't know where else to go."

Rick reached out and took her arm gently then led her inside. "It's okay, Peanut. Just tell me what's going on."

She looked up into his concerned eyes and felt her cool composure shatter. She burst into tears, and when Rick pulled her into a hug, she cried harder. "Rick, everything is so messed up. Hayden's lost her shit. I mean, really lost it."

Rick gingerly stroked her hair and rocked her softly from side to side. "What do you mean?"

"I thought she was just high last night," Sadie said with a sniff. "But when I saw her today... I don't know how to help her."

Rick held Sadie back and said, "What do you mean she's gone crazy? What has Hayden done?"

"She told me she saw Tony and his friends kill some girl on Old Rock Road. And then she introduced me to this guy who tells me shit you wouldn't even believe." As soon as the words left her lips she started to laugh and then cried some more. "Apparently I'm dating Dracula, or some version of him, according to Hayden's new friend."

"Come over and sit down, Peanut." He led her to the sofa. "Can I get you some water or maybe a glass of wine?"

She shook her head. "No, thank you. I'm so sorry I just barged in on you."

Rick sat down beside her and placed his hand on her knee. "Sadie, I told you to always come to me if you need anything. There wasn't a time stamp on the matter."

"I think I'm screwed up, too," she whispered, wiping at her eyes.

"Screwed up how?"

"Do you know Tony's last name?" she asked, looking up at him.

"I can't say that I do."

"Well, neither do I. I don't know anything about him. Where he lives, where he works, all I have is a cell phone number."

Rick nodded. "That's not such a big deal. You haven't known each other long."

"I slept with him," she said, not even caring if this knowledge embarrassed him and humiliated her. "I don't do that, Rick. I don't sleep with people I don't know."

He averted his eyes and cleared his throat nervously. "You like this boy and when you really like someone, Sadie, it can make you do things you wouldn't normally do."

"Maybe," she sighed. "There's something else though." She had her hand on the pendant and was about to tell him all about it when she was cut off by the sound of a woman's voice.

"Rick, honey, do you want me to put the vegetables on simmer?"

They both looked in the direction of the kitchen where a pretty woman with white blonde hair wearing a sweater with a plunging neckline and a pencil skirt was standing in the archway. When she saw Sadie, she looked surprised.

"Oh, I didn't realize you were having anyone else over."

Rick rose to his feet and smiled warmly at the blonde. "Angela, this is Sadie. She works for me. Sadie, this is a friend of mine, Angela Baxter."

"Nice to meet you," Sadie said, already standing. "I'm not staying," she assured the woman. "I just needed to give Rick some information on the bar. Thanks, Rick. I'll see you tomorrow."

The blonde flashed a sly smile before heading back into the kitchen. Sadie was almost at the front door when Rick stopped her. "Peanut, just sit back down. You're not leaving as upset as you are. Let me go have a word with Angela for a moment, and then you and I will finish our talk."

"I don't want to mess up your night."

He squeezed her shoulder. "You're not, I promise. Just sit here and wait, please."

She nodded and went back to the sofa, not wanting to ruin their date but not ready to leave either. As she waited, she looked around at Rick's home. It wasn't what she imagined. It was modern almost to a fault. The furniture was art deco with sharp edges and glossy surfaces. It felt cold and stale, not like Rick at all.

Her eye caught sight of two sliding doors at the end of a hallway. They were dark stained oak with a strange circular design carved into the wood. The doors were slightly open, and Sadie could see what looked like a wall of bookshelves illuminated by a dim blue light. She knew it wasn't polite to snoop around Rick's house, but was it really being nosy or just curiosity about someone she admired so much? She looked back towards the kitchen and could hear the muffled voices of Angela and Rick as they talked.

She made her way down the hall, and when she reached the doors, she felt an intense desire to see what was on the other side. Sadie opened the doors a little wider, just enough that she could squeeze through them. The room was larger than she expected. The walls were comprised almost entirely of bookshelves. A desk, made of the same wood as the doors, sat in the center of the room. There was an old fashioned quill and inkwell on the surface along with a pile of papers.

Sadie examined the spines of the books; some looked so old and tattered she was sure they would crumble under her touch. She moved around the room and stopped at a shelf that did not hold books at all, but framed photographs. Rick was immediately recognizable to her. It was odd. The pictures appeared aged, vintage relics, but Rick looked exactly as he always did. She moved to another photo and felt her entire body stiffen; adrenaline shot straight through her.

She snatched the gold frame and held the image directly in front of her face. Rick was standing next to a mint green car she could only define as a classic. He was wearing a sweater vest and wide brimmed hat. To his right was a young man with dark, slicked back hair and piercing eyes that seemed to look right through her. His arms were crossed, and he was wearing an open collared shirt with a white T-shirt underneath. Alex.

She recognized the man on the other side of Rick, too. His hair was shorter, and his skin was free of tattoos, but it was most definitely Tony. She flipped the frame over in her hands and removed the cardboard backing so that the photo could slide into her fingers. On the back, written in a hand she knew was Rick's, it read: *Rick and his boys, Tony and Alex. Summer, 1953.*

The frame slipped from her fingers and hit the floor with a shatter. Still clutching the picture in her hand, her head spinning and legs weak, she started backing out of the room. As she did, she started to notice other things that made no sense. A master's degree hanging on the wall dated 1905 with Rick's name underneath in rich black calligraphy. More photos from decades past filled the shelf. Tony and Alex together with Rick. Sadie's heart was pounding so loud she was sure Rick would hear it. As quietly as she could she left the room and made her way to the front door. Her hand was on the knob when Rick's voice called out to her.

"Where are you going?"

She turned to look at him over her shoulder, tears teetering on the edge of her eyes. "I need to get home. I've got to check on Hayden." With her hands behind her back, she turned to face him and stuffed the photograph into her back pocket. "Thank you for everything."

"Are you sure you don't want to stay?"

"I'm okay now," she told him and reached behind her to open the door. "Goodnight, Rick."

The door was closed before he could respond, and Sadie was sprinting down the walkway back to her car. None of it made sense. Everything was tumbling around in her head, and she couldn't get a grip on it. She thought about Hayden, about the terrified look in her eyes, and knew that she had to get back to her. She put the car in drive and slammed on the gas, speeding back towards the pier.

Hayden had never been more scared in her life than she was at that moment as Oscar held her in his arms. She had stayed at Tanner's store, unsure when she could go back home. Sitting in the back room she thought about Sadie and wondered how she could ever protect her from something that Sadie would never believe was real. Then she heard her name being called. It was Oscar's voice, and it was loud inside her head.

Hayden. Come on down here darlin'. Come down to the beach and see what we have for you.

There was no thinking being done on her part, just the desire to follow his voice and commands. As the sky darkened into indigo, Hayden found herself walking in a zombie like haze toward the pier.

That's right, girl. Come here. No one is going to hurt you.

She walked down the steps of the pier slowly, Oscar's rich, melodic voice urging her on. Then, without ever hearing the footsteps, someone grabbed her and took her flying into the night. She tried to remember all the things Tanner told her, but her mind was an empty space now filled only with Oscar's laughter.

Her face was buried against his chest, eyes stinging as the cold air hit her skin hard. The clouds were a fine mist and there was a sense of weightlessness as they flew toward the cliffs and their home. She felt something poking her in the hip and remembered the vial Tanner gave her. That woman in New Orleans said to think of it as mace. It was the same thing he gave Sadie. He said it would hopefully, at the very least, give her a chance should she ever find herself cornered.

Her mind began to clear, and the fear that she should have felt all along gripped her tight. They were descending toward the ground. She could feel the pressure popping in her ears, like she was on an airplane, and the altitude had changed.

Oscar's feet hit the hard earth with a thud making Hayden's teeth clamp down on her tongue. She winced with pain and tasted blood in her mouth. Oscar flinched, sniffing at the air before lowering his eyes to her. He chuckled when he saw fear spread across her face. He put her down and held tight to her arm as they walked toward the house. Her eyes were wide as she took in the sight of it, wondering how no one in town knew it was there.

"In we go," he said and gave her a shove through the front door.

Oscar took her to the parlor and sat her down on one of the high backed chaise lounges. Alex, Tony, and Dylan came into the room and stared hard at her. She felt something warm on her lips and dabbed at them with her fingers. There was blood staining her skin, and she quickly wiped it on her pant leg. The metallic taste burned her throat, and her head throbbed with a sharp pulsing beat focused at her temples. A cold feeling, deep and penetrating, spread through her. She drew her knees to her chest and closed her eyes.

Dylan sat down on one of the stools next to the bar. "She's kinda cute," he said. "Seems like a waste to kill her now."

"We're not killing her... yet." Alex smiled knowingly. "We need her. She's going to be the bridge Sadie walks over to get here."

Hayden looked away from them, fighting back tears. Tanner was right. They didn't want to kill Sadie. They wanted to make her one of them. It was all too real now, and she wished for something to help her escape reality, even for a moment. Her mind drifted back to Sadie. Hayden was praying to a god she wasn't even sure existed, that Sadie had gone back to Pineview and left Brave Beach. But Hayden knew better than that. Sadie would go home so she could try and work things out. She would push Hayden to go to the doctor, still convinced this was all part of a psychotic break. She also knew Sadie would attempt to save her if she knew Hayden was in danger.

"Go to her house," Alex ordered Tony. "Let her know what the game is and how we play it." His cold gaze fell on Hayden. "Let her know the stakes have gone up."

She watched as Alex spoke to Tony, who chewed his lips with anticipation of the night ahead. Alex gave him a pat on the back, and Tony was already heading for the door. Hayden knew there was nothing she could do, but she also knew she had to try. She jumped up and ran at him, grabbing hold of his arm and tugging him backward. He laughed with surprise and looked from Alex back at the crying girl.

"Don't do this to Sadie, please! Just leave her alone."

"You offering yourself in her place?" Tony asked, as if it were actually a viable option.

She let go of his arm and stepped back. "Will you leave her alone if I do?"

He stepped towards her, and she took another step back. Alex watched the strange dance with amused eyes while Dylan and Oscar simply snickered to themselves. "Come here," Tony said.

Hayden was frozen. What would happen if she did let them turn her into whatever the hell they really were? What would the process be like? Would there be pain? After she was changed, would she hunger for Sadie like he did? As her mind churned with questions, Tony grabbed her and pulled her into his chest. He pressed his palm against her cheek and forced her head to the side so that the long slender line of her neck was pulled tight. Her heartbeat called to all of them as she gave in to the fear she could not control. Tony pressed his nose against her skin and inhaled the scent of rose petals and honey. His tongue made a slow path up her throat to her ear. She could hear the others breathing, waiting for whatever bloody conclusion was to come.

"Mmmm," he growled. "You taste good enough to eat." She tried to pull away, but his grip tightened. "We'll take her together," he said. "You and I can bathe in Sadie's blood. Is that what you want, Hayden? Do you want to take her place at my side?"

"No," she whimpered. "Don't do this."

"I think we should all get a sample," Dylan said. "What do you think, Oscar?"

"Seems only fair," Oscar responded with a shrug.

"No, no boys," Tony laughed, his grip on her hair tightening more. "She wants to take Sadie's place, and Sadie is mine."

"Stop playing with your food," Alex rolled his eyes. "You know she's just an appetizer to the main course."

Tony looked down into her terrified eyes. He licked at the lines of her lips and tasted the blood that had dried there when she bit her tongue. Tears were falling in thick rivers down her cheeks. "I have a better idea," he said.

There was a sudden stinging to her right earlobe, followed by dull heat. Her ear began to throb against the cool air, and she felt Tony tugging on the earring with his teeth. His breath was warm against her skin as he licked at the lightning bolt shaped earring she always wore. Then, without warning, he snapped his head back and Hayden felt the flesh rip apart. The sound of all that sinewy tissue stretching seemed to echo. Her scream pierced every corner of the room as Tony latched his lips to the shredded lobe of her ear and sucked at the blood that flowed. She pushed at his chest, the slurping sounds and harsh grunts a frightening soundtrack to the events. Tony pushed her back hard, snarling at her as his lips drew back to showcase the tips of his fangs. She stared at him, the monster wearing a Tony mask, and screamed until her voice was cracking.

Alex met Tony in the center of the room and took the earring from him. "I think this will be a sweet gift for Sadie. Let her know this little morsel doesn't have a lot of time left."

Tony gave her one last look, and with a flurry of movement, he was gone. Hayden held her hand over her injured ear and began to sob. It was burning fiercely, and she could feel blood dripping down the side of her neck, pooling into the well of her collarbone. She grabbed onto the lounge and dug her fingers into the fabric. The others started walking toward her, their eyes alive with aroused hunger at the smell of her blood. She slipped her hand into the pocket of her jeans, her fingers wrapping around the small jar Tanner had given her. She feared what might happen when she threw it at them but was more afraid of the outcome if she didn't. There was not much, certainly not enough to thwart all three of them, but it was the only protection she had. She held the vial in her shaking hand and showed it to them.

"Don't touch me," she screamed. "This is a spell, and I'll throw it on all of you, I swear it." Her voice sounded shrill in her ears, the squeaking demands of a girl way in over her head. She knew she looked ridiculous as she held the jar out in front of her while the three monsters looked at her with amusement.

"What do you think that's going to do to us?" Alex asked, his voice sounding both angry and annoyed.

"I don't know," she answered honestly. "But I will throw it in your fucking face so I can find out."

He took a step toward her but stopped as she plucked the stopper from the mouth of the jar. "Throw it, baby," he snarled. "I want you to."

"Come closer," Hayden whispered.

Oscar stepped up behind Alex and talked to her in that same calm tone she had followed to the beach. "That's not going to kill us, Hayden."

"It might sting," Dylan interjected. "But not so much that we won't be able to rip you apart."

Oscar rolled his eyes and gave Dylan a look that told him now was quiet time. He met Hayden's eyes again and she smiled, falling into the song he sang in her head. The jar fell from her hand, and before she knew what happened, it was nothing but shattered glass under Alex's shoe.

"What else you got, sweetheart?" Alex asked with a laugh. He grabbed her by the throat and lifted her until her toes were skirting the floor. "You can't win, Hayden. Truth is you can't even play the game." He looked back over his shoulder. "Boys? Who's ready to have some fun?"

Sadie had one thing on her mind when she went back to the strip. She had to find Hayden and avoid Rick and his boys, whoever they really were. There was nothing rational in her fear, and deep down she knew that. After all, it wasn't possible that the photograph she saw was really taken in 1953, nor was it possible that Tony and the others were vampires. The thing that scared her was Rick lied to her about knowing them, and the uneven heaviness in her chest was enough encouragement to stay away.

She scanned her surroundings. The regular array of tourists and locals were out that night but there was no sign of Tony and his friends. She kept her head down as she made a beeline for Tanner's shop. As soon as she stepped through the door and was met with the cool air and sweet smell of sage, she felt a relief wash over her.

"Sadie? What are you doing here?" Tanner asked as he emerged from behind the tapestry.

"I came to see Hayden."

"Well, she's not here I'm afraid. I went to pick us up some dinner a few hours ago, and she was gone when I got back."

"Shit, maybe she went home or to her aunt's house."

"What happened to you? Why do you believe her now?"

"I don't believe her," she said with frustration. "But she's my friend, and maybe there's a logical explanation for what she thinks she saw. I was angry because she was acting so irrational and so..."

"Afraid," Tanner stole the word from her.

"Vampires aren't real," she said softly. "Maybe Tony is a bad guy and maybe he is dangerous and they're all monsters inside, I don't know. I can't pick everything apart right now. I just have to get her and get out of town for a while. We can figure this all out."

Tanner smiled softly at her, but his eyes looked worn and sad. "I hope you do. If you ever need anything, you have a friend here too."

"Thank you."

As she walked back to her car, she couldn't stop scanning her surroundings. She expected Tony to show up at any moment, but he never did. Half of her was so thankful, but the other half, the selfish part of her, wanted so much to find out about Sarah and the necklace. Confusion was mounting at a pace she couldn't keep up with. As soon as one thought surfaced with a logical explanation, it would be devoured whole by the unbelievable scenarios she was stuck in.

She pulled into the driveway of the beach house, dimming the headlights but leaving the motor running. Hayden's car wasn't in the driveway. The windows were dark, and the house looked undisturbed. Swallowing down any apprehension she carried with her from the strip, Sadie withdrew the keys from the ignition and slowly got out of the car. As she walked up the steps of the front porch she stopped, suddenly aware of how quiet the beach was that night. No couples out for a romantic walk, or kids hanging out. There was only the sound of the surf and thunder in the distance. She pushed open the front door and stepped inside to silent darkness.

"Hay? Are you home?" Her voice seemed unnaturally loud, and it made the house feel that much emptier. It was possible Hayden left her car at the strip and took a Lyft home. Maybe she was still too upset to drive. It didn't really make sense, but Sadie wanted to believe it just the same.

She dropped her purse onto the sofa and without turning on the lights started down the hallway towards Hayden's bedroom. She had to force her legs to keep moving as her mind seemed determined to will her body back toward the front door. The urge to scream or run slithered through her. The picture she took from Rick's was still in her back pocket, and her fingers itched to take it out and examine it again. Instead, she opened Hayden's door and peered into the room.

"Hayden, are you in here?"

The bed was made, Hayden's robe still slung over the end of the mattress. She backed out of the room and closed the door, stiffening when she heard a faint noise behind her. Then she smelled an earthy aroma of sandalwood and orange trees; it was the scent that lived on Tony's skin. She had once felt arousal at the smell, but now she was consumed with fear. She turned over her shoulder but saw nothing except shadows dancing on the walls.

"Tony?"

"Boo," a voice whispered beside her.

Sadie screamed and spun around only to find empty space. She backed herself against the door and tried to even out her breathing. A shadowy outline emerged at the end of the hall. Tears stung her eyes and spilled down her cheeks.

"I missed you," he said, his voice low and purposeful. He wanted to frighten her. He wanted her to know and understand the magnitude of the danger she was in. "Did you miss me?"

She searched for her voice, but all she managed was a breathy whimper as Tony slowly walked down the hall toward her. Her entire body was trembling as she pressed herself against the door harder, hoping to just disappear inside it.

"What are you doing here?" Her voice was soft.

"Aren't you happy to see me?" he asked, his smirk appearing in and out of the shadows as moonlight from the window caught his face. When he reached her, he could smell her dread and see it reflected in her big blue eyes.

"I want you to leave," she said, flinching as he reached out to caress her hair between his fingers.

"Leave? That's not very nice, Sadie. I thought you wanted to be my girl."

He pouted and then started to laugh darkly as he pressed himself against her, his hunger aroused by the sound of her blood pumping in her ears. She let out a helpless sob and turned her face away from his advancing lips. He grabbed her face and squeezed her round cheeks between his fingers.

"We shouldn't be playing this way, Sadie. Not when we both know why I'm here."

"I don't," she cried, her eyes pleading with him. She inhaled a sharp breath as his hands moved away from her hair to her shoulders and down her arms until he gripped her hips.

"I know she told you," he growled. "Stop playing dumb with me."

Sadie's eyes went wide. He was talking about Hayden and the story she told about them on Old Rock Road. The picture in her back pocket wasn't some illusion meant to confuse her. It was real. "What do you want from me?"

Tony took her by the arms and slammed her hard into the door. Her mouth opened and the air in her lungs expelled in one painful push. "I want your blood," he hissed, his mouth over her ear. "I want to drink every drop, baby. But I can't. I can't because Rick doesn't want to lose his little Peanut."

"No," she sobbed. "That's not true."

His hand tightened around her throat making her eyes go wide with panic. "No? Don't be so dense, Sadie. Not when I know how smart you really are." He leaned in and pressed his cheek against hers, his fingers tightening just a little more around her throat. "Don't make this hard. I don't want to hurt you, but I will if you make me." He loosened his grip, and she gasped at the air.

A thousand thoughts went zooming through her head. All the madness had spiraled into a single reality she couldn't deny. "Where is Hayden?"

Tony studied her, cocking his head to the side, wondering if brutal honesty would be enough to have her walk into the house holding his hand. "If you come back with me we'll let her go. Do you want to know how we did it? She was on the strip surrounded by people. We're a lot of things, baby, but stupid isn't one of them." He ran his thumb over her bottom lip and enjoyed the way she shivered under his touch. "We got inside her pretty little head and called her. She went right into Oscar's arms."

Her eyes danced over his face. "Then why don't you..."

"Why don't I jump inside your head and fuck it sideways? I can't do that with you, Sadie. None of us can."

"Why?"

Tony's grin spread wider, and he pushed himself harder against her. Her warm flesh against his cold skin was like a hymn she sang only for him. "You're something special. We've only ever known one other person like you, someone who could resist our call."

Sadie was trembling so much that it rattled the knob on the door he held her against. "Where are they now?"

"She's dead," he breathed into her ear. "Alex killed her. He wanted to turn her, to see what our power would do mixed with her blood. But he couldn't stop himself. He told me that her blood was sweeter than anyone else before her." His breath turned hard as he felt himself getting ready to shift. "I wonder if you taste the same."

Sadie closed her eyes. Everything was coming together now. The mystery was solved. "My necklace," she whispered. "It was hers, wasn't it?"

"Yes."

Tony didn't get the necklace at a pawn shop. He plucked it from her dead sister's body after Alex murdered her. She forced her thoughts away from the scene they were conjuring and focused on the little bottle Hayden gave her earlier. She had no idea what was in it, but she was more than willing to find out. It was in her purse on the sofa, and all she had to do was get there. Without warning, she rammed her knee into Tony's groin. He howled in pain, stepping back and cupping his injury. The pain ignited his fury, and he shifted completely. Sadie saw his face, his glowing eyes, and screamed as she ran past him. He reached for her with a growl, but she was too quick.

She charged down the hall and was almost to the couch when she was struck from behind with a force that threw her forward. She hit the sofa and rolled off it with a thud. Her purse and all its contents were scattered on the floor. Sadie saw the bottle roll across the carpet toward the picture window. Ignoring the way her chest hurt and her muscles protested, she got to her knees and started clambering toward it.

A scream crawled up from her throat as a strong hand wrapped around her ankle and pulled hard. She clawed at the carpet, tears blurring her vision but her will still strong. Lights from outside swept through the house. Beach patrol was out, and Sadie readied her lungs for the wail of terror that would have them charging her house with guns drawn.

Tony fell onto her back and wrapped his hand around her mouth, fingers over her nose. "Stop it, Sadie," he demanded. "You're making this so much harder than it has to be."

She struggled under him, her body fighting for the air he was denying her. With one hand still covering her mouth he used the other to grip her hair. He pulled her head back and then slammed it hard into the floor. Stars erupted behind Sadie's eyes, and there was a ringing in her ears that was deafening. With her dazed, but still conscious, Tony flipped her over and held her arms down at her side. Blood was leaking from a gash under her eye, and he couldn't have denied himself even if he wanted to.

He leaned forward and let his tongue slide across her skin. Alex was right. There was something special about her, and he could taste it in her blood. It was like the sunlight he abandoned so long ago. Vision tunneling, she stared at the nightmarish face above her until the sweet black abyss of nothingness took over. As she faded into unconsciousness, she heard him tell her it would all be okay. Then she felt herself flying.

CHAPTER TWELVE

When Sadie opened her eyes, she saw *The Raven*.

She blinked hard, her head throbbing, and it was several seconds before she realized she was looking at a painting. A sharp pain in her wrists woke her further, and she grunted a little when she realized she couldn't move her arms. Tony was behind her finishing up the knots on the rope he used to bind her hands behind her back. The nightmare had become reality.

"Where's Hayden?" she asked softly.

Tony tightened the rope more and smiled at himself when she bit back the pain. "She's here," he promised. "When it's time, you can see her."

He moved so that he was standing in front of her and then crouched down to meet her eyes. He admired the crusted blood below her eye and the purple bruise forming beneath it. Should he tell her that once she took a drink, all the hurt would fade away? No, he rather liked the idea of having her suffer these last moments of human life. He had chosen her, true, but not for this. This was all Rick, and part of Tony wanted to punish her for it.

"Why can't I see her now?" She looked into that boyish face, still not able to accept the truth it was hiding.

Tony reached out and ran his finger gently up and down her cheek. She released a tiny whimper as her body tried to curl away from him. "Do you remember the night you let me fuck you?"

Sadie bit her lip. The way he said it, the way he laid the words out so nonchalantly, made her feel sick. Maybe they didn't make love, but Sadie never thought she "let" Tony do anything. She had given him a part of her she had been holding onto so fiercely because she trusted him.

"What about it?" she asked, still refusing to look him in the eyes.

"You liked it when I touched you then." His hands moved down, stopping briefly to caress her neck. She drew in a harsh breath and a whole new slew of tears cascaded down her cheeks. "Do you like it now?"

This time she did look at him and spat out, "No! I don't want you to ever touch me again."

Tony dropped his hands and stood up with a laugh. "Forever is a long time, baby. I think you might change your mind."

"Then you don't know me at all. I'm nothing like you."

Alex stepped into the room with a smile, emerging like a ghost from the darkness. "And that, my dear, is what we're all counting on." A beam of moonlight shone brightly through the parlor windows, and Alex stood in the center like a ringmaster. He looked at her with cold eyes. "This isn't for us. It's for Rick."

Sadie looked away from him and pressed her cheek against her shoulder. Why would Rick do this to her? He wasn't like them, was he? Rick was her friend; in so many ways he had been like a father. "Where is Rick?"

Alex walked to the bar and poured himself a glass of wine. "Well, this part here, it's the dirty work. I don't think he has the stomach to see what's going to happen to his little Peanut."

Her heart thumped viciously. "What do you want from me? Just tell me what you want. Let Hayden go, and I'll do it."

Just then Oscar and Dylan joined their brothers in the room. As soon as Sadie saw who they were holding, she screamed Hayden's name. Her friend had been stripped down to her bra and panties so that Sadie could see every scratch and bite mark.

"We know you will, sweetheart," Alex smiled. "That big soft heart of yours will do anything to save her."

It was still so strange to look at the teenager before her, shorter and lankier than his companions, yet still able to command them with just a nod of his head. Dylan threw Hayden to the ground at Sadie's feet.

"Stop it," Sadie pleaded, her eyes on Tony. "Please make this stop."

There was a moment when Tony met her gaze, and this time he was the one to flinch. She was looking at him with such a hopeful plea it made his skin hurt. This wasn't as much fun as he thought it would be. Suddenly he was no longer interested in hurting her; he just wanted to get the whole thing over with.

"Do you think he wants to help you?" Alex laughed at the absurdity of the idea. "He was playing you, Peanut. The only thing he wants from you is your blood."

"Let's just do it already," Tony sounded bored. "The quicker she drinks, the quicker we can get out of here."

"Why do we need to leave?" asked Oscar. "We already have our dinner." He kicked Hayden in the side. She barely made a noise.

Alex looked at Tony and saw the blank stare in his eyes. He needed to get him back on track. Tony was one of the most brutal killers Alex had ever known, but there was a part of him that would never shake off the humanity Mary Ann scarred him with. Her demise had made Tony hate the human weaknesses of death and fragility, but at times it also made him envious of them. Alex eyed the glass of wine in his hands and then handed it to Tony.

"You do it," he said. "She's yours."

He took the glass and stared at it with fond remembrance. It wasn't the wine, but what was in it that had all of them shiver, their bodies remembering the moment when they took their first sip. A sire would be connected to his childe for all the days to come, and there was a bond created from that blood that even a human mother could never understand.

Rick was a part of all of them; his blood flowed in their veins because it birthed Alex, and he in turn had given the gift to them. Their loyalty was to Alex above anyone or anything else. They were Rick's gift to his childe. Eventually, they would sire children of their own. It was Rick's greatest hope to have a family that wound through the centuries, riding the years on the basis of his blood.

Tony stepped over Hayden's body and knelt in front of Sadie. "Don't fight this," he warned her. "There's no other way this is going to go. If you make this harder than it has to be, Hayden's the one that will suffer for it. Do you understand?"

Sadie nodded, inhaling deep breaths for courage, terrified of what was to come. She looked at the glass in his hand and then at Hayden who lifted her head off the ground to pierce Sadie with bloodshot eyes.

"Don't do it," she whispered.

"Shut the fuck up," Dylan said and then gave her a sharp kick to the side to emphasize his point.

"Sadie," Tony said her name and brought her attention back to him. "You ready?"

"How will it work?" she asked, understanding that there was no choice but still needing time to accept that. Above all, she had to save Hayden. It was her fault her friend was lying there now. If Sadie could save her, she would.

Alex was the one to answer. "You mean, will you drink this and then turn around to kill your friend?"

She lifted her eyes to him with a glare. "Yes."

Tony touched her cheek and kept his voice soft, his face calm. This had to go smoothly. She was Rick's pet project, and although he would never admit it to the others, he did not want to torture her anymore. He just wanted it to be over. "It will take a few days or more to complete the process, but you'll feel a change the moment you drink."

"You'll be a monster," Hayden said, trying to push her weakened body off the ground. "You'll be a killer, Sadie. Just like them."

Oscar stepped forward and pressed his shoe against the back of her neck, forcing her back down. "Open your mouth again and I will flay you right here."

Sadie felt the room closing in on her as the hands of her past and future began to pull her in opposite directions like she was the rope in a game of tug o' war. She looked into Tony's eyes and asked, "Did you mean any of it?"

He looked back over his shoulder at his brothers then faced her. "When you're like me, you'll understand." It was the only truth he was willing to give her.

She closed her eyes, clenching them tight, and opened her mouth waiting for him to pour the cursed drink down her throat. She could hear Hayden whimpering next to her and forced her attention to the thunder rolling in the distance. If she focused on that, it would make it easier. She felt cool skin against her cheek, soft fingertips brushing gently over her lips. Tony was moving closer, and his chest pressed firmly into hers. Then she tasted his kiss and the wine he shared with it.

Warm liquid spilled into her mouth. Sadie tried to pull away from him, but Tony gripped the back of her head and sealed her lips with his. The drink was sweet and coated her throat in a way that eased it down. She tried again to pull away from him, the deed done, but he did not let her go. He kissed her harder as Dylan urged him on. Suddenly he released her and stood up. He wiped his mouth with the back of his hand and gave the glass back to Alex.

Sadie wouldn't have noticed the differences if she had not been expecting them. She could still taste the blood in her mouth; the tears that had been so steady were completely gone now. Everything appeared just a little clearer, like a film had been removed from her eyes. She looked at Tony, who was panting, blood and saliva dripping from his lips, and for a moment she forgot everyone else, even Hayden.

And then she felt her. Sarah.

Sadie's eyes widened; her mouth parted as a breath of disbelief escaped her. Her sister was standing in the corner of the room with long brown hair and eyes so similar to her own. "Sarah!" She started to wiggle and pull at the ropes binding her. The men looked behind them, trying to see what she did.

"Who the hell is she talking to?" asked Dylan.

Sadie watched with wonder as Sarah stepped into the candlelight. She smiled at Sadie and put a finger over her lips. Then she knelt beside Hayden and looked at the broken girl with sad eyes.

"Help her!" Sadie pleaded.

"This bitch is nuts," Oscar mumbled. "No wonder Rick likes her."

But Alex knew better. It was the blood. It was doing something to her it had never done to any of them. "Tony, untie her."

"Why? Let's just go already."

Tony did not want to untie her. It was done. He wanted to get the fuck out of that house and go find some hot piece of tail that would make him forget all about her.

"We're not leaving," Alex said, his eyes fixated on Sadie as she stared at something his eyes were blind to. "We have plenty of action here."

"I'm hungry," Tony snapped.

"Then by all means," Alex swept his arm down towards Hayden and said, "bon appétit."

Tony made no move toward the girl on the floor and no motion to untie Sadie. Alex grumbled and walked over to Sadie, who was desperately trying to get free. He reached around her, smiled into her wide, unblinking eyes, and undid the ropes. When he stepped back, Sadie was slowly standing.

Sarah smiled at her. How long had Sadie been dreaming and hoping for this moment? All those years of staring at her sister's face behind a frame, wanting so deeply to know her. So desperate to find the missing piece that would complete the puzzle of who Sadie was.

"Don't go," she whispered and reached out her hand to the dead sister she had been longing for.

I won't leave. I never did. I've always been with you.

Alex stood behind Sadie and put his hands gently on her shoulders. He leaned into her ear. "What do you see? Tell me."

She didn't answer him. She couldn't because Sarah was not alone anymore. They came out of the shadows, children, adults, all races and classes. Sadie stumbled back into Alex as her eyes fell on Kevin and Kristen. They were covered in blood; Kristen's right eye was a frightening black hole of emptiness.

"Get away from me," she whimpered and trembled at the terrifying images before her. "Go away!" More of them filled the room.

Sadie, I'm sorry for what I did to you, Kevin started to speak as he held tight to Kristen's hand.

She turned into Alex's body, burying her face in his chest and clinging to his shirt. She could feel herself shattering, pieces breaking away in chunks. Alex's arms wrapped around her, and his smirk was aimed at Tony who could only stare dumbfounded. When Sadie glanced back, the people were still there. Some had their throats splayed open while others had hands with missing fingers and blood spilled from open wounds on pale skin. Sarah had resumed kneeling beside Hayden, and now Sadie could see the blood on her sister's white shirt.

"What do you want from me?" she cried and turned to look up into Alex's face. "Make them stop, please!"

"There, there, sweetheart. You just hold onto me and tell me what you see."

Tony took a step forward and narrowed his eyes. "What the fuck do you think you're doing?"

"She's scared, Tony. Look at her. She just needs someone to hold her." He laughed deep in his throat, enjoying both the jealousy beaming from his childe and the excitement of Sadie's turn.

Tony shifted so fast it even caught Alex off guard. He reached down and yanked Hayden up off the ground, her frail form hanging limply in his arms. "Say goodbye, Hayden," he growled into her ear.

Hayden called for her friend, blood gurgling in her throat and pooling at the corners of her mouth. Sadie unwound her arms from around Alex's waist and turned around. The people, all those people, were coming forward to stand behind Sarah.

"Hay, she's here," Sadie whispered. "I think she came for you. They all did."

She walked toward Hayden, and Alex didn't stop her. He wanted to see what she did next. As though she couldn't see the monster clutching Hayden in his arms, Sadie reached out and touched her cheek. She knew she didn't need to say anything, not out loud. Hayden knew how much she loved her, how sorry Sadie was that she had brought these demons into their lives. And Sadie knew Hayden forgave her.

"Enough of this bullshit," Tony snapped and threw his hand into Sadie's chest with a force that sent her careening into Alex.

Her eyes locked on him, and the terror she saw staring back sent her mind reeling. Tony opened his mouth wide and sank his fangs so deep into Hayden they scraped bone. Hayden's mouth opened but no sound other than gasps and gurgles came from her. Blood spilled in dark rivers down her body.

Oscar and Dylan shifted and waited for their turn. Within minutes Hayden was lying on the ground, three vampires slowly devouring her. She did not scream, did not cry, just held Sadie's stare.

Then she saw Hayden standing next to Sarah and knew her best friend was gone. The others were fading back into the shadows. *Sadie, you must be strong. You don't have to be like them, baby sister. You're special. You know that's why they wanted you.*

"This is my fault," Sadie cried. "I did this."

No. They did this, and you have to find a way to stop them.

"I can't," she said, reaching out for Hayden's hand but only able to touch the cool air. "Don't leave me here."

We'll always be here, Sadie. When you need us, we'll come.

"I need you now!" Sadie yelled. "Stay! Stay!"

But they were already gone.

Tony stood on the porch with his arms crossed. He watched as Oscar carried Sadie out the front door, her body limp and seemingly unconscious. After screaming for ten minutes and clinging to her friend's dead body, she simply passed out. It had already been decided that the house was not the safest place for Sadie to turn. She would need to be watched closely and restrained during the day, considering she was there against her will. Tony would take her to Rick's secret spot deep in the woods, hidden beneath the ground. She would complete the turn there.

"Why do I have to do this?" Tony asked as Oscar passed Sadie into his arms.

Alex chuckled. "Oh, you don't want her anymore?"

"She just watched me eat her best friend. I don't think we're going to pick up where we left off."

Alex reached out and tucked a strand of Sadie's hair behind her ear. He was in awe of how innocent she looked, no sign of the devil slumbering inside her. Of course, he would never let her know the true potential of what she was. It was like he told Tony before; she would be a vampire in name only.

"You chose her," Alex said, his cold gaze meeting Tony's eyes. "If you want, I'll stay with her. I would love to ride the turn with her. To see what she becomes with our blood."

Tony adjusted Sadie in his arms and smirked. "It's too bad Rick chose me then. Guess you'll have to sit this one out."

"Touché," Alex smiled.

"I thought we were just going to drink from this bitch?" Dylan said and lit a cigarette. "Although, for the record, if all her blood is going to give me is hallucinations, I think I'll pass. I had enough bad acid trips in high school to last forever."

Tony and Alex both laughed. "She's got to complete the change," Alex reminded and threw his arm around Dylan's shoulder. "Then we'll drink from her."

"And you discussed this with Rick?" Tony asked. "I'm not about to crack open his Peanut without permission."

Oscar lifted his hand. "I second that."

"Do you want this permission in writing?"

"That would help," Tony grinned.

Alex made his face like stone, but soon the corners of his lips were pulling upward into a smile. "Get out of here," he said and playfully smacked Tony's arm. "We'll be by tomorrow with your dinner."

"Appreciate it, man." Tony gripped Sadie tighter then lifted off into the night.

Rick's hideaway was about fifteen miles from the house, so the flight was a short one. His feet hit the ground hard and jostled Sadie in his arms. He looked down into her face to find her still sleeping. With a sigh he set her down on the damp grass while he began the process of moving sticks and leaves away from the door camouflaged in the ground. Tony dug the key out of his pocket, and in less than a minute was carrying her down the stairs.

Rick built the hideaway in the sixties during the height of the Cuban missile crisis. At the time, those with the means were building underground bunkers. Rick, who spent nearly seven hundred years accumulating his wealth, made sure his bunker was as luxurious as possible. He never actively used the space but still upgraded it consistently.

Tony used his shoulder to flip the light switch that flooded the interior with a soft glow. Unlike their own house which lacked electricity, the bunker used a generator. He put Sadie down on the leather sofa and watched her. Part of him was furious that he was there, babysitting a fledgling that, if Alex had his way, would be nothing but a drinking fountain. He turned away from her and gripped his hair, took a breath, and tried not to think too much about it. Alex was crazy if he thought

Rick was going to let them do anything to Sadie. They were only meant to help her ease through the turn. After that, Rick would want his little Peanut to himself and all of Alex's fantasies would remain just that.

There was a stereo set up in the corner, and Tony turned it on to kill the silence. Van Morrison tore through the room, and he felt his body relax just a little. He left Sadie on the couch and went down the hall to the bedroom. The bed was a king sized sleigh. Tony was used to his wrought iron full back at the house, but he supposed he could live with this. How long had it been since he slept in bed with someone else? He couldn't remember. It must have been when he was still alive, when he would wake up beside Mary Ann and brush the blonde hair out of her eyes while the sunlight bathed them in warmth.

He stepped out of the room and closed the door hard. He leaned back against it while he took deep breaths and forced his mind to shut away the memory that was slowly forming. Tony had not thought about Mary Ann for so long. The first twenty years or so after the change were hard, but over time he started to forget her, and with every year that passed it became easier to pretend she had never been there at all. It wasn't until Sadie came into his life that Mary Ann was resurrected and he hated Sadie for that.

Tony stomped his way back into the living room and grabbed Sadie roughly off the couch, holding her up by her arms as he stared into her face. Her head lolled to the side. Whatever was happening to her had not happened to him. Bouts of sleepiness during the day were one thing, but to be so lost in slumber was not unlike his own sleep as a fully formed vampire.

"Wake up," he said, shaking her hard. "Wake the fuck up, Sadie!"

There was nothing, just her limp appendages moving under his force. The anger was rising again. He was beyond pissed that he was forced into this and tricked by Rick, just like Sadie. Of course, Rick knew Tony would be attracted to her. He knew whatever it was about her that kept her mind closed to him was the very thing that would draw them all to her. Rick also knew she would remind Tony of what he had lost. It was cruel in a way even Tony could never be.

He let her go and watched as she toppled to the shaggy rug beneath their feet. What would Rick do if he were to drink from her now? Would he destroy Tony over this girl whose only uniqueness came from her ability to shut them out? Fuck him. Tony earned her blood, every drop.

He knelt over her, pushing his body between her legs. He turned her face to the side and zeroed in on the beautiful blue vein that seemed brighter now due to the change happening inside her. He traced the line with his tongue and wondered if her vampire blood would be sweeter than human blood. Tony had never tasted a vampire's blood besides Alex, and that was only once, to initiate his death and rebirth.

It was something Rick told them vampires never do. Human blood was theirs to consume and devour, but to drink from or harm one of their own was an abomination. Tony smiled against her skin. Knowing how pissed Rick would be if he saw what was about to happen made the idea even more appealing. He shifted, his mouth salivating as he pressed the tips of his fangs against her neck. He couldn't drain her, but he could drink until he had his fill. By the time she saw Rick, the wounds would be healed, and no one ever had to know.

His fangs pierced her skin and there was a sharp pop as they broke through. Her blood filled his mouth, and he responded with a moan. She was exquisite, like nothing he had ever tasted before. There was a static charge that moved through him as he drank; the hairs on his arms and the back of his neck stood straight up. He pressed his body fully onto her, gripping her hair tightly in his hands. He tasted her power as sure as he felt it moving through him.

He pulled back, took a breath, and sunk his fangs into her again. Tony felt her move beneath him, her arms twitching at her side as her mind tried to defend what her body did not have the strength to. He couldn't stop, even after he passed a point that he knew he should. Then he heard Sadie whisper, "Mary Ann."

Tony was off her in one quick move. He stared at her with wide eyes and watched the blood dribble down her throat onto the rug. His whole body was shaking. Maybe he didn't hear her say anything at all. Maybe he imagined it while lost in the throes of the feeding. He could see her lips moving, her eyelids fluttering rapidly. Slowly he inched his way back to her and turned his head so that his ear hovered above her mouth. Her voice was quieter than a whisper, but he heard what she said.

"Mary Ann."

This time his shock kept him rooted to the spot. When she started repeating Mary Ann's name, Tony couldn't stand it anymore. He pressed his hand over her mouth. "Shut up," he hissed even as her lips moved against his palm. "Shut up, Sadie!" There was a dark warning in his tone, a warning her slumbering ears could not hear. He put his lips against her ear and pleaded. "Don't make me kill you."

"Mary Ann. Mary Ann."

Tony scooped her into his arms. He tried to ignore the tears he could feel stinging his eyes and the perspiration dotting his forehead. He took her into the bedroom and dropped her onto the bed. She was still bouncing a little as he walked quickly out of the room and slammed the door hard behind him. He wanted to call Alex, to tell him what he had done with the hopes that his sire could reassure him it was nothing, and that Sadie's words were nothing too. But he couldn't bring Alex into this. He wasn't supposed to drink from her, not until the change was complete and Alex tasted her first.

He pressed his forehead to the door. Her whisper was still calling to him, reaching slender fingers under the crack and caressing his senses. Tony slammed his hands into the wood, fury and fear igniting. "Shut up you fucking bitch! Shut up!"

He went back into the living room and sat down on the couch, his hands over his ears, and waited for the sun to rise and draw him into a sleep where her voice wouldn't find him.

Chapter Thirteen

When Sadie opened her eyes, the dream was still present. In the dream she was on the cliffs again, watching as the woman named Mary Ann jumped to her death.

Sadie understood now that her dreams of Tony's wife were not dreams at all, but memories. They were Tony's, and she had found a way inside them. It had happened off and on when she was a kid. Once she dreamed she was walking through open fields in Vietnam, trailing behind a slimmer and younger version of her father. Sometimes, she was with her mother, only in the dream her mother was five years old and standing over a grave clutching a single red rose. The dreams stopped sometime around age fifteen. Now they were back, and she knew Tony was the reason.

Slowly she sat up and looked around the windowless room. Where was she? This didn't feel like the house she'd been taken to the night before. This place had a warm charm that Tony's icy home lacked with its gothic ambiance.

Her neck ached, and when she touched it she could feel something sticky and wet. She got off the bed and walked right out the door. Logically, she knew she should be afraid, fearful of this strange place and the man who brought her there, but she wasn't. The fear was replaced with anger.

As she stepped into what looked like a small living space, Sadie stopped cold as her eyes fell on Tony who was sitting on the couch reading a book. She did not know what to do. Images of Hayden's final moments swarmed her mind. She wanted him dead, wanted them all dead, and she wanted to be the one to do it. As she looked around for an escape route, she found there was none. There were no windows and no doors leading outside.

Her head was hammering. Images of Sarah, Hayden, and all those other people consumed her. Again, she internally chastised herself for getting involved with Tony at all. Her actions were so reckless, every move steered by pure impulse. It was so unlike the person she had always been. If only she'd ignored her intrigue of him, Hayden might still be alive now.

"Are you just going to stand there?" Tony asked, not taking his eyes off the book in his hands.

Her entire body stiffened at the sound of his voice. She could only stare at him. Now that she knew what he really was, just a monster inside a human shell, she felt nothing for him but disdain. He wanted to make her just like him, and Sadie knew she would die to keep that from happening.

"Where am I?"

"Somewhere safe," he told her in a bored tone, turning the page and smiling at something he just read. "How do you feel?"

"I want to see Rick."

She deduced that it was Rick who wanted her to drink the tainted wine. Somehow, he was the person in charge of what happened to her, not Alex and not Tony. If she could see him, look into his eyes and ask him why he did this to her, maybe it would lessen the anguish. Deep down she knew that wasn't the real reason she wanted to see Rick at all. The truth was so much darker and uglier. She wanted him dead just like the others.

"Well," Tony drawled and set the book aside. "He doesn't want to see you. Don't take it personal, Peanut. I didn't see Rick for five years after my turn."

"What did you do with Hayden? Where is her..." The words lodged in her throat as tears welled up in her eyes. "Where is her body?"

"She's gone."

"You don't think people are going to be looking for her? Her family? They'll call the cops."

Tony released a booming laugh. "Shit, Sadie, you really don't get it, do you? We can make people forget all about her. If we tell them that she called Mommy and Daddy and said she was hightailing it to the south of France, they'll believe that's what happened. You have so much power to look forward to."

Sadie took a step toward him, the anger propelling her. "She deserves a funeral. Tell me what you did to her so I can at least give her that."

Tony locked his hands behind his head while his feet went up on the coffee table. "She had a funeral, Sadie. It was a burial at sea. Truth be told, sugar tits, there wasn't that much left of her. All we gave the sharks were scraps."

She ran at him. Rage and hatred combined with her new blood made her bolder. Tony was stronger, though, older, and he was ready for this confrontation. The last few hours while she slept, he had been readying himself for it.

His hand was around her throat before she had time to blink, and he pressed her against the wall with crushing strength. "Do you wanna fight, Sadie?" he asked, his eyes glowing. "Because if you do, baby, I'm game."

"Let go of me!" She clawed at his hands, her feet thrashing at the wall as he kept her in place.

"Look at you," he said, amused. "I like this side of you. I've always enjoyed it rough, but humans are so fragile. You won't break that easily, though. You might be just what I need."

"Did Mary Ann like it rough?" she hissed.

Suddenly she was on the floor, holding her throat and panting. When she looked up, Tony was staring down at her with wide eyes, the amber faded back to green.

"How do you know that name?"

"I don't know," she lied.

Tony charged her and threw his open palm against her cheek. She couldn't help but scream, more out of surprise than pain. He grabbed her by the arms, lifted her off the floor, and held her to the wall again. His eyes were on fire, burning hot flames as his face shifted right before her. When he spoke again, she could see his fangs, the sharp points glistening.

"How the hell do you know about Mary Ann?"

Sadie clenched her jaw tight. She would not tell him. Next to him she was weak and defenseless, but knowing that she could infiltrate his memories was the only weapon she had. She needed to protect it. He dug his fingers harder into her arm, making her wince.

"Do you really want me to make this ugly? Maybe you would like me and the boys to pay a visit to your parents."

All of Sadie's pretenses shattered. Of course, they would use her parents against her, the same way they used Hayden. She started crying in earnest. Tony pulled her back from the wall only to shove her against it harder, demanding she answer his question.

"I dreamed her," she cried, her voice breaking. "I dreamed your memories."

Tony's face faded back to the human mask. "How?"

"I don't know. It's something I did a lot when I was a kid." She felt his grip loosen and the reprieve in pain allowed her to get hold of her trembling voice. "I used to dream about things I couldn't possibly know, like my father in Vietnam. It wasn't until now that I understood they weren't dreams, but memories. I haven't done it in years."

Tony leaned into her and glared. "If you ever say that name to me again, I'll kill you. Fuck Rick and fuck Alex. I'll drain you." She kept her eyes down and would not look at him. He tipped her chin up so that she was forced to see his dominating stare. "Do you understand me?"

"Yes."

He took a deep breath and gave her a nod to signify the end of the conversation and the sealing of their agreement. "Good. Now come on, we have to get you cleaned up before the others get here."

He took her by the hand and led her back down the short hallway to the last door on the right. It was the bathroom, complete with Rick's latest home improvement, a standalone shower. "Sit down," he told her, motioning to the toilet, something Rick put in just for show. Everything Rick surrounded himself with was designed to make him seem as human as possible. Maybe that was why he survived for so long.

She sat down and tried to steady her breathing. She was still shaking. Tony's outburst of violence left her with fear she thought had retreated. He wet a rag and started to wipe at the dried blood on her neck. "Did you do this to me?" she asked softly.

"Yes," he said, noticing a lot of blood had gone down past the collar of her shirt. "And you're not going to tell anyone about it."

"Why?"

"Because I said so," he told her bluntly. "I shouldn't...it was a mistake. I won't do it again." He set the rag on the sink and looked her straight in the eyes. "I didn't want this. I didn't want to turn you."

"What did you want?"

Tony sighed. "I wanted to know you. I guess I wanted to know why you couldn't hear me in your head. Apparently, I wasn't the only one."

"So, Rick is like your boss?"

"Boss? No, and he's not like a father either." He searched for the words to better help her understand the family tree. "I guess you could say he's like a grandfather."

She looked away from him. Sadie couldn't understand how Rick, someone she felt so close and connected to, could have hidden such a dark truth. Did he care about her at all, or was it all about the internal blocker she had against their mind games?

"Take your clothes off," Tony said.

She wrapped her arms around her middle and shook her head. "No."

"Don't be such a brat. You need to shower and wash all that blood off." She didn't move so Tony leaned in closer. "If I wanted to, I could just take you. Remember that. But right now, all I want you to do is get cleaned up. Now please, get in the fucking shower."

A single tear escaped the corner of her eye. "Okay. Get out and I will."

Tony stood back, amused. "I've already seen the best parts of you, baby."

"And you'll never see them again," she snapped, glaring at him. Sadie's eyes were teary, but there was still a fiery resolution reflected by the vampire she was becoming.

His smile faded. "We'll see," he told her. "I'll leave clothes on the bed." He slammed the door hard behind him as he left.

Tony waited outside for the others. He stood on top of the hidden door and tapped his feet against it nervously. What if Sadie told Alex he drank from her? What if she told Rick? He would just have to make sure she understood what would happen to her and anyone she cared about if she did. So what if she had something on him, he had plenty of hers to bargain with.

He heard his brothers before he caught sight of them between the branches of the trees. Soon they were walking towards him with Tony's dinner in Dylan's arms. The boy was young, younger even than Alex had been when he passed from one life to the next. He looked about fourteen, and his cheeks were smeared with dirt. His body was clothed in a threadbare shirt and jeans. Runaways were easy prey. They were not immediately missed, and they always followed a stranger who promised money or food. The young always tasted just a little better, but Tony knew no one would ever taste as good as Sadie. His stomach rumbled at the memory, and he wiped his mind clear of those thoughts.

"Please," the boy was saying, looking up into Dylan's face. "Let me go. I won't tell anyone."

"Sure thing, kid," Dylan said, gripping the boy's hair in his fist as he led him towards Tony. "Just be patient."

"Where is the little lady?" Alex inquired with a smirk.

Tony looked down at the door he was standing on and pointed.

"How are things going?"

"She's a pain in the ass," Tony huffed. "She's asking to see Rick."

Dylan laughed. "Awe, that's so sweet. Already she wants her daddy."

Alex shrugged. "Rick doesn't want to see her until she's complete. He wants her to feed before she is his, and since we're going to make sure she doesn't, that could be a long time."

Oscar and Dylan seemed pleased by this, but Tony was unconvinced. Yes, Rick would wait until she experienced every aspect of her new life because she would be completely his at that point. If she saw him now when so much of her was still human, her emotions would override the vampire nature. She would hate Rick, and he wouldn't be able to stand it. Yet, there would come a point when they would not be able to hold him off anymore. He would want to see her, whether she fed or not, even if it was just to force-feed her himself.

"There's nothing weird happening to her, you know." Tony chewed his bottom lip and hoped Alex would not see through the lie. "It's a slow turn, just like ours."

Alex shook his head. "No, there's something different in her change. You saw her back at the house. Whatever she saw was real, and it was something only she could see. Something the blood gave her."

"Maybe," Tony mumbled under his breath.

Alex nodded to Dylan. "Go get her. I'm ready to get this night started."

Dylan stepped toward the door and looked at Tony expectantly when he did not step aside. Tony turned to Alex. "Wasn't her seeing me turn her friend into sushi enough? She already hates me, man. I'm the one who has to stay here with her in this fucking hidey-hole." He pointed at the crying kid in Oscar's grasp. "Let me feed, and then I can go back to babysitting."

Alex's lips stretched into a knowing smile. "We have something else in mind."

Oscar tossed the kid to the ground. "We're going to have a good old-fashioned hunt."

"No," Tony said fervently. "It's too soon."

Alex snickered at the misunderstanding. "We're not trying to teach her how to hunt. We want to show her how we do it, so she'll know we can always find her."

"So, tell her that," Tony responded flatly. "She knows what we can do. We killed her best friend."

"This is different. Besides, when's the last time we got to chase dinner?"

Tony still looked uncertain.

Alex calmed his tone. "We send Sadie and the kid off together. We'll even be fair and give them a head start. If the kid makes it back to the strip, he can live. And Sadie will be the one who saves him."

"What's the point? We know we can find them both," said Tony.

Oscar laughed deeply. "She doesn't, though. In her head, she thinks she can outrun us. It's not like we explained how the blood works before you literally spit it in her mouth. This will be fun."

Tony's head was spinning. The whole thing with Sadie and Mary Ann still felt wrong and isolating. His plan was to spend the night interrogating her about his memories and just how much she knew about his past. After feeding he would be stronger, and there was no doubt in his mind that he could get her to talk. He didn't want to chase the dinner his brothers were supposed to just deliver. He didn't want to go hunting Sadie either, even though the idea was somewhat appealing.

He wanted her to complete the transformation so he could get back to the house and his boys, then Alex could do whatever he wanted. Tony already told himself he would never drink from her again, convinced he would not be able to stop if he did. Even as he stood there, hiding his guilty lips behind his hand, he was craving her.

"Tony," Alex said, lifting his brows. "This isn't up for debate."

He knew there wasn't a choice. He would do whatever Alex wanted. He stepped off the door, and Dylan nodded his thanks before disappearing underground. A few minutes later he returned with Sadie. Her hair was wet from the shower; her skin showed no signs of Tony's betrayal. She had healed, the vampire within made sure of that.

"Good evening, Sadie," Alex smiled. "How are you feeling?"

"Can you take me to Rick?" she asked. It was obvious Alex, no matter his appearance, was in charge of the others. Maybe she could get somewhere with him.

He looked at Tony who rolled his eyes as if to say, 'I told you so.' "Rick is a difficult being to understand. He doesn't want to see you until you've completed the turn."

"When will that be?"

Alex put his arm around her shoulder like she was an old friend. "There's no real timetable to this, Sadie. Every vampire is different. I should warn you, in case your teacher didn't, the hunger will become excruciating."

Sadie dropped her eyes to the leaves under her feet. "I can't kill anyone."

Alex's smirk turned into a deliciously evil grin. "But you will. Every day more of the person you were will die inside you. One day you'll think back on the human you are now and despise her."

Oscar and Dylan cackled, and Tony laughed too, just to keep Alex off his back. The moon was bright and full, a fat opal hanging above them. She was brought back to the situation at hand when she felt someone grabbing her arm. The boy was pleading with her, but Sadie could not decipher what he was saying. Her hearing was tunneling in and out, picking up something else very far away. It took her a moment to realize it was the sounds of Brave Beach and the people inhabiting it.

"Are you even listening?" Dylan asked as he waved his hand in front of her face while the kid continued to cling to her.

The sounds faded until all Sadie could hear were the vampires around her, the kid's pleas, and the cicadas singing a late summer song. "What did you say?"

"Him," Oscar said and pointed at the crying boy. "He's yours to save if you accept the challenge."

She looked to Tony; her first instinct was still him. "What is he talking about?"

Alex was the one to explain the game, though. After going through the details Sadie understood she and the boy were both being hunted in a fucked up version of hide and seek. Alex let her know what she would win should she beat them. "Make it back to the strip and he lives."

"What about me?"

"You?" Alex asked. "If you make it to the strip, you can see Rick. He'll be at the bar right now."

She looked down at the crying boy who now had his arms wrapped around her thigh, holding onto her like the savior she was intended to be. Then she eyed the four vampires, still unsure what powers they held. Sadie did not even know what she was becoming, but she believed the answers were with Rick. If she could get to him and convince him of her loyalty, maybe there was a way to reverse all of this. Either way, she would destroy them all.

"Okay," she said, lifting her chin defiantly. "I accept. Shouldn't there be rules to make it fair, though?"

Alex's attention turned to Oscar and Dylan. They were shifting their weight from one foot to the other, trying to stave off the hunger and prepare for the hunt. Then his eyes were on his oldest. "Tony, what should the rules be?"

He looked at Sadie and felt a violent surge of hate. This was all her fault. "Give them a head start," he stated, though the enthusiasm seen in the others was completely absent.

Alex said, "Seems fair. I guess you better get going, Peanut."

She ignored the taunting and grabbed the boy by his arm. Without glancing back, she started to drag him deeper into the woods. It was strange because she could see through the darkness in a way she never had before. After walking for ten minutes, she stopped and grabbed the kid by both shoulders to shake him a little.

"You have got to stop crying," she snapped. "It won't be much of a chase if they can hear us."

The kid hiccupped and pulled in a staggering breath. "Please," he whispered. "Don't let them kill me."

It was not her intention to lie to him. She had no idea if he would survive the night. "I'll try," was all she could manage. "But you have got to help me by being quiet."

He nodded and his chest puffed out with determination. "What's your name?"

"Sadie."

"I'm Marcus." He held his hand out to her, and she shook it. When he intertwined his fingers with hers, she didn't pull away.

"Okay, Marcus. Let's go."

Chapter Fourteen

Sadie was feeling the effects of her time without food. She had ingested handfuls of water from the sink after her shower, but her body wanted more. The hunger was not like anything she had felt before. It was more than just a clinching pain in her stomach; it was like a burden she was hauling alongside her. There were times when all she could focus on was her body's demands for nourishment. Sometimes she would glance over at her companion and wonder what his blood would taste like.

"Why don't we just fly out of here?" Marcus asked just as he ducked a wayward branch.

"I can't fly," she said, a small laugh to emphasize how ludicrous the idea was.

"You're like them, aren't you?"

She clenched her jaw tight. "I'm not like them at all."

The boy could sense the conversation was over, so he stayed quiet and let his curiosity fizzle out. Sadie came to a stop so suddenly that Marcus bumped into her. There was a feeling in her that someone else was with them. When she looked to her right and saw Sarah, she breathed with relief. "You're here. I knew you'd come back."

Yes, sister. I'm here. You can't save the boy if he stays with you.

"I'm his only chance."

They will always find you, and they are already close. Your blood is linked with theirs. It won't matter where you go or what you do, they'll always find you. He must go on his own. That's the only way you save him.

"No, I have to get to the bar," she said with teary eyes. "I have to get to Rick."

You'll never make it. Save the boy, Sadie. That is how you are different from them.

She closed her eyes, and when she opened them, Sarah was gone. It made sense, what Sarah said. Their blood was a part of her now, and it was a connection that could not be severed with distance. Marcus was not attached to them, though. It was his scent they were tracking.

A foul odor caught her attention, and she sniffed at the air, aware that like her eyes and ears, her sense of smell had also become highly attuned. Marcus watched as she followed the stench to the carcass of a dead deer hidden under the branches of a tree. Whatever animal had taken the doe down had left an ugly scene behind. If she could mask Marcus's scent, then they would only be tracking her and the call of her blood. They would assume the kid was with her.

"Come here," she said, motioning to Marcus. He approached on unsteady feet. "You can't stay with me. They can find me, and if they find me, they find you." He immediately started to cry, so she took hold of his arms and looked him straight on. "You're going to be okay. You just have to trust me."

Knowing he had no other choice, Marcus nodded and wiped at the tears on his cheeks. She knelt next to the deer and tried desperately to ignore how her stomach growled and longed for the raw meat in front of her. She stuffed her hands into the gaping wound of the doe's midsection, then smeared the blood and pieces of flesh onto Marcus's clothes and skin. He looked like the unfortunate victim of a slasher movie when she was done, but he would be safe.

"Don't try and make it back to the strip tonight. When the sun comes up you can go to town. When you get there, take a bus home. Don't ever come back to Brave Beach, do you understand?"

"Yes," he said and put his hand over his mouth to hide the gag reflex that was triggered by the aroma of rotting deer meat. "What do I do till morning?"

"Lie here and I'll cover you in sticks. Even if you see them, don't move from this spot."

He was willing to do whatever she told him. After she covered him with debris and wished him luck, he grabbed her wrist. "Thank you."

"I mean it. Don't ever come back here."

The slow and steady walk she had been utilizing was replaced with a run as she sprinted into the trees and away from Marcus. The deer blood was sticky on her hands, and pieces of tissue were caked under her nails. It took every ounce of willpower not to stick her fingers in her mouth and taste what was on them.

The moon, which started big and bright, had become eclipsed by thickening clouds. She could sense the subtle change in temperature that followed a hard gust of wind. A storm was building. If the four of them were close, she didn't feel it. Would she even be able to sense them now, or would that only happen after her turn was complete? She looked up and let her eyes scan each patch of sky. She didn't see anything but the fast moving clouds.

Sadie had no idea how long she had been walking, but the hunger inside her was growing more persistent. She wasn't craving anything that walked upright on two legs, though. As odd as it was, she really wanted something from Better Burgers on the strip. Of course, she would have to order it rare. At least that's what her body was telling her.

Time rolled forward, and she wondered why they hadn't shown themselves yet. If what Sarah said was true and they could find her wherever she went, then why drag this out? Deep down the answer was already known to her, though. They were monsters, evil, and they wanted to torment her just for the fun of it. She came to a hill covered in loose gravel and weeds growing wild. It dawned on her that she ran in the opposite direction of the strip. At the time, it was to draw the boys as far away from Marcus as possible, but it also meant taking her farther away from Rick.

The hunger pangs were slowing her down and the hill was a dead end. She could turn around and head back into the woods to try and wait out the sun like Marcus, or take a chance and see what was waiting for her up top. Gathering what energy she had left, Sadie started up the hill, falling several times when her weakened legs simply gave up on her. When she reached the precipice, she was standing on the edge of a cliff that extended on both sides of her, reaching far into the darkness. Without giving her next move much thought, she turned to her right and started walking fast, making sure there was a considerable gap between her feet and the edge. There was nothing but the black night and below her the sound of water.

Her ears caught the sound of shifting footsteps followed by Tony's familiar scent. She wanted to turn around but couldn't. He invoked a fear in her now that froze her to the spot.

His voice, low and gravelly, sang out to her. "Ah, distinctly I remember it was the bleak December, and each separate dying ember wrought its ghost upon the floor." Poe's words dripped off his tongue as he started to make his way to her. "Let my heart be still a moment and this mystery explore; tis the wind and nothing more."

Sadie balled her hands into fists and slowly turned over her shoulder. She knew if he wanted to kill her, if any of them really wanted to kill her, she would be dead. Rick wanted her alive, in some sense, and Tony couldn't really hurt her. Logic deflated, however, when he continued to advance in her direction. She quickly turned away from him and kept going.

She glanced back once more to see him standing with his arms crossed and a smile pulling at the corners of his lips. Whipping her head back around to focus on the path in front of her, she came to a sudden stop when she saw Alex standing just a few feet ahead of her. A scream tore from her throat and she lost her footing when she tried to back up. She fell back onto the ground with a smack as her head collided with a sharp rock. For a moment all she could focus on was the throbbing pain at the base of her skull. When she sat up and looked around, she saw no one.

It took a while before she was able to stand up again. The moon was gone, swallowed by the clouds. The only light the sky provided her now was in the form of lightning. The first drops of rain fell, and then it was pouring. She squinted into the rain, still looking for the monsters hunting her. "Come back and get me, you fucking cowards!"

Laughter filled the air, and it seemed to be everywhere. They were playing with her. This was all just a game to them. She might not be able to win, but she would play, and if it was a chase they wanted, she would give it to them.

Under her feet the earth felt less stable. The water was weakening the side of the cliff, and Sadie knew this was a mudslide waiting to happen. "Shit," she said, not sure if she should run or jump. She decided she wasn't quite ready for a leap of faith and continued forward.

Suddenly, a hand reached over the edge of the cliff and grabbed hold of her ankle. Her stomach flipped as she swayed over the edge and saw two gleaming eyes glaring at her.

"Let go of me!" she shrieked and pulled her leg away. The hand slipped off her and disappeared back into the darkness.

Not bothering to look back, she got to her feet and started to run, her blurry eyes focused on trying to see what was in the distance. Her feet halted when she saw the three human shapes before her. The laughter rose again.

Then it hit her. Why was she running? This would be the easiest way to end everything. She would be with Sarah and Hayden. There really was no choice to make. Her stomach was still spasming, demanding the one thing she could never give, but she was unsure how long she would be able to deny it. This was the only way to stop her from becoming like them. She faced the edge of the cliff and closed her eyes. She was ready to end this nightmare. There was no fear as she took a step toward the edge. Then something hit her in the back and arms were wrapped around her. Her eyes shot open as she kicked her legs trying to get free.

"It's not that easy, Sadie," Tony seethed in her ear.

He lifted her off the ground with strength no human man could have possessed and threw her over the side of the cliff. She was lost in her subconscious before she ever hit the water.

When she opened her eyes, she was staring at the ceiling, lying on the bed she woke up in the night before. She tried to sit up but was stopped by a pull in her arms. Her wrists had been tied to the headboard, and when she glanced down at her feet, she saw her ankles tied in the same way. The pain from her hunger was now agonizing. It seemed to dig into every pore, every fine line of her skin. Tears fell as memories of the cliff and that long black fall came back to her.

You did good, Sadie.

She turned her tired eyes in the direction of the sweet voice reaching out to her. Her best friend was sitting on the end of the bed. "I miss you so much, Hay."

I miss you too but just know that I'm okay now. And you know what? Marcus made it. He's on a bus back to Oklahoma right now.

Sadie's chapped lips stretched apart into a smile. There was a feeling of accomplishment in saving that boy's life. There was also justice in knowing she rose above her tainted blood and beat them at their own game.

"I'm so hungry, Hay. It hurts so much."

I know. He's punishing you for outsmarting them.

She heard footsteps in the hallway, and both she and Hayden looked at the door. Sadie started to tremble, and she tugged at the ropes binding her in a fruitless attempt to escape. She shut her eyes tight and clenched her teeth as the pain inside her seemed to multiply. It forced a scream, and when she opened her eyes, Hayden was hovering above her.

You can survive this. You're strong and kind. Don't let them win.

The pain hit again like a knife slicing through her. She bit hard into her lip until she tasted blood and thrashed against her restraints. After several minutes the pain started to recede until it was a dull ache, but she knew it would become even worse the next round. Hayden was gone, but Sadie was not alone. Tony stood in the open doorway, his arms crossed over his chest and a knowing gleam in his eyes.

"It hurts, doesn't it? I remember. Do you want me to make it better?"

She let out a defeated sob. "Yes."

He turned and walked away. When he returned holding a white paper bag from Better Burgers, Sadie nearly screamed with happiness.

She kept pulling at the ropes, trying to reach for the sack that held what she needed to make the pain stop. Tony set the bag on the nightstand next to the bed, laughing softly to himself as Sadie's teary eyes looked at the sack with yearning. He sat down beside her and started to trace her jaw with his finger.

"I don't know how you did it, Sadie. Alex was shocked as shit when he realized that kid got away." His thumb ghosted over her bottom lip, and Tony loved the way she recoiled into the mattress. "But I wasn't surprised. I tasted it in your blood. You really are special."

Her back bowed off the bed as another wave of pain rolled through her. "Please," she breathed, the ache stealing the strength of her voice. "Let me eat. Make the pain stop."

Tony smiled down at her sweetly then leaned forward to press his lips against her wet cheek. "Of course, baby. But there's something we need to get out of the way first." He got up and left the room. When he returned, he was holding a young girl by the hair. She had been gagged and her arms bound behind her back. Her frightened eyes locked on Sadie.

"This is Carolyn," Tony said and tossed the girl onto the bed between Sadie's tied ankles. "She's fourteen, in the 9th grade, and wants to be a ballerina when she grows up." He met Sadie's eyes. "Of course, thanks to you, she'll never get the chance."

"What are you doing?"

"You lost my dinner," he snapped at her. "So I had to go find a replacement. You could have just let me have that little street rat, but instead, I'm going to dine on the finest cuisine Brave Beach has to offer." On cue, the girl started to wail behind the gag.

"Stop it, Tony, please!" Sadie could feel the girl's terror as if it was a living entity all its own. "Let her go. I'm sorry!"

He gripped a fist full of Carolyn's sandy blonde hair and lifted her face, so her eyes were on Sadie. "Apologize to her," he snarled. "You're the reason she's going to die. You know, I could make it painless, but I won't. I'm going to make it as painful as possible, and you're going to watch."

She shook her head, pleading eyes locked on his angry face. "Don't! Please, what do you want me to do? I'll do anything just don't hurt this girl."

Tony dragged the crying girl to the side of the bed and shoved her face directly over Sadie's. "Tell her. Tell sweet Carolyn how sorry you are."

"Please, I'm begging you, Tony. Don't do this."

"Tell her! So she knows who's really killing her."

"I'm sorry," Sadie sobbed. "I'm so sorry!"

Tony howled with laughter and shifted into the demon Sadie knew was his true identity. He pulled Carolyn's head back, tiny veins in her neck straining, and ground his mouth onto her with a ferocious growl. Blood sprayed outward and slapped Sadie's face. She continued to pull at the ropes, so desperate not to be there, to not watch this girl die all because of her.

Carolyn tried to scream but there was no sound, only the burble of blood in her throat. It dribbled from the corner of her lips down her chin. Tony flipped Carolyn over onto her back, and the pressure of his body made her shoulders snap and break from the awkward way she fell. Carolyn's head was lying on Sadie's chest, her blood coating all of it. Tony lifted his head and dropped it again to sink his fangs into the side of her face, ripping a hole from her ear to nose. Somehow Carolyn managed to get the gag out of her mouth. Sadie could only watch in horror as blood and saliva spilled between her lips while she spoke a gurgle of jumbled pleas.

Tony released his fangs and fixed his blistering eyes on Sadie. "This is how it should have ended for you," he seethed and tore away a chunk of Carolyn's throat. He spit it into Sadie's face. The girl's eyes stared unblinking at the ceiling, and her mouth, with white teeth stained pink, hung open as the last breath left her. A moment later Sadie caught a glimpse of Carolyn standing next to Hayden in the corner of the room.

"I'm so sorry," Sadie cried, Carolyn's blood on her lips and in her mouth, the taste easing some of the pain. "Oh, God, I'm so sorry."

Hayden took the girl's hand, and in the blink of an eye, they were gone.

"Save your breath," Tony said, the human face he wore so well was back. "She can't hear you anymore." He licked his lips and tossed Carolyn's dead body onto the floor. "This is what will happen to everyone you love if you ever fuck with us like that again."

She looked up at him with defeat. "I hate you."

"Girl, I'm the best friend you have right now."

She turned away from him, the hunger pains starting up again. She wanted to hide it from him, but her muscles twitched involuntarily, and the painful cries she tried to hold in escaped her lips before she could stop them.

Tony sat down next to her on the blood soaked sheets and untied her wrists. With a sigh, her arms collapsed beside her. The ropes burned two perfect red circles into her skin, but Sadie understood they would not last long.

He grabbed the sack of burgers and tossed them to her. "They're rare. Just the way I know you'll like them."

He moved down the bed and untied the ropes around her ankles while she tore into the sack and stuffed pieces of bread and nearly raw meat into her mouth. The pain started to subside almost immediately, and Sadie heard herself whisper, "Thank you."

"After that, I'll take you to the shower, and this time when I tell you to strip, you'll do it like the good girl I know you can be."

She wanted to protest but there was no room to argue or fight. He was stronger and always would be. And now she knew he would torture others to punish her. So, she nodded her head and kept on eating. Was this what Rick had wanted for her?

Rick sat back in his chair, eyes blurring a little as he focused on the bookshelves that surrounded him. He missed Sadie. He hated that he had to do this in a way she would not understand until she completed her turn. But he knew this was how it had to be. Too much time had passed since he experienced his own turning. He didn't feel he could fully sympathize with her nor have the patience to help her through it.

He told Leah Sadie quit, too distraught over the disappearance of her ex boyfriend and Hayden leaving. She questioned him again, wanting a number to call or an address to visit. He told her Sadie requested privacy and time to grieve. Rick promoted Leah and let her hire a replacement. A little extra cash soon made the questions stop. He knew money was the ultimate importance for Leah. That was only one of the reasons he didn't choose her for his family. Sadie, on the other hand, was everything he could want in a daughter. He just needed to be patient and wait for her to come to him. Once she was like them, she would be grateful.

"She's having hunger pangs," Alex said, stepping into the room and holding a glass of scotch he'd helped himself to. "All she seems to want, though, are burgers."

Rick sighed. “She’ll fight the urge; her willpower is strong. Eventually, though, she’ll give in.” He removed his glasses and leaned back into his chair. “Has she asked for me?”

“Nope,” said Alex. He walked over to the bookshelf where the framed pictures of past decades sat. “I wouldn’t take it personal. Don’t worry, though, she’s comfortable and I promise we’re treating her with the utmost respect.” He couldn’t help but laugh a little. “Anyway, now that she’s on her way to being one of us, what about Tony?”

“What about him?”

Alex turned over his shoulder. “Well old man, you promised if he could get her in you would let him have her.”

“I did. Are you questioning my word, Alex?”

“Not at all, Rick. I’m just wondering if the idea of Tony banging your sweet little Peanut is going to sit so well with you after she’s finished turning.”

Rick steepled his fingers in front of his chest and lifted his brow knowingly. “Somehow I doubt Sadie is going to feel the same way for Tony she once did.”

“Does that matter?” Alex asked and sipped his scotch. “A promise is a promise, and you said he could have her.”

“What are you suggesting? Are you saying that I should allow Tony to ravage my daughter if that’s what he wants because, as you say, a promise is a promise?” He shook his head with disappointment. “Alex, we are an evolved species. We are not animals.”

“Well, it seems only fair he should get something out of this. He’s locked down there in your weird little bunker babysitting while the rest of us are out having the time of our lives.”

“She’s going to be a part of our family. I didn’t choose her so you and the boys could have a plaything.”

Alex gulped the rest of his drink and set the glass down on Rick's desk. "You do know she hates you, right? Don't fool yourself into thinking she doesn't know who really did this to her."

Rick stood from his chair and glared hard at his childe. "Sadie is mine. I chose her, and I have sired her. I let you sire the boys because it was my gift to you. They are yours, but she is mine. Tony has no claim, and neither do you."

Alex pointed his finger at Rick and said, "Actually, there's something you should know about that."

"And what is that?"

"I didn't give her your blood, Rick. It was Tony's. So, while your blood is a part of her, he is her sire."

Rage filled Rick's eyes as he stumbled back into his chair. "You intolerable brat! Do you even know what you have done?"

"Yes," Alex said with a smile. "I added a beautiful new addition to my pack. And I gave Tony back his Mary Ann. That was my gift to him."

"I should destroy you for this."

Alex lifted his hands and shrugged his shoulders. "But you won't. Face it, this pack doesn't need a daddy anymore. We're big boys, and we make our own decisions."

Rick got out of his chair and started toward Alex, whose smugness was replaced with respectful fear. "Get out," he snapped. "And don't come back until my daughter is complete. Don't come to me for anything, do you understand? Let's see how well you and your pack of miscreants do without me."

Alex looked afraid for only a moment, but it was replaced quickly with the arrogance that suited him best. He bowed his head and said, "Until we meet again."

He left the room and laughed all the way to the front door. Sadie would soon be ready to taste, and he could already imagine the power she would give him. With Rick out of the picture for now, Alex had no one to stop him.

Chapter Fifteen

The night was almost over, and dawn was coming around the corner when Alex, Dylan, and Oscar made their way back to the house. Oscar and Dylan waited outside Rick's while Alex went inside to talk. When he emerged twenty minutes later, it was with a victorious smile. He told them Rick knew the truth about Sadie and the true proprietor of the blood she drank. They didn't speak of it again until arriving home.

"Are you going to tell Tony?" Dylan asked.

"Why would I do that? Besides, it could have been any of us. There's a reason I keep our blood handy, Dylan. I want all of you to be happy, and I realize that having your own offspring is important. At the end of the day, this was a gift and Tony will appreciate it."

"He's her sire," Dylan said, confused. "Won't he figure it out?"

Alex took off his jacket and hung it on the back of a barstool in the parlor. "I told you; the sire doesn't feel the full connection until the childe has completed the turn. When she does, he won't care that he's her maker."

Oscar sat down on the lounge with a huff. He glared at Alex but didn't say a word.

"You have something you need to get off your chest?" Alex's eyes were inviting a challenge.

Oscar looked at Dylan, who shook his head with wide eyes, a silent encouragement to let the matter go. He couldn't do that, though. "It's not right, man. He should know."

"And he will," said Alex. "She's only halfway through the turn. Once she's finished, we'll bring them both back here, open Sadie like a fine bottle of Merlot, and see what happens."

Oscar sat forward on his knees. "This is wrong, Alex. He thinks she's Rick's, and Tony should know she's not. You told us the sire connection was stronger than anything. Won't he look at her the way you see us?"

"She's not like us, and she never will be. So, it stands to reason that he won't feel anything for her like I feel for you. He can't stand her." Alex walked slowly toward Oscar and looked down on him with a stare that said the conversation was over. "I'm your sire. You remember that. If either of you say a word to Tony about that bitch, I'll make you wish you hadn't. Are we clear?"

"Crystal," said Dylan, who honestly didn't care either way.

Alex lifted his brow. "Oscar?"

He held Alex's stare but eventually had to look away. "Yeah, man. I get it."

"Good," Alex said and clapped him on the shoulder. "Now, let's get some sleep."

Sadie opened her eyes and had to force them to remain that way. She had never felt so drained, her entire body fighting against the need to sleep. Her head turned to the right, and she saw Tony lying beside her, hands resting on his unmoving chest. It took all her energy to sit up, and as soon as she did, there was an unnatural gravity pulling her back down. She dug her hands into the sheets and willed her legs over the side of the bed. Her stomach was rumbling again with a slight ache she knew before long would become unbearable.

She glanced back at Tony and waited for his eyes to open, but they never did. It was strange to see him look so innocent; that cherubic face hid the truth under his skin. She thought back to the first time she saw him in the bar, the way her eyes were drawn to his face. It made her hate him more. With renewed strength, she stood up and wobbled all the way to the door, using the frame as leverage to propel her out into the hall. The dull pain was becoming more persistent, and she had to take deep breaths to stop herself from moaning.

After what felt like hours, she made her way into the living room and collapsed onto the sofa in frustrated tears. Not willing to give up, she got back on her feet and walked into the small kitchen. She opened the refrigerator and moaned when she smelled raw hamburger. The pleasure of knowing she was about to eat was almost orgasmic. Sadie slid down to her knees and tore away the plastic on the package. Within seconds, she was scooping the meat into her mouth until the only thing left was bloody fluid coating the Styrofoam. Her mind told her to lick it and not let a single drop go to waste. She stared at it for a moment before tearing it into pieces, eliminating the temptation altogether.

The strength she got from eating was amazing. She was still sleepy, but standing up and walking around no longer felt like the energy stealer it had before. A few cups of water later and she was feeling almost like her old self again. Quietly she moved around the space and went up the short staircase that led to the door she couldn't open. Aggravated, she slammed her palm against it hard. She had to get out of there. The sun wasn't going to kill her, not yet anyway. She was still the same old Sadie, albeit with a few extra additives, and she promised herself that no matter what happened to her body, that would never change.

She eyed the lock on the door. All she needed was the key, and she knew just where to find it. With no windows and no clock, it was impossible to know what the time was. She assumed because of Tony's deep sleep and her sluggish awakening that the sun was still up, but for how long? In the end, it didn't matter. She had to try and get the hell out of that pit while she had the energy.

In the bedroom, she stood next to the bed and stared down at Tony. There was no movement from him at all. With a breath of courage, Sadie eyed the pockets of his jeans. Carefully, she slipped her fingers inside, biting her lip, afraid she was moving too much. The tip of her finger brushed against something cool, and she nearly screamed in elation as she withdrew a small brass key.

She backed away from the bed slowly and clutched the key so tightly the grooves were breaking her skin. Once out of the room, she ran for the stairs. Adrenaline had her shaking. She dropped the key more than once and had to start over. It only took a minute to get the door open, but it felt like an eternity. She was up the stairs and outside before she knew it. Her brows creased in confusion as she took in her surroundings.

The sky was an iridescent blue, a color that signified the end of the day and the first few minutes of night. When the realization that she had been tricked hit her, she knew it was already too late. She swung around and met with Tony's grinning face.

"Going somewhere?"

Sadie thought about lying, but what was the point? "I have to get out of here," she told him. "I'm going crazy."

He held out his hand to her. "Give me the key."

"Please, just take me to the strip."

"Give, me, the, fucking, key."

Knowing her attempt was over, she bowed her head and dropped the key into his open palm. He grabbed her roughly by the arm and dragged her back down the stairs, then tossed her onto the couch and stuffed the key back into his pocket. When he looked down at her, she was trying not to cry.

"He doesn't want to see you," he told her, his voice firm.

"It's not even about Rick," she said and looked up at him. "I have to get out of here, even if it's just for a few hours. What's the big deal anyway? You can find me no matter where I go."

"Do you even know what's happening to you? You think you're the same person you were before you drank the blood, but you're not! When you complete the turn, we'll go back to the house. Then maybe we can talk about going other places."

She crossed her arms over her chest and said, "This is bullshit."

"You're telling me," Tony mumbled as he headed into the kitchen. He saw the torn pieces of Styrofoam scattered on the floor and looked back at her. "Do you think this is fun for me?"

"Isn't it?"

He opened one of the cabinets and removed a stainless steel tumbler. He opened it and took a swig, wincing as the blood slid down his throat. Tony hated that he was being forced to feed this way. The blood was cool and lumpy from the time it spent coagulating. Alex had promised to come by that night and relieve him for a few hours so he could hunt with Dylan and Oscar. Part of him was aching to get the hell out of there. The other part wasn't sure he wanted to leave Sadie with Alex. He was torn on why. Was it because he feared she would tell him Tony drank from her, or because he was worried Alex might drink from her, too? He finished his deeply unsatisfying snack and slammed the tumbler into the sink. Sadie flinched on the couch.

"No," he finally said. "This isn't fun for me."

"Then why..." She couldn't complete the question, and she didn't have to. Tony already knew what she was going to say.

"I didn't know Rick wanted to turn you, not until after we had already started talking. But he knew I would be drawn to you." He walked over to the couch and sat down beside her. "He knew you would be drawn to me."

Sadie was weary of this side of Tony, the calm, serene man who looked at her like she was something more than just a science project. Yet, she could sense his openness and wanted to take advantage of it. "How did he know that?"

"Because I couldn't get inside your head."

She looked down at her hands. There was a sting of rejection, and she hated the feeling. Sadie didn't want to care that Tony's attraction to her had only been based on some freak ability she possessed. She didn't want to feel hurt that his feelings weren't akin to what she felt for him, and yet it hurt just the same.

"And because of Mary Ann," he said suddenly.

She looked up at him with surprise. He told her he would kill her if she ever mentioned that name and now, he was bringing her up. "Do I remind you of her?"

Tony leaned back into the couch. He wasn't sure why he told her the truth, but some part of him felt he owed it. He had stolen so many lives and killed with no thought about the person whose blood he was taking. Everything was based on his own primal need. Sadie was different, though. He wasn't just ending her life; he was leading her into a hell Alex was setting up for her. The truth was the only thing he could offer that made him feel even a little better about what was happening.

"You're strong like she was."

"Did you love her a lot?"

He sighed a little and closed his eyes. "I loved her as much as I could. But I wasn't very good at love."

Tony felt a sense of relief sweep over him. He hadn't spoken about Mary Ann or his life before the darkness in so long. Now he was desperate to release all the memories, if only to lose even a part of the leftover guilt he carried with him. Sadie looked at him with eyes that begged to know all the answers to questions she was too afraid to ask. He cast his gaze around the room and focused on the painting of a castle. It was Rick's home once upon a time.

"I thought I wanted to be married and have a family. Family was very important to my father. Even though I left Italy and came to America to start fresh, that tradition was kind of engrained in me. I met Mary Ann, and I was ready to be a good husband, but as soon as we had our own house and she was talking about children, I realized I didn't really want any of it. I wanted her, but I didn't want that life. When she became pregnant, I started roaming the streets at night, drinking in bars till they kicked me out. It was just too hard to be with her and see her belly getting bigger, knowing that when that baby was born my life, the life I wanted, would be over."

Sadie soaked in every word he said. She could tell he was debating whether to keep going or leave it as is. She didn't want him to stop; she was thirsting to know everything. It surprised them both when she placed her hand over his. "What happened to your baby?"

"He died. I wasn't there when he was born. I was with another woman in an alley behind our home."

Sadie withdrew her hand. The way he said the words, so casually and without reverence, sent a chill through her. There was no remorse in his voice for the child who died. His child. "I don't think we should talk about this anymore."

Tony laughed. "Why? Because you imagined that before I was this, I was some sweetheart with a wife and kids I adored? I loved Mary Ann, and I wanted her with me forever, but she made her choice."

"Some choice," Sadie said without thinking. "Be a killer or throw yourself off a cliff. Obviously, she made the right decision." As soon as she finished the sentence, she regretted it. She felt Tony stiffen beside her, and she was trying to get up off the couch when he grabbed her by the waist and pulled her back down.

"Were those the memories you dreamed?" he asked, green eyes starting to simmer.

"Yes."

He pulled her into him, so his face was an inch from hers. Damn him for letting his guard down and allowing her in. "I don't know how you got in my head, Sadie, but if you ever do it again..." He let the words and the threat that came with them hang in the air. When she said nothing, he dug his fingers deeper into her arm until she winced.

"I can't help it sometimes," she said and let out a pained gasp when Tony grabbed the hair at the back of her head and yanked hard.

"This wasn't a bonding moment," he spat. "You aren't Mary Ann, and you never will be. You were nothing but a fuck to me, Sadie." He watched a tear trickle down her cheek, and he couldn't stop from licking it away. "You'll always be just a fuck. You're Rick's girl. You're only mine when I want to get laid."

She threw her hands into his chest and wiggled away from him. He only let go of her hair because he was afraid she might rip it off her head in her attempt to get free. She stood up, huffing and glaring down at him. If he looked hard enough, he could see flecks of amber in her eyes.

"You will never be with me again."

He laughed and put his feet up on the coffee table while his hands went behind his head. "Never say never, Peanut."

"Stop calling me that!" she screamed at him.

Tony smiled. He could see the subtle changes in her. Those soft blue eyes became hard and darkening as her chest heaved. He didn't want it to, he knew she was nothing but trouble, but her fury was turning him on. For the first time since his turn, there was a girl that could match him, that could survive the rough touch of his temperament. He drew his tongue over his lips.

"Did I touch a nerve?"

His own eyes were smoldering, his shift coming closer. He was ready to make his time down there worth it. What had he said to her? She was only his when he wanted to get laid. Right now, it was all he wanted.

Sadie was crying now, but only because she was so enraged. How was it possible that one single moment, one stupid flutter of flirtation, could change her world so completely? She could feel all that pent up fury heating inside her until she was sweating. The sound of her heart pounding in long, slow beats was thunderous in her ears. Something was wrong. She could hear him mocking her on the couch, but there was another sound rising above him until it was all she could hear. Voices were calling to her, hundreds of them, screaming and crying for help. She felt her knees buckle and collapsed to the floor with her hands over her ears.

Tony stood up and walked over to her, amused at the childish way she tried to shut him out. "Get up," he said, looking down on her with a grin.

Her eyes were stinging, like a fever inside was trying to seep out. Her vision distorted and her clothes were damp with sweat. She wiped her eyes, then doubled over as a wave of deep, vicious pain coursed through her. It was not like the hunger pangs she experienced before; this was something else. This was a pain that had no words to describe it. She fell back, her body twitching involuntarily. The voices were everywhere, above her, below her, inside her.

"Help me!"

Tony could only stand there dumbly while she sobbed and screamed, skin flushed red. She started to tear at her clothes, telling him she couldn't breathe. He had no idea what was happening or why. Then her body started to rise upward, a slow levitation until she was suspended in the air level with his chest. She was sweating so profusely that her hair was soaked, and she clawed at her skin until it was split and bleeding.

"It's, it's okay, Sadie," Tony said, even though none of this was okay.

He reached for her, prepared to hold her even as the air tried to claim her. Suddenly her body flew across the room and slammed so hard into the wall the picture frames crashed onto the floor. Sadie landed on her stomach atop the broken glass. Tony ran to her and knelt to carefully turn her over. She stared up at him, eyes alight and face contorting with pain.

"Please," she whispered. "Tony, please help me."

He didn't know what to do. His turn wasn't like this. He understood hunger and lethargy, but this was something else. Whatever made her different was making the turn different, too. Blood dripped from her nose and ears. The tears that streaked her cheeks were tinged with it, as well. She lifted a shaking hand and touched his face. He didn't think about what to do next; his instincts took over. Tony scooped her up and carried her to the bathroom. Sadie shook violently, red streams spilling from both corners of her mouth.

"I'm here," he promised her. "Just hold on."

He sat her down on the toilet lid, and for just a moment he was almost afraid of her. If she could have seen herself, she would have seen the monster inside clawing to get out. Those pretty blue eyes were now wicked orange flames.

"It's so hot," she shrieked and raked her nails down the side of her neck.

He undressed her quickly, noticing the small sighs of relief with each piece of clothing he rid her of. He started the shower and helped her step inside. Her body kept twitching, and every few minutes she would scream horribly. He stepped into the shower fully clothed and put his arm around her waist.

"Hold onto me," he said gently.

She wrapped her arms around his neck as another stab of pain shot through. Her screams were not just the sound of a body dying, but a soul dying with it. She clung to him while his hands supported her head. The cold water fell over them, and Tony could only hold her close as more seizures wrecked her. Then she went still, and her head fell back. There was peace that shone on her face. The pain stopped.

"Is it better?" he asked.

She pressed her head against his chest. "Yes, it doesn't hurt anymore."

He put his fingers under her chin and gently lifted her face. Her eyes were blue again. "I think you'll be okay now. You should lie down, though."

She nodded, too tired and weak to argue anyway. He turned the water off and let her lean against him as he helped her back to the bedroom, grabbing a towel off the rack along the way. Carefully, he sat her down on the edge of the bed and wrapped the towel around her shoulders.

"There are clothes in there," he said, pointing to the sliding doors of the closet. "Oscar got a lot of your stuff from the beach house. The boys will be here soon, and they'll have food for you." He stood up, his mind still a chaotic mass of confusion over what he saw. For a moment there, he thought she was going to die, and he didn't want to confront the part of him so thankful she didn't.

"Don't leave me," she pleaded. "Stay with me." She couldn't be alone, not after that. There might be evil inside her, but Sadie was still human. She needed someone to hold her. Even if that was Tony, the prince of her dreams turned horror.

Tony held her eyes, then let his own drift over her. His body was responding to the sight of her, and the feel of her wet naked skin pressed against him. "You don't really want me to."

"Right now, I really do."

He looked down at the ground then gave a resolved nod of his head. She watched as he opened the closet doors and pulled clothes out of a duffle bag on the floor. Then he handed them to her with a soft smile.

"You should change, too," she noted. "Your clothes are wet."

He lifted his shirt over his head and started to unbutton his jeans. He saw the way Sadie wrapped the towel tighter around her shoulders and looked away from him. So he turned around and kept his back to her. He wasn't sure where the chivalry was coming from. He had already seen her naked, been so deep inside her she would never forget how he felt, and yet he still wanted to appease her.

After he was dressed, he heard her crying behind him. He turned around to see her looking down at the faded T-shirt she was wearing, clutching the hem in her hands and rocking gently back and forth. "What is it?" he asked.

"This is hers," she said with a sob. "This is Hay's favorite shirt."

When she looked up at him and their eyes met, he could see the change in her so clearly it startled him. Whatever just happened to her body was a turning point. The innocence he once saw in her eyes was replaced with deep, knowing sadness. There was something else looking at him from behind her gaze, something he couldn't place. A secret she would never share.

"Why?" she asked.

"What?"

"Why did you kill her? You didn't have to. You knew I would drink to save her, so why did you do it?"

Tony felt a lump in his throat. "Get some rest," he said, heading for the door.

She jumped off the bed and slammed the door shut, closing him into the room. Sadie wedged her body between him and the door. Hayden was her family. She had tried to warn Sadie, and in return, she had pulled Hayden into a death trap.

"You owe me an answer," she said.

"I don't owe you shit. I killed her because that's what I am. She didn't mean anything to me, and in time she won't mean anything to you. Face it, girl. You're like me now. I see it in your eyes, and one day soon you're going to bite."

"You don't really believe that," she told him with a knowing grin. "I could never be like you. Before Alex turned you into this, you were already a monster. What kind of man could have no compassion for his own child? Mary Ann saw you, too; she knew exactly what you were."

Tony grabbed her by the throat and shoved her hard against the door. He knew he was hurting her, but the grin never left her face. "We could be friends, Sadie. I could help you through this. But if you think I won't make you shut that smart mouth of yours, you're wrong."

"She killed herself because being with you was already like being dead!"

Tony squeezed her throat tighter. "You think Rick can save you?" His fangs were pressing against his gums, aching for a taste of her.

"Then kill me," she spat. "Do you think that scares me? I'm not afraid to die, Tony. That's the difference between me and you."

With his hand still around her throat, he pulled her away from the door. She was trying to push away from him, but he was stronger. He threw her down onto the bed and fell on top of her.

"Nothing scares you, huh?" He let go of her throat and grabbed both wrists, pinning them above her head as she struggled under him. "I know that's not true."

"What do you know about me?"

"I know you like me on top of you right now. That your body wants me as bad as it wants blood. And that, my sweet Sadie, scares the shit out of you." He couldn't stop his smile when he felt her still beneath him.

"Get off me," she demanded.

He leaned into her neck and licked her skin. "That's what really scares you," he whispered into her ear. "That you know what I am, and you still want me. Let's stop fighting. I mean it, Sadie. I can help you get through this."

She turned her face away from him and stared at the wall. She hated him so deeply, despised everything he was saying because in the end she was afraid some of it was true. Sadie had wanted him before she knew the awful truth, and she wanted him still. He loosened his grip on her wrists and began planting soft kisses down the side of her neck, and God help her, she didn't want him to stop.

"This is who you are now," he breathed against her cheek, aching so much for her it was making him crazy. He slid his hand under her shirt, caressing the soft skin on her belly, and tried to kiss her. Once more she turned away from him. "Do you want me to say I'm sorry?" he asked.

Her eyes returned to his face. "What would be the point?"

"You're one of us now. It's who you are."

"No, Tony. It's not who I am. It's what you made me."

He closed his eyes and took a deep breath. "I'm sorry."

"No, you're not," she said delicately. "You're incapable of it because that's what he made you."

They stared at each other, neither one able to move forward from the moment or ready to step back. Laughter came from the living room, and Alex's voice echoed out through the small space.

"Tony! We're here."

He looked at her a second longer then rolled away. Without a word, he walked out of the bedroom to meet them. Sadie could only lay there, eyes fixed on the low ceiling, tears falling silent. She knew they were both right.

Chapter Sixteen

Tony stepped into the living room to find Alex and Dylan sifting through Rick's record collection. When Alex looked over his shoulder, he took in Tony's appearance, the wet hair and fresh clothes, then said, "Did we interrupt something?"

"Hardly," Tony said and rolled his eyes, hopeful the lie was convincing.

"That's too bad," Dylan laughed.

Alex grabbed a sack of burgers off the coffee table and held them up. "Well, here's her dinner. Are you ready to go get yours?"

"She's asleep," said Tony. "We can all go."

"And who will watch over Rick's precious princess?"

"The door locks, man. She couldn't get out of here even if she tried."

The truth really was that simple. The other half of that truth was Tony didn't want to leave Sadie alone with Alex. He didn't want him to know what happened that night and how close she was to completing the turn. As much as he hated that hole in the ground, he wasn't ready to leave it.

Alex looked at Dylan, who was nodding with a huge smile stretched across his face. They'd been missing their brother and earned a night without the stress of Sadie hanging over them. "All right," he said. "Let's get going. Oscar will meet us there."

"I'll leave these on the nightstand," Tony said, grabbing the sack. "She can eat them when she wakes up."

He stepped into the hallway and listened to Alex and Dylan walk up the stairs. When he opened the bedroom door, Sadie was standing next to the bed. "I'll be back," he told her while handing over the food.

"Okay."

She could barely contain the urge to rip open the sack and gulp down everything inside. The hunger was the worst, and the fact that she was going to live with it forever made the idea of living at all less appealing. Tony's finger lifted her chin upward, so she was looking him in the eye.

"Don't do anything stupid. I meant what I said about not fighting anymore. It's a waste of energy." He grabbed her face and clasped it between his fingers. "But that doesn't mean I won't make you sorry if you fuck me over. Got it?"

"Yes," she said, her breath heavy.

Tony dropped his hand and took a step back. "I'll be back before sunrise."

Outside the bunker, he inhaled a deep breath. He could smell the dying summer as autumn galloped toward the starting line. They met Oscar by the Ferris wheel and started along the perimeter of the strip, looking for a meal that would satisfy them all. Tony's eyes swept over the array of bodies, but his mind was back in the bunker with Sadie. Something changed when he saw her slowly dying in his arms. She was like him now, and her power, whatever it might turn out to be, was dangerous. He looked over at Alex and felt an overwhelming need to protect her from him.

"So," Alex said, rubbing his hands together. "What are you in the mood for tonight, Tony?"

Dylan answered instead. "Right there," he said and leaned on Tony's shoulder. He pointed to a group of girls standing together outside the movie theater. "And wouldn't you know it, there's one for each of us."

Tony's stomach growled. "Yeah, those girls are exactly right."

"Which one do you want?"

"He wants the honey blonde," Alex said, as though it should have been obvious. He knew his childe had an affinity for blondes because they reminded him of Mary Ann. When he killed them, in a way, he was killing the memory of her, too.

"It is my favorite flavor," said Tony.

After a series of short introductions and a bit of mind trickery, the boys won the girls' trust. It helped that they each saw Alex as a kid, the baby brother who got to hang out with the older guys for the evening. People trusted him; they saw him as a nonthreat. It made it more fun that way. Alex loved to watch the look in their eyes when they realized what he really was.

Tony had an arm around his chosen meal, Tiffany, and tried to ignore her incessant need to talk about bands she liked or how much she loved his tattoos. He wondered what Sadie was doing right then and if he made the right decision by leaving her alone after everything she'd been through.

"That's so scary," Tiffany said, pulling Tony from his thoughts.

"What is?"

She pointed to a flyer that had been taped up in one of the theater's windows. It was a warning from the police about being safe and staying in groups. Undoubtedly, this was all about them. They had been eating too close to home as of late because of Sadie. Soon, they would have to start sampling fare elsewhere.

"Yeah, that's pretty scary," Tony said, trying to sound truly affected.

Oscar caught his eye and smirked. "Lots of crazy people out there, girls." He pulled his pick, a dark haired dance instructor, closer to him. "It's a good thing you have us to protect you."

Alex walked behind the rest of them. It was funny to watch these girls with them, so trusting and unaware. They looked at Tony, Dylan, and Oscar like all good girls who think they can tame bad boys. Honestly, it made sinking their fangs into flesh even more satisfying. He and his boys were not just bad. They were eternal devils, and nothing but the sun would ever tame them again.

Oscar was growing tired of the formalities involved with dinner, so he suggested they head over to the Brave Beach graveyard, which wasn't a graveyard at all. It was an old section of the strip that at one time had been something like a carnival. Now, it was home to several rusting rides and a group of dilapidated buildings. The girl under his arm looked up at him and shook her head.

"No way," she laughed. "I'm not going in there."

"Come on," Dylan prodded. "We'll protect you." He pulled the girl he had chosen closer. "You want to, don't you?"

She nodded enthusiastically and looked at her friends. "It will be fun."

They arrived at the graveyard, but the smallest girl, whom Alex had silently placed dibs on, was still apprehensive. A part of the surrounding chain link fence had been torn away and never replaced, a perfect spot for them to gain entrance. Alex's girl still refused to go in.

"It says no trespassing," she said and pointed at the large sign. "Can't we just go to the pier or back to the strip?"

Alex met her eyes. It only took a small push of his quiet suggestion, and she was going through the fence like everyone else. Dylan lit a joint and shared a knowing look with the others. The girls inadvertently led themselves farther into their own demise with every puff they took. The hazier they were, the more fun the boys could have.

"You know what we should do," Dylan suggested. "We should play hide and seek."

Tony nodded, his lips twisting into a lopsided grin. "Definitely."

Alex's chosen meal was still apprehensive. She wanted to leave, afraid of getting caught by the police. Alex knew there was another reason. Her intuition was fighting against his persuasion and told her that something was wrong. He liked a challenge, so he let her stew in her own misgivings for a moment while her friends goaded her. Then he sent one final push into her mind, calming and soothing her. Soon she was following her friends into the maze of buildings.

"Let's give them a few minutes," he smiled. "Then we'll go seek."

Dylan and Oscar split up, but Alex stayed with Tony, wanting to take a moment to discuss Sadie. She should have completed her turn by now, or be close, and when she was complete, Tony would know instantaneously he was her sire. While Alex felt he might be grateful for the opportunity, Tony was prone to fighting against Alex's hierarchy over them. Tony was the strong willed first born, and Alex needed him in a place that would allow him to see Sadie the way Alex did. She was simply a means to an end. He wanted her unknown power and was desperate to taste her blood.

"Rick is okay with it, you know," said Alex as they watched Dylan fly to the roof of one building and disappear feet first through a broken window. "He says as long as she's not really hurt there's no harm done."

Tony could not hide his surprise. "Are you serious?"

"You don't think Rick is curious about her, too? He just doesn't want to be the first to take a bite. I mean, the old man really does care about her. But she's a gift, Tony. She's a once in an eternity chance to make us more than we could have ever dreamed."

"But you don't know that. Her blood might not do anything to us at all."

"True. But it's worth a try, isn't it?"

Tony looked back at the buildings and broken rides that were left to rot and crumble. "No," he heard himself say. For a moment, he couldn't believe he let the word loose.

"Excuse me?"

"It's not worth the risk if she's really going to be a part of this pack."

Alex swallowed hard. He didn't expect those words, nor did he expect to feel like putting his fist through Tony's face. Still, if he was ever going to get a taste of Tony's progeny and explore all the possibilities in her blood, he would have to play smart. It wasn't that he wanted to lie to his childe. He didn't. Alex knew Tony was connected to Sadie in a way none of them ever would be. She was a reminder of what he wanted when he was turned, and Rick took advantage of that vulnerability. The clever bastard.

"You're right," Alex said, smiling as he saw relief cross Tony's face. "She is going to be a part of this family. It's not worth it."

"Thanks, man," was all Tony could think to say. He was more than a little surprised but relieved that Alex had let the idea die so quickly.

"We better go find our dinner," said Alex, inhaling deeply. "I believe Oscar already found his."

The scent of blood hung heavily in the air, and a few moments later, the sound of Dylan's laugh and the brunette's scream shattered the silence.

"I'll race you," said Tony before lifting off into the wind.

Their feeding frenzy made them drunk off blood and adrenaline. The morning approached before they knew it. Tony left the others and flew back to the bunker alone. It was dark inside, and he kept the lights off as he walked to the bedroom. When he opened the door, he saw Sadie lying on her back, asleep.

He slipped off his clothes until he was only in boxers. His victim's blood was still pumping through him. It left him feeling warm, and he still wanted what Sadie denied him earlier. He slid into bed beside her and propped his head up so he could watch her. Her chest rose slowly, breathing almost nonexistent. She was close to completing the turn, and he wasn't sure he was ready to share her with the others, not even Rick. Even if she never lived any of her immortality with them in the house, staying with her maker instead, the blood bond would never sever. She would still be a part of their pack.

He had no doubt that eventually she would accept and even love what they gave her. Until then, he wanted to earn her trust. She may have been Rick's daughter, but she was his in ways none of them would ever know. Tony tried greatly to deny his feelings, to believe they were just born from residual guilt over Mary Ann. That afternoon, though, when he saw her in the throes of pain, all he wanted was to protect her. And he did want her. That was a truth he and the others would have to accept.

"Sadie," he whispered, smoothing his hand over her hair. "Are you asleep?" She didn't respond. The sun was coming and pulling him into a sleep nothing would wake him from. He could only assume she had already been claimed by it. "I'm going to make this okay," he promised. "I'm going to get you through this."

He kept his eyes on her face and lowered his lips to hers. She was still warm, her humanity not yet lost. Tony turned onto his back and stared up at the ceiling as the death sleep pulled him into a dark and dreamless abyss.

Sadie slowly turned her head, watching him with careful eyes. When she was positive he wasn't faking it, she slid out from under the sheet and off the bed. Her stomach was clenching with hunger, but she bit back every groan her body wanted to release. She crawled to the pile of Tony's clothes and sifted through the pockets until she found the key. As quietly as she could, she exited the bedroom and went back to the kitchen, where she'd hidden the sack of burgers in one of the lower cabinets.

She had to ration the food if she was going to have the strength to fight both her need for sleep and whatever effect the daylight might have on her. At this point, she knew it wouldn't kill her. She could still feel her humanity. Besides, even if the sun destroyed her, she was almost okay with that. Tucking the sack under her arm, she climbed the steps that led to the door. Ignoring hunger and insatiable drowsiness was not easy, but her resolve kept her moving. When the door swung open, she was doused in dappled sunlight filtering through the trees.

She stepped outside and lifted her hand to shield her eyes. Sadie took two steps and looked back at the open door. If she went back inside now, locked the door, and returned the key, Tony would never even know she left. The thought was tempting, but her determination was stronger than her fear. She walked into the woods, each step harder than the last. A few bites of the burger helped, but it wasn't enough. After only a few minutes, she had eaten everything in the bag. There wasn't much time left before the sun would force her to stop altogether.

It felt like hours passed. The more she walked, the more afraid she became. The woods seemed to go on forever, and she had no idea where she was going. Her body felt like it was weighted, each tread leading her to total exhaustion.

You're almost there, Sadie. Just a few more steps.

She looked over to find Hayden standing beside her. "I can't do it," Sadie said, leaning against a tree and slowly sliding to the ground. "I want to, Hay, but..."

Yes, you can. If anyone can do this, it's you. Get to the road, and someone will be there to help you.

"Help me? No one can help me anymore."

Get up, Sadie! You're so close.

She took a deep breath and grabbed hold of the tree, gripping the trunk hard as she forced herself to her feet. Sadie looked back and Hayden was gone. Her eyes were heavy, and her lids kept closing as though someone else was controlling them. It took everything to compel herself to take three more steps. The last one sent her falling, face down, onto a gravel road. The sound of tires crunching over loose rock was damn near an angelic choir. Seconds later, she heard a car door slamming, and then someone was gripping her shoulders to turn her over.

She knew that face and those kind eyes. "Tanner," she smiled. "She told me you would be here."

Then everything went black.

Sadie's eyes shot wide open, the birth of night drawing her from sleep. She sat up, her mind spinning as she remembered the last moments when she fought her way through the trees and fell on the road. For a second, she was afraid they had found her and she was in the bunker. As her eyes took in her surroundings, she knew that wasn't the case. She was in the room behind Tanner's store, the last place she had been with Hayden. Part of her was dreading seeing Tanner and having to explain to him how wrong she had been.

There were no words Sadie could ever say that would make anything better or would accurately explain how torn apart she was inside. Words were useless, but Hayden led her to Tanner, and he helped her. That was enough to keep her going despite the story she would have to tell him.

She slowly got off the floor and stepped through the tapestry. She looked around for Tanner but stopped dead in her tracks when she was greeted by Hayden's smiling face. Her photo was perched on a bundle of flowers with candles lit on either side of it. It was a memorial; she understood that she didn't need to tell Tanner anything. The boys might have convinced Hayden's parents and maybe even the police that she had simply gone away to find herself, but Tanner knew. Tears welled up in her eyes as she approached the shrine.

"So, it's true," a voice came behind her. "They killed her, and they turned you."

Sadie looked back at Tanner and could only nod and heave a sorrowful breath. She opened her mouth to speak, to tell him she was so sorry she didn't listen from the start, when a strange feeling moved over her. It was as if there was an invisible rope wrapped around her, and somebody just tugged it hard. She heard Dylan's distinctive cackle, and her eyes went wide. Tanner didn't need her to explain.

"Come on," he said, then took her hand and dragged her back behind the tapestry. He grabbed a bundle of herbs off the round table, lit them, and ran the smoke over her. "This will mask your scent for a while." The bell above the shop door rang. "Stay hidden," he told her.

Sadie crouched down behind a pile of large pillows and waited.

"Gentlemen," Tanner greeted. "How may I help you?"

Alex's eyes were moving over the store. "We're looking for a girl."

Tanner laughed and clapped his hands together with amusement. "I'm afraid I can't help you there. If it's tarot cards you're wanting or perhaps some rose quartz for a special lady, I've got you covered. If you're looking for a little fun," he winked knowingly, "I hear some ladies of the night hang around the pier."

Tony stepped forward, but Alex held out his arm to stop him. He caught sight of Hayden's picture and walked straight to it. "Well, isn't this lucky," he said. "It's Sadie we're looking for."

"That girl isn't named Sadie," Tanner said, his welcoming tone becoming curt. "That is my friend who went missing, apparently."

"Apparently missing, huh?" Alex grinned. "Apparently missing is exactly the problem we're having. Sadie Daniels, she was Hayden's best friend. Surely you know her."

"I don't. You could say that Hayden and I had a private friendship."

"Quit fucking around and tell us if you've seen Sadie." Tony was in a panic, still not able to believe Sadie managed to get out of the bunker, let alone make it to the strip by herself. He could sense she was close, but pinpointing her exact location was not as easy as it would've been if she had finished the turn.

"She came in here," Tanner said. "She seemed pretty messed up."

"Which way did she go?" Tony asked.

"She said something about going to the bar on the other side of the strip. Rick's Something-or-another."

Alex's jaw clenched. "If she comes back here, tell her she needs to come home." Then he and the others hurried out the door to get to Rick's.

Once they were gone, Tanner locked the door and went back to Sadie. He helped her up and rubbed her back as she descended into sobbing hysterics. "It's all right," he told her. "They're gone, for now."

"I don't know what to do," she said. "I need you to help me."

"Sweet pea, I'm not an expert in vampires. Everything I know is based on literature and media."

"But you believed Hayden. You have to know something."

"I believed her because I know that things lurking in unreality are the things most likely to be true. My grandfather studied them, but even he is limited in what is fact and what's fiction. Example: does garlic cause you to break out in hives? Can you eat regular food? If you bite me, will I become a vampire?" He shook his head sadly. "Sadie, I want to help you, but I don't know how. Whatever I know, I've already told you. The best I can do is give you more of that potion, but since you're one of them now, it might hurt you, too."

"So, there's nothing I can do to stop them?"

"I don't know. The truth is I can't get involved any more in this. They killed Hayden, and I can't risk my own life. I'm leaving Brave Beach, and I'm never coming back." He took her hand and squeezed it. "I'm sorry."

She returned the gesture with a hug and said, "Don't be."

Tanner leaving was the safest move for him, and she had to respect that. When she released him from the embrace, there were tears in his eyes. He took off one of his many necklaces and put it around her neck.

"It's black tourmaline. For protection."

"Thank you."

"You better go," Tanner said and wiped his eyes. "They'll come back here when they can't find you."

"Goodbye, Tanner."

She left the store and didn't look back.

"She's not here," Tony growled as the four stood in front of Rick's bar. Tony grew more agitated with every second that passed, and Sadie's presence grew dimmer.

"She's here somewhere," said Alex stiffly. "We just have to find her."

"Should we split up?" asked Dylan. "I can still feel her, but just barely."

"No," said Alex. "We stick together. That way when we find our little escapee, she can't get away so easy."

Tony chewed nervously on his thumb. He knew what they were all thinking because he was thinking it, too. Sadie had gotten under his skin, and he was the reason she got away. The ropes were still tied to the bed, and he should have used them, but he wanted the trust between them to bloom, so he hadn't.

"Sorry," he mumbled.

"It could have been any of us," Alex said.

Inside, he was furious, raging at Tony, wanting to smack him upside the head for being so stupid. The only thing holding him back was the need for Tony to be an active participant in Sadie's future taste test. She only helped his cause by running away.

"But it wasn't," Tony snapped. "It was me."

"Wait," Oscar suddenly said, his eyes wide as his chin lifted. "Did you feel that?"

Alex shivered. He felt the roll of energy move through him from his toes to the top of his head.

"What the fuck just happened?" Dylan asked nervously, having never felt the sensation before.

Alex looked at him with a frown. "Our little Peanut just completed the turn, and I'd say she also fed." When he looked over at Tony, it was to find his childe's eyes glowing amber, his chest heaving as he stared his sire down. "Pull it in, kid," Alex demanded. "People can see you."

Tony closed his eyes, breathed deeply, and when he opened them again, they faded back to green. "You lied to me," Tony snarled.

He stomped toward Alex and grabbed him by the collar of his shirt. Then he pushed Alex back into the nearest wall and held him there while Dylan and Oscar made moves to pull him off. Alex held his hand up, stopping them, and continued to let Tony spit ire into his face.

"I'm her fucking sire."

"Yes," Alex said, lips forming a grin. "Congratulations, Daddy, it's a girl."

Tony let Alex go and stepped back. He tugged at his hair, using all his willpower to hold in the shift. He turned his back on them, feeling not only Sadie's hunger and shift, but her fear as well. She needed him now.

"Where are you going?" Dylan called after him.

"To find her," he yelled back.

His walk turned into a run as he felt his body being pulled closer to her. Sadie's panic and confusion was loud in his ears, like a voice screaming at him. He followed his instinct toward the beach and the pull of his childe's cries.

Chapter Seventeen

When Tony found Sadie, she was under the pier in a dark corner where the sand and surf mingled together in a frothy mess. She was kneeling in the sand, her back to him, and the body of a man was lying motionless in front of her. A whimper drew Tony's attention to a young girl sitting on the other side of Sadie, one hand over her mouth as she tried not to scream. When she met Tony's eyes, he knew what he was supposed to do. Even if they could erase the memories from the minds of their victims, they didn't. They always killed anyone who might have seen them.

This time, however, he absorbed the girl's fear, perhaps because of Sadie. He told her to go home and forget everything. Once she was gone, he approached Sadie slowly and with his hands up like he was approaching a wild animal.

"Sadie?" He whispered her name, afraid someone on the pier above might hear them and investigate. Gradually she turned to look at him, blood caked around her lips, pieces of the dead man stuck in her hair. "It's okay, I'm here now."

"He was hurting that girl," she told him, eyes still burning. "He wouldn't stop even when I told him to."

Tony crouched down beside her and gingerly took her hand in his. "You have to pull it in before someone sees you." It was the most awkward place in the world to teach her about what she was and how to control this new part of her, but he was her sire and couldn't leave her now.

She closed her eyes, body trembling, and when she opened them again, Tony was staring into a sea of blue. "Good girl," he told her, cupping her cheek in his hand. "Good girl." He repeated the words again, trying to encourage her to calm down so they could move on to the next step.

"I killed him," she cried. "I did that."

Tony gripped her face and forced her eyes to his. "We're not going to think about that now, understand? We're going to get rid of him, and then I'll take you back to the bunker where you'll be safe."

Suddenly, her body gave a violent jerk and fell back into the sand. She started twitching, and he was spun back, remembering what happened to her before. Saliva and blood began to spill from her mouth in the form of pink foam. He leaned over her and clutched her shoulders as she thrashed back and forth. Her eyes rolled back in her head so all he could see was the bloodshot whites. Then, just as suddenly, she went still. Her eyes were staring up at the pier above them, unblinking.

Tony could hear the foot traffic over them increasing as more people arrived to enjoy the cool evening. He moved away from her and grabbed hold of the mangled remains of her prey. It was then he saw that not only had she removed his throat, she ripped off his manhood as well. It was vicious, and if he wasn't in such a panic, he might have even been proud. He dragged the corpse into the water until it was up to his chest. Without needing to take a breath, he slipped beneath the undulating waves and swam as fast as he could, his dark gift giving him sight into the blue-black darkness.

The man's blood turned the water crimson. Tony soon sensed new predators arriving, their thirst barely matching his own. He let go and watched as the broken body started to rise to the surface before it was snatched by strong jaws. He admired the sleek way the shark arched and disappeared back into the shadows. Tony turned and swam back toward the pier, unsure what he would find in Sadie when he got there.

She was still lying there with her eyes trained on the pier. He scooped her up in his arms and looked down into her face. "Talk to me," he pleaded, so unsure of what to do. He was her sire, but it was a role he never imagined having. It would have pleased him to stay Alex's childe forever; the responsibility of another was something he never wanted. Yet, she was his, and a part of him felt a need to protect her so intensely, tears stung his eyes.

"I killed him," she said.

Tony pulled her closer, and she wrapped her arms around his neck, sensing what was going to happen. He stepped out from beneath the pier, and she tightened her grip before he shot into the sky, leaving anyone who might have seen them unsure what they really saw.

Sadie was steadily crying when they made it back to the woods, her face turned to the side of his neck. He carried her down the still open door of the bunker and wondered what to do next. He had been frantic when he woke up and she wasn't there, the door wide open, her scent fading into the trees. His panic had turned to fury, a feeling of intense disloyalty that fueled his rage. At that moment, all he could think about was what he was going to do as punishment for not heeding his warning.

Now, though, knowing she was his, he only wanted to help her. He understood the strange feelings that a vampire experienced after their first kill. Tony had sobbed over the dead body of his first while Alex admonished him. He didn't cry over the next. Thinking back, he could see himself with Alex as they stood over the bodies of a young couple, their blood dribbling down his chin.

He carried Sadie to the bathroom and sat her gently on her feet. "Get cleaned up, and then we'll talk." As he was nearing the door, she reached out and grabbed his wrist.

"Don't leave me. I can't be alone right now."

"I'll stay," he told her, then turned his back while she got undressed.

He listened as her wet clothes hit the floor, and moments later, the water turned on. He turned around and watched her silhouette through the frosted glass on the closed shower door. Then he heard her softly crying again.

"Sadie, are you okay?" He bit his lip. It was such a stupid question. Of course she wasn't.

"I'm like you now," she said.

He took another step toward the shower, then another, until he was an inch from the glass. "Yes."

"There's more, isn't there? I can feel it, I just don't understand it."

"I didn't know," Tony said, pressing his palms against the door.

The connection he felt was so deep now, like the ocean he had swam in a thousand times but could never find the bottom. It was a blood bond only matched by the one he shared with Alex. Her pain, confusion, and fear could all be felt in him right then, emotions he had not experienced since his days as a human.

"It was your blood," she said.

"I swear, I didn't know. Not until you finished the turn."

Sadie looked down at the red tinged water swirling around her feet. She could still taste the blood in her mouth, thick like syrup and just as sweet. "I told him to leave her alone, but he wouldn't. Then he came at me, and I couldn't stop."

She tried to bite back her tears and pressed her back against the wall, knowing it was done. Sadie Daniels was dead. Whatever lived inside her now would never know the person she used to be. The shower door opened, and she met Tony's eyes. He stepped in beside her, his gaze never breaking from hers.

"You're mine, Sadie. It's my job to protect you."

"Why? I thought you hated me."

"I'm your sire. It's in my nature."

She looked at him and let her eyes drift down over his bare chest, down farther to that part of him she had only ever known in the dark. The pull she felt earlier was magnified, a push that sent her only in his direction. He reached for the bar of soap sitting on a dish in the wall. Without a word, he took her gently by the wrist and pulled her to him. His eyes stayed locked with hers as he began to rub the soap over her shoulders, fingers moving to her neck, where the slow pulse he once felt was now absent.

"Trust me," he said softly, his hands ghosting down her arms, touching the sides of her breasts tenderly. "I could never hurt you, not now."

She wanted to scream at him. She wanted to take her nails and rake them down that bronzed skin until it was his blood covering her. She wanted to demand he tell her why he couldn't have done this for her before, when she trusted him so completely. Deep down, she knew why. She felt it. The pull toward him and the longing to have him there was because of their mingled blood. Its truth laid dormant until the moment the human melted away and the man under the pier made such a fatal mistake.

Her teeth dug into her lip hard as his hands cupped her breasts, fingers gently tracing her nipples until they were hard and aching. Sadie's mind shut off, all those human feelings sliding away with the blood down the drain. Without thinking or calculating her next move, she wrapped her arms around his neck and pressed her lips to his, surprising them both. Then, slowly, he opened his mouth, their tongues tangling, the rich taste of blood heavy on her lips. He pushed her back into the wall, his mouth moving down her throat to bite gently at her neck while her fingers gripped his shoulders.

Sadie felt her gums aching as the fangs slowly descended. Every touch was a cool caress, and she wanted more. Her shift called to Tony, and when he looked up from the soft skin above her breast, he was stunned. Head tilted back, mouth wide, fangs sharp, he couldn't remember ever seeing anything so beautiful before. His shift took him over, and when he grabbed her face and forced her tawny eyes to his, she looked at him not with fear, but pure desire.

He lowered his mouth to lick her skin, to bite with the tip of his fangs until he tasted her blood. She tasted stronger and, as if it were possible, more delicious. Sadie tangled her fingers in his hair and guided his mouth back to hers. The taste of her blood on his lips made her hunger roar. Tony could see it in her eyes. He leaned into her, his mouth next to her ear.

"Do it," he breathed.

The moan he released when her fangs pierced his skin echoed through the small space. She whimpered with want as his blood flowed past her lips. Tony couldn't keep himself from pressing fully against her, encouraging her to bite him again.

She pulled away and leaned her head back against the wall, panting as her tongue ran over her lips, soaking up his blood like it was the only nourishment she would ever need again. She looked at him and her eyes faded slowly back to blue. He pulled in his own fiend to share the moment with her. He cupped her face and pulled her as close as he could, their blood smearing against wet skin.

"Promise me," she said, eyes searching his for the Tony he might have once been.

"What?"

She didn't know what to make him promise. It seemed unfair to make him promise anything at all. He had been a vampire for so long now, and Sadie, who was still so close to her humanity, couldn't know that promises were just words to their kind.

"I don't know," she said, looking away.

Tony leaned down so that he could look up into her eyes. "You're mine. You don't have to worry about anything or anyone else ever again."

"What does that mean? I'm yours."

He stood straight and took a small step away. She felt cold without his body against hers.

"It means I protect you." He immediately thought of Alex, of the plans he had once been hatching for Sadie and her blood. "It means you stand with me."

"And Alex?"

Tony looked confused. "What about him?"

"You stand with him, don't you? You're his like I'm yours."

It was his turn to look away. Things were becoming far too complex in that tiny space. "We'll talk about it later."

He closed the distance between them and kissed her hard, then dropped his head and swiped his tongue over her bloody skin until she melted. Soon she was cradling the back of his head and guiding his mouth lower until his lips were wrapping around her nipple with tender precision. Suddenly, he stood up and looked over his shoulder. Seconds later, Sadie felt a chill move through her. Someone was there, someone whose blood was, in some way, connected to hers.

"Sadie! Peanut, I'm here!"

Tony growled deep in his throat. Rick was there; he felt Sadie's turn like they all did. He turned to see her eyes lit up, and she was already reaching around him to open the shower door. Tony put his hands on her shoulders and held her against the tile.

"Stay here," he told her.

"But it's Rick. You said I would see him after..."

"That was before I knew. Stay here, do you understand?"

She shook her head. "Why?"

"Because I told you to." He didn't bark at her like he once might have. He said the words calmly. He leaned in to kiss her gently on the cheek, and she found that she did understand. His words were her law.

Tony grabbed a towel, wrapped it around his waist, and stepped into the hallway, nearly colliding with Rick. He shut the bathroom door behind him and glared up into Rick's face.

Rick looked surprised for a moment, and then said, "Meet me outside."

Tony dressed quickly and told Sadie to wait in the bedroom. He wanted to keep her out of this as much as he could. When he emerged, he saw Rick staring up at the moon with a dreamy gaze.

"It was very clever of you boys to give her your blood," he said. When Tony didn't respond, he turned to face him.

"I didn't know it was my blood until tonight."

Rick couldn't help but laugh. "What a devil our Alex is. And now Sadie is your childe. That is, if you want her to be."

Tony kept his face emotionless, but his eyes gave away confusion. His blood was the ingredient used to change her, and whether he wanted it or not, he was her maker. "What are you talking about?"

"I see Alex didn't pass down everything I taught him. Maybe I was wrong to let him sire you all. You can release her to anyone. Relinquish the responsibility of teaching her all the endless things you don't know yourself." He placed his hand on Tony's shoulder and said, "Give her to me. You know deep down you never really wanted her."

He looked at Rick's hand and then back into his face before shrugging him off. "She's mine. Alex is more like you than you even know. You played me just like he did. You both put me in the middle of your sick idea that she's something special, that her blood will make us stronger. I've tasted her, Rick. She's delicious but, there's nothing there."

Rick's eyes began to burn. "She was supposed to be mine. Release her to me, Tony. Do it, and I'll have Alex grant you permission to sire anyone you want."

"I want her."

Rick crossed his arms over his chest. "How long do you think you'll be able to control her? Do you even remember what it was like to be a young vampire? She's liable to kill anyone she comes across. It puts us all in danger."

"I can handle it."

"Fine, if that's what you really want then we'll see how this plays out. I want to see her though, please."

"She doesn't want to see you right now, Rick." He could see the hurt wash over Rick's face, believing Tony's lie.

"Very well, if that's what she wants, I'll wait for her. Just remember, being a sire isn't doing only what's right for you. It's your job to make sure you do what's right for her, too."

"Obviously," Tony huffed, although there was apprehension growing under the heaviness of Rick's words.

"Good, you can start by taking care of a mess Sadie's former life has created for us."

"What do you mean?"

Rick removed his glasses and wiped the lenses with his shirt. "Her parents have been calling up to the bar. With Hayden gone, I'm their go-to search engine. They want to know why she won't return their calls. The Daniels are threatening to come here if she doesn't get in touch soon. The last thing we need is Sadie disappearing like Hayden did. Persuasion and mind tricks won't work on police if we keep giving them reasons to look at us. She's connected to a lot of people who aren't here anymore."

"What do you want me to do?"

"Take her to them. Have her convince them she's fine, and then she needs to say goodbye. Surely my offspring taught you that. This life cannot have any part of the one before."

Yes, Alex certainly taught him that. "I'll take her."

"See that you do." He looked over Tony's shoulder as though waiting for Sadie to appear there. After a brief pause, he sighed and said, "When she's ready..."

"I'll bring her to you," Tony finished.

Rick turned on his heel and became a blur with the sky. Tony kept his eyes on the stars even after he could no longer sense him. There was immense weight on his chest, the burden of all he had to teach Sadie and still learn himself. A movement behind him caught his attention and he turned around. She was standing at the bottom of the stairs looking up at him.

"You okay?" he asked. She nodded, but he could see nervousness reflected in her eyes. He walked down the steps and closed the door behind him.

"I'm tired," she said softly.

"Dawn's coming in a few hours. Later you won't feel so sleepy until right before the sun rises." He reached for her, and her hand slipped into his with complete trust. "Let's go to sleep."

He helped her into bed and watched her eyes flutter close, a death sleep he knew all too well. Could he do this? The idea that Alex gave her his blood and planned to keep her in that house as nothing more than a blood bag, it made his entire body ache. "Why did you do this, Alex?" he whispered to himself.

Because she was a gift you would never give him.

Tony turned his head quickly. The voice had been so clear, sharp like a piece of glass. He sat up, eyes roaming the darkness. He knew that voice, knew it like he knew his own, but it wasn't possible he would be hearing it now.

She stepped out of the shadows, hair wet, and her dress brushing the floor leaving behind a puddle. There was an iridescent quality to her, like she was a mist that had found shape and form. Mary Ann smiled sweetly at him. He was trembling. He had never felt fear like this, not even when Alex revealed himself that very first time. "You're not real."

I've always been here, my love. She gave you the ability to see me. Her blood that you so eagerly lapped up tonight, it brought me into your sight.

Tony could feel himself rising off the bed, hands reaching out to her. "Mary Ann." He breathed her name, and it felt like a song. He was so close to her now that he could see the scratches on her skin and the beads of water clinging to her dress. "Forgive me," he said, choking on the words.

Forgive you? For which part, my love? The moment you abandoned me for his blood? Or perhaps for the nights you found yourself lost in another's arms. Oh, my sweet Anthony, there are so many trespasses to forgive. How could I ever begin to grasp them all?

He shook his head, still reaching for her. "I loved you. You know that."

You don't know how to love. You'll abandon her just as you did me.

"Fuck you," he hissed. The devil inside rising to meet the angelic foe before him. "She's stronger than you could have ever been."

He wants her blood. You'll do anything to please your master. Even serve her up to him like one of his fine wines. Look at what you have already done.

"I won't," he said, but his voice was not quite as strong now. "Sadie is mine."

But for how long, lover?

He charged at her, but she was gone before his hands could touch her. The force of his movement had him tumbling forward, and he had to press his palms against the wall for support. The coming sun was weakening him. Tony hurried back to bed and reached for Sadie. He wrapped his arms around her unmoving body and pulled her close. "It's just a dream," he said out loud.

He buried his face into Sadie's neck and fought back fearful tears. It was just a dream. Mary Ann was dead, and ghosts were not real. He had been alive long enough now to know if they were. Tony thought back to his childhood. The stone house he was raised in, filled at night with odd sounds and dark shadows. He had believed it was haunted and would wail for his mother. She assured him there was nothing to be afraid of and read him poetry until he fell asleep.

Filled with images of Mary Ann's ghostly presence, and falling captive to the sun, he whispered poetry against Sadie's ear. He recited their lullaby, the words that marked the beginning of it all.

"Deep into that darkness peering, long I stood there wondering, fearing, doubting, dreaming dreams no mortal ever dared to dream before..."

Alex stood next to the water, watching as the surf crashed against the bottom of the cliffs. He could feel Oscar behind him, so he turned to face him. "Just say it, Oscar. I know you want to."

His childe looked back with eyes that betrayed him. There was wisdom in Oscar that existed before he drank Alex's blood. The wise old man he was now, living forever in that youthful shell, knew that Alex lost, even when his sire didn't.

"Why didn't you just tell him?"

Alex looked back at the ocean. "He wouldn't have understood. Even you don't understand."

Oscar took the last few steps necessary to bring him to Alex's side. "Then explain it to me. Help me understand why you did all of this."

He sighed and dropped his head. "Before I turned Tony, I spent months watching him. I invested because I saw the darkness in him no one else did. He wanted to love his wife, but Tony couldn't give up his desires, even for her. Times were different then. Marriage and children were expected the moment society deemed you a man. He was twenty-five when I met him in a brothel, drinking and fucking until they threw him out. Twenty-five back then was considered too old to be without a wife and family. Tony did what was expected of him."

Oscar didn't fully know Tony's story. Each of them had a past that was only known to the ones that came before. It felt awkward standing there under the full moon listening to Alex spin stories about Tony and the man he once was. It was such a contrast to the immortal Oscar had always known. Alex continued, his eyes locked on the bright sphere in the sky.

"His wife gave birth to a stillborn son, and while she was bringing death into the world, Tony was with a whore in the alley next door. I watched him and knew, at that moment, that Tony was only ever meant for this life. And he was hungry for eternity. The only problem was that bitch that took his name. He wanted her, too. But I knew she would never cross with him. Hell, you could see the light radiating off her like she was the sun. The darkness had no chance claiming that."

"You gave Sadie his blood so he'd have what his wife wouldn't give him?"

If only it were that simple.

"Partly," Alex said. "I did it because I knew there was something inside her that could be ours. I knew it when I drank that artist on the beach; I knew she was special. I've always regretted not forcing her to take my blood. Sadie was drawn to Tony, you saw it just like I did. Rick saw it, too. He deserves her power. We all do."

"Your whole plan was to keep her drained and helpless. How did you think that was going to work once he realized he was her sire? You know what it means to be the one whose blood brings life. Why didn't you just give her your blood?"

"She was a gift, something only I could give him. A replacement for what he lost, and maybe I thought he would know I deserved her blood in return."

"So just ask him, Alex. I know what I owe you, and so does he. Taste this bitch and then bring Tony back here where he belongs."

Alex couldn't help but shake his head and laugh. His children knew so little, in part because he'd been lazy and never gave them all the knowledge Rick had given him. If he was really being honest, he kept things from them to ensure they would never feel empowered to leave him the way he left Rick.

The connection Tony had with Sadie now was more powerful than the one he had with Alex. She was born from his blood, and Alex had come to realize that his childe would be hard pressed to share even a drop of her. It was the same reason Alex knew he could turn Sadie with Tony's blood, and Rick would do nothing but scream and yell. He could never really hurt Alex.

He thought about giving her his own blood, then he wouldn't need anyone's permission to drink from the well of his own creation. In the end, he gave her Tony's because Alex knew how much he wanted her. He knew how much Mary Ann stole from Tony, and he hoped Sadie would give some of it back. It was their bond that led him to make such a foolish decision.

"I will taste her," Alex snapped. All his carefully laid plans had collapsed, but he would pull his desire right out of the rubble. He would rebuild Tony's trust, and soon he would partake of the power he longed for. "And you and Dylan will help me."

Alex could feel Oscar wanting to say no. He could see the left-over humanity wanting to argue with the vampire that had crushed it. But he also knew Oscar would follow wherever he led.

"Yeah," Oscar said with a sharp nod. "Always."

Chapter Eighteen

Sadie opened her eyes and found the space beside her empty. There was a moment of panic. She sat up and glanced around the room, her eyes able to take in every detail despite the darkness. She got out of bed and stepped into the hall, where she could hear cicadas and frogs coming in through the open bunker door. Outside, she found Tony sitting on the top step, looking up at the sky.

"Hey," he smiled at her. "How do you feel?"

"Awake," she said, sitting down beside him. All her senses took in the night like she had never seen it before. She could see every blade of grass and hear an owl somewhere in the trees swooping down on its prey.

"I remember that. It's like seeing the world for the first time."

She dropped her eyes and thought back to the man she killed, the one who was trying to hurt the girl and would have hurt her, too, if she hadn't done what she did. Part of her felt horrified that she allowed the genie out of the bottle, but the other knew the man got what he deserved. Only now, she was hungry, and a burger wasn't going to cure it.

"We'll go to the strip," he said. "Grab some dinner and talk about stuff."

Sadie could sense his uneasiness. His smile seemed forced, and the look in his eyes was sorrowful. "What's wrong?"

He looked away and shook his head. "Nothing, just thinking about Alex and the boys."

"You miss them." It wasn't a question. He was missing his friends like she was missing hers.

He nodded his agreement. "It's just, there's a complication now that I don't know how to handle."

"Me."

"Yes," he said softly.

She lifted her eyes to the cluster of stars above. They were so bright and beautiful she couldn't help but stare at them in awe. Had she ever noticed how beautiful the night truly was? "Why don't you go be with them?" she said.

"It's not that simple, Sadie."

She took a breath, out of habit now as opposed to necessity. "I promise I won't let what happened last night happen again. I'll do it where no one can see me, and I'll get rid of the body."

"Why don't you want me there?"

"It's just something I think should be private."

It wasn't the truth. The real reason she didn't want him there was because Sadie had thought long and hard about this new life forced upon her. She understood the hunger was never going to go away; it would be with her forever. While so many things about her changed and were maybe lost forever, there were other parts that would never leave. She couldn't kill innocent people. So, she would kill the ones who weren't innocent at all.

"I can't let you," said Tony. "Not right now. It's for your own safety as much as mine and the boys." He could see the disappointment on her face. He thought back to Rick, to the mess Sadie's parents were about to make. If he was going to get her to go along with the eternal goodbye, he would have to give something in return. "But, I'll make a deal with you. Tonight, you let me watch you hunt, and if I think you can handle it, I'll let you do it on your own next time."

It was not a conventional way for them, and while they did occasionally feed on their own, most of the time they were together. Even with Tony's blood coursing through her veins, she would never really be a part of their group. Maybe, deep down, he didn't want her to be. The four of them were too close to add someone in who didn't even want to be there.

She shrugged her shoulders and relented. "I guess that's fair."

Then he kissed her. As he sat back, an awkward silence stretched between them. She lowered her eyes, unable to look at him. There was so much about their relationship that confused her, and she was unsure exactly what they were to one another now.

Tony placed his hand gently on the side of her neck to pull her closer. "It will get easier," he promised.

"What part? Being a vampire or being yours?"

He dropped his hand and turned away from her. This wasn't going to be easy. Before he knew the truth, he had been cruel just because he could. He killed the ballerina to punish Sadie, blaming her for the separation from his brothers. Now, all he could feel was an intense desire not to lose her. His relationship with her came from the most complicated place, and eventually, he knew they would have to discuss it, but not tonight. Tonight, he just wanted to be away from everyone and everything except her.

"We should head out," he said. "Go get changed."

She did as she was told. When she returned, Tony was standing between two trees with his arms outstretched to her. Sadie walked into his embrace and wrapped her arms around his middle. He didn't say a word, just lifted like a flare into the sky.

He could feel her arms tighten around him. She would gasp occasionally as they skimmed the top of a tree. As soon as they were over the open ocean, however, the only sound coming from her was laughter. So, he sped up, dipping low enough that their toes skirted the water. By the time they made it to an isolated part of the beach, she was beaming.

"That was amazing," she said.

"It will always be like that. You will never be tethered to one place ever again."

Sadie wanted to say something, but she couldn't find the words. One minute it felt like they were having that very first date, and the next she was reminded this was no date at all. It was forever. They walked silently, hand in hand, up the beach to the pier. She felt a shiver move through her and recognized it as the call of someone connected to her blood. Tony felt it, too, and turned over his shoulder to see the silver Beemer pulling into the strip.

"Stay here," he told her. She nodded absently, her eyes looking not at him but at the people around her. Tony took her by the arm to get her attention. "I mean it, Sadie. Don't leave this spot."

"I won't," she said, pulling away from him defiantly. "Can I at least go stand by the railing?" She didn't know if she would ever be able to understand or accept the dichotomy of their relationship. Was he her lover? Was he her friend or parental figure? Or did being her sire mean he was all those things rolled into one.

"Of course," said Tony, feeling a little guilty. "I'll be right back, okay?" He waited for her nod of compliance before he walked away to meet his brothers.

"So, you two seem to be bonding," said Alex.

Tony lifted his shoulders in a shrug, trying to make the entire thing seem casual. "What else are we supposed to do? I'm stuck with her now, right?" He let his eyes linger on Alex's face for a moment before turning to Dylan and Oscar. "You guys eat?"

"We were waiting for you," Alex said, moving between Tony and Dylan. "Don't you think we should be bonding with her too?"

"She's not ready for that."

Alex chuckled. "Will she ever be?"

"I'm taking her to feed tonight. You guys go on without us."

Alex's smile fell away. "That's not how it works, Tony. If she's a part of this pack, then she feeds with this pack. And she gets her ass back to our house where this pack lives."

"You know," Dylan said, taking a hesitant step forward to insert some peace before the conversation turned into an argument. "Maybe Tony has a point. Think about it. After everything we put that chick through, there's no way she's coming to the house before she's ready."

"If I want your opinion, I'll fucking point at you," Alex glared.

Dylan held his hands up and stepped back. "Whatever, man. I'm just trying to help."

"Tony is her sire," Oscar said. "He decides what she does. That's how it works, right?"

Alex flashed angry eyes at both of them. He was their sire! Had he not already made it perfectly clear he wanted Sadie's blood, and they were supposed to be instrumental in helping him attain it? Instead, they were siding with Tony and throwing Alex's inherent power completely off balance.

"Look," Tony said, his eyes soft on his sire. "She's just not ready. Come on, man. You owe me a chance to make this right."

He moved closer to Alex so that he could look into his eyes, hoping their connection would make him understand. Yes, he was furious with Alex for the deception, but at the same time, he wanted all of this to right itself. He had no idea how he would ever juggle his pack and Sadie when he knew the two were magnets pulling in opposite directions. He just needed more time to teach her, get to know her, and then he would know what the next step was.

Alex's eyes were focused over Tony's shoulder. He smirked and said, "Well, you're right about one thing, Tony. You definitely need time to learn how to control your precious Peanut."

"What's that supposed to mean?"

"It means she took off."

Tony whipped around and saw that Sadie was no longer where he left her. "Dammit!"

Dylan scratched his head, the immortal youngest, and said, "Um, I think I just felt her shift."

Tony paused and realized Dylan was right. Sadie shifted, which meant she was about to feed. "Fucking hell!"

"Do you want us to help you find her?" asked Oscar, still so calm even as a storm was growing around them.

"No," Tony mumbled and pushed past them. He could feel she was close. When he was on the steps leading down to the beach, he looked back to see the three of them disappear into the crowd. At that moment, every part of him wished he was with them.

The night started out clear and windless, but Sadie could feel the turbulence of a storm brewing. She knew Tony was close, just like she knew he would find her when she left the pier and followed two men down the beach. She'd listened intensely to their conversation, some inner beacon homing in on them as they discussed the heroin in their back pockets. All she saw was the chance to feed and rid Brave Beach of some terrible characters at the same time.

At first, the men didn't want to leave with her, more inclined to do their deal in a back alley. She convinced them to follow her down to the beach. As she listened to them talking back and forth, she realized she could hear them even when their mouths weren't moving. It was as though there were five people walking instead of three.

They were afraid the police were on their trail. Four overdose deaths were all linked to the same batch, the latest victim being a college football player. They both knew it was theirs. Sadie was doing the city, maybe the world, a great favor.

Their deaths were not painless or quick. As she drank from one, the other tore off down the beach screaming for help. She caught him, too. When it was all over, there was nothing left but their dead bodies and the death powder in their pockets. She regretted nothing.

While she was disposing of body number two, the wind picked up and rain started to fall. Taking her cue from Tony, she dragged the corpses into the water until she was up to her chin. Then she simply let them go. On her way back to the beach, she saw Tony sprinting through the sand. She readied herself for whatever was about to take place. She knew all too well how quickly his feelings for her could sour. The only difference now was they were playing on the same field, and she was a worthy opponent.

"What the actual fuck, Sadie?" His voice boomed over the thunder and rain. "What part of stay put did you not understand?"

"I was hungry. I couldn't wait for you to finish your fight with Alex."

He shook his head, beads of rain clinging to his dark hair. "It wasn't a fight. It was a conversation. I mean, you want me to trust you, but then you go behind my back."

"I don't want you watching me feed!" Her voice was shrill and desperate. She knew he wasn't stupid. He would pick up on her master plan before she finished choosing her marks, and then he would stop her. Bad guys looked out for other bad guys, didn't they?

"Why? What's the big deal?"

She looked back at the sea, purple waves rising high into the air as the storm grew stronger. "This isn't what I want to be. I know I have to feed. I know I have to kill if I want to live. But that doesn't mean it's what I want. I need this part of my life to be only mine. I don't want to share it with you."

It was the truth, even truer than the plan behind her kills. Sadie was now a monster, a shadow hiding from the light. Those moments when she took something out of the world needed to be her burden alone. It felt euphoric when the hunger took over and she unleashed the vampire within. Once it was over, though, she was left to stare at the destruction of her need. As terrible as her prey were, they were still human beings.

"Tell me what you want from me," he pleaded.

She shook back the tears. Sadie didn't know what she wanted from him any more than she knew what she wanted from herself. It was all so new, this unnatural existence. How could she accept who she was when creatures like her only lived in the pages of books or on the screen of a theater?

"Do you want me to be yours, or do you want me to belong to your pack?" It was the only question to ask.

"It's not that easy. I never wanted to be a sire. I don't know how to be here for you."

"But you are here," she said gently. "Right now, when I need you."

He reached out and gripped the side of her neck. Then he pulled her into him. Her kiss was everything in that moment. Even with the vast vocabulary he acquired throughout so many years, there were no words to describe how he felt right then. All he knew was that it was the two of them, standing together under a rain-soaked sky, the ocean dancing beside them, and she was his.

She kissed him back with need. When they finally separated, she was smiling up at him. He caressed her cheek, refusing to release his stare. This moment was something he thought would never happen again after Alex bestowed him the gift of his blood. Tony had been with many a woman, enjoyed the softness of their skin, but none of them lasted. Sadie outlasted them all, even Mary Ann.

"What do we do now?" she asked.

"We can go anywhere. There's no place that isn't ours."

"Where do you go?"

He kissed the top of her head, the smell of blood still clinging to her hair. "Do you want me to take you to my favorite place?"

"Do they ever go with you?"

"No. It's just mine."

"Then yes, I want to go."

He stepped away from her, removed his shirt, and tossed it into the sand. His lips bent as he kicked off his shoes and unbuttoned his jeans. She eyed him curiously. When he was down to his boxers, he pointed at her and said, "Your turn."

She didn't ask why or about the destination. None of that mattered. She took off her clothes and placed them onto the pile with Tony's. She raised a brow and waited for him to make the next move.

"Give me your hand."

She slipped her hand into his and let him lead her farther into the water. When it reached their chins, she said, "Wait! I can't swim good."

He couldn't help but laugh. "It's okay, Sadie. I promise you won't drown."

"What about sharks?"

"You don't have to be afraid of anything. Everything fears you."

She swallowed hard, her eyes looking around at the choppy, white-capped seas. Thunder was coming in closer intervals, and more than once a fork of lightning sparked in the distance. She was about to tell him she wanted to go back when his hands wrapped around her waist and drew her close.

"Trust me," he whispered against her ear.

She didn't say anything, simply wrapped her legs around his waist and her arms around his neck. Trust had become like a fairy tale to her, beautiful in concept, destructive in reality. Perhaps that would change and evolve like she had.

Tony pulled them both under the surface, arms cradling her as he swam farther from shore. At first, her human instincts kicked in, and she began to fight for breath. He held her closer, never breaking eye contact, until she suddenly seemed to realize that she didn't need air at all. She smiled and unwound her arms from his neck so she could hold his hand instead.

Sadie marveled at everything around her. She lifted her eyes to the surface above. Lightning brightened up the darkness every few minutes so that she could see the colors of the aquatic life that had now joined them. It was another world, one she had only ever seen in books and National Geographic specials.

Tony swam circles around her, his fingers caressing bare skin. There was no up and no down, only the vast ocean with its never-ending promise. He turned a somersault, like a kid enjoying a new pool, and Sadie only watched with a smile. It wasn't just her surroundings that were magical; it was seeing him as something more than just a monster. He was hers, for always.

The hours passed like a dream that had no hint of realism but somehow still made sense. An eel swam past them, its body undulating against the current. Tony reached out and took the creature in his hands. It struggled only a moment before nuzzling its head against his shoulder. He encouraged her to come closer, then released the eel into her hands. Sadie marveled at the soft and velvety texture against her fingers. This experience was a gift, one she could have as many times as she wanted. And it was all because of him. She cradled his face and sealed her silent promise with a kiss. When they both sensed the late hour, they surfaced together and laughed all the way back to shore.

"So that's your special place, huh?"

"It's not just mine anymore. It's ours."

The rain stopped, leaving behind a pleasant mist. She looked back at the water, the waves calmer and the moon peaking in and out of the departing clouds. "Do you really want to share this with me?"

"I'm yours as much as you're mine. I want to share everything with you."

He meant it. These were secrets he kept from the others because they seemed so wrong in comparison to the demon he really was. Maybe he was afraid Alex and the others would laugh if they knew Tony liked to swim alongside dolphins and explore the ocean. The truth he didn't want to face was that he was afraid to find out.

"What if you weren't my sire? If it had been Rick's blood or even Alex's. Would you still want me with you?"

"It is my blood in you, Sadie." He didn't want to discuss unpleasant what-ifs.

"I want to hunt and feed on my own. I want you to help me understand this life, but I still need something that's just mine."

His eyes were soft and never left her face. "So, we find a way to make it work." He would have to accept her desire to keep some things to herself; it was only fair. There were so many parts of him he could never give to her. "We better get back. The sun is coming."

Sadie felt the finality of the conversation like the slamming of a door. She knew it would come up again, but for now, it was done. Tony scooped her into his arms as he took flight, and she clung to him tighter than was necessary. Somewhere in the distance, she thought she heard Sarah calling her name. It was too late for that sweet voice to find her though. Sadie was already gone.

Chapter Nineteen

They were still laughing when they got back to the bunker, riding high on their shared experience. As soon as they were on the ground, Sadie's arms were around Tony's neck, rising on tiptoes so she could press her lips to his. His fingers spread through her hair, and he deepened the kiss. He hadn't fed, and while the hunger was there, it was eclipsed by his hunger for her.

As he led her backward down the steps, their kisses never broke. Morning was a few hours away, and Sadie could feel her body getting heavier by the second. She wasn't ready to end the night yet, so she fought sleep and focused on the feel of his hands.

They stumbled into the bedroom, fumbling with each other's clothes while their heavy breaths filtered the silence. When they were down to underwear, he laid her gently on the bed. Her eyes begged him not to stop. He kissed her neck tenderly, holding her closer as a long, satisfied sigh blew through her lips.

He held her breasts in both hands, kneading them while he licked and nibbled the side of her throat. Each moment that passed made them hotter for the finale, but Tony wanted to elongate the time. He had only ever been with her the night she was drunk, and he was so unsure. There was no hesitation now. It was more than just his blood inside her, more than the way she tasted on his tongue. Sadie was like him. She had crossed over into the shadows. While she hadn't done it willingly, she wore darkness as though it was meant for her.

She lifted her body off the bed enough so she could reach behind and unhook her bra. With reverence, he pulled it away from her and lowered his mouth to her skin. She sucked in a breath then exhaled a pleasured moan.

He kissed his way down her body. Her hand touched the top of his head, fingers gripping his hair as she welcomed him to give her something no one else had. The first tentative lick of his tongue made her flinch, and the grip on his hair tightened. He took his time, wanting this moment of eternity to be one she always remembered.

Tony kissed his way back up her body, and she held him closer. All the uncertainty and fear she felt when it came to her sexuality dissolved. Was it the blood that had her craving more of him? Not just his body, but the look in his eyes.

He held her gaze and reached between them. With agonizing slowness, he pushed his hips forward until there was no space left. He panted against her lips and began a slow rhythm, watching her expressions change as each move seemed to find some new unclaimed spot.

She closed her eyes tight, feeling the compression in her stomach that signified impending release. Her mind was everywhere, breaking apart and scattering as she lost herself to him. When her eyes opened, she focused on the shadows over his shoulder, the way they blended into the wall. Then the shadow took form.

There was a woman standing in the corner, watching them. Sadie couldn't see the accents of her face, only the gleam in her eyes and the outline of her long dress. She dug her fingers into Tony's back while he breathed hard in her ear. She couldn't tear her eyes away from the figure, the woman's presence filling the room like static electricity. Tony gave one last push, his groan of pleasure warm on her face. The woman stepped out of the shadows fully and stood at the end of the bed. Her eyes narrowed with anger. Sadie held him tighter as she stared wide-eyed. This didn't feel like when she saw Sarah or Hayden. This was terrifying.

Tony rolled away and immediately missed the warmth of her body. He looked at her and saw she was staring into the darkness. "What is it?" he asked.

Sadie swallowed the lump that had swelled in her throat. The woman stepped away from the bed and blended back into the shadows, disappearing before Tony looked her way. It didn't matter. She knew he couldn't see the things she could. It was her affliction, something she never even knew was inside until the blood awakened it.

"Nothing," she said, forcing a smile.

He snuggled into her side. "If there's something wrong you can tell me. I don't want you to keep anything from me."

"Honestly, it's nothing."

"Sadie, I'm sorry." The moment he said the words, Tony wished he could take them back. He shouldn't have to be sorry for the things he did before he knew it was his blood that brought her to life. But he was sorry, and he needed her to know it.

She turned on her side so she was facing him, his hand on her hip, fingers tracing patterns without even realizing it. She looked into his eyes, and, for the first time since discovering his truth, she believed him. "Don't do that. I don't want to spend forever going back and forth with apologies."

"But it's the truth," he insisted.

Sadie closed her eyes. She could see Hayden in her mind, those final moments when the monster took her life. In the hours before, with Tony under the waves, she had almost forgotten that monster was him. "I know," she sighed. "I don't ever want to talk about any of it again."

"Part of me hates him for not telling me. The other part is so fucking grateful for the chance."

She rolled onto her back and looked up at the ceiling. "I can't even grasp it. Forever, it's impossible to believe it can really last that long."

"It won't always feel like that. Soon you'll measure time in a different way."

She supposed that made sense. Like everything else in life, this would be a slow adjustment. Eventually, her brain wouldn't hurt as she tried to understand a life that had a beginning but no end.

"I need you to do something for me, Sadie. Something important."

She looked at him. "What?"

Tony sat up and tried to center his thoughts. This conversation was heavy, and the gravity of it could not be overstated. Sadie seemed to sense this, because she sat up herself and faced him head on.

"Your parents have been calling up to the bar. They want to talk to you or they're coming to Brave Beach. We can't have that. I need you to go see them."

"And tell them what?"

"That you're okay," he said, taking her hand in his. "That you love them but won't see them anymore."

There was a stab of sudden grief that overwhelmed her. She was never close to her parents, always feeling like a poor substitute for the daughter they lost. Still, they were her family, and the idea that they'd been seeking her out felt almost joyful. What would it do to her parents to lose another child?

"So, I won't see them again." That made sense. Sadie was going to stay the way she was right then forever. Her parents would continue to grow old, until they eventually moved on from this life to a place she would never know. "But I can still call, check in with them and stuff."

"No, Sadie. It's goodbye forever."

"But they're my parents. I know I can't see them, but you can't really expect me to never talk to them again." She felt strangled by the thought.

"You're not the Sadie you used to be. That girl is dead. There's no room in this life for the one you had before. It's hard, I know, but that's the way it has to be."

"You make it sound so easy."

"I know it's not easy. It still has to happen." He cupped the back of her neck and pressed his forehead to hers. "I'll get you through this. Trust me."

There he was again asking her to trust, when he'd been part of what butchered her belief in the concept. Even though she accepted Tony as her companion, she couldn't forget those times the vampire asked the mortal to trust him, and she did. She trusted him and Rick so very much, and they led Hayden to death and Sadie to eternal blood lust. Whatever she once believed trust to be died when she did.

"I'll go tomorrow," she sighed.

He smiled, pleased with how easy it was for her to accept the inevitable. "I'll take you."

"No," she shook her head. "This is something I have to do by myself."

There it was, that damn stubbornness and independence Tony knew he would be fighting forever. He got off the bed and reached for his discarded boxers. "I'm taking you. We're not discussing this again."

"You ask me to trust you, but why don't you trust me? These are my parents you're asking me to never see again. The least I'm owed is a chance to say goodbye in my own way."

Tony slammed his hands against the wall in frustration. "You still don't get it, do you? Whatever you think you feel about your parents isn't real. You'll take one look at them, smell their blood, hear their hearts beating, and kill them before they even finish saying hello. I'm going to be there so you don't make some epic mistake I can't save you from."

"And you don't get it either." She got out of bed and padded across the carpet straight out the door.

He followed behind her until she stood naked in the center of the living room with tears in her eyes. "What don't I get, Sadie? Enlighten me."

"I'm not you!" she yelled. "I know I could never hurt my parents or anyone else I love. You were already dark." She could see the way he flinched when she said those words, and she could see the rage building. But she couldn't stop herself. She needed him to understand, even if that understanding came at a cost for her. "I'm not going if you insist on going with me."

There was finality in her tone that she hoped resonated with him. She started toward the bathroom, but he grabbed her by the arm.

"Why do you do this?" he growled. "Why can't you just accept the way things are?"

Her eyes danced over his face as she searched for the right words. "Because, I'm not you, and you're not Alex. You don't have to do things like he does, Tony. We can have our own life." His grip on her arm loosened, and she stepped away from him before he could grab her again.

"He's my sire. They are my pack."

"But they're not mine, and they never will be." She looked away from him. "That's the truth, isn't it? They never wanted me to be there, and neither did you. This was all Rick's idea, and if Alex hadn't slipped me your blood, you wouldn't care what I did."

"But it wasn't Rick's blood," he said, stalking toward her. "It was mine. Nothing is ever going to change that. I'm taking you to your parents tomorrow, and you're going to say goodbye." She rolled her eyes like a petulant child who doesn't take parental threats seriously. "We do it my way, Sadie, or I kill them to stop them from fucking things up. Take your pick."

Her mouth opened to protest, but he had already turned his back on her and was heading into the bedroom. The door slammed hard behind him, and she recoiled. She wanted to follow him, to argue her point until he finally relented, but she knew this wasn't an argument she could win. The sun was coming, and her body was shutting down. Sadie stumbled her way back into the living room and collapsed on the sofa. There was no way either of them could sleep side by side when they both knew what lay ahead.

Rick let Tony borrow his car, and he and Sadie were on their way to Pineview and her parents as soon as the sun dipped below the horizon. She sulked the entire drive, and when he tried to hold her hand, she snatched it away.

"Just so you know," she said as they headed up the walkway, "my parents are going to hate you."

"And I care why?"

She ignored him and pressed her finger against the doorbell. There was deep hope that her parents weren't home, that they had gone out and she could prolong this. Hope was not on her side as she heard shuffling footsteps and her father's gruff cough as he approached. When the door swung open, he took one look at her and frowned.

"We've been calling," he said. "For weeks we've been calling, Sadie."

"I know, and I'm sorry. I've just been really overwhelmed."

Her father stared hard, his eyes scrutinizing her, sensing a change he couldn't define. It wasn't until Tony cleared his throat that Mr. Daniels even noticed him.

"This is Tony," said Sadie, her voice not giving even a hint of emotion.

"Nice to meet you," Tony flashed a smile. He reached his hand to her father who shook it, but his eyes conveyed a very clear message. He did not like Tony, and he didn't like him standing beside his daughter.

"Can we come in?" Sadie asked. "We won't stay long."

Her father gave a curt nod and opened the door, allowing them inside. "Julia! Sadie is here."

The house smelled of her mother's cooking, smothered pork chops she knew were her father's favorite. Sadie's mother hurried out of the kitchen, flour and cooking oil staining her apron. She was shocked when her mother grabbed her in a tight embrace. It was the most genuine hug she could remember ever getting from her.

"Oh, Sadie, I was so worried. Are you okay?"

"I'm fine." Sadie held onto her tight. "I'm sorry I didn't call."

"You're here now," she said, stroking her daughter's hair. "That's all that matters."

Mrs. Daniels' eyes fell on Tony, and she held onto Sadie tighter. She immediately equated Tony with the reason her daughter had disappeared, and she wasn't ready to give her back. Finally, she broke away but held Sadie's hand in hers.

"Is this your boyfriend?"

"Yes," Tony cut in before she could deny it. "It's a pleasure to meet you. Sadie's told me a lot about you."

"Funny," Mr. Daniels grumbled as he sat down in his reading chair. "She hasn't told us one goddamn thing about you."

"Jim!" her mother said. "Now is not the time."

Her father laughed and reached for the can of beer on the end table next to him. "Not the time? Look at her, Julia. Really look at her. That is not our daughter. I don't know what this punk has done to her, but that is not Sadie!"

"Don't be ridiculous." She turned back to her child, and when she looked into her eyes, she noticed her husband was right, something was different. "What's happened to you?"

"Nothing," Sadie said, shaking her head. "I just..."

Tony knew the conversation was never going to happen if he wasn't the one to put it into motion. There was no easy way for this to go down. He knew that a sweet and simple goodbye wasn't ever going to be possible with people like the Daniels. It was up to him to instigate the upheaval that would make Sadie's permanent departure the best thing for everyone.

"We're moving," Tony said, ignoring Sadie's wide, confused eyes. "To the East coast, and I brought Sadie here to say goodbye."

"What?" Her mother looked from Tony back to Sadie. "What the hell is he talking about?"

Sadie fumbled over unintelligible words. She had no idea what Tony was doing.

"Moving," Tony repeated as he sidled up next to Sadie and wrapped his arm around her shoulders. "Splitting, taking off, starting a new life together. Whatever settles best for the two of you."

"Get your hands off my daughter."

Mr. Daniels was rising from his chair with a fury that filled the room rapidly. Tony couldn't help but laugh. He was still pissed at Sadie for her outburst the night before and ruining what had been an otherwise perfect evening. Fucking with her parents was the most fun he'd had in a long time.

"Pardon me?" Tony asked with feigned politeness.

Mr. Daniels walked right to him and glared. "I said, get your hands off my daughter, and get the hell out of my house."

"Don't you want to say goodbye to her?"

"Oh, she's not leaving. You are leaving right now, but Sadie is staying."

While Tony and her father were having their little sparring session, Mrs. Daniels had taken her daughter and was holding her so tight it was leaving impressions on her skin. Sadie was looking at Tony with a pleading stare; she didn't want things to happen this way.

"Sadie, come here." When she didn't move, Tony narrowed his eyes and said, "Now!"

She untangled herself from her mother's grasp and walked to him. She held his arm and looked up into his eyes. "Please stop. I'm sorry, Tony. I'll do it right now, just stop this."

"Tell Mommy and Daddy who you belong to."

She shook her head and tried to hold back tears. "Don't do this."

"Sadie Marie," her father called, his hand reaching for her. "Come here. You don't have to be afraid, honey."

"Look who suddenly cares," Tony mocked. "Neither of you seemed to care much for her before. Now, suddenly, you're vying for Parent of the Year."

"Let's go," Sadie pleaded, trying to steer him toward the front door.

Tony leaned into her father. "You lost her, old man. When you ignored her all her life and pretended she didn't exist, you drove her right to me."

Her mother held out her arms and motioned for her to come. "It's okay, baby. He can't hurt you; we'll protect you."

Tony whipped around to face Julia, his eyes glowing, fangs shimmering under the overhead light. She screamed and fell backward into the wall with her hand over her heart. Sadie watched in muted horror as her father lunged for Tony, not able to see the monstrous features his wife had. Tony stopped the man's momentum with a fist to the face.

"What are you doing?" Sadie screamed and was moving toward her father when Tony grabbed her around the waist and held her.

"Trying to show you the truth," Tony snapped. "I can see right inside their heads, and so can you if you try. They don't love you; they never did. They only want you now because they don't want to be left alone."

"That's not true," she whispered, even as her eyes held her father's and his thoughts started spilling into her mind. They were confused and mangled from his disorientation but clear enough that Sadie heard him say he wished she was Sarah instead.

Tony turned her so she could look at him, and he cupped her face gently. "It is true. I'm here, Sadie. I won't abandon you like they did."

"Get out," her father mumbled as he struggled to his feet. "Both of you get the hell out."

Sadie's teary eyes tried to reach him. "Daddy, I'm sorry. I never meant for this to happen."

"We should have left you at the damn hospital. Sarah left because of you." He glanced at his wife who had slid down to the floor, still clutching her chest. "Get out of here. You're no daughter of mine. All you've ever been is a burden."

Sadie couldn't see the smirk on Tony's face as she stared with disbelief at her father. He had drawn the words from Mr. Daniels' thoughts and siphoned them out through his lips. It didn't matter that he never intended to say those things to his child. The fact he thought them at all seemed reason enough for Tony to make sure Sadie never felt an ounce of guilt for leaving them behind.

She put her hands over her ears and turned into Tony's chest. He rubbed her back and said, "Go wait for me. I'll take care of this."

"What are you going to do?"

"Make them forget this. They'll believe this was a happy ending where we all got what we wanted."

She could still hear her father speaking behind her, horrible things that made her feel like the smallest creature. She took one last look at her mother and ran out the door, trusting Tony to finish it.

For his part, Tony hurried through the process of changing the narrative in the Daniels' minds. They would believe they told Sadie not to come back and she agreed it was best for all of them. They would never think about it again.

As he was walking toward the door, his eyes were drawn to the fireplace, to the picture on the mantle of a pretty girl with dark hair and round blue eyes. She looked so much like Sadie. Then it hit him, and the awareness was so strong he stumbled back a little. It was the artist on the beach, the one Alex had wanted so badly to turn.

"Fuck me," he whispered to himself.

The necklace he had given Sadie was hanging around her sister's neck. He whipped around, half expecting Sadie to be there. Did she know? He thought back to that night when he took her home for the turning. She had asked him if the necklace she wore belonged to the artist Alex killed.

Tony's head was spinning, but he was sure of one thing. Alex could never know who the artist was, or that Sadie knew it was Alex who took her sister from her. He didn't know what would happen if those things came to be, but he knew none of it was good. Tony would never tell his sire the truth, and he didn't question his decision. He would do it for his childe, to protect her.

Chapter Twenty

Alex enjoyed interesting people, even when they were dead. He propped the woman up behind the wheel of her car, using her long hair to hide the bloody side of her throat. He first noticed her when they arrived at the strip that night. Still feeling like Dylan and Oscar had turned on him where Sadie was concerned, he broke from his boys and took to the streets alone. Everything felt wrong as he walked through the crowds, hands in his pockets, his mind unable to focus on anything but Sadie's blood and the upheaval she caused in their lives.

As he was passing a sports bar, he noticed a blonde woman enjoying cocktails with co-workers after a long shift at the hospital. Even from behind the window, Alex could smell the sterilization on her scrubs. He watched her for a while, biding his time until she was alone and walking back to her car. Just as she was preparing to leave, a man near the bar began to wave his hands and a hysterical woman was screaming that her husband was choking. With mesmerized eyes, he watched the blonde quickly hurry to the man, and in only a minute, save his life.

Maybe that was what attracted him to her so much. Here he was, a walking form of death, and she was an advocate for the advancement of life. Theirs was a match made in vampire heaven.

"That was impressive," he said as she exited the bar, blushing as the cheers of drunken patrons followed her.

When she first turned around, it was with the intention of dismissing him. She didn't talk to strange men as a habit. Seeing this teenager, dressed so nicely and wearing an appreciative smile, softened her entire demeanor. "It was nothing," she shrugged. "The Heimlich maneuver, I learned it my first week of nursing school."

"Well, I'm still impressed."

"That's really nice of you."

They stood there for a moment in silence. Then he asked if he could walk her to her car to make sure she got there safely, and she was sold. Like a good Boy Scout would, he walked beside her with his hands behind his back, feigning interest in her education and job title. When he pushed at her with his persuasion, she immediately asked if he needed a ride home. He accepted with a smile.

"What's it like?" he asked as she turned onto the main road.

"What's what like?"

"Saving someone's life."

"I don't know. I guess it feels pretty good."

He reached down and turned her radio off, wanting silence instead. "You don't mind, do you?"

She shook her head and turned her eyes back on the road. His influence no longer a factor, he could sense apprehension starting to bloom in her. After ten minutes, she realized they were driving into a part of town unfamiliar to her. Post-war houses in varying stages of decay stood on either side of the road.

"Turn down that way," said Alex, pointing toward a turn-off that had no street sign.

She did, pressing her foot against the gas a little harder, wanting this strange kid out of her car. She had to slam on her brakes to stop them from colliding with a chain link fence. She slowly looked at him, understanding quickly that he was not just a nice kid needing a ride home.

"Please get out," she said, her bottom lip quivering.

Alex moved in his seat so he could face her. "Have you ever seen someone die?"

"What?"

"You must have. Being a nurse means you might save some lives but not all of them."

She nodded slowly. "Yes, I've seen people die."

"How did it make you feel?"

"Why are you asking me these questions?" Tears dribbled down her cheeks as her hand reached for the door handle.

"I'm a studier of human nature. Watching you save that poor schmuck tonight was... it was magical. I suppose I never really looked at life like that before. The only magic I ever saw before tonight was the beauty of it ending."

She took her chance and swung the door open; Alex was quicker. He reached across her and pulled the door shut, then clutched her face in both his hands. Her heart was beating so loud it nearly hurt his ears.

"Please," she cried. "Don't hurt me."

"I don't want to," he told her gently. "Death doesn't always have to be about pain. Sometimes it comes down to a choice."

"What choice?"

"Do you want me to make this experience painful, or would you rather it be something else?" He wiped away the tears on her cheeks with his thumb and added, "Something magical."

"I don't want to die," she said, trying to pull away but finding herself frozen in his gaze. "No one wants to die."

"Sure they do," he said very matter of fact. "Look at all those people who throw themselves off cliffs and down a fistful of pills, too fed up with this bleak existence and all its disappointments."

"I'm happy!" she insisted, her fingers around his wrist trying to pry his hands away.

He looked inside her head and knew she was lying. While she went to great lengths to appear happy, she was anything but.

"Your fiancée leaving you for a younger woman didn't make you happy. The credit card debt you're swimming in and the loneliness you feel because you have no real friends, those things don't make you happy either."

Her eyes widened with disbelief. "How do you know about that?"

"I know everything, sugar."

The fear in her eyes was gone. "Are you an angel?"

"Fallen," he whispered against her ear.

His lips moved to her neck where he peppered her skin with gentle kisses. He felt her body relax and dropped his hands from her face so he could spread his fingers into her hair. The blonde let out the softest moan when she felt his tongue swipe against her skin.

"Let me send you to your happy place."

He sunk his fangs into her flesh and she barely flinched. Sometimes Alex enjoyed the pain he inflicted more than he enjoyed the blood he took. Then there were times like this, where he found the person worthy of a departure that was graceful and erotic. When she was on the brink of death, her heart barely beating, he pressed a chaste kiss to her lips and sent her into the beyond with a smile on her face.

"Are you sure you don't want me to stay?" Tony asked as they pulled up in front of Rick's house.

"No, this is something I have to do alone."

After the devastating goodbye to her parents, Sadie begged Tony to let her see Rick. She needed to talk to him and get answers Tony didn't have. She could hear the hum of soft jazz coming from the house as they stood at the end of the long walkway.

"I'll be back later," he told her and dropped the keys to Rick's car in her hand. "Then we'll go get you some dinner."

"How about I just meet you there?"

Tony looked away from her with his jaw clenched in annoyance. "Whatever."

"Don't be mad. I thought you understood."

"I'll see you later," he said as he stepped out of the car. He was gone before she opened the door, leaving her burned once again by his sudden shifting moods.

The long walk up to Rick's door seemed to take forever. The door opened before she had a chance to ring the bell. He looked at her with the bright, calm eyes and smile she had come to know.

"Peanut!" He reached for her, the smile fading as she stepped back. "I'm sorry, I'm just so glad to see you."

"I only came to talk."

He opened the door wider and stepped aside so she could cross the threshold. The house smelled like autumn. The scent of freshly carved pumpkins wafted in from the kitchen, and on his coffee table were Halloween decorations he was preparing to put up at the bar.

She pointed at the paper skeletons and cartoonish witches and said, "Getting a head start?"

"Well, you know this is my favorite time of year."

"A vampire who likes Halloween, who would have thought?"

He gestured to the sofa, and Sadie took a seat. He sat next to her, making sure there was a cushion of distance between them. "How are you?"

"I'm a vampire," she said, narrowing her eyes. "That's how I am."

Rick took off his glasses and rubbed his eyes. "It wasn't supposed to happen like this, Sadie. I hope you know me well enough to believe that."

"I don't know you at all. I don't think I ever did."

He shook his head and leaned toward her. "That's not true. Everything I've done, I did because I care about you. I wanted you to have this gift, not curse you. This world is a miracle, and I wanted to share it with you because you mean so much to me."

"Hayden is dead because of your gift," she spat. "She's dead, Rick, and nothing you could ever give me will make that okay."

There were so many things he wanted to say to her, but no words he uttered would make her understand why he chose her. She was still so new, her human emotions clinging to her and not letting go. One day she would understand and forgive him, even thank him. But now... He stood up and disappeared down the hall through the sliding doors Sadie entered the last time she was there. When he re-emerged a moment later, he was holding a photo album. He sat back down and ran his hands over the leather binding with a soft smile.

"I remember when the camera came into being and photographs were born. It was such a momentous time for me. Finally, I could document the road of my life with visual aids." He opened the album and released a hearty laugh. "This is me," he said, pointing to a small black and white photograph. "I'm shaking hands with JFK after his inauguration." He could see the intrigue in her eyes and took it as an invitation to scoot closer. "What an extraordinary man he was," Rick said thoughtfully.

"What's it like, living so long and seeing the world change so much?"

He lifted his eyes and thought about his answer. Were there words to even begin to explain what this gift had given him? "It's wonderful, truly. After a while, it became a lonely world, though, and then I met Alex."

She shivered at the sound of his name. "There's something wrong with him."

He couldn't help but laugh to himself. "Alex was so young and sickly. I saw it in him, though, the will and want to live. He took to being a vampire like a duck to water. I knew he would, and I knew he would be a wild beast that I would have to try and tame. It took some time, but Alex learned control. He gained understanding of what it means to be immortal in this place of temporary existence. I love him very much."

Sadie was surprised to see tears teetering on the edge of his lids. "Why did you do this to me, Rick? Is it because you couldn't get inside my head?"

"No," he said firmly. "I saw how special you are. I've known so many humans, and none of them carried your light. Yes, your abilities caught my attention, but your heart, your sincere hopefulness in something better, captivated me. I wanted you to be my childe. I wanted to love you and give you all those things your parents didn't."

Sadie felt a warm tear drop down her cheek. She wiped it away and swore there would be no more. "Why did you push me and Tony together?"

"I knew you would be drawn to him and him to you. The same things I saw in you are what Alex saw in Tony. Maybe those things are standing on opposite sides, but they are still so similar. Tony has always been a shadow; the darkness was a part of him the moment he was born. You are light. I knew I wouldn't be able to keep you from him, so I just allowed it to happen as it did."

"But you wanted it to be your blood I drank, not his. You used him to bait me, to keep me close."

"I gave you someone who could help you transition," he said. "You liked him, and I knew you would trust him in ways you might not be able to trust me. Yes, it should have been my blood, but if Alex was going to play his dirty trick, then I'm certainly glad he chose Tony as the pawn."

She let out a sigh and leaned back into the sofa. "I don't know how to do this, Rick. I know I'm bound to him forever, but he's bound to Alex. I don't want to ever be in that creepy house."

"Sadie, the house is where your family is. It's where you belong."

"No, it isn't. They aren't my family; they aren't my pack. I belong to Tony, maybe, but I will never be like them." There was a pause before she said, "I want to stay in the bunker alone. I want it to be just mine."

"Sadie, I..."

She took his hand and gave it a squeeze. "Please, give this to me. After everything, it's all I'm asking."

"Oh, my sweet girl," he said, touching her cheek. "If it was my blood inside you, I would give you anything and everything you want, but it isn't. You're not my childe. Only Tony can decide where you will stay. I cannot make that decision."

"I can't be there, not with them." She leaned her cheek into Rick's hand, knowing he was the only one who could make it all okay. "Will you talk to Tony?"

"Of course I will."

She sat back, still angry but a little relieved to know he would always be there to help her make things right. She reached for the photo album. "I can't even imagine living in all these times."

She flipped through the pictures and stopped on one of Tony, Alex, and Oscar standing in front of a marquee where it said The Beastie Boys were playing. The year 1995 was scrawled across the bottom corner.

"Where's Dylan in these pictures?"

"Dylan is still very young. Alex turned him in 2004." He turned a few pages until he stopped on one of Dylan sitting on the beach beside a fire, a lit cigarette dangling from between his lips. "I think Dylan is probably glad you were turned. I know, at times, he's felt very alone in his pack. So young and green, always making Alex mad with one misstep after another. He asked Alex to turn a friend of his, a musician. Alex wouldn't do it."

"Why?"

Rick shrugged his shoulders. "Alex is a complicated creature, Sadie. Maybe he wanted to teach Dylan a lesson, forcing him to grow up faster. Or maybe Alex didn't see anything in his friend worth turning." Rick took the book from her lap and closed it. "Sometimes I think I should have sired them all."

"Why didn't you?" she asked, turning her body to face him. "Why did you give them to Alex if it was a family you were trying to create for yourself?"

"Because he is my son. He wanted to be a sire, to have his own children, and I wanted him to have it all."

She looked at him in a way she hadn't thought of looking at him before. He loved his boys, and he loved her just the same. Rick was the father she needed for all those years, and maybe losing her humanity was the price she had to pay to find him. She laid her head against his shoulder and felt him sigh with relief.

"I don't hate you, Rick. It will take time for forgiveness, but I guess time isn't a problem anymore."

"No, Peanut, it isn't."

Sadie stood alone on the pier, leaning against the railing and staring down into the water. She didn't want to admit that she missed Tony, and as the hours passed, she knew he wasn't coming back to her that night. A sudden shiver moved through her before she heard the words spoken from behind.

"Are you going to stand here all night?"

She turned over her shoulder and saw Alex standing under the street lamp with his hands in his pockets and eyebrows raised. She immediately looked back at the water, wishing him away.

"I'm just waiting for Tony," she said.

Alex walked up to the railing and stood beside her. He felt her flinch a little, and it made him smile. If he was ever going to taste the blood inside her that smelled so damn good, he would have to change his approach. All he needed was a carefully manipulated situation.

"Sweetheart, the sun is rising in four hours. You have to know he's not coming back tonight."

"He'll be here. He said he would."

"Tony's with the boys. They're feeding together right now, and I can promise you he won't be back before dawn." Alex pouted and shook his head with what he hoped would convey his disapproval. "Let me take you home," he said softly.

"I'm not going to that house."

"I meant the bunker, your home."

When she looked up at him, he knew he had her. She did not want to be in that house surrounded by the memory of her dead friend and four vampires who weren't the most welcoming of housemates. Alex might not be able to read her mind, but he could read her face. All those years of studying expressions and body language had taught him plenty.

"What's it like being a sire?" she asked. "Why are you here and he isn't?"

Alex had to think about his answer. In the end, he decided she would see through him if he lied, so he told her the truth. "It's a connection that nothing can break. When you sire someone, it changes everything you think about this life. And when you're a childe, you desire to be with the one who made you. I know you think what I did was cruel, giving you Tony's blood instead of Rick's. But it wasn't."

"How do you figure?"

"Because I am Rick's childe. If I had a choice between him and Tony, I would pick the latter."

Sadie was taken aback. "Why?"

"Look, I don't want to talk trash about my maker. I'm sorry, it's just some things are better left close to the vest."

She returned her attention to the water. Alex placed a hand on her shoulder and squeezed gently. It surprised them both when she didn't pull away. Tony wasn't there, nor was Rick, and at that moment, Sadie needed someone just so she didn't feel so disconnected from the space around her.

"Come on," he said. "Let me take you back."

He had stolen the car from a quick snack, and she didn't ask him about who owned it or why she had never seen it before. He could sense her drowsiness growing, and he counted on that. Being so new meant she couldn't stay awake as long as he could. So, he took his time driving back to the woods, leaving the car on a narrow dirt road so they could walk into the trees together.

"You don't have to walk me to my door," she laughed.

"Well, that's true, but a gentleman would," he winked.

When they arrived at the secret door in the ground, she said, "Thanks for the ride."

"No problem," he replied, pulling open the door for her. He lifted his eyes to the sky and his face dropped. Sadie noticed the sudden look of weariness.

"What's the matter?"

"I didn't realize it was so late," he said. "I don't think I have enough time to make it back."

Sadie bit her lip. "Just leave the car on the road," she said, clearly trying to find a way around having him stay. "Fly to the house."

Alex tried not to snarl and instead made up something he knew she wouldn't be able to disprove. "I haven't fed," he said, looking down at his feet and hoping his boyish face looked innocent enough. "I don't have the energy to fly back. Shit, I can't believe I let this happen."

Sadie studied him for a minute. He came to her when Tony didn't. She might have stood on that pier all night, frying in the sun when it rose because she didn't know where to go. Alex was kind to her, and she wondered if all her qualms about him were wrong.

"You can stay here," she finally said, but added rather quickly, "on the couch."

Alex tipped his head toward her with a smile. "Thank you, Sadie."

He followed her down the steps, amazed and elated his plan worked.

Chapter Twenty-One

Alex locked the door behind them and watched as Sadie began stumbling with each step she took. The sun's coming rays were pulling the new vampire quickly toward sleep. He would be able to stay awake until the sun peeked over the clouds, which gave him plenty of time to take advantage of the moment.

"Are you okay?" he asked and caught her around the waist.

"It hits so fast."

"Let me take you to bed."

"No," she mumbled, pushing her hands weakly against his chest. "I can do it."

Alex snickered to himself while her body went limp and her eyes rolled back in her head. She was fighting sleep, even as it pulled her under. He scooped her up and carried her to the bedroom, then laid her gently on the bed. It was as if the mattress were an altar and she was an offering meant only for him. Alex looked around the room and frowned in disgust. It was domesticated, like Rick, and so unnatural to the world he and his boys lived in. He shrugged off his jacket and unbuttoned his navy blue shirt. It was important that no trace of her blood made it back to the house with him, not that he'd waste a single drop.

"So, this is where you've been keeping my progeny," he said. "I hate to break it to you, Sadie, but this will never be enough. If Mary Ann couldn't keep him happy, I'm not sure what makes you think you're so special."

He rounded the bed and reached out to touch her face, skin cool and smooth like his own. There was a flurry of excitement rippling through him, touching something that Tony never intended for him to enjoy. It was astonishing to him that she could look so innocent. He supposed it was something they had in common. Leaning into her, he ghosted his nose across her skin, inhaling her scent. She smelled so much like the artist on the beach, sweet like summer strawberries and salty like the ocean breeze still clinging to her skin. It was the power beneath those subtle scents making Alex's body tight, aching to taste her.

Alex plucked a button on her shirt loose, just enough to give him access to more skin. He splayed the material aside to reveal the nape of her neck. Then he lowered his cheek to hers, nuzzling a little before guiding her head to the side. He closed his eyes and breathed in deeply, wanting to savor the moment, though he knew it wouldn't be long before the sun drew him to slumber beside her.

She might never remember the feel of his fangs penetrating her flesh, but he was in love with the notion that he could steal something so precious from her, from Tony and Rick, too, and none could stop him. He swiped his tongue along her throat and bared his fangs. He pressed the tips to her skin, already trembling at the wonder of what might happen when the blood passed through his lips.

He stopped suddenly and sat back, eyes focused on the very spot where he brought forth a single fat drop of blood. Tony's scent permeated from the healed scar he couldn't see but smell. She had already taken the blood when she was bitten. Alex's fingers gripped the sheets as rage bubbled and spilled over. He was supposed to be the first to taste her, to know her power. Tony, his favorite, had betrayed him and drank first. To Alex, it was a betrayal surpassing his own.

"Bitch!" he roared at her. She didn't move, no acknowledgment he was even there. Death would not release her until the night released the moon.

His hunger for her grew with his increasing fury. He would make her pay for what she did. She would heal the rift between him and his childe, and she would do it with her blood. With a growl, Alex tore at the buttons on her shirt, listening as they bounced against the dresser on the other side of the room. He zeroed in on the single, glistening drop of blood with excitement. If only Tony was there to see what Alex did to those who went behind his authority. He could never really hurt Tony, it would be too much like hurting himself, but Sadie? She was the perfect conduit to help him release all the bitterness.

He rolled on top of her. It didn't have to be this way. Tony could have offered her with the reverence Alex was owed, and in turn, he would have drunk with respect. It was their fault his tasting had to go down like this, in the dark and in secret. Alex was going to use her like the blood whore Tony had forced her to become. Of course, now that he was there, he wouldn't have it any other way.

"I'm going to bathe in your blood," he whispered, giving her neck a gentle nibble. "Even after the sun sets, you'll never even know I was here."

With a deep chuckle, he felt his fangs descend again. Unable to hold back any longer, he sank them into her until there was nowhere else to go. A moan escaped his throat the moment her blood touched his tongue. Never, in all his years roaming the Earth, had he ever tasted anything so wonderful. Even the beautiful artist on the beach was no match for Sadie. He knew it was the vampire blood, their blood, that enriched her essence.

He extracted his fangs and lapped at the open wounds like a kitten with a bowl of milk. Yes, this is what he wanted the moment he knew she was to become one of them. There was power in her. He could feel it burn as the blood slid down his throat. He turned his focus to the spot below her collar bone and clamped down hard. Was it possible she was becoming more delectable with every bite he took?

Alex drank from the spot for several minutes then threw his head back with a maniacal laugh. Nothing would stop him now. Rick himself could charge through the door, and Alex still would have held his claim to her. He sat up and straddled her, watching a river of blood flow down the curve of her neck and over the round hump of her breasts. Drunk from adrenaline and her unbelievable taste, he nibbled his way down her stomach. Then he bit deep into the spot above her belly button. Her blood was thick and sweet, the more he drank the more he wanted. He knew it was time to stop. He was dangerously close to a point where she would need more than a day to heal. Still, he kept drinking.

His bare chest was smeared with her blood, and it painted the sheets in a grotesque but oddly beautiful way. He moved to her wrist and made small bites, the blood not quite as thick but just as sweet. Finally, he worked his way back up to her neck, sinking into the side Tony hadn't touched.

Get away from her, Alex.

He sat up with a start and looked over his shoulder, certain he heard a voice. There was no one there, only darkness and the smell of Sadie's blood filling the air. Convinced it was nothing, he returned his attention to her. The wounds were already beginning to heal, and Alex took great pride in ripping them open all over again.

Alex!

He sprung off her like a jack in the box. "Where are you?" he asked, his voice a dangerously low hum.

Right here.

His eyes focused on the space in front of him and he scurried backward, falling over Sadie's lifeless body and tumbling off the other side of the bed. When he stood, the owner of the voice was still there, smiling at him, her long brown hair moving with a nonexistent breeze.

"I killed you," he heard himself mutter, recognizing her instantly. The artist on the beach he wanted so badly to turn but could not keep from killing.

Did you? Or did you just set me free?

Alex rubbed his eyes and blinked hard. She was still there, moving closer to the bed and looking down on Sadie. When she brought her gaze back to his, he could see rage reflected in her glassy eyes. It was the first time he felt actual fear since his turn. "You're not real," he said, his voice a stranger to his ears.

I am very real. I've been watching you all this time. We all have.

"What do you mean, we?"

She stared at him, her smile stretching the line of her lips. Alex gripped the edge of the dresser to hold himself up. The shadows on the walls began to twist and spread outward until the dark shapes became people. He recognized them all, every last bloodied body that emerged behind her. A vampire always remembers the faces of his kills.

For years Alex hated the idea that those faces would always take up space in his mind, little snapshots of a life cut short by his thirst. After a while, however, he looked to those images as nothing more than fond remembrances. Like a serial killer taking trophies, Alex cherished every face he collected. They'd been his to treasure, only now, seeing them glaring from the darkness, he wanted to release them all.

Still want Sadie's power? Was she worth it?

His body tightened, muscles freezing like blocks of ice. She started to laugh, and soon the others were laughing with her. Alex ran for the bedroom door and swung it open with so much force the hinges creaked. His body collided with something hard, and Alex could hear himself scream as his arms thrashed wildly. He only stopped when he recognized the voice speaking to him.

"What the fuck, man!" Dylan shouted, his eyes looking at Alex's blood-smeared skin and then into the bedroom. "What the hell did you do, Alex? You said you were only going to taste her!"

Dylan flipped on the bedroom light and hurried into the room, examining Sadie before stepping back from the bed with his hands to his head. Alex stayed in the hallway, eyes darting around looking for the artist from his past, for all the dead she brought with her. He regained his control and would deal with the logical explanations of his hallucinations later. Now he had to handle his childe panicking at the sight of Sadie.

"Dylan, what are you doing here? I told you I had this covered."

"Tony's asking for you, dude. I tried calling to you, but I guess you were too busy draining her to hear me." He fixed his sire with a serious stare. "You need to get back to the house, I think he knows something is up."

Alex surveyed the room. Blood was all over the sheets, all over him, and all over Sadie. "How much time do I have?"

"Two hours, maybe a little less."

"I'll get me and her cleaned up. You get rid of those sheets."

Alex walked to the bed and hauled Sadie up over his shoulder. It was imperative that neither Tony nor Rick knew what happened that night. The feed had gotten away from Alex, and he swore he'd never taste even a drop of her blood again. Even as he thought this, he licked his lips to savor what was left.

Dylan stepped into the door frame blocking Alex's way. "I'll clean her up."

"Why would you do that?"

"You almost drained her, man." He shook his head, afraid to challenge Alex, but more afraid of what would happen if he didn't.

Alex told them he would just take a sip, a sample to stamp out his curiosity. What Dylan saw was anything but a simple taste test. It was a bloody mess that reminded him of the aftermath of their feeds. Sadie was not a human. She was one of them. Even among vampires, there had to be somewhat of a moral code, and Alex crossed it. Dylan was still an infant in his immortal life, but he knew that much, and now there was a heavy guilt settling on him because he helped make this happen.

"Fine," Alex huffed, pulling Sadie off his shoulder and practically throwing her at him. "Clean her up, change her clothes, and put the little Peanut back to bed."

Dylan hooked his arms under Sadie's shoulders and dragged her down the short hallway toward the bathroom. He leaned her against the wall and took off his shirt to keep her blood off his clothes, and then found several folded washcloths under the sink. He wet them, lathered them with soap, and turned back to the unconscious vampire at his feet.

A sudden urge to taste the blood still on her skin filled him. This was his chance to have what he would never be allowed again, to experience the blood that had driven Alex to such levels of deceit. Maybe if he just tried it, he would understand why his sire risked so much for her. He shook his head hard, trying to dislodge those intruding thoughts. He continued the task at hand, scrubbing at her skin until there was no blood visible. Then he dragged her back to the bedroom where crisp new sheets were on the bed, and a pair of sweatpants and a tank top were lying atop the covers. He dressed her quickly then backed out of the room. When he turned around, Alex was standing in front of him, clutching the stained linens and Sadie's clothes.

"Crisis averted," he said. "We have plenty of time to get back to the house. I'll burn these in the fire pit."

Dylan followed Alex out of the bunker, and they flew home. Tony was already asleep, and Dylan could barely keep his eyes open. Alex burned the evidence and stepped into the house feeling his own exhaustion take him. It wasn't just the sun, it was everything that happened that night. He wondered if he should talk to Rick, but his father made it clear he didn't want to see Alex. His secret about what really lived in Sadie's blood would be filed away with everything else he never told his boys.

"Looks like he had a good time," said Alex, eyeing the dead bodies on the parlor floor. He started up the stairs and looked back at Dylan. "Thank you for helping me."

Dylan nodded, grateful for Alex's praise. The truth, however, wasn't that he cleaned up Alex's mess for his sire. He didn't even do it for the poor girl they'd condemned, he did it for Tony. In the end, their blood would always be a bond worth protecting.

Sadie could hear Tony's voice calling to her from very far away. As her eyes slowly opened, she focused on a pinprick of light that grew larger until she was staring into Tony's concerned eyes.

"Are you okay?" he asked, helping her sit up. "The sun set two hours ago."

She rubbed her eyes and groaned as her stiffening muscles protested the movements. She looked around the room and down at her clothes. Had she changed before bed? The last thing she remembered was Alex standing with her outside the bunker as she thanked him for the ride. Her memories were pieces, and she couldn't quite fit them together. It was like waking from a dream and trying to hold onto the images until they fade into nothingness, as though it never happened at all.

"I'm fine," she said, tugging her arm away from him. There were some things from the night before she could remember clearly. Standing on the pier waiting for him to come and he never did.

"You need to eat," he reasoned. "I'll take you to the strip."

She shook her head and pushed past him to the closet where she started sifting through clothes. "You go to the strip. I have my own plans."

"Oh yeah," he laughed. "What are those?"

"I think I'm going to see Rick. I'll go somewhere else to feed later. I don't want to go to the strip. I'm so sick of that place."

Tony's jaw went taut. He could sense her anger, even as she was trying to hold it in. Their connected blood let him know she smelled the girl on him from the night before and now she would try to punish him. To go see Rick and feed outside the boys' hunting grounds was her polite slap in the face.

"In case you don't remember, you don't go anywhere unless I let you."

Sadie's calm collectiveness shattered when she heard him say the words. "If you were so concerned with where I go and what I do, you sure didn't show it last night. I waited for you, and you never came. I could have fried in the sun!"

Tony rolled his eyes. "But you didn't, obviously."

"Disappointed?"

He threw his hands up, frustrated. "Are you fucking kidding me? After everything I've done for you!"

"What have you done for me, Tony? You killed my best friend, destroyed my family, and cursed me to live for fucking ever in this shithole town! Thanks a lot!"

She shook her head, not wanting to waste a single tear on him. She had felt it coming, knowing this was going to happen. Whether it was two weeks from now or fifty years in the future, there would never be another outcome. They were living in the same world, but a glass wall was between them. He took her by the arms and tried to kiss her.

"Get off me!" she yelled and pushed him hard. "You can't fix things with a fuck every time they get difficult."

"There's nothing for me to fix," he said, trying to kiss her again to no avail. "Listen to me, this isn't a marriage. It's a blood contract, and there is nothing deeper. Tell me why you're really pissed."

"No," she said, not willing to admit she was jealous, plain and simple.

"You act like I've betrayed you."

"If it's not a betrayal, then what the hell is it?"

Tony's face softened. He didn't want to hurt her, he only wanted her to understand. Monogamy was for human relationships. What they shared was something else, something that surpassed sexual intimacy. Their connection would always be more important than whether he got his rocks off with a human.

"She was just food," he said, swiping his thumb gently over her cheek. "You are my blood."

"Is that what you think I'm mad about? That you slept with another girl?"

She smelled the woman's scent the moment she woke up. It clung to Tony even after he showered to rid himself of it. Sadie was hurt at first, but she soon realized it wasn't the woman that sparked her envy. Tony gave Sadie his blood and entry into the long hereafter, but he never promised fidelity. No, her feelings came from somewhere else.

"Isn't it?" he asked.

"You left me for them. That's how this is always going to end, Tony."

He dropped his hands from her face and took a step back. "You can't understand," he said, pointing an accusing finger at her. "You can't know what it's like to have your pack always there. We're bonded by more than blood. We've walked this world together for over a century."

"You're right. I can't understand." She took a step toward him and reached for his hand. "And I don't want to."

His eyes glistened with tears he wouldn't release. Evidence of the human being still lurking very deep inside him. "Tell me what to do, Sadie. What do you want me to do?"

"Let me go," she said softly, reaching up to touch his face. "Release me. Rick told me you could."

He shook his head and pulled her into him. "No, I won't do that. I can make this work. We can make this work."

"You know we can't. I know we both wish we could. You need them and I know that. I see it in your eyes when you think I'm not looking. I don't want you to have to make the choice, because I won't be able to stand it when the time comes and you choose them."

Tony wrapped his arms around her and pressed his cheek to the top of her head. "I never wanted this. Once I knew you were mine, though, I never wanted to hurt you again. I know that's all I've done, Sadie. From the moment we met, I did nothing but hurt you. Then I found out you were mine, and all I've tried to do since then is find a way to make it right. But I won't release you to Rick," he said, holding her back so he could see her face. "I just can't do that."

"Then release me to myself."

"What are you talking about?"

"Let me be on my own. You go back to your brothers, and I'll stay here. I don't want to belong to anyone else." She shrugged her shoulders, feeling at a loss for words to make him understand. "I just want to be."

He smoothed the hair away from her face. "And what about us?"

Tony wanted her to say she would always be his, even if he released her to immortality without him. She would never replace what the pack meant to him any more than they could replace what Mary Ann took from him all those years ago. He needed his brothers and Sadie in ways he never fully understood until this moment. When she was asking for something only he could give, a freedom he would never know.

She smiled gently. "We have the ocean, right? I'm always going to need you." It was the truest thing she knew about their relationship.

"Kiss me," he said, not ready to say the words that would untie her from him.

Sadie wrapped her arms around his neck and drew his lips to hers. He breathed hard against her mouth, soaking up her taste and knowing he wanted just one more night with her, unsure if it would be their last.

He made love to her for the rest of the night, unable and unwilling to stop. It wasn't until he felt the pull of morning that he finally let himself go. For a while they just lay together, Sadie's head on his chest while his fingers tangled gently in her hair.

"You did something to me," he said. "You know that, right?"

"What did I do?"

"Remember when I told you that I wasn't very good at love? I wanted to give Mary Ann the world. That was always my intention from the moment I saw her. I wanted her to have everything, but I couldn't give it to her. Do you know why?"

She held him tighter. "Tell me."

"Because I'm a selfish asshole, Sadie." He laughed to himself only to keep from crying. "I always have been. Alex was right when he said this was the life I was meant for. I couldn't love Mary Ann wholly because I loved myself more."

"You did love her. I saw it, remember?"

"That wasn't love. That was me wanting to damn her so I wouldn't be damned alone. I won't do that to you." He rolled his body so that he was leaning over her. He could see her eyes closing even as she struggled to keep them on his face. "I release you, Sadie," he whispered and sealed the deal with a kiss. He had taken so much from her, and while he could never give it back, he could do this.

Her lips pulled at the corners, the softest of smiles. "Thank you, thank you..." She kept saying the words until the sun finally silenced her.

Chapter Twenty-Two

It had only been a week since Tony released Sadie, but it felt longer. Alex was ecstatic when he found out, which left Tony feeling confused. He couldn't understand how his sire went from wanting Sadie's blood so badly he tricked them all into giving her Tony's, to being completely done with her. His happiness at having her out of their daily lives spilled over into Dylan and Oscar. The week was spent with nights celebrating Tony's return. They traveled to neighboring towns and hunted their prey, sometimes coming home filled and drenched in blood. It was like old times, and yet Tony felt totally disconnected from it.

He thought being back in the house, surrounded by his brothers, would leave him sure he did the right thing where Sadie was concerned. It didn't, though. If anything, being around them only made him miss her presence more.

The connection between them had not severed like he thought it would. They were all bound by the blood they shared, and when she shifted, they all felt it. Tony could feel her pull whenever she was close by. All he wanted now was to sever the tie he had previously been so desperate to maintain. Was it even possible if his blood lived with hers?

He stood on the beach, eyes trained to the pier where he could see Sadie walking along with Rick. If she felt Tony's presence there, she didn't show it. He hated the way Rick held Sadie around the shoulders, pointing things out to her with a goofy grin. Rick was probably regaling her with stories of his past, all the years he saw come and go. He had shared them with Tony, too. More than anything, Tony despised how much he wanted her there beside him.

It reminded him of those first few years after Mary Ann died. Tony drowned himself in blood and the beds of sweet girls and hungry boys who became dinner after he was done with them. Debauchery became second nature. All the things he had done when he was alive, he could do as an immortal without any fear or guilt attached. Still, it took decades to erase the need for Mary Ann. Things were clearer now with a century behind him. He wasn't sure anymore if he ever really loved his wife or simply loved the idea of her.

When he thought about her now, the angry vengeful spirit promising to haunt him, he felt weak and unnerved. Nothing was supposed to frighten him. It was Alex's promise when offering the blood. He swore that Tony would never know the terrible sting of death and that all creatures of the Earth would cower at his feet.

He turned his gaze to the water, inhaling the ocean air while trying to calm his impending shift. The human emotions that were eating him were all coming from Sadie, from her blood. This meant none of what he felt was real. The longing, the ache to touch and taste her, or the fear she might never be his again, were illusions manifested by what flowed in her veins. If only there was a way to purge himself of her blood and lift the curse, he would give anything.

It doesn't work that way, Tony.

He swung his head to the side and saw Hayden standing there. She smiled sweetly, blood dripping slowly down her neck.

"I'm sorry," he heard himself say, his mouth spitting words faster than his mind could form them. "What the hell do I have to do to make you disappear?"

I don't really know. Maybe the only way you stop seeing your sins is after you atone for them.

"Tell me how," he pleaded.

How do you think you make up for all the lives you've destroyed? What's fair in the grand scheme of things?

"It wasn't personal," he said, trying to touch her arm and watching his hand go right through her. "It's what I am. Do you judge a lion for taking down a gazelle?"

You trapped me here, always afraid and always lonely. Sometimes, I think there must be someplace else. Where is the heaven I was told to expect? Even dead I fear you, and I repeat my death over and over. You keep killing me, and I don't think it will stop until you die, too.

He took a step away from her. "I'm immortal."

That's where you're wrong. Everything dies, including you. It's just a matter of how long it will take. We won't go away until we can rest, Tony. We can't do that until you've paid for what you did to us.

"Then I guess you'll be suffering forever," he shot back, trying to keep the tremor of fear out of his tone. "I'm not going anywhere, sweetheart. I am death and life rolled into one, and you? You're just a dead bitch."

And what is Sadie?

"She's like me," he said, chin rising with absolute belief in his words. "She loves this world I've given her. She was made for it."

Then why did she want to be free from you? If she loves your world, why would she want to walk it alone?

Tony looked away from her. He knew if his heart could still beat, it would be pounding. Anxiety was rising in him as her words settled. Did he deserve the pain of Sadie's absence?

You will die, Tony. One day, when you least expect it, death will take you, too.

There was no time for a response as she simply faded into nothingness. He could only stand there, chest heaving as he looked around the quiet beach, half expecting Mary Ann to appear. But it was just him and the waves. A sudden tug inside him forced his attention back to the pier. He saw Sadie walking down the beach, moving toward him with a smile. It took everything he had to turn his back on her.

"I thought I felt you," she said, moving next to him and reaching for his hand.

He snatched it away. "Yeah, I guess letting you go didn't accomplish all it was supposed to."

"What's that supposed to mean?"

He looked at her with angry eyes. "It means I don't want you here. Giving you freedom was supposed to separate us."

She dropped her eyes, stung so suddenly by his words she didn't know how to respond. "I thought... I thought we were still going to be here for each other."

He let loose a mocking laugh. "You said it yourself; we can't make this work. I don't need you to be here for me, Sadie. I have my pack. They're all I'll ever need."

"Tony... I need you."

He huffed. "Well, maybe you should have thought about that before you asked me to let you go. If I could take it back, I would."

"My release? Why?" There was a hopeful tinge in her voice that made him want to run from her.

"So I could do it right. I'd release you to Rick. Maybe that's why I can still feel you every fucking second."

She stared at him with disbelief. "Why are you doing this?"

"I told you; I'm a selfish bastard. I'm a monster," he snapped. "I don't love you. I never did and I never will. If that's what you think this was, you're wrong. We don't love. We can't."

The tears she had been holding back finally fell. She couldn't keep herself from reaching for him. When she brushed his shoulder, he turned and shoved her hard. She stumbled, barely holding her footing. All week she had been haunted by her sister and those sad souls pleading with her to avenge them. It was never going to happen. What she felt for the man before her was too powerful. He said they weren't capable of love, but she knew she did. Maybe it was a lie, but she wanted it to be true.

"Fine," she said, wiping away her tears. "I'll go."

He looked back at the water. "Good. And next time you feel me close, just ignore it. That's what I do."

Sadie walked away, not even stopping to glance back at what she was leaving behind.

Tony's chest expanded as he struggled to hold in the dam of emotion threatening to burst. Her blood had revived everything Alex's was meant to destroy. The very blood Tony had hungered and longed for was now a cancer eating him slowly. It was devouring the demon and pulling his humanity back to the surface. Tears streamed from his eyes. He gripped his hair and screamed so loudly his sire felt it. They all did.

Time moved in a steady stream. Sadie could feel the loneliness of her eternity already. Nights were spent scouring for criminals to feed from and then back to the bunker where she sat on the sofa until the sun called her to sleep. Sometimes she would feel a tug inside her and know her maker was close. There would be a flicker of excitement before she remembered his words on the beach. He didn't want to be saddled with her and never would.

As she stood on the strip watching Rick's bar, the grief finally took over. She saw Leah through the windows, bouncing her head to whatever music was coming through the overhead speakers. Part of Sadie wanted so badly to be there, pouring drinks while Rick sat in his office reading the paper. She missed the little house on the beach, the one Hayden's family sold when their daughter disappeared. That life seemed so long ago now. She turned around with a sigh, managing one step before running smack into someone. She was spewing apologies when she looked up into Dylan's smiling face.

"What are you doing here?" she asked, shaking off his hands as he tried to help steady her.

"Oh, yeah, I have to see the big man about something. But now that I'm here I can feel he ain't so..."

"He never works Fridays," she said absently.

"Oh well, guess I can stop by tomorrow."

"Where is everyone?" She hoped the question sounded casual.

"They went out of town," he said, laughing at the surprised look on her face. "What? You don't think we spend every second in this place, do you?"

"I never thought about it. Where did they go?"

Dylan sat down on a nearby bench and plucked a pack of cigarettes from his shirt pocket. "Rick has a place in Seattle. We go there sometimes, you know, spice things up."

"Why aren't you with them?" she asked, immediately wishing she hadn't when Dylan's smile dropped.

"Not my scene," he said with a casual wave of his hand.

She knew it was a lie and thought back on what Rick told her about the youngest vampire in the pack. It was all over his face. He was the baby brother who constantly got left behind, metaphorical legs not able to catch up.

Sadie sat down beside him and took the cigarette he offered. "Hayden and I went to Seattle once. I didn't really like it either." It wasn't true, but lying to make him feel better seemed the right thing to do.

They sat in silence for several minutes, Dylan's legs bouncing as the seconds passed. He hated sitting still for too long. "Have you eaten?" he asked her.

"Earlier." She always fed early, getting it out of the way. Even though she had taken down a woman who was eyeballing girls for a prostitution ring, it was still the thing she hated most about her new existence.

"Me, too," he sighed. He would have fed again, though, just to relieve the boredom. "Do you want to go do something?"

"Like what?"

"Shit, I don't know. We could go jump the cliffs. Tony and I used to do it all the time before..." he let the words trail off.

"Before me," she finished softly.

Dylan looked at her briefly then turned away. His mind wandered to his brothers, and part of him was so jealous it stung. When Alex said they were taking Tony to Seattle to cure him of his sulking, Dylan was excited. They always had fun when they were there, going to strip clubs and feeding on new flavors. Then Alex told him he wasn't going with them. Assigned instead to keeping an eye on Sadie, Dylan argued, and his sire quickly put him in his place, just like he always did.

"What do you mean, jump the cliffs?"

"It's just something we do for fun. We go to the highest point and jump. Then we fly back to the top right before we're going to hit the water. I know it sounds kind of lame, but it's a blast."

Sadie looked down at her hands. "I don't know how to fly."

"Seriously? Damn, girl, that's one of the best parts of being us." He stood up and reached for her hand. "Come on, I'm taking you to the cliffs and teaching you how to fly."

She stared at his hand for several seconds. Dylan was just as responsible for all the torment and loss she had experienced. Sarah told her there was no one in the pack worthy of reprieve. In that moment, though, Dylan was offering Sadie something she needed. He was offering her a friend, even for one night.

She accepted his hand with a shake. The boredom of eternity, for now, was forgotten.

Sadie looked down over the cliffs, water smashing against the rocks with a thunderous roar. "No way," she looked to Dylan and laughed nervously. "I am not jumping."

"Don't be a pussy. It's not like the fall would kill you anyway."

"It will still hurt like hell. You do it; I can have just as much fun watching you."

Dylan reached for her hand. "We'll do it together. I promise not to let you fall."

"I can't," she said apologetically. "I'm not ready."

He dropped her hand with a disgruntled sigh. When he could see she wasn't going to give in, he took a seat on a large rock and motioned for her to join him. "You'll never be ready. The only way to do it is just jump. The first time I jumped I was scared shitless. Tony kept telling me it was the best way to learn how to fly. You know, because instinct and self-preservation kick in so your body just does what it knows deep down it can do. I wouldn't do it, though. Shit, you should have seen me standing here blubbering like a big baby while Tony's shouting, 'Jump, fucker! Just fucking jump!'"

Sadie couldn't help but smile. It was nice to hear stories that humanized them and made them seem more like her. "So, you finally jumped?"

Dylan shook his head. "Nope, and you know what Tony did?"

"What?"

He leaned forward with a crooked grin. "He pushed me off. I screamed the whole way down, and just before I hit the water, bam! I was flying straight back up."

"I can't believe he pushed you."

"It's what we do, girl. We push each other to be more." He looked over at her with calming eyes. "I know you're not part of our pack, and I know you miss him. He misses you, too."

She could feel the tears pricking her eyes but held them in.

"It's not easy being the youngest," he continued. "I'm not anymore, though, thanks to you. I know you and Tony are done, but you'll still need someone to teach you stuff. So, I'll do it."

"Why?"

"Because deep down you are one of us."

Sadie became so overwhelmed with both Tony's absence and Dylan's kindness that she burst into tears.

"Hey, now," Dylan said, not sure how to react. Usually, when he was around crying women it was because he was about to kill them, so consoling one was unfamiliar territory. "Come on," he encouraged, rubbing her back. "I told you I'll help you, and I will."

She wiped at her eyes and looked at him. "Thanks."

He dropped his hand, ensuring the moment was nothing serious. It struck him that if Alex or even Tony knew what he was doing right then, and who he was sharing time with, they might not see it the same way. So, he said, "Just don't tell Tony or the others, okay?"

"Wow, do they hate me that much?"

"It's not a hate thing, Sadie. It's a pack thing."

"I won't tell them."

Dylan smiled his thanks. She wasn't the bitch Alex had made her out to be, not at all. He realized he was enjoying this time with her, and maybe he felt a little sorry for her. She had been forced into immortality instead of seeking it. They turned her, then abandoned the responsibility of teaching and guiding her. Tony didn't want the burden, so maybe Dylan could pick up some of the slack.

"You ready to jump?"

She took a deep breath and clutched his hand tighter. "You ready to push me?"

Dylan laughed and stood up, pulling Sadie to her feet. They stood on the edge of the cliffs looking at one another, her eyes getting wider as he began to count down. "Remember," he told her. "It's your mind that tells your body what to do. You can fly, Sadie. Just believe it."

She heard him yell "One!" and then both their feet were leaving the rocks. His hand slipped from hers, and Sadie's screams echoed out over the cliffs. She could see the water getting closer and hear Dylan above her screaming encouragement. Her eyes shut tight, and in her mind, she willed herself not to hit the water below, but to rise above it.

It wasn't until she felt Dylan's hand on her shoulder that she peeked. She was surrounded by white mist, the wetness clinging to her skin. It took her a few pauses to realize it was the clouds. Her eyes widened as did her smile. "I'm flying!" she said, looking down at her feet as they dangled in the air.

"Pretty cool, huh?" Dylan swept backwards and turned a somersault.

It was like being in the ocean; a whole world she didn't know existed was now hers. She willed herself forward, brain urging body to go faster until her eyes were stinging as the cold air met her face. Dylan caught up with her and grabbed her hand, descending her toward the water only for them both to zoom back up in a flash. When the coming morning signaled with a shimmering blue sky, they went back to solid ground. She was exhausted but exhilarated, wishing the night could last just a little longer.

"I could do this all the time," she told him.

"Well, if you ever want a jumping buddy, just come find me."

"I will," she promised, and she meant it. "Are you going back to your house?"

Dylan nodded, eyes turned upwards to the moon. "Morning will be here in a few hours."

"When are they coming back from Seattle?"

He shrugged. "Who knows? I guess when they get bored."

"If you want, you can come by my place tomorrow. Maybe we can find a new adventure."

"Sounds aces," he said. "Need a lift home?"

She shook her head with a grin. "Nah, I think I'll fly."

Chapter Twenty-Three

Tony stood at the end of a walkway that led up to a small yellow house. He told Alex and Oscar he needed to be alone. They fought him a little but eventually conceded, if only to be rid of his sulking. Slowly, Tony reached down and lifted the latch on a white-washed gate. He stepped through and focused on a sign in the yard that read:

ANGELA BAXTER WORLD RENOWNED PSYCHIC AND MEDIUM

The words were accompanied by a photo depicting a pretty blonde woman with large round eyes and a toothy smile. He glanced behind to make sure Alex and Oscar hadn't followed him but saw only the empty street. As he neared the front door, he was stopped by the overwhelming feeling that he was being watched. He swung around and fell back onto the porch steps. Mary Ann was standing a few feet away from him. She wasn't alone. Tony could make out Hayden, Sadie's sister, and a dozen other former kills looming behind her.

"Fuck off," Tony growled, eyes glowing. "What the hell do you want from me?"

Why are you going in there, my love? Do you really think that witch can help you?

"Maybe, maybe not, but I'll try anything to get rid of you." Then it hit him. Mary Ann wasn't there to frighten him at that moment, but to lure him away. "She can help me, can't she? That's why you're here trying to stop me."

My darling, listen to me. You still love me, Anthony. I can feel it, like your kisses I still feel on my lips.

"I don't love you," he spat and hurried up to the door. He banged on it hard and glanced back to find Mary Ann and her companions gone. No one answered so he banged again, then jabbed his finger into the bell.

The door finally opened to reveal Angela Baxter standing in the doorway wearing a thin red negligee and a frown. "Do you not see the sign that says closed?"

It was only then he noticed the neon sign lit up in the front window. "Sorry," he mumbled. "I'm Tony." He gave her a soft smile and waited for her to recognize him.

Her eyes raked him up and down before they sparkled with recognition. "Oh yes," she crooned and opened the door wider. "You're one of Rick's boys."

"Yeah, I am."

"Well, come on in, sweetie." She closed the door behind her. "What can I do for you?"

His eyes gawked at the surroundings. The walls were painted deep purple, and the air smelled floral. He knew Angela was older than him and that Rick had met her sometime in the 17th century. While not an immortal, she used magic and potions to keep herself alive and youthful. In this new era, she found that calling herself a psychic made her more money. She was well known among celebrities. She toured occasionally with rock stars and spent time with actors on movie sets.

"I'm having a problem," he said, trying to keep his voice steady.

"Are you now?" She walked a circle around him, fingers tracing the tattoos on his arms. Then she leaned into his ear and whispered, "Your little girlfriend is still here, you know. She thinks she can hide from me, but she can't."

"You mean Mary Ann? She's here now?"

Angela's eyes lifted to the ceiling. "Oh yes, waiting outside for you. And she's not a very happy girl, is she?"

"No," he said, defeated. "She's definitely not happy."

Angela took his hand and began leading him towards a dark hallway. She opened the last door on the right, and he was met with candlelight and gothic-inspired furniture. Tony stepped through the door and immediately felt like a weight fell off his shoulders. It was cold and dark; a red velvet sofa sat at the foot of a canopy bed with wrought iron posts.

Angela sat on the sofa and crossed her legs. She watched him with curious eyes, excited by his nervousness. It was amusing, considering he was an immortal killing machine. But she was more powerful than he was, and they both knew it. "I'm assuming your problem is the woman that was standing outside my house."

Tony hurried through the story of Sadie, her blood, and the spirits that haunted him now that he had tasted it. As he got farther into the tale, his voice became louder, his movements more animated. Could she make the spirits go away?

Angela listened patiently to everything. When Tony was done, she motioned him to sit next to her. She brushed her fingers through his hair. "Poor Tony," she said. "Of course, I can help you."

"You can?"

She nodded and scooted closer to him. "But everything comes at a price."

"What do you want?"

"I want you." She took his hand in hers, stroking his palm with her fingernails and enjoying the shiver that ran through him. "Give me what I want, and I'll make all those nasty spirits disappear."

Was she serious? Tony could feel his arousal growing as she leaned into him. It couldn't be that simple. Angela was a beautiful woman, capable of having any man she wanted bow at her feet. Why would she give him magic in exchange for sex? There was a catch and he knew it. "What do you really want?"

"Clever boy," she smirked then sat back and grabbed a pack of cigarettes off the table next to her. "Your blood," she said simply. Her seduction routine was no longer needed; her entire tone turned to business. "Give me some of your blood, and I'll give you the remedy to your problem."

Tony shook his head. "I can't do that. Rick decides who becomes a vampire. Besides, I sure as shit don't want to sire anyone else."

"You immortals are all the same. Always thinking your gift is the greatest. I don't want your blood so I can become like you. I need it for my magic."

He looked away from her. The idea of willingly giving away his blood left him feeling cold all over. Rick told them their blood was sacred, and to give it away or take it from another vampire was not just unforgivable, it was dangerous. He probably should have listened closer to that part. If he hadn't feasted on Sadie, he wouldn't be there now.

He looked over at her and lifted his brow. "Can't we just fuck instead?"

Angela took a long drag off her cigarette and let the smoke escape slowly. "Oh, we can fuck, cupcake. I never say no to handsome vampires, but if you want my magic, you're going to have to pay my price."

Tony could feel the two sides of him fighting with one another. Giving this witch his blood while not knowing what she would do with it was terrifying. The idea of spending any more nights in fear of the ghosts following him was scarier. "Okay," he said with a sigh. "I'll give you my blood. Just make this stop, please."

Without a word, Angela got off the sofa and walked across the room. She opened a glass cabinet filled with tiny bottles, each one with a different color liquid inside. As she sauntered her way back to him, he caught the mischievous gleam in her eyes.

"It's only temporary. When you need more, I'll give it to you. Of course, you'll give me more blood."

"Temporary? How fucking temporary?"

She sat beside him, her finger tracing a line up his thigh. "A month or possibly more. It all depends on the spirits and how strong they are. How much they want to torture you."

"I'd say they're pretty hell-bent on making me suffer."

"Your girl must be very special," she said thoughtfully. "I've heard stories about vampires who bring out the dead. I've never been lucky enough to meet one, though. If you were to give me her blood, I'd give you this potion until the end of my days."

"I won't give you her blood," he said flatly. "But I'll give you mine."

"Well," she said, reaching to the table again for an empty vial and long-handled knife. "If you ever change your mind, you know where to find me."

Tony held his arm out to her, wanting to get the transaction over with so he could get the hell out of that house. The longer he was there, the more apprehensive he became. What would Rick do if he knew

Tony sought Angela out? What would happen to Sadie if any of the others knew what swam in her blood?

She dragged the tip of the blade up his arm and turned it over, so the blood flowed steadily into the vial. He winced as she squeezed his arm tight, making sure to get every drop. When the blood stopped flowing, she put the vial aside and handed Tony what he paid for.

He gawked at the bright orange liquid with sorrowful eyes. "If Mary Ann was like she was before, I wouldn't need this. Maybe I would like having her around."

"Mary Ann will never be what she was before. Murder rips a soul apart, Tony. What's left is nothing but vengeance. They want revenge for the life you stole."

"But I didn't kill Mary Ann," he insisted.

She lifted her eyes to the ceiling again, cocking her head to the side as though listening to something Tony could not hear. "She killed herself for you. In her mind, it's no different than if you pushed her yourself."

His eyes dropped back to the elixir in his hand. He wanted Mary Ann and the others to go. He wanted to go back to feeling like he used to. Back to feeding without remorse, fucking without feeling, and most of all, not falling for the girl who brought all those feelings back.

"Drink it," Angela whispered into his ear. "Go on."

He slugged it back in one long gulp. It tasted like shit, and he had to force himself to keep it down. She took the empty vial from his hand and ran her palm up his thigh. "I better go," he told her.

"If you really want to," she quipped, biting her bottom lip as her hand inched closer to his crotch. "But if you want to stay for a while..." She let the words drop as she pressed her lips to the side of his neck, hot breath on his cold skin.

Even as Tony was telling himself to get up and get out, his hands were reaching for her. Her kiss tasted dark and delicious, but Sadie dominated his thoughts. He wondered what she was doing, and if she was thinking of him.

"Forget about her," Angela urged and straddled his lap. "Just for a little while."

He accepted her then, fingers gripping her hips as she ground against him. He emptied his mind, determined to take back who he was, even if it was only in that room and just for a little while.

Angela fell over Tony, laughing with exhilaration as her orgasm subsided. She kissed his cheek and rolled over onto her back, hands sliding over her sweaty skin as she smiled.

He looked up at the ceiling, eyes focusing on a spider in the corner of the room spinning a web. He could feel the pull of sleep and wondered how long he had to get back to Rick's house. "I better go," he said, sitting up and reaching for his jeans on the floor.

Angela got on her knees and leaned into him from behind. "You can stay," she offered. "This room is light tight, honey. Rick always stays over."

Tony grimaced, hating the idea that he just slept with someone Rick fucked, too. "Yeah, well, I'm not Rick," he said, pulling on his t-shirt.

She leaned back into the pillows. "And I'm not your sweet little Sadie."

"Don't say her name," he warned, turning over his shoulder glaring at her.

"Honey, you really need to gain some perspective. That was fun just now, and if you weren't so screwed up over this girl you would lay back in this bed, sleep the day away, and be ready for round two when the moon rises." She grabbed her cigarettes and lit one, watching as Tony tried to ignore her while looking for his shoes.

"You don't know anything about us." He grabbed his jacket off the end of the bed and made for the door. "I'll see you in a month."

"I know more than you ever will," she said. "I know that she's in danger, and her clock is ticking." A wicked smirk spread across her lips as his hand halted on the doorknob.

"What are you talking about?"

Angela took a deep drag and exhaled slowly, the smoke taking on the shape of a ghostly smile as it met the air. "The spirits you see, they go to her, too. Only they don't try and scare her like they do you. There are all kinds of souls, Tony. Death is different for everyone, and while some souls accept their departure from this world to the next, some can't. You're a vampire; your soul was dissected soon as you drank your sire's blood. When you kill your victims, their soul latches on to you."

Tony shook his head. "That doesn't make any sense."

"I don't make the rules. It's a price you pay for the gift of eternal life. They've always been there. The first girl you killed all the way to the group of teenagers you all drank on the hill in town. You just never knew it. Enter your Sadie with her very special blood, and suddenly they have a way to communicate with you."

"And what does that have to do with Sadie? What danger is she in?"

"The spirits don't just want you to pay for their lost lives. They want her, too. After all, she's one of you, isn't she? They are not the same souls that once loved her. They are broken and torn apart, decaying with every second they remain on Earth. Your girl walked into the shadows, and when she did, she made herself their enemy. Oh, they'll sweet-talk her and play her until she's in a place where they convince her the only way back to life is death. They'll lead her right into the sun."

Tony hurried back to her side of the bed and sat down, offering his arm. "Take more of my blood. Take as much as you want. Just give me more of that stuff so I can give it to her."

She took another drag and walked her fingers up Tony's forearm. "It won't work on her. She's got a different makeup than you. I'd have to make it special, and it comes at a price I don't think you're willing to pay."

"Anything," he pleaded.

"Her blood, and not just a vial full either."

"If you drain her, you'll kill her," he spat.

"But if she is only taken to the edge, she'll bounce back. Then I'll give her the potion she needs to block them out."

Tony didn't know if he should believe her. She was clever and manipulative. Rick told Tony he offered Angela immortality, but she refused. She was in control of her future, knowing if she wanted to die as a human and go into the beyond with a human soul, she only had to stop making her potion. A vampire would live forever, and if they did die, there was no beautiful afterlife waiting for them.

He decided to switch his approach and reached for her breasts, caressing them gently as she sighed. "Come on, baby. We can work something out, can't we?"

She pushed his hand away with a cackle. "You're a good fuck, sweetie, but I want her blood more."

"Fuck you," Tony growled and got off the bed.

"Oh, don't take it personally. Besides, our deal still stands. Your blood for my remedy. But if you want to save your little muffin, you know the price."

Tony felt himself starting to shift, so angry at her that all he could think about was ripping her apart. She could see it in his eyes and called him out.

"If you kill me, my little immortal, you'll be haunted forever, and Sadie will be burnt toast. Think about that before you let those fangs drop."

He bowed his head, squeezing his eyes shut as the vampire inside retreated. There was no way he could let anything happen to Angela. He still needed her, and so did Sadie. He finally opened his eyes and felt sick at the smile on her face.

"Come back here," she patted the empty space beside her. "The sun is almost up, and you know you're not really mad at me."

Tony stood there for a moment before finally dropping his jacket onto the bed. He kicked off his shoes and crawled into the bed beside her. If he was ever going to convince her to help his childe, without sacrificing Sadie's blood to do it, he was going to have to play nice. She stroked his hair and ran her lips along his neck. He wasn't focused on her, though; he could not think of anything except the one he pushed away.

Chapter Twenty-Four

Alex watched from the shadows as Dylan and Sadie walked along the surf. If his childe was older, he might have sensed his sire lurking. Then again, Dylan was never one to spend time honing his gifts. Part of Alex wondered if he had tasted Sadie, too, and if that was the reason he was standing in Tony's place. After some thought, he concluded that Dylan was with her because she was younger and would look up to him. She would need him in ways his brothers didn't.

They laughed like they had known one another for decades instead of mere weeks. They looked around the beach, making sure it was empty, then shot off into the sky like a black smear. Alex smiled to himself, knowing exactly where they were going.

He followed them, landing gracefully next to the door in the ground. He crouched to his knee and focused his energy on listening to the muffled sounds under the chirping crickets and hum of the wind. His hand reached for the door handle, tongue licking his lips as he prepared to interrupt and make his presence known.

Alex had spent a lot of time thinking about Sadie and where she stood now that Tony released her. Since her blood had already infected him and he couldn't get the taste out of his mind, he would employ blackmail to get what he wanted. Sure, he knew nothing happened between his youngest offspring and Tony's spawn, but that wasn't the story he planned to tell. Alex wanted more of her blood, and it was driving him crazy.

He would tear into her human way of thinking and let her know what he told Tony would not be innocent. The truth was, Tony probably wouldn't care if Dylan spent some time in her bed, but Sadie had fooled herself into thinking Tony was her mate, her one and only. Alex would make her believe Tony would see her relationship with Dylan as a betrayal. For Dylan's part, he could only do what his sire told him to.

Besides, Alex had grown used to seeing the victims who followed him. Sometimes they would shout at him, calling his name and growling obscenities. At first, he was unnerved and maybe even a little frightened, but after a while, he realized he had nothing to fear. They were just air with a voice. Nothing they did could ever hurt him.

Why don't you just let them be?

Alex popped up and swung around, his eyes narrowing on the spirit he did not immediately recognize. She was smiling at him, wet hair clinging to pale skin. When she became clearer, he couldn't help but laugh.

"Mary Ann! You look like shit, sweetheart."

You don't really want to keep them from having such a good time, do you? Dylan is teaching her things Anthony never did.

"Ah, I see. You're miffed over Tony finding a replacement for you. That's why you want me to stay up here and let whatever happens down there play out."

Replace me? Don't be silly, Alex. Anthony will never be able to forget me. I am slowly driving him mad, and one day soon he is going to waltz into the sunlight just to be with me again.

Alex's lips curled into a snarl. "You're wrong, bitch. Tony's stronger than that. I'm not scared of you, and neither is he."

He turned his back on her and reached down for the door handle again, ready to get what he came for. His stomach was growling. He had deliberately skipped feeding so he could enjoy his Sadie snack even more.

Alex? Before you go, there is someone here who wants to see you.

He rolled his eyes and stood up, ready to face whatever new ghost was waiting. When he saw the woman standing next to Mary Ann, though, his legs turned to jelly, and he fell to his knees in shock. "No," he breathed hard, his fingers grasping the leaf-strewn ground beneath him. "Not you."

He could have handled any spirit that made their way to him, trying to make him feel bad for ending their miserable lives. He wasn't prepared to run into one he had only ever known as a human, the woman who only ever knew him as her son.

Hello, my boy. You've grown so much. Of course, you'll never really grow up, will you?

Alex's mind reeled backward, images flipping like the pages of a photo album. He could see himself as a small boy, black hair shining in the sun as he watched his mother digging a hole in the ground. Her own hair was up in a bun, tendrils flying loose and glistening with the sweat of her exertion. She looked over at him, blood and dirt smeared across her cheeks.

They had been in the fields behind their small farmhouse. His mother was standing high in the hole. "Hand me that piece." She pointed her finger at the bloody hump next to his bare feet.

He reached down, little hands picking up the severed foot of a man. The blood made it slippery, and he lost his grip before quickly picking it up again. "Sorry, Mamma," he said, bottom lip trembling as he approached her. He never wanted to make his mamma mad.

"That's all right, child," she smiled, taking the foot from him and tossing it into the newly dug hole. She wiped her hands on her apron, the long blue dress underneath smeared red. "Now, be a good boy and hand me the head." She laughed deeply as his face screwed up in fright.

Little Alex swallowed hard, turning his back to her and walking slowly toward the head of a man his mother invited over that afternoon. Milky eyes stared at him, the bloody lips parted open, and a beady black fly landed on the slightly protruding tongue. Alex took another step and then slammed his hands over his eyes.

"I can't!" he screamed. "Please don't make me."

A sudden smack across the back of his head sent him tumbling to the ground. He turned over his shoulder and watched his mother take a handful of the dead man's black hair and lift the head up. Tears began streaming down her face as she stomped back to the hole.

"What am I supposed to do with you?" she shouted. "I am the only one to take care of you, and this is how you show your thanks? You leave me to do it all."

He watched his mother slump to the ground, face buried in her hands. Slowly he got to his feet and walked to her, one tiny hand falling on her shoulder. "I'm sorry, Mamma," he whispered. Then he picked up the shovel and finished the job for her.

She wiped her eyes then reached into her pocket and pulled out a wad of paper money. It was the dead man's money, and she had taken it from his pocket right after he dropped dead from her poisoned coffee. She was not a whore and certainly didn't appreciate any man who thought so. There was only one male she would keep around, and he was standing right in front of her, burying her crimes like she taught him to. One day he would grow up, and men would not be her only victims. Alex would bring her women, too. His future usefulness might have been the only thing that kept him alive.

Alex's memory dissolved as he stared up at the woman with wide fearful eyes. "You can't be here," he said, then turned his attention to Mary Ann. "She can't be here!"

But I am here, son. Oh, I have been with you all along. Now that you can see me and hear my voice, we can finish what we started.

He shook his head, clapping his hands over his ears and shutting his eyes tight. More flashes of his childhood erupted like lightning behind his eyes. His mother at the kitchen stove, their new house bigger than the little farm he was born on. She was using a long-handled butcher knife to chop at a hunk of meat on a cutting board.

"Make certain you cut off the fat," she told him, dark eyes landing on the twelve-year-old boy. "Mamma doesn't like any fat on her meat."

What's the matter, son? You always liked my special stew. Is it so different from the blood you feast on now? I am so proud of you, picking up right where Mamma left off.

Another memory, the worst, was so clear in his mind he doubled over in pain. His mother being led up the scaffold, hands tied behind her back, defiant eyes glaring at the crowd of spectators there to watch. Alex hid behind a group of men, peering over their shoulders as the executioner fitted the noose around her neck. Then her eyes found him in the crowd, and she held his stare right until the floor broke underneath her and the rope snapped her neck.

"I had to do it," Alex heard himself say. "I had to be rid of you."

You certainly did a fine job of that. What kind of man turns on his own mother? The woman who birthed him, loved him, and cared for him. Now, you'll never be rid of me. You will live forever, and so will I.

He listened as she laughed, a deep cackle not unlike his own. When he opened his eyes, she was gone. Only Mary Ann stood there, looking down on him with pity.

You can make her go away, Alex. Make us all go away. Save your sanity and Anthony's, too.

"How do I do that?" He didn't recognize his voice; it sounded meek and small.

Go to Rick's witch. She'll tell you how.

"Angela? She can fix this?"

Oh yes. Go to her and be free again.

"Why do you want to help me? You hate me, you always have."

Because there is only one thing I truly need to be free of this Earth, and she's standing in my way.

"Who's standing in your way?"

Go to the witch but do it soon. Mother is very anxious to see you again.

Mary Ann disappeared into the air, leaving Alex on the ground with tears in his eyes. He pushed himself up, staring at the spot where his mother stood moments before. Maybe ghosts couldn't hurt him, but his mother could. He shot up into the sky, flying like a bat out of hell straight back to Seattle and the witch who could help him.

Dylan and Sadie made their way up the side of a giant sequoia, hopping from one branch to another until they reached the top. Dylan leaned back against the trunk, while Sadie stretched out on the branch above him. The last few weeks had been her happiest in a long time. It came from the normalcy their friendship provided. While they were connected, it wasn't like the connection she shared with Tony. There was no ownership or arguments over who was in charge. It was just the two of them existing in the same space and time.

"It's going to suck when they come back," said Dylan, tucking his hands behind his head. "It'll be any day now."

"Why do you say that?"

"They've never been gone this long," he surmised.

"No, I mean why do you say things will suck when they get back?"

He looked up at her with a grin. "Well, I won't be here with you for one." He waited for her smile to match his, appreciation for what he was saying. She didn't smile, though, and her lips drew down into a frown.

"But I thought..." she stumbled over the words. "I thought we were going to still hang out."

Dylan sat up fully, dropping his legs on either side of the branch. He motioned for her to come join him, and she slid down to sit opposite him. "We will," he promised. "We're always going to be buds, girl. Who else is going to count stars with me? I'm just saying that when the guys get back, we won't have as much time."

"I don't understand."

"It's been a blast hanging with you, I mean it. When they come home, though, I'll be back at the house. Things will pretty much be the way they were before. You and I have something really cool, and I meant what I said. I'll always help you if I can."

He waited for her to acknowledge her understanding, and when she didn't, he felt his stomach sink. She just stared at him with confused eyes, and he felt himself growing more frustrated. "Come back with me," he said and took both her hands in his. "You and Tony can work shit out, and then you'll really be a part of our pack."

She looked away from him, trying to hold back tears. Sadie thought about it, going to the house, being with those like her, and not being alone. When she asked Tony for her freedom, she truly believed it would make her happy. She never stopped to think about the long road of eternity or how lonely it would be to walk alone. It was when she thought about going into the house to stay, however, that slammed something shut inside her.

Sadie felt like she was being torn apart, ripped straight down the seam. One half of her wanted to embrace the vampire she had become and the other wanted to avenge all those deaths, including her own. It hit her then; the awareness there would never be a balance for her in the world because she was so unnatural, split open and straddling the light and dark.

"Come back with me tonight," Dylan encouraged. "When they get home, we'll surprise them. You and Tony will be back together, and we won't have to hide hanging out."

"It's not that simple."

"Yes, it is. Things started off rough for you with us, and I know that. Shit, girl, forever is a long fucking time to keep pretending like you don't need us."

"That house is where I died. It's where you killed my best friend."

Dylan shook his head with disbelief at her sudden mood shift. He noticed the amber gleam forming in her eyes. "The house is where we saved you. Don't think of it as death but rebirth."

"Give me a break," she huffed. "That's Alex talking."

"Watch it, Sadie," he pointed at her with a stern warning.

"Just say what you really mean."

She felt so stupid. All those days with him, and she truly believed they would teach one another, exploring new places without the pressure of being what history dictated. There had been a sense of hope that she might have found a way to navigate the darkness. Now it was all crashing down around her. He was only there with her because the others were gone.

"That is what I really mean. Why should I waste time saying things I don't?"

"Why would we have to hide our friendship? You said Tony didn't own me, that I could do what I wanted."

"And you can, but it's not the same from our side. We want to be with each other, not because of Alex's blood but because we're a family. The pack is who I am, and I'll always want to be with them."

He dropped down off the branch and landed on the ground with a thud. Dylan hated complications, and Sadie was complicating things on a massive level. He heard her land behind him and turned over his shoulder to face her fully. It was time he laid it all out, made her understand what their lives were supposed to be before she pulled him into her universe where everything was so unbalanced. He saw the tears in her eyes and suddenly hated everything about her. She was too close to the human she once was, unable and unwilling to embrace the vampire they had made her.

"I like you," he said simply. "I really do. I want you to come back to the house and be part of this family. But I will never choose spending time with you over being with them. It's your choice. Live in there like a goddamn hermit or come back with us and really be free."

"You think you're free?" she took a step toward him. "None of you are free. If you were, then it wouldn't matter if Alex knew that you liked to count stars on the beach or jump off cliffs just for fun. You're not free, Dylan, not really."

"Don't do that," he said. "Don't try and turn your choice to be an antisocial weirdo onto me. We're free because we choose the blood over anything else. We are all that matters."

"Then why don't I feel that?" she asked, anger turning to confusion. "Why is it so simple for all of you and not for me?"

Didn't he understand that she would give anything to feel like he did? Able to kill without guilt, to feel pleasure with abandon, and live without restraint. Why was being a vampire so easy for all of them and so very hard for her?

"I don't know," he said softly then placed his hands on her shoulders. "Maybe it's because you didn't drink the blood wanting what it would give you. You're fighting so hard not to give into what your body tells you it wants. I know you want Tony more than anything; I know your blood is constantly seeking him out. It's how we feel about our maker, so let go. Stop trying to control yourself when the whole point of who you are now is that nothing will ever control you again."

"Except all of you," she shook her head sadly. They looked at each other for a few moments then she said, "You should go."

"Sadie, come on. We're still friends. I don't want to control you. None of us do, we just want the best for our pack."

She didn't turn back or answer. Sadie went inside to the only place she belonged.

Alex waited until the following night to see Angela. He told Oscar and Tony he was going to visit Rick and check on Dylan. After Tony casually mentioned Sadie, Alex reminded him that she was no longer their concern. He arrived at the little yellow house and pounded so hard on the door it started to crack. When the door flung open, he stepped inside and grabbed a bewildered Angela's arms to pull her close.

"You have to help me," he said, shaking her slightly. "Please, help me!"

"Back off, you little monster," she spat, wiggling out of his grasp. She looked him over then sighed loudly. "Oh perfect, another one of you. Let me guess, you drank Sadie's special sauce, and now you've got some unwanted company."

"Yeah, how do you know that?"

She smirked at him then started walking down the hallway. "Come on, Dracula. Let's get the introductions over with and start talking a payment plan." He hurried after her into the bedroom. She sat down on the sofa and patted the seat next to her. "I don't bite," she giggled.

"How do you know about Sadie?" he asked, a sudden calm coming over him.

"Her sire was here four days ago looking for the same thing you are."

She plucked a cigarette from a gold case on the end table then blew on the tip till a red ember sparked. Angela looked him over and then slowly nodded her head. She pointed her finger at him and drew a circle into the air.

"You wicked boy. He doesn't know about you and her. In fact, she doesn't know you drank from her either, does she?"

"So Tony is seeing them too?" Alex asked, side-stepping her questions.

"He certainly is, and lucky for him he came to me when he did. A few more months of that torment and he'd be a crispy critter right about now. Even vampires have a breaking point."

"So, you helped him?"

"Sure did, honey. I helped him in more ways than one," she snickered.

"Help me," he said imploringly. "Whatever you did for him you have to do for me."

She flicked her ash over the side of the couch. "You vampires and your overinflated egos, always expecting everyone to fall at your feet as if we owe you. Look, magic isn't easy, and it takes a lot to keep the balance. If you want my help, it's going to cost you."

"You want money? I'll get you whatever you want. Please, just make this stop."

"Money?" Angela started to laugh so hard she doubled over. "Look around you, pumpkin. Do I seem destitute to you?"

His eyes swept the room. A ruby-encrusted frame hanging on the wall, the painting it cradled recognizable as a Picasso. The diamond rings on her fingers and hanging from her ears told him Angela was not hurting financially.

He lifted his brow. "So, what do you want? My blood?"

"That deal has already been struck. Your childe is going to keep me well-stocked in vampire blood for a while."

"But I'm older," Alex said. "Isn't my blood better?"

Angela's shrill laugh pierced the air as she clapped a hand against her thigh. "Oh, Alex, you are a funny one. No, your blood isn't better." She leaned into him and inhaled deeply. "In fact, your blood is a little too dark for my taste. Of course, your blood was dark before you took Rick's into you. She made sure of that."

Alex shivered as he tried to keep memories of his mother out of his head. "Quit fucking with me and just tell me what you want."

"Very well. I want her blood."

"Sadie?"

"She's special," Angela said thoughtfully.

"She's Tony's childe. You know I can't give her to you. If she dies, he'll feel it and so will Rick."

"My goodness, you and your brother are so similar. Killing her would defeat the purpose. No, I want to experiment with her. I'll just take a little at a time and she'll come back like it never happened at all."

"You don't understand," Alex hissed. "She'll never let me close enough to get her blood, and she's obviously not going to give it to you."

Angela sat back with a sigh. "Then I'm afraid there isn't a bargain for us to make. I hope you're looking forward to more time with Mommy Dearest. You have no idea how excited she is to bond with her baby boy."

Alex's eyes flashed gold, his face shifting in seconds as he lunged for her. She held up her hand in his direction. It felt like someone punched him hard in the chest. His body crumpled and hung suspended in midair for a moment before she made a motion with her arm and sent him flying across the room. She stood to her feet, chest heaving as she glared down at him.

"You stupid, arrogant boy, do you think you're stronger than me? You have no idea how much power I have accumulated over the centuries of my life."

He struggled to his feet and his shoulders slumped in defeat. He knew Rick was not the only creature more powerful than he was, but he never imagined that power would exist in a human soul.

"I'll get it for you," he relented. "But it will take some time. If we're going to do this, you have to let me set it up. She has to trust me."

Slowly, she sat back down, eyeing him with victory. "All right, I'll give you a month. That's how long the potion lasts. When you need another dose, you come see me. But you won't be alone, will you, Alex?"

"No," he said. "I'll have her with me."

He had no idea how he would get Sadie's blood. All he knew for sure was that she was the price he was willing to pay. He would do anything to make the demon of his human life disappear. Anything.

Chapter Twenty-Five

Tony waited at the end of Rick's walkway. He stood by the picket fence chewing at his fingers nervously while he waited for Sadie to emerge. He went to the bunker first and felt she wasn't there, so he walked all over Brave Beach looking for her. It wasn't until he was flying high over the cliffs that he felt her pull and followed it to Rick's. Tony didn't know what he would say to her. Weeks had passed since that night on the beach, and he knew she might dismiss him altogether. Angela's warnings were fresh in his mind, and protecting his childe was the only thing he could focus on. Lost in thought, he didn't hear the front door open or notice the footsteps coming toward him.

"What are you doing here?" she asked, crossing her arms over her chest. She tried to look angry, but her face gave away the lie. There was a relief in her eyes that no one else might have noticed. Tony saw it immediately.

"I felt you," he said softly.

"Why didn't you just ignore it?" Her brow lifted as she threw his cruel words back to him.

He looked away from her. "I can't ignore it." When his attention returned to her face again, he reached for her hand and said, "I don't want to."

She held back at first, tugging her arm away until he clutched her wrist and pulled her closer. When his arms slipped around her waist, she stopped fighting altogether.

"I'm sorry," he said, dipping his head to try and meet the eyes she kept cast downward. "I really am."

"Why did you say all that to me?"

Her question froze him. There was no answer he could give that wouldn't reveal everything he was trying so hard to protect her from. Angela said Sadie would be resistant to giving up the spirits attached to her. They weren't victims after all, at least not to her. They were her sister, her best friend, two people who meant the world to the human girl he stole. There was another truth, one he knew had been there all along.

"I was wrong," he said, cupping her face. His thumb brushed across her bottom lip as it trembled. "I never wanted to let you go, Sadie. When you asked me to, I thought I was doing the right thing for you. It wasn't. You aren't meant to be here forever alone. You'll always be mine, and I'll always be yours."

Her eyes filled with tears. She longed for this moment. Even when he wasn't there and she filled the empty space with stargazing and cliff jumps, she still ached for him. It was the blood, stronger than anything she could have ever imagined. Maybe she didn't understand the mechanics of her new life or the body she possessed. There was one thing so clear to her now it was blinding.

Tony was a literal part of her. Although she knew there wasn't a soul inside her anymore, her body was home to his blood. She cradled and carried it with her, like she once carried the soul now lost. In the end, only Tony made her feel whole.

"I take it back," she said, her arms around his neck. "I take it all back."

"What?"

"I don't want to be alone. Wherever you are, that's home to me." She leaned into him and pressed her cheek against his chest. "They were just words, weren't they?"

"Yes, they were just words."

"You're my ocean, Tony. You're wild and so deep I feel like I might drown sometimes, but you're what I want."

He held her back, eyes dancing across her face. "Come back with me," he said. "This pack needs you."

Sadie had been fighting the house for so long it was almost ingrained in her to say no. She was unsure of that place, of the memories it held. All the time she was away from Tony, one thing became clearer. He belonged to his pack, and she belonged to him. There would be no separating any of them. Wherever Tony went, Sadie would always be with him. Their blood was a magnet, pulling them closer even as they struggled against it. She didn't want to be in the house, probably never would. It still frightened her to think back on that room bathed in candlelight, where she first saw Sarah and watched Hayden die. That cold room where Sadie took her last human breath might be her enemy forever. She needed Tony though. She wanted him even when the reason why was impossible to answer.

"I'll try. Can that be enough for now?"

Tony knew it would never be enough until she was like all of them, but for now, it would do. He kissed the back of her hand and said, "Yes."

"Then take me home."

When they arrived at the house, Tony felt Sadie stiffen as they reached the front door. The others were gone, out on the strip hunting for their dinners. He fed earlier and sensed she had too. That was important, because he needed time to introduce her to the house properly. She had to see it as a home and not a prison with ornate walls. More than anything, he wanted her to see the old house like he did. It was their Neverland, a place where they could be themselves and truly free.

He led her through the front door and bypassed the parlor. Her human life ended in that room. It was crucial to introduce her to the other rooms before reacquainting her with the space that held her last human moments. They walked down a hallway to a large door. Candles littered every surface. The walls were comprised mostly of built-ins, like at Rick's house. The shelves held books and other relics from their pasts.

"I figured you'd like this room the best," he said as she stepped inside. "Alex is the only one that really uses the library anymore."

For a moment her thoughts drifted back to the parlor and what happened there. She closed her eyes and fought those images away. It would never leave, the memory of Hayden's death, but for now she had to push those moments away. There was no room in that house for Sadie's mourning. Not just for Hayden or Sarah. Her own death must be tucked away as well.

When she opened her eyes, she gave herself permission to really take the space in. So much history and lost secrets were hidden in the walls. That was beautiful. Nestled within the other books was the one she loaned Tony. She ran her finger down the spine then plucked it from the shelf. She flipped through the pages, found their poem, and began reading aloud.

"Once upon a midnight dreary, while I pondered, weak and weary, over many a quaint and curious volume of forgotten lore,"

Tony recited the last line. "And my soul from out that shadow that lies floating on the floor, shall be lifted,"

"Nevermore," she finished and smiled at him. On one of the shelves was a framed photo of all four of them, taken on the pier, Alex just slightly at the forefront. "Tell me why you love him. Is it just that his blood gave you life, or is it him?"

Tony sighed and then joined her next to the shelf. He remembered the photograph and the night it was taken. Dylan had ingested the gift two weeks before, and they were celebrating. There was so much blood spilled that night all over the coastline. Why did he love Alex? Could he ever explain such complicated reasoning with someone like her?

"Do you remember the night you met him, at that party?"

"I remember."

"You were shocked that he was so young. Alex was only nineteen when Rick saved him. It was 1868, a few years after the Civil War. Alex was sick with tuberculosis, but he refused to leave his house even when they threatened to drag him to the sanatorium. Rick offered salvation, and I don't think either of them thought about what that really meant at the time. Imagine being so sick that your body can't gain muscle and grow into the man you're becoming. It fucked with Alex for a long time. He's 151 immortal years, more powerful and stronger than a hundred men, yet when he walks into a room no one even notices him."

"Isn't that a good thing?" she wondered. "I mean, for a vampire, isn't being unnoticeable an edge? No one would ever suspect him of being dangerous."

Tony gave a nod. "That's true, but Alex isn't nineteen years old. The man inside that body wants to be desired, like we are. Not by girls, but by women. When we go to a bar to find pretty meals, he's never with us. You see, as powerful as he is, there are still things he can't do simply because of his immortality. Does that make sense?"

"Did he ever want to sire a girl?"

"Yes, he did."

"My sister, right?"

"Sadie, you have to let that go. I know what I'm asking, and I know it will take time. I blamed Alex for Mary Ann, and then I blamed myself. There's no room for blame in this life. Promise me you'll never talk to Alex about Sarah."

She lifted her chin, ready to argue, but the feeling faded when she saw the sincerity in his eyes. "I promise."

He took her hand and toured her through the first floor, up to the second where she stepped into what was now her bedroom. Tony lit the candles, and she sat down on the bed. Her hands caressed the bedding, dark blue and silky. The room was full of antiques and treasures collected over the years. Tony brought many of them from Italy when he was still human.

"How did you find this house?"

He sat down beside her. "I was here when Rick owned it." He closed his eyes and pictured the house as it once was. "I wish you could have seen it, Sadie. The floors were imported marble, and the walls were covered in all the great artists. Rick kept this place a members-only club and over time, after technology bloomed, people forgot about it. You know, that's the thing about secrets. If you're good at keeping them safe, they'll never hurt you. We wanted this house, me and Alex. We killed every member who knew it existed."

"You killed all those people just to protect this house? Why not have Rick build you a new one, like he has?"

"Sometimes you have to be willing to do anything to keep something important."

"I dreamed this house. She died here, didn't she?"

He knew she was talking about Mary Ann, about his memories she accessed. "She did, but I don't want to talk about her."

"I know Dylan was turned in 2004, Rick told me. Where was Oscar?"

"We met him in Brooklyn. It was 1992, and he was trying to be a screenwriter. Turns out that wasn't his calling."

She leaned back into the pillows. "Can you tell me about it?"

Tony chewed his lip as he pondered her question. Was it right for him to share the story of how Oscar came into their world, or was it only his story to tell? He already told her more than Alex would want known. In the end, she needed to know them from Tony's point of view. He wasn't sure they would ever share it with her themselves.

"Rick was pretending to be a literary agent. At the time we would volley between coasts, and that summer we stayed in New York. We would pretend to be different people; we had plenty of money to make the scam work and it was fun. Rick took us to this event attended by publishers and agents. He thought we needed to broaden our palettes, so to speak. Anyway, Oscar was there shopping this script he'd written. He was dressed to the nines, and there was something about him that drew Alex in immediately."

"A darkness," she said softly. "Like what he saw in you."

Tony pushed the hair away from her shoulders. "Sort of, but Oscar's darkness was different. His was about hiding."

"From what?"

"From the life he didn't want to live. His father was CEO of this big medical distribution company, and he wanted Oscar to be just like him. That wasn't going to happen, though. You see, Oscar was creative and free. He hated knowing his life was already planned out for him. So, he left Chicago and went to New York to be a writer. He checked into the Plaza, of all places, with a suitcase filled with booze and his screenplay. In the drawer next to the bed was a gun."

"I don't understand."

"Oscar believed he had nothing left if he couldn't sell that script. His father was going to cut him off, and he couldn't give up being himself."

"He wanted to die."

Tony nodded. "If the script didn't sell at the event, yeah, that was his plan. Alex read his mind and used persuasion so Oscar would hang out with us that night. Alex gave him the option to die and live again. He didn't even need time to think it over. You see, Oscar knew we weren't damning him like his father was with all his rules and regulations. We were saving him. Like Alex saved me, and I saved you."

She sat up and leaned her cheek against his shoulder. They sat there like that for a while until they heard the door close downstairs. Tony felt her body go rigid beside him. "It's okay," he promised and took her hand in his. They went downstairs together and entered the parlor where his brothers gathered. They both felt the tension.

"Hey," said Tony, running his hand awkwardly through his hair. "I didn't think you guys would be back so soon."

"It's raining," said Alex. "The strip was deader than we are." His gaze fell on Sadie whose eyes showed how nervous she was. "Hello, Sadie, so nice to see you again."

She mumbled her hello and looked away, feeling like she was a stranger imposing on all of them.

"What's she doing here?" asked Oscar.

Tony glared hard. "This is her home as much as it's mine," he warned.

"Not much fun being alone, is it?" Alex asked with a smirk as he poured himself a glass of wine at the bar.

"No," she said, looking up at Tony and wondering if she was making a horrible mistake.

"Well, I'm glad she's here," Dylan smiled, lighting a cigarette. "Welcome home."

"Thanks, I appreciate that."

A wicked smile pulled at the corners of Alex's lips and settled over Sadie like the dark stare in his eyes. "You two seem awfully familiar. I thought you had only met that one time."

Sadie shivered, knowing he was referring to the night she drank the blood. She hated him fiercely for bringing it up.

Dylan could see her recoiling under Alex's veiled accusations. She was there, though. Their last conversation obviously meant something. This wasn't just Alex's pack after all, nor was the house only his home. It belonged to all of them and now it belonged to her too.

"We hung out while you guys were in Seattle," he shrugged.

Tony looked at Sadie with surprised eyes. "You did?"

"We sure did," Dylan jumped in before she could answer. "I taught her to fly, didn't I, girl?"

Sadie could feel all their eyes on her, but it was Tony's stare she met. Was he mad at her? She couldn't tell and she needed him to say something, anything, to let her know if things had changed in the seconds Dylan let their secret out of the bag.

Tony's lips spread apart into a smile. He flopped down onto the chaise lounge and pulled her next to him. "You jumped the cliffs, didn't you?"

She felt the relief run through her. "Yeah, I didn't want to, though."

"She just needed a push," Dylan said, and then he and Tony were laughing at the shared memory of Dylan's first flight.

Alex watched with silent contempt as Dylan and Sadie relayed the stories of their adventure atop the cliffs. He already knew everything anyway. After all, he was an invisible spectator of their annoyingly normal friendship. He grimaced as he remembered the night his mother first appeared.

Having Sadie in the house ruined everything Alex planned. How was he supposed to get her to Angela and get more potions if Tony was by her side every second? Now that she had Dylan as a sidekick, it would be even harder. The month was nearly up, and Alex could almost feel his mother's putrid breath on the back of his neck. There had to be a way to get this done.

He looked across the room at Oscar who was sitting on one of the barstools, dark eyes trained on Sadie. Alex wasn't sure what was hiding behind that sharp gaze. Was it suspicion or just apprehension at having this newbie suddenly thrust into their lives that had him glaring at her with hooded eyes? Knowing Oscar, it was anger that she walked into the house willingly. Her being there upset the delicate balance the four of them shared, and she had been nothing but trouble since she drank the blood.

Alex sat back in his chair feeling a little more relaxed. There was at least one other immortal in that house who wasn't ready to welcome Rick's princess with open arms, and he was counting on Oscar's distrust to help put his own plan into action. Alex was going to get that bitch to Angela, and his childe would help him do it.

The five of them stood at the end of the strip, their eyes sharp and searching for a group large enough to feed them all. Tony could sense Sadie's apprehension; her desire to feed alone was something that didn't change when she stepped into the house. He leaned down and whispered into her ear; a moment later she was heading off into the crowd alone.

"Where's she going?" asked Dylan, confused.

"To feed," Tony said.

Alex asked, "Is she too good to feed with us?"

"It's what she needs." Tony turned to face them. "What's the big deal?"

"We're a pack," said Oscar. "We're our strongest when we're together. How strong can we be when we have to spend all night worrying about her and why she wants to be separate from us?"

"It's not like that," Tony insisted. "She came to the house, didn't she? Sadie's trying, man. But shit takes time."

"I'm with Tony," Dylan announced, earning an eye roll from Alex. Of course, Dylan would side with Tony; he always did. "It's not a big deal really. So, she has some eating issues. She's a girl, dude. None of 'em like eating in front of guys."

"Your insight into the female psyche is astounding, Dylan," said Oscar.

"Thanks, my man." Dylan was never good at discerning sarcasm.

Alex stepped forward. "You know what? I think I'll take a page out of Peanut's playbook. Let's all just go out on our own tonight. What's the big deal, right?" He saw the pinch in Tony's brow and knew he had struck a nerve.

"Don't do this, Alex," Tony warned. "She's mine. It's my job to look out for her and make sure she's okay. You made sure of that when you gave her my blood."

Alex's lips curved into a snarl as the cause of complaint was placed solely on his shoulders. If he had known then what he knew now, he would never have given her Tony's blood. He wouldn't have given her Rick's either. It would have been his blood and his control. Alex couldn't argue Tony's point, though, so he did what any good leader would do when faced with an impossible scenario. He turned his back on it. They stood side by side and watched Alex move through the crowd, his hair dancing with the breeze.

"She's already tearing us apart," Oscar said. "Get her in line, Tony. There won't be anything left of this pack if you don't." He shook his head with disappointment before running off to catch up with Alex.

Tony and Dylan stood beside one another in silence. Part of Tony understood where they came from. They did everything together and rarely split up. Then again, Alex was the one who brought Sadie into their pack even if it wasn't his original intention. He knew what it meant to be a sire, what the connection felt like, and he was still holding it against Tony for trying to play the part right. All Tony could do was help her adjust, and if feeding alone was what she needed to sleep day after day in his bed beside him, he would give it to her. What other choice did he have?

Dylan sighed. "I know you don't want to hear this, but Oscar's right. We can't be a pack if a part of us keeps breaking off. She needs to trust us."

"What the fuck do you guys want from me?" Tony asked with irritation. "For fuck's sake, I never wanted any of this. This is all Alex's fault!"

"You're right," Dylan said. "It is his fault. But she's your problem. I like Sadie, man. She's sweet and funny, but eventually she'll have to be ruthless if she's going to survive." He clapped Tony on the back. "Just talk to her. Get her to understand."

With one last encouraging smile, Dylan walked away and left Tony feeling, once again, like he was losing everything that mattered to him.

"What's she doing?" asked Oscar as he and Alex watched Sadie from a distance.

She had been standing in the same spot for half an hour, biting nervously on her lip as she eyed the crowds passing her. There had been a dozen easy marks that walked by. She seemed oblivious to them. Her choice of meal was confusing them both. As a baby vampire, it should have been in her nature to go for prey that would be easy to take down. The drunken girl leaning over a trash can a few feet away from her, or the young man in his letter jacket that spent all the money in his pocket to throw basketballs into hoops with the hope of winning a giant stuffed rabbit. It was like she didn't see them.

"I don't know," Alex said thoughtfully. He was as intrigued by her hunting method as he was confused by it.

"Well, as much fun as I'm having spying on Tony's little lady, I'm hungry." Oscar ran his hand over his stomach, certain Alex could hear it rumbling even over the noisy crowd.

"Wait," said Alex, his eyes widening as he watched the subtle way Sadie suddenly straightened. "I think she's found her mark."

Sadie took a step forward, eyes trained on the alley between the saltwater taffy shop and a burger joint. Soon she was walking with a steady speed that quickly became a run as she disappeared into the shadows.

"Well, this should be interesting," Alex chuckled, following her with Oscar trailing behind.

Sadie entered the narrow passage between shops, her nocturnal vision giving her a clear image of the three drunken men surrounding a teenage boy. They were taking turns pushing him until finally one of them landed a punch to the boy's face that sent him tumbling to the ground.

"What's the matter? Wishing your mommy was here to save you?"

The kid looked up, tears and blood smearing his cheeks. "I don't have any money," he said, pleading with them to leave him alone.

"That's too bad for you," one of the other men laughed. "If you had money, we would call it Even-Steven. You've wasted our time, though, and now we're just gonna kick your ass."

Sadie didn't wait any longer to make her presence known. She stepped forward, her sneakers squeaking against the wet asphalt and alerting everyone that she was there. "Leave him alone," she said, her voice so soft it barely made it above the roar of the bar patrons one brick wall away.

"Look what we have here," the biggest man smiled. She could smell the beer on his breath even from a distance. "Are you his big sister or something, honey?"

"No," she responded stiffly.

He laughed and looked at his friends. "Baby, you just made our night." He smiled, two black holes where his teeth once were before the meth rotted them away. "We'll fuck you silly after we finish with this piece of shit. Would you like that?"

Sadie's keen eyes were trained on the man speaking and the crying boy at his feet. As his cronies started to move toward her, she felt her body begin its shift. It started with her eyes, a change that came about so subtly none of them noticed. It wasn't until they had her surrounded that she heard one of the men gasp in surprise. She looked right at him, amber eyes blazing as her mouth opened to reveal the weapons she was holding.

He stumbled back into his friend, smashing the man into the wall. Sadie sprang forward, ripping out his throat before the scream could meet the air. She grabbed the hair of the man behind him and smashed his head as hard as she could into the brick, knocking him out instantly.

When she turned on the leader, it was to share her bloody smile. "Still want to fuck me silly?"

He had no time to answer as she pounced on him, holding his thrashing body still beneath her as she drank from the gaping wound in his throat. When she lifted her head to the crying boy, she said, "Go!"

He crawled backward until he found his footing and sprinted toward the opposite end of the alley. Sadie heard movement behind her and watched as the unconscious man woke up and went running. She was on her feet and after him when she slid to a stop, blocked by the figure standing in front of her.

Alex was holding the man by his neck, smiling at Sadie with a grin that made the warm blood she'd just ingested go cold. He shifted in the time it took her to blink and dug his fangs into the man's neck with a satisfying crunch.

She walked backward away from him as he let the body fall to the ground with a pronounced thud. He started walking toward her, one hand wiping a trickle of blood from his chin and licking it off his fingers. She turned and ran in the same direction the boy had, wanting to get away from Alex and find Tony. What was Alex doing there in the first place?

She didn't get far. Oscar stood at the opposite end of the alley with the dead body of the crying boy in his arms.

"You forgot one," he growled, his eyes glowing against the darkness.

She turned over her shoulder watching as Alex came closer. Just moments before, she was the hunter, and now she felt like prey. She charged toward him, panic fueling her on. Just as she was about to side-step him and escape back into the noisy safety of the strip, he had her around the waist, his other hand coming up to cover her mouth.

"Not so fast, Peanut," he whispered against her ear, smiling at Oscar as he came toward them. "I think we have a few things we need to talk about."

Chapter Twenty-Six

Alex kept his hand over Sadie's mouth while Oscar began the process of disassembling her crime scene and throwing the pieces in the trash. Luckily for them, the dumpster wasn't full, and the bloody limbs could be easily hidden beneath trash bags. By the time someone noticed the odor, they'd be long gone. It wasn't how they would normally dispose of their kills, but being in an alley with hundreds of people walking by called for creativity.

"It's alright," Alex said, his free hand wiping the tears off her cheeks. "We're going to go find Tony and Dylan just as soon as Oscar finishes cleaning up your mess."

Sadie wasn't comforted by Alex's words. She knew she had made a terrible mistake, one she might not be able to bounce back from in their eyes. When the last arm was deposited into the dumpster, Alex removed his hand and turned her around to face him.

"You realize you just fucked up big time, right?"

She bit down on her shaky bottom lip and nodded her head. "Yes, and I'm sorry." Her eyes swept over to Oscar who was trying to clean blood off his hands with a discarded newspaper. "I wasn't thinking. The hunger just took over, and I acted on instinct."

Oscar rolled his eyes. "We can't stand in this damn alley all night."

"No, we can't," Alex agreed. "But we can't go back out there with her looking like Carrie after prom. I'll go get something to clean up with."

"Good," said Oscar. "And while you're gone, me and the Peanut are going to have a talk."

As Alex walked away, Sadie felt relief that, for now, he was gone. His presence had a way of soaking up the air and suffocating anyone in the vicinity. Her relief was short-lived when she looked back at Oscar, whose eyes were on fire as he stalked toward her. She barely had time to take a step back before his hand was on her chest, pushing her roughly against the brick wall.

"Do you even realize what you just did?"

"I... I should have killed them somewhere else. I know that. It was the hunger,"

"Save it," Oscar snapped. He barred his arms around her, caging her against the wall with no escape route. "It has nothing to do with your location choice. Although, killing in an alley while the entire strip is at its liveliest is certainly ballsy. You could have handled the cleanup, though."

Sadie was still frightened, but confusion was overtaking that emotion. "Then why are you so angry?"

"The kid," Oscar hissed and leaned in close. "You let him get away."

"I would have gone after him," she lied. "I was going to, I swear."

"You're lying," he ground out the words. Then he grabbed her face, squeezing her cheeks tight. "I'm not going to let you ruin this pack, do you hear me? Tony's blinded by his bond with you, but I see you, Sadie. I see you bright and clear."

"I'm sorry." She was more afraid of Oscar in that moment than she had ever been of anyone else, even Alex.

"Kill who you want. None of us can take that away from you. If being a fanged Batgirl and taking out bad guys is your thing, go for it. But we don't leave survivors, ever. Do you hear me?"

"Yes," she whimpered, a tear dropping down her cheek.

Oscar let go of her face and stepped away. She kept her back pressed against the brick. Her only relief came from regaining personal space. Minutes later Alex emerged from the end of the alley with a bottle of water and a stack of napkins. His eyes locked on Oscar, who gave a soft nod, letting his sire know his alone time with Sadie had been a success. Whatever Oscar said that left Sadie silently crying would be instrumental in Alex gaining more of her trust. Every bad cop needed a good cop, after all.

"Go find Tony and Dylan," said Alex roughly. Oscar lifted his brow at the harsh tone, but saw the corners of Alex's lips twitching and quickly caught on to the game. Oscar nodded and then, for good measure, glared hard at Sadie before disappearing down the alley. Alex motioned her to him. "Come on, let's get you cleaned up."

She looked at him warily, waiting for him to begin chastising the way Oscar had. But Alex wasn't looking at her with malice. The look in his eyes was one of concern, and she took a hesitant step forward.

"It's okay," he assured, opening the bottle of water and drenching one of the napkins. "We'll get you cleaned up, and Tony won't ever have to know."

"You're not going to tell him?"

He shook his head and began wiping the damp napkin over her cheek until it was soaked with blood, and he got a new one. "Lean your head back," he instructed. Gingerly, Alex wiped at the dried blood until her skin was clean. "There, just like it never happened."

"Thank you," she said, still nervous.

Alex shrugged his shoulders and threw the bloody napkins and empty water bottle into the dumpster. "We all fuck up, Sadie. We all make mistakes. But you understand now that this can't happen again. Tony should have explained our ways better to you."

"It's not his fault," she said with a sigh. "And it won't happen again."

"Then no harm done," he smiled.

"But what if Oscar tells them what happened?"

"Oscar won't do anything unless I tell him to. He knows better than that. Look, Tony cares about you. He wants you with us and I care about him. So, making you feel safe is all that really matters right now. You could be good for this pack. Maybe you're just what we need."

Sadie swallowed hard, grateful for his words but uncomfortable with the wide toothy smile that seemed so mocking. Then she noticed movement behind him and felt her body stiffen as Sarah stepped out of the shadows.

Don't listen to him, Sadie. He's lying to you. He'll tell Tony everything, and then they'll all punish you. Alex saw her eyes focusing on something and turned over his shoulder, half expecting to see a host of ghosts glaring at him. Then he remembered they could not get to him while Angela's magic was working.

"What is it?" he asked her. "What do you see?"

"It's nothing."

Get out of that house! Go back to the bunker where you're safe. How will you ever be able to destroy them when you're busy playing house with our murderers?

"Can we go now?" Sadie asked, looking up into Alex's face. "Please."

"Sure, sugar." He reached down and took her hand. "Let's get you back to Tony."

She let him lead her toward the lighted end of the alley. When she glanced back, Sarah was still standing there, joined now by others, including Hayden. They all stared at her with accusing eyes. Without a thought she gripped Alex's hand tighter. He looked down at her with smiling reassurance. He was delighted with how easy it was to mold Sadie to his side. At this rate he would have her at Angela's in days. He would never have to worry about the poison her blood infected him with again.

Alex stood on the witch's doorstep with his head hung low. He thought it would be a simple process after his bonding moment with Sadie, but he was wrong. She clung to Tony every second. The only time she was away from him was when she fed, and it seemed she had mastered the art of killing in an hour or less. As soon as he thought he might have time to find her, she was already back at her sire's side. Angela opened the front door, eyed Alex for a moment, and then slammed it right in his face. He pounded his fist against the door until she opened it again.

With one lifted brow she said, "What are you doing here?"

"It's wearing off. I can feel them. I can't see them yet, but they're there."

"Of course, they are," she laughed. "They can't wait for my magic to break down. Especially that mother of yours."

Alex closed his eyes and shook his defeated head. "Come on, sugar. Have a fucking heart. Can I please get another dose?"

Angela crossed her arms over her chest and leaned her shoulder into the door frame. "I just gave Tony my last dose. Sorry." She went to close the door when Alex stuck his foot out stopping her.

"You gave Tony the rest of your potion?"

"Well, unlike you, Tony kept his part of our deal. And, just between you and me, he's a wild cat in the sack." She giggled to herself. "Now get your foot out of my damn door before I send you flying."

Alex withdrew his foot but pushed against the door with his hand. "I'm trying to get her to you, but it's not that easy. She's a lot smarter than I thought."

Angela smirked. "Women always are."

"Please, I'll get you her blood, I just need more time. And maybe a little help."

She studied him for a moment before finally opening the door fully to let him enter. Angela shut the door and started toward the kitchen, Alex right behind her. He wrinkled his nose as the fumes of whatever she was cooking on the stove met his nostrils.

"Have a seat," she said, nodding to the kitchen table. "I'm just cooking up what you came for."

He sighed with relief and slumped down in one of the chairs. He ran his hands through his hair and watched as she looked down into the cast iron pot. "So, you're fucking Tony?"

She put the lid on the pot and grabbed her cigarettes off the counter. "It wasn't originally part of our deal, but it just seems to happen every time he's here." She lit her cigarette and gave him a wink.

Alex sat back in his chair. "If Sadie finds out, she'll be heartbroken."

"So, tell her," Angela mused. "Maybe she'll fuck you in retaliation. Wouldn't that be ideal? I do love the idea of one woman eviscerating a vampire pack with nothing but her cunt."

"She's not like that. Stupid bitch is gobsmacked for Tony. She wouldn't sleep with me to get back at him. All she'd do is go back to her hole in the ground."

Angela grabbed a bottle of Scotch off the counter and poured two glasses. Then she sat down in the chair next to Alex and handed him a glass. "Why don't you tell her though? If she left, wouldn't that solve part of your problem?"

Alex picked up his glass and stared down into the pale gold pool. "It would hurt Tony if she left again, and that would hurt the pack."

She laughed softly and downed her Scotch. "And they say vampires are heartless creatures. Little do they know."

"Will you help me?" he asked, looking up at her.

"I don't know," she said. "Truth is, I don't really like vampires much. You're all just egotistical vultures who think all the answers to life's mysteries live only in your head. Still, your blood is very powerful, and I wouldn't be here now if not for that."

"Look, I don't give a shit about Sadie," he glared. "But she's Tony's childe and it would destroy him to lose her."

"Just as it would destroy you to lose him," she said thoughtfully. "And while it's frowned upon for parents to have favorites, he's yours."

"Yes," he said through clenched teeth.

"There's more though. You don't want to lose him to her. You would have killed her a long time ago if you didn't think it would send him down a hole you could never save him from. But above all, you're jealous."

"Jealous of Rick's little princess? I don't think so."

"You're jealous because Tony's bond with her is stronger than it is with you. You're jealous that Rick chose her for his blood and that's the real reason you gave her Tony's. Oh Alex, you couldn't stand the idea that your master could love someone more than he loves you. Now you're stuck in the great sea of irony, atop a boat of regret, because you made all of this happen. You silly egotistical vulture."

Alex ground his teeth, the sharp lines of his jaw pressing against skin. He hated the smirk on her face and hated even more that all he could do was sit there and take it. "There has to be a way I can get her blood to you without Tony or her ever knowing."

"I have a way, but it still won't be easy. You'll have to get Tony and Sadie apart, and according to you that's not really happening."

"I'll make it happen," he said. "Just tell me what to do."

"Follow me," Angela curled her finger at him.

He followed her through the house, down the hall, and into her bedroom. The bed was still mussed from Tony's visit. He knew sex with Angela meant nothing to Tony. It might not mean anything to Sadie either, if she weren't a defective vampire. She wasn't like any vampire he had ever known. She was different. The mortal she once was lived beneath the surface. She was a vessel of light and darkness, always fighting the natural instincts of both sides.

Angela opened the glass cabinet filled with various vials and grabbed one. "This will put her to sleep." She crossed the room and handed it to him.

"How does it work?" He lifted the bottle to his eyeline and watched the black liquid inside bubble.

"You know what chloroform is?"

He looked at her like she was stupid. "Yes, I know what chloroform is. But it won't work on a vampire."

"You know, kiddo, it's no wonder Rick chose you of all people to lead a pack. That big old brain of yours must keep you really busy with all that thinking it does."

"Go fuck yourself," Alex snarled, knowing sarcasm when he heard it.

"Testy, testy," she laughed and sat down on the red velvet sofa. "That potion you hold is like chloroform. Only this is specially made for supernatural creatures such as yourself."

"So what? I just put it over her face, and she goes to sleep?"

"Pretty much."

Alex smiled wide and tossed the bottle into the air before catching it again in his hand. He stuffed it into his pocket and said, "Done deal, witch. I'll have her here before the week is out."

"Oh, Alex. Sometimes I ask myself how you ever made it this long."

"What the hell is that supposed to mean?"

"It means nothing is ever that simple, you arrogant piece of shit. If smothering sweet Sadie with that potion was all it took, don't you think Tony would have taken me up on my offer to do the same thing?"

"Why would he? You're giving him the potion in exchange for blood and dick. Seems like a pretty good deal to me."

She leaned forward and fixed him with a hard stare. "She sees them, too, you idiot. And these spirits that follow her are very clever. They'll drive her into the sun, after they get her to stake all of you."

Alex felt his entire body seize a little. "Stake us? That bitch could never kill us."

"Vengeance is one of the most powerful emotions in the world, Alex. The need to protect one's family is even stronger. Think about those mothers who inherit superhuman strength to lift cars off their children. Sadie's family has been acquainted with you and your pack for years, even before she was born. They don't just want revenge, sweetie; they want the absolute extinction of your pack."

"And Tony knows this?" he asked, fuming at the realization that his childe had brought a ticking time bomb into the house and knew it.

"He knows the basics. I told him she was in danger; I failed to mention that he was, too." She shrugged her shoulders with a giggle. "Silly me, I just lose my train of thought whenever that Italian fox is anywhere near me."

"This family of hers, how do we know them?"

Angela stubbed her cigarette out in the ashtray. "I think it goes back farther than even I can see. Maybe all the way to Rick."

"Rick?"

"Families are lineages dating back thousands of years. Somewhere along that timeline we've all connected. But let's not go back that far," she said with a wave of her hand. "Let's start with you."

"You're saying I killed someone in her family."

"Most definitely," Angela said. "And not just one, either. It seems like you've been drawn to Sadie's bloodline." She could see Alex trying to work it out in his mind, flipping through the images of his kills and coming up empty. "Think, Alex. Think really, really hard."

Suddenly his eyes widened, and Angela gave a nod of her head, knowing the light bulb had just been switched on. "The artist on the beach," he said, more to himself than her. "She's Sadie's sister."

"Give that boy a gold star," she laughed. "But she's not even the start of it. Remember that sweet pregnant woman and her little girl that you and Tony met in the 50s? The ones you killed and never told anyone else about? You've kept that secret from Rick all these years because you know kids aren't on his approved food group."

Alex's face drew down. "Yeah, I remember."

"That was Sadie's grandmother, and the little girl was her mom."

"I think your crystal ball is fuzzy," he said with a casual laugh. "Tony chased that little girl into the woods and killed her, so you see, no way she's Sadie's mother."

"Did he?" Angela asked with a raised brow. "Or did your fledgling lie to you, because even as dark as he is, none of them will ever be as dark as you?"

Alex sat back, his mind trying to focus on that night almost fifty years earlier. There had been blood on Tony's lips, but Alex had never seen the little body it belonged to. He glared at the witch, knowing she was right.

"So, Tony doesn't know her dead family is trying to kill us all?"

"I'm afraid not. He only knows that I could make a potion, special for Sadie, that would block them from her. But he's not willing to sacrifice a drop of her blood, even for that. It all goes back, my simple-minded friend, to the egotistical vulture theory. He thinks he is strong enough to protect her. But he's wrong."

Alex felt his stomach drop. He hated Sadie, but Tony was his childe and he knew that losing her could be the thing that took his firstborn from him forever. If Angela could stop Sadie from seeing the spirits, and it would ensure the safety of the pack, then Alex would make sure it was done. "Will you make it for her? If I get her here and you get the blood, will you give her that potion?"

She gave him a sideways grin. "Maybe you're not as dumb as I thought."

"Will you do it?"

"I'll do it," she said and reached out her hand. "Partners?"

He looked at her hand then back at her face. After a pause, he shook it while his lips formed a grin to match her own. "Partners."

Chapter Twenty-Seven

Oscar listened as Alex told him everything. He started with the night he nearly drained Sadie and ended with Angela telling him she would help him only if he brought her Sadie's blood. Oscar was sitting on a tree stump while Alex paced in front of him, grey eyes glistening with tears he would never let fall. There was so little time left before the potion wore off and the ghosts came back. He was nowhere near Sadie alone. He needed help. And Oscar was the only one of his children he could trust when it came to the topic of Sadie.

Oscar let the story settle over him. It was almost too much to take in. Every word that came from Alex's lips felt surreal. How was it possible that they had been connected to Sadie for centuries, maybe longer? And more importantly, how had they let something so dangerous infiltrate their pack?

"I can't help you, Alex," Oscar finally said, seeing the shock and then anger take over his sire's face. "I'm sorry, man. But what you're proposing is more than dangerous, it's betrayal."

"Like hell it is! I'm trying to save that little bitch as much as I'm trying to save myself. What happens if these spirits get her to walk into the sun, huh? What do you think that will do to Tony?"

"I don't know, but what happens when Tony finds out you're drugging his childe and taking her to the witch so she can siphon bits of her at a time? You want to talk about something that will destroy this pack, that's it right there."

"He doesn't have to know," Alex said. "Neither of them will ever know."

Oscar looked away. "It just doesn't feel right. Like it's all too easy to be the real deal."

"Easy?" Alex laughed. "Trust me, none of this is fucking easy."

"Do you trust her?" asked Oscar. "Do you really trust this witch? Do you trust she won't take so much blood she kills Sadie?"

Alex thought about it for a moment. He didn't trust Angela at all. She was cunning and had been alive for centuries without having to sacrifice her soul to do it. Alex knew she was smarter than him, but she was also the only one who could keep them all safe. She blocked the spirits from reaching him or Tony, and she could do the same for Sadie. Alex had no choice but to trust her. And Oscar had no choice but to trust him.

"I won't let her go that far," Alex assured. "I gave you this life and saved you from your own hand. You owe me, Oscar, and it's time to pay up."

"What do you want me to do?" Oscar relented.

"You're going to tell Tony you want to spend some time with her, just the two of you."

"Are you serious?"

"Think about it," Alex said, relishing in a plan that was foolproof. "He's so desperate for her to bond with us, to become part of this pack. He'll throw her at us if he thinks it's what we want, too."

"Isn't it what we want? Why bother saving her if you don't?"

Alex grumbled in annoyance. Leave it to Oscar to take something relatively simple and turn it into a theological discussion. "I want Tony to be happy," he said bluntly. "I want all my children to be happy. And for whatever reason, Sadie makes him happy."

"Fine," Oscar sighed. "So, I get her alone and then what?"

"We use Angela's potion to knock her out, fly her to Seattle, give Angela what she wants and voila! We're all free from that poisoned blood."

"The Angela part of this still seems too easy, Alex. You really believe she'll keep curing you guys just for some of Sadie's blood? Eventually she's going to want something more."

Alex lifted his eyes to the moon. He knew Oscar was right. Angela would eventually up the price, and Alex could only guess what that would be, none of it good for their pack. But right now, she was the only thing keeping him sane. Alex would give Angela whatever she wanted to make sure his mother stayed away. Even if what she wanted was Sadie.

Alex was right about Tony relinquishing Sadie to Oscar for the evening so he could get to know her. Because she was still so new, Sadie fell asleep before they did and woke up an hour later, too. It gave Alex time to pretend to go see Rick, while Tony and Dylan headed over to the next town. That was Alex's suggestion. They were killing too many people in Brave Beach and Rick wanted them to start spreading out. Not a lie so much as a preemptive jump. Rick hadn't said any of that yet, but Alex knew it was coming.

Tony knew Sadie wouldn't want to be without him for a bonding session with Oscar, so he left. He trusted that Oscar would explain it all to her. The importance of her knowing the boys was crucial to her continued blending into their family.

"That couldn't have gone better," Alex laughed deeply as he entered the house through the back door once Tony and Dylan were gone. "I told you he would take the bait."

"Still feels wrong," he mumbled.

"Right or wrong, it's fucking happening," Alex said. "And you're my partner in this so don't go soft and mushy on me now."

Upstairs they heard Sadie's feet shuffling against the floor. Alex reached into his pocket for the bottle of Angela's potion and the rag he'd kept with him from the moment they made their deal. He gave Oscar a knowing stare and quietly slipped into the shadows just as Sadie stepped into the parlor.

She looked around, her eyes searching for Tony, but all she saw was Oscar sitting on the chaise lounge. He was leaning forward with his elbows on his knees and dark eyes fixed on her. "Where's Tony?" she asked politely.

"Gone."

Sadie could feel the tiny hairs on her arms standing on end. Something about the air didn't feel right. She swallowed the lump building in her throat and purposefully walked backward out of the room.

"See you later," she said, her eyes glued to him.

The only part of him that moved was his eyes as they followed her. She was almost in the entrance hall when Oscar was suddenly standing directly in front of her. He moved so fast, but the only thing he disturbed were the flames of the candles as they wavered against his sudden wind.

He said nothing, just kept that dangerous glare on her face, watching as the uncertainty and fear began to etch across her features. Sadie took a step backward, taking another as he inched closer. It was his silence that unnerved her the most. She kept backing up until her body met with something solid. Sadie knew who it was even before she turned to face him. Alex smiled at her, the white rag held in the palm of his hand.

"What's going on?" she asked, her voice not far above a trembling whisper.

"Don't ask questions you don't want the answers to," he said. "This doesn't have to be hard, and when you wake up you won't even remember it happened. So there really isn't any reason to fight, Peanut. It just brings unnecessary pain, and you don't want that, do you?"

"What are you talking about?" Her feet were sliding against the hardwood floor as she backed away from him. She couldn't hold in her scream when she felt hands suddenly gripping her arms and holding them at her sides. "Stop!" she shrieked, trying to pull out of Oscar's grasp while her brain frantically searched for reasoning.

"I'm trying to help you," Alex told her, lifting the rag up and moving forward as the candlelight flickered in his eyes. "You may not understand now, but one day you will. You'll thank me."

"Tony! Tony!" It was all Sadie knew to do. To cry for her sire.

"Hurry the hell up. Tony will sense her fear," Oscar snarled while Sadie thrashed her head from side to side.

"Hold her damn head still," Alex barked, frustration growing as he tried to smash the rag against her face.

Oscar let one arm go and gripped a handful of hair at the back of her head. Her wide eyes filled with tears as Alex came toward her holding the rag. The rancid scent of decay and rot was all she could smell as the rag was placed over her nose and mouth. Even with her vampire strength, she was no match for the older vampires. Oscar kept her immobile as Alex looked at her, his lips curling into a sideways smile when her eyes began to flutter. She felt like she was falling into a cool black abyss, and Alex's image grew smaller as the darkness swallowed her.

"Give her to me," Alex said, dropping the rag back into his pocket and reaching out with both arms.

Oscar was glad to be rid of her and pushed her toward his sire with a rough shove. "What now?"

"We take her to the witch," said Alex as he hoisted Sadie up into his arms. "And we do it fast."

Alex didn't use Angela's front door this time. He and Oscar landed in her expansive backyard so no one would catch sight of them carrying around a comatose girl. Alex carried Sadie up the back steps and kicked the door with his foot. He glanced behind at Oscar who was rocking nervously.

"Get a hold of yourself," Alex snapped.

The door opened and they met with Angela's satisfied smile. "Look who finally came through." She eyed Sadie's sleeping form in Alex's arms and seemed to marvel at the sight of her. "Funny, I didn't imagine her like this at all." She looked over Alex's shoulder at Oscar and said, "Hello, handsome. You must be the strong, silent type."

"Quit fucking around," Alex said as he shifted Sadie in his arms. "Take her blood so we can get back to Brave Beach."

Angela stepped back and opened the door wide. When Oscar didn't follow his sire up the stairs she asked, "Are you coming?"

"I should stay here," he said, a feeling of deep unease coming over him as he met her eyes.

She gave him a pitied frown. "You don't have to be afraid, Oscar. I'm not going to do anything to Sadie that will cause her real harm.

She'll wake up tomorrow believing the two of you had a wonderful heart-to-heart."

"How are you going to do that?"

She smirked. "Magic."

"Oscar!" Alex called him from inside the house. "Get your ass in here."

Oscar knew he could not disobey his sire, so he reluctantly allowed his feet to propel him forward, up the porch steps and inside the house. Angela closed the door and pointed toward the hallway leading away from the kitchen.

"Take her into the living room," she said, then retrieved two glass mason jars.

Alex disappeared down the hall while Oscar watched Angela place the jars side by side on the counter. With a black sharpie she labeled each one as SADIE, and with an excited gleam pulled a silver-bladed dagger from the counter drawers.

"What are the jars for?" he asked.

"For her blood. Didn't your sire tell you why you were bringing Tony's precious muff here?"

"He told me," Oscar said, taking a hesitant step toward her. "But you can't really mean to fill both those jars with her blood. It's too much."

Angela huffed. "She's a vampire, sweetness. Two jars worth of blood isn't going to kill her. Weaken her? Sure. But it's nothing she won't bounce back from in a couple of days. Besides, I'm giving Alex a potion that will help her. By the time it wears off, I'll be due a new batch of Miss Sadie. If I take less blood, I'll need more of it sooner. Do you really want to do this again so soon?"

Oscar shook his head with bewilderment. "What are we supposed to tell Tony? How do we explain her being a veggie for two days?"

Angela sighed and leaned against the counter, her icy eyes fixing him with a deep stare. "Hasn't your sire ever told you about Thalxemia?"

"What the hell is that?"

"I'll take that as a no. Thalxemia is a condition some vampires get when feeding on diseased blood. It doesn't affect all vampires, but for some it makes them weak, fatigued, and sometimes leaves them close to their death sleep for several days. All Tony needs to know is that Sadie has Thalxemia. It makes complete sense."

Oscar's eyes started to burn amber. "Tony will never believe that shit."

"But he will," she said, matching his glare with her own. "Because he trusts his brothers implicitly and he'll have no choice but to believe his darling is sick. And since he won't know which human Happy Meal is going to set her off, any time she comes back here and goes home a little under the weather can be explained away."

His eyes cut from her back to the jars, which were looking incredibly large now that he knew what was going in them. "It's too much," he said again. "Just do one."

Angela's patience fizzled and she slammed her hand hard against the counter. "I'm taking two," she hissed. "Alex and I made a deal."

"Are you coming?" Alex yelled out. "The clock is ticking!"

Angela smiled at Oscar and picked the dagger up, clutching the handle between her teeth as she grabbed hold of the jars. At first, Oscar didn't want to follow. He didn't want to see what horrible things were about to happen. If he didn't see them, maybe there would be less guilt after. In the end, though, Oscar felt like he had to be there. Not particularly for Sadie, or even for Alex, but for Tony. If Alex wasn't looking out for her well-being, then he would.

Oscar stepped into the living room as Sadie was being laid out atop a round wooden table. Angela unscrewed the tops off the jars and sat them down beside Sadie's head. Alex occasionally poked her in the side to make sure she was still out.

"Do you have it?" Angela asked.

"What?"

"The potion, you imbecile. Do you still have it with you?"

Alex reached into his pocket and withdrew the vial filled with bubbling black liquid. His eyes cut to Oscar who pretended not to notice the way Angela talked to him, or how he took her words with nothing more than a small flinch.

"Give her some more," Angela ordered. "We don't want her waking up in the middle of our little transaction."

"You said she wouldn't wake up," Alex reminded.

"And she shouldn't. But better safe than sorry, yes? So, give her some more, and when I come back, we'll get started." With that, she turned her back on them and disappeared down the hallway toward her bedroom.

Alex doused the rag with the liquid again and smashed it against Sadie's face. "I wish I'd never given her Tony's blood. I wish he would have killed her that first night."

"But he didn't," Oscar said. "And you did give her his blood."

"Yeah, and now I'm paying the price. You have no idea what it's like to be bombarded by a past you were never supposed to know again."

"You're wrong," said Oscar, his voice soft but eyes hard. "We're all paying the price for your selfishness."

Alex moved away from Sadie and was about to confront his childe when Angela came back into the room. Only she was not alone this time. A man with long black hair wearing tight black pants and no shirt was with her. He ambled into the room, eyeing the two vampires with amazement.

"Who the fuck is this?" asked Alex.

Angela looked at the man and said, "This is my apprentice, Nick."

Oscar shifted nervously. "He shouldn't be here."

"Oscar's right," Alex said. "We didn't agree to this."

Angela wrapped her arm around Nick's waist and let her manicured index finger draw an invisible line from his belly button up his bare chest. "Nick is learning, and Sadie is a terrific study." She turned her attention back to Alex. "You don't make the rules here, vampire. This is my domain, and if you want my help, you'll keep your mouth shut until I tell you to open it. Besides, my baby knows how to keep a secret."

"Just do it," Alex growled. "Get her blood, give me the potions, and we'll get out of here."

"I love it when you play dominant," she winked. "But you're right. We've wasted enough time." She took Nick's hand and pulled him closer to the table. "So, why don't you get her shirt off, lover, and we'll get what we need."

Nick reached for the hem of Sadie's T-shirt but was stopped suddenly by the crushing grip of Oscar's hand around his wrist. "Why are you taking off clothing?" he asked, looking from Angela back to Alex. Wasn't it bad enough they were stealing her blood? Did they have to steal her dignity, too?

"So we don't get any blood on her clothes," Angela said flatly. "Besides, haven't you ever wondered what your sweet packmate looks like underneath those frumpy clothes? Consider this your opportunity."

Oscar's shift took him over and his fangs dropped without notice. He gnashed his teeth at Nick who took a huge step back, fear covering his face. Angela wasn't the least bit phased. In fact, she seemed almost amused by it all.

"I'll do it," Alex said. "Step back, Oscar."

Oscar looked at him with something that resembled hurt. "She's part of our pack, Alex. You're really gonna strip her on this table and let this crazy bitch and her psycho boy toy do this to Tony's childe?"

"Step back," Alex ordered again, his own eyes beginning to shimmer with an orange gleam. "She's right. We get Sadie's blood on her shirt and Tony will smell it." He pushed Oscar back with a force that had him nearly falling. "I want what this witch promised me."

Oscar pulled his shift back in, knowing he wouldn't win against his sire. He stepped away from the table as Alex grabbed a handful of Sadie's hair and pulled her body into a sitting position. He gripped the hem of her shirt and yanked it over her head, then tossed it to Oscar. She fell back onto the table with a loud smack that made him cringe.

"Hurry up," Alex said. "We have to get her back before Tony and Dylan get home."

With a final wink to Oscar, Angela moved to the table. Her seductive stance was replaced with strange professionalism, like she was a surgeon about to operate. She handed one jar to Nick who knelt next to the table with the jar poised beneath Sadie's outstretched arm.

Angela took the silver dagger and dug the tip into the crook until she felt it hit bone. Then she ripped it upward and a thick stream of crimson began to flow freely. Oscar and Alex both flinched as the scent hit the air. Alex had to look away, his mouth filling with saliva as he remembered how good that blood tasted.

Oscar couldn't look away though. He watched as the jar slowly started to fill, and when her blood reached the brim, Nick quickly slid the empty jar into place. Sadie's skin was losing the pink blush it usually held. She was turning a sickening grey, and by the time the second jar was full she resembled a corpse. Her arm was already healing, but Angela used a hand towel to clean up what was left. As soon as she moved, Oscar was next to the table trying to get Sadie's shirt back on.

When he couldn't quite get her arms into the sleeves, he looked at Alex sharply. "A little help, please?"

Alex didn't argue or reprimand Oscar for his tone. He helped him pull the shirt over her head. Angela returned from her bedroom with two vials. She gave Alex the orange liquid and he downed it in one long swig. She then handed him the other filled with a purple liquid that seemed to shimmer.

"Give it to her now," she said, pulling the cork from the vials. "It will last three full moons. You can come back next month for your own potion, but when it's time for Sadie's next dose, you'll bring her back to me. Do we understand each other?"

Alex looked at Oscar who was lifting Sadie into his arms and heading toward the back of the house. "I get it," he told Angela without looking at her.

"Good boy," she smiled.

The house was empty when they returned to Brave Beach. Oscar laid Sadie on the chaise lounge and stared hard at her face. There was nothing there to show she was alive in any way. The only way Oscar knew she wasn't dead was because she still existed. If Angela's draining had been lethal, Sadie would be nothing but ashes now.

"How do we explain this," he asked, looking over at Alex who was sipping whiskey from a bottle by the bar.

"Thalxemia," Alex mumbled. "That's what we tell him. And Rick will back us up. He'll think she has it, too."

"Why have you never told us about this before? What else haven't you shared with us, Alex?"

"I've taken care of you," Alex said. "I've always taken care of my children. From the moment I saw you in that hotel room, wanting to blow your head off or be saved, I saved you, Oscar."

"I know one thing for sure," Oscar said, touching the side of Sadie's face gently. "Our blood is the only thing that matters. And she's part of that."

Alex slumped down into his chair in the corner. "What would you have me do, Oscar? I'm trying to keep her safe. You don't know what these spirits are like. They would have driven her into the sun and Tony into his grave."

"And you?" Oscar asked.

"I would have followed them," he answered softly.

"You're a bastard, Alex. You ruined this girl, you know that, right?"

"No," he said with a frown. "I saved her just like I saved you. Her mortal life was a pathetic existence. She should be thanking me for this gift, not trying to punish me for giving it to her."

"She's yours, mine, and Dylan's just as much as Tony's," Oscar said sadly. "I felt it, Alex. When that bitch was touching her and those jars were filling up. I knew."

"You knew what?"

"She's our sister."

"She's my mistake," Alex corrected. "Sadie was never meant for this family. She goes out and kills the bad guys, so she doesn't have to feel guilty. But we don't feel guilt over the lives we take, and that's just one reason I know she'll never really be one of us."

"Regardless," Oscar said, rising to his feet. "You brought her into this pack, and we protect her, like we always protect each other. The witch said she has three months before the magic wears off and those spirits can get to her again. You had better figure out a way to fix this without sending Sadie back there. Because that witch won't stop with two jars and you know it. Next, it will be three and then four until she drains her dry."

Alex heard the veiled threat behind the seemingly innocent words. He stood up from his chair and pierced Oscar with sharp eyes. "And if I don't?"

"I'll go to Rick. I'll tell him everything you've done."

"I'm your sire," Alex warned. "I lead this pack."

"Yeah, and you're leading us straight to hell. Fix this, Alex. Or I will."

Alex was stunned into silence. Before he could tell his childe exactly where the hierarchy stood and just how far he could push Oscar down the ranks, they heard their brothers' laughter coming close to the house. Tony and Dylan came into the parlor, smiling and wiping fresh blood off their lips. When they saw Sadie lying there on the lounge, grey and motionless, no one was laughing anymore.

Chapter Twenty-Eight

Tony moved Sadie into their bedroom, and when the sun rose, they all slept. The next night Tony stayed behind with Dylan while Alex and Oscar headed into town. They would have stayed, but Tony made it clear he wanted them gone.

He held Sadie close, eyes fixed on her pale face. Thalxemia. That's what Alex said was wrong with her. She fed on blood that was diseased, and her body rejected it. Tony hated Alex for not telling them something on the list of top ten important things all vampires should know.

Dylan slowly sat down on the end of the bed. He didn't know what to say. He stood in the background while Tony went first for Oscar, asking what he'd done to Sadie. For his part, Oscar just stood there and took it while Tony held him against the wall and gnashed his fangs, demanding answers. Dylan looked at his sire, waiting for Alex to stop the madness, and eventually he did. But it was too late. The damage was done. Sadie was lost in a death sleep the sun couldn't wake her from.

"She'll be okay," Dylan promised. "You heard what Alex said. Give it a few days and she'll be back to normal."

"And why are we just now hearing about this Thalxemia, huh? What else has he kept from us?"

Dylan could only shake his head. "I don't know, man."

Tony had never felt this before. It was more than just having feelings for the girl in his arms. This was a need so rooted in him, it was all consuming. He felt his hatred for Alex burning so bright it overpowered the love. Tony didn't trust his sire anymore, and that was a pain he was not ready to contend with.

"Something's not right," Tony mumbled. "This is all wrong."

Dylan chewed his lip and tried to ignore the clench in his stomach that reminded him he hadn't fed. "She's a strong girl, Tony."

Tony lifted his eyes and forced a smile. "Get out of here, man. I know you're hungry."

"I can stay."

"No," Tony insisted. "Go eat. I'll stay here with her."

"Don't you need to eat too?"

"I'm older," said Tony simply. "I can go longer between feeds. Just leave, Dylan. Maybe she'll have woken up by the time you get back."

Dylan slowly slid off the bed and gave a reluctant nod. "I hope so. If you need me..."

"We'll be fine," Tony cut him off. "I've got it covered."

And he did. Alex wasn't the only one who withheld things from his brothers. Angela may have been Rick's witch, and she certainly came in handy over the past several months, but what Tony needed now was the advice of a vampire who had walked the Earth longer than even Rick had. And Tony knew just where to find him.

He held Sadie tight and flew as fast as he could, north toward Vancouver. Her color was getting better, but the grayish tinge to her skin was still present. It was a little after midnight when Tony reached the bottom of a steep hill surrounded by towering trees. Above him, high atop a cliff, was a three-story house with a sloping roof and large picture windows. The grey stone exterior was covered with climbing vines, and large gnarled oaks lined the property. The only part of the house Tony had ever entered was the greenhouse behind the main home. It housed hundreds of plants, each one coming from a different part of the world, and cared for by the vampire who was master of the house.

As Tony reached the top of the hill, he could see that all but a few windows were lit with an orange glow, and he could hear the chorus of laughter and music coming from inside. A multitude of expensive cars lined the pebbled driveway, and Tony had to weave in and out of a metal maze as he made his way to the front door.

Sadie's cheek was pressed against his chest while the lashes on her closed lids fluttered softly against the gusting cold wind. With his elbow he pressed the doorbell, not surprised when no one answered immediately. Even his vampire ears would have had a hard time hearing the chiming bell over the incessant roar of laughter and music. Tony hit the bell again and kicked his foot against the door until it finally opened.

A man he didn't recognize was smiling at him, eyeing the unconscious girl in his arms. "Is this dinner?" the man asked, his British accent thick and gravelly. He turned over his shoulder and called out, "Did someone order takeout?"

"I'm here to see James," Tony said, his grip on Sadie tightening to a point that, if she had been awake, would have been painful.

"Is he expecting you?"

"Tell him Tony is here."

The man gave a hearty laugh and said, "I'm no pigeon, boy. Tell him your damn self." He opened the door wider, allowing Tony entry.

When he stepped over the threshold, the overwhelming scent of evergreen and cinnamon struck him hard in the face. A pine tree that was nearly as tall as the ceiling was nestled in the corner of the room, covered in colorful tinsel and twinkling lights. Dozens of beautifully wrapped presents sat underneath it. Holly hung from the thick wooden columns that lined the hallway leading away from the front foyer all the way to the back of the house. Tony had completely forgotten about Christmas being just around the corner. Other than Rick's affinity for Halloween, the boys had left holidays and the human need to celebrate them behind.

A scattering of people dressed in tuxedos and glittering cocktail dresses left Tony feeling like one of the bums who hung out by the pier begging for change. It was the first time in a long time that Tony felt completely out of his element. Within the city limits of Brave Beach, he and his brothers were kings. But this wasn't Brave Beach, and Tony could tell by the glaring eyes peering at him from behind champagne flutes that he and his worn jeans weren't welcome there.

An old man with a balding head of white hair approached Tony, his body hunched over as he carried an empty silver tray in one hand. "Mr. McClennon is in the game room," the man said, pointing down the hall. "It's the last door on your left."

Tony adjusted Sadie in his arms before making his way down the hall, his sneakers a glaringly out of place distraction against the long oriental runner under his feet. It wasn't just vampires surrounding him in the house. There were humans, too, and Tony had the distinct feeling they knew what he was. He reached the last door on the left and let out a sigh of relief to find James sitting at the end of the table. The man who answered the front door was seated beside him.

"Well, hello, Tony," James said cheerfully, brown eyes fixing on Tony's face, his accent a mirror to the man from the door. "To what do I owe the pleasure?"

James was the oldest vampire Tony had ever met, and despite the baby face and elegant accent, Tony knew James was a powerful and terrifying force. They met seven years earlier, when Tony ventured north alone and made the mistake of feeding on a woman who turned out to be James's human companion.

Images of James's red eyes and long sharp fangs crowded Tony's memories, filling him up with a terror not even Rick could impose. Tony was never sure why James hadn't killed him, not just for murdering his companion, but for encroaching on his territory. Whatever the reason, James was fond of Tony and let him live. They had developed a friendship of sorts over the years, with James filling in all the gaps of knowledge Alex didn't share. If anyone could help Tony make sense of all that had happened, it was James.

"I need your help," Tony confessed. "We both do."

James looked at Sadie admiringly. "So, this is your childe, eh?"

Tony nodded.

"What did you do to her, mate?" the man from the front door asked as he reached for a pile of cards sitting on the center of the polished table.

"I didn't do anything. That's why I'm here."

James and the other man shared a knowing smile. "I would have won this round anyway," he laughed, then flicked his wrist and sent the cards in his hand flying toward the pile. They landed one at a time onto the deck like magic.

"Well, I fully intended to win the next," the man beside him huffed.

James rose from his seat, ran a hand through his mop of chestnut hair and turned his attention to Tony. "Let's go upstairs and take a look, shall we?" He looked at the man from the front door and said, "John? Fetch our guests some dinner."

"My pleasure."

Tony followed James up the wide staircase, his eyes drifting over the banister to watch as John approached two blonde women standing beside the fireplace. As one of the women laughed loudly at something he said, John let his eyes find Tony's. He shared a knowing smile before returning his attention to the blondes. John was an old vampire; Tony could sense that much. Maybe he was even older than Rick.

"In here," James said, stopping at a door near the end of the hall.

They stepped inside and Tony knew this must be James's bedroom. Candelabras littered every conceivable surface of polished furniture while thick red velvet drapes hung beside the French doors leading out to the terrace. A painting hung on the wall of a man dressed in silver and gold armor with a sword in one hand. Behind the figure, a stone castle took up most of the background. The face belonged to James, painted centuries earlier when he was a distinguished Duke in England.

"Lay her on the bed," said James.

Tony did as he was asked and brushed the hair away from Sadie's eyes. If only she would open them and assure him that she was okay. They could go back to Brave Beach together and forget about everything that happened.

James took off his suit jacket, loosened the tie around his neck, and unbuttoned his vest. The twinkling lights that hung off the balcony and decorated the large bay windows danced with shadows in the room. Rolling up the sleeves of his shirt, James stood next to Tony by the bed, both looking down at the seemingly dead girl lying before them.

"You've never been inside my house, have you?" asked James.

"No, I've only ever been in your greenhouse. I didn't think you wanted me in here."

James chuckled. "Oh, that's right. In all fairness, you did devour my Peggy."

"Can we focus on Sadie, please?" Tony wanted to get his questions answered then leave that house. As much as he liked James and enjoyed him being Tony's secret, being there was making him feel weak.

"Very well," James said, sitting down on the edge of the bed and leaning into Sadie's face. "How did this happen?"

"I left her with my packmate, and when I came back, she was like this. Alex said it's caused by Thalxemia. Is that a real thing?"

"It's definitely real," said James, and he sniffed at Sadie's lips. He leaned back and looked up at Tony. "But this girl is not a victim of Thalxemia. She's not even fed, Tony."

Tony felt his hands clench into fists. Alex lied to him. "Then what's wrong with her?"

"Someone has bled her."

"Fed on her?" Tony asked, everything coming together in his head. Alex had been after Sadie's blood from the beginning.

James shook his head. "She wasn't bitten. Whoever took her blood did it with a blade. If you look close enough you can see the scar." He pointed to the inside crook of Sadie's arm, but Tony saw nothing. "Your eyes are not as strong as mine," James said absently. "But trust me. It's there."

"Why would Alex or Oscar take her blood that way? She's a vampire, and they wouldn't have marked her. It doesn't make sense."

James rose to his feet and walked across the room. A bottle of red wine, infused with willingly donated blood, sat on a round table in the corner. He poured them both a glass. "I don't think they were the ones who bled her," James said, taking a sip. "This looks like the work of a witch."

"A witch?"

Tony's mind flashed on an image of Angela, spread out on her bed with that wicked smile, enticing him with her body while trying to convince him to give her some of Sadie's blood. He swallowed hard, his eyes burning as he tried to control his shift.

"Why would a witch want vampire blood? What could she do with it?"

"I've known many a witch in my day," said James with a smile of fond remembrance. "Blood working has always been a time-honored tradition in magic."

"What do they do with it?"

James moved away from the bed and stepped out onto the balcony with Tony following behind him. "A vampire's blood would keep them alive, wouldn't it? The same as it has kept me alive and you, as well. Only they use it in potions, manipulating the blood so that when they drink it, they remain technically human. They want their souls, you see. Even if it is dark and decayed as some witches are, they still can't let it go. You've given a witch your blood, haven't you? And she wanted your childe's, as well."

Tony thought about lying and denying James's accusations, but there wasn't a point. James was ancient and would see right inside Tony's relatively young immortal mind, then pick it apart as easily as the boys could do with humans. If he wanted help in saving Sadie, it was crucial James hear the entire story. So, Tony told him everything. Human Sadie able to block his advances, Alex tricking them all by giving her Tony's blood instead of Rick's, the spirits that manifested into his sight after he drank from her. He left out no detail and spoke for almost an hour until the entire story had been told.

When he was finished, they both stood in silence, the wind whipping at Tony's hair and blowing wayward strands around his eyes. He looked out over the steep hill to the black waters of the lake below. The enormity of everything pressed down on him and he felt the tears slipping down his cheeks before he could stop them. Brave Beach seemed so far away at that moment, and there was a part of him that didn't want to go back. He wanted to stay inside James's stately house on the top of a hill and not go back to that cold Victorian ever again.

"I gave the witch my blood," Tony said sadly. "If she wants our blood to keep herself alive, then why go through Alex to get Sadie's?" He paused, inhaled a deep breath, and said what he'd been thinking ever since James mentioned the word 'witch'. "Alex drank from Sadie. He went to Angela for the same reasons I did, and when I wouldn't give her Sadie's blood, Alex did." He dropped his head. It was a betrayal deeper than the ocean. Tony knew he should never forgive it, but, even as his anger boiled over, he knew he'd forgive Alex still.

In truth, Tony might be angrier with himself more than Alex. If only he had ignored Sadie that first night. Left her to Rick and gone on to be the demon he was. There were so many ways he should have played this game, but, in the end, wishing he had done things differently didn't change the present. Sadie was his and he was hers. And now she had been bled by a witch because he couldn't stand seeing Mary Ann and what he did to her. This happened because he was selfish and weak.

The sky was darkening, and thick clouds were rolling in from the west. Tony could smell the storm. The air was already damp with approaching rain. He glanced back over his shoulder at Sadie asleep on the bed, flames from the candles casting shadows across her sleeping face.

"You're asking yourself the wrong questions," James said. "And that is why the answers you find leave you unsatisfied."

"I really can't deal with your philosophy and pomp right now, James. Just tell me what you know. Tell me what to do for her."

Deep knowledge stared at him from behind James's eyes, and Tony was desperate to know everything. Tony had been alive and on the Earth for a hundred years, but he still knew nothing about who and what he really was. It was so unfair of Alex to slip his blood into the wine bottle and feed it to Sadie. Not just unfair to Tony but unfair to her. She deserved better than him, better than their pack of wild hellions. She deserved someone like James who could teach her the ways without killing everything that made her Sadie.

"Haven't you asked yourself what it is about Sadie that makes her so special? Don't you want to know why this witch hungers for her blood so badly?"

"Something about her brings spirits into our line of sight," Tony said. "That's what is special about her. And when we drank from her, we somehow can see them too. I don't know why Angela wants Sadie's blood. Maybe because Sadie is different from us, and Angela is a collector of the unusual."

"The question you aren't asking is why does Sadie see spirits? What is inside her that allows her to see the souls of others only when she is hovering in technical death?"

"I don't know," Tony huffed, getting frustrated with James for not just spitting it out. He focused on the lake's white caps. The storm was getting closer.

"When you drank the blood, you gave up the humanity you had always known. You parted with your soul, your conscience. It is unnatural and goes against the laws of nature for those like us to carry a soul within. But after you drank Sadie's blood, you felt it, didn't you?

Those feelings of guilt, sorrow, empathy, and love. The feelings you left behind when Alex's blood became a part of you."

"What are you saying?"

"Sadie's soul is intact. It never left her. That is why she can see the souls of others. And when you drank from her, you took part of her into you, as did Alex."

"It's not possible," Tony said, shaking his head. "Our souls die inside us the moment we drink the blood. It's just the way it is. Even Rick told us that much."

"You wanted to know why she is special, and now you do. Why does she feed alone, away from you and the others?" He waited for Tony to answer, and when he didn't, James answered for him. "Because she feeds on evil, it is the only thing her soul will allow."

"This is crazy," Tony whispered.

It all seemed so impossible, but Tony knew they were creatures who lived in a realm of impossibility. They were nightmares come to life, fairytales written in shadows, and yet he was very real. Of course, when he really thought about it and dissected the last months, it all made sense. It was why Sadie's turning had been so frightening and painful. His blood tried to kill her soul, but it fought at every inch to hang on. She was the reason he started to experience the emotions he hadn't felt since he was human. Part of Sadie's soul was inside him, and as he stood on the terrace and felt the first spray of cold rain against his face, Tony could feel that part of her stirring within him.

"And Angela?" Tony asked, swallowing down the pain. "Why does she want Sadie's blood?"

"I can only speculate."

"Then speculate," said Tony. "You're probably right anyway."

"Yes, I probably am." He turned and went back inside, with Tony following. James lit a fire in the stone fireplace, and Tony felt the warmth of the flames fill up the room even as the cold night air blew in through the open terrace doors. They each took a seat on chairs next to the hearth. James was still sipping at his wine while Tony fidgeted in his seat, glancing back at Sadie occasionally, half expecting her to suddenly sit up and ask where they were.

"I've known many witches in my years. Most of them are lovely men and women, secure in the magic they call upon themselves. They are happy to be a mortal in a world where immortality can be obtained. But there are others who desperately want our power, which over time, will always be greater than theirs. At some point, a witch is as powerful as she will ever be, but vampires grow in both power and knowledge with every year that passes. Why, just look at me. As powerful as I am, I'll only become more so as time goes on."

Tony only nodded. He didn't know what to say. On one hand, it was a comfort to know that, eventually, Tony would be more powerful than Angela and killing her would be a possibility. However, he wasn't sure Sadie had much time when it came to the witch and Alex. If Angela had given Alex the same potion she gave him, it would wear off and his sire would always need more. He knew Alex well enough to know that if he had gone to Angela, there were some souls he couldn't face for eternity. Just like Tony and Mary Ann. So, he would always need more of Angela's elixir, and she would always want more of Sadie's blood.

"What do you think she's hoping to achieve with Sadie's blood?" he asked.

"I believe your witch wants to drink Sadie and absorb not only the vampire but the soul that still dwells within her. It is this witch's greatest desire and yet never attainable. Or at least it wasn't until your darling came along."

"So, why doesn't she just drink the blood she took from Sadie already? If what you say is correct, then whoever drinks from Sadie takes a part of her soul."

"She's most likely testing her theory. Making sure Sadie is what she thinks she is. And after she concludes that your childe is a vampire with a soul, she'll take the rest."

"The rest of what?"

"Her blood, Tony. If the witch is going to have a soul and be an immortal, she'll need all the soul. Not just a piece like you and Alex carry."

Tony stood up so quickly it knocked his chair back. He turned to Sadie and then back to James, his chest heaving. Angela would kill Sadie. That was the only possible outcome if what James hypothesized was true. Draining Sadie would kill her, and he wasn't strong enough to protect her from Angela's magic. None of his pack could. Maybe even Rick wasn't old or strong enough to keep her safe. There was only one vampire who could protect Sadie and dispatch Angela. James.

"You know what I want to ask you," Tony said. "Don't you?"

James nodded.

"Will you do it? Will you kill this witch to save my childe?"

James looked down at the wine glass in his hand, swishing the liquid inside it before inhaling deeply. Then he took a long, slow sip and closed his eyes as though relishing each drop of bitterness on his tongue. Finally, he looked back up at Tony. "And if I do? What will you give me?"

"What do you want?" Tony's eyes looked around the room. The Oriental rugs, the silver tea service, and the glittering chandelier hanging above his head told him that there was nothing he could ever give James that wasn't something he already had. "I don't have anything, James. I'm just a vampire living in a rotting Victorian in the woods."

"You beautiful boy," James said with an admiring smile. "Still too young to understand how precious his dark world truly is." He set the wine glass aside and leaned forward so that his elbows were resting on his knees. "There is something you have that I would very much like. You're asking me to fight a powerful witch. Even if I can defeat her, it won't be easy."

"What is it? Whatever it is, it's yours. Just get rid of her. Make Sadie safe."

"I've sired many children, Tony. The man you met downstairs, John, he's mine. A little devil, much like your sire I imagine. But I love him. You understand that love now, don't you? Look how far you've already gone to protect it."

Tony could feel that stirring inside him again, the piece of Sadie that danced around to the melodic rhythm of James's voice. "I feel it, and I understand it," he finally said. He dropped his head and when the tears started to fall, he did nothing to hide them. "And I know what you want. You want Sadie."

James stood up and met Tony in front of the fireplace. He placed his hands on the young vampire's shoulders and gave a gentle squeeze. "She is special, my boy. Far too special to be raised by one as young and inexperienced as yourself."

"I can't," Tony said, wiping his eyes and looking back at her. "I need her."

"You need to grow, to learn. You'll never be good for her or any childe until you do. If you release her to me, you'll be releasing that tiny piece of her soul that lives inside you. Those spirits will go with her, and you'll be free."

"I let her go before," Tony said. "And I still saw them."

James gave him a soft smile. "You didn't mean it, Tony. You never really released her at all."

"No," Tony yelled, pushing his hands into James's chest and barely making the older vampire move. "You can't have her! She's my childe."

"And what kind of life will she have if you keep her in that house? You'll always be looking over your shoulder, wondering if Alex will go behind your back and taste her again… or worse. Killing this witch may save her life, Tony, but staying with you will keep her from ever really living it."

Tony turned his back on James and hurried to the bed. He scooped Sadie into his arms and held her close, ready to bolt. When he looked back at James, he was expecting to see that red stare, the older, stronger vampire prepared to take what belonged to Tony alone. But he only stood there watching Tony with understanding eyes.

After a few terrible moments of silence, Tony said, "I don't know if I can go on without her. I'm a part of her." He looked down at her sleeping face. "And she's a part of me."

James was right. Deep down Tony knew Sadie was never meant for their decaying house or the bloody night they inhabited. She wasn't meant for Rick's bunker either. Always hiding, alone, afraid to be the creature they damned her to be. Tony was no good for Sadie, no matter how much he wanted to be.

"You gave her life eternal, Tony. Nothing will change that. I will let her be the vampire she is and teach her how to live in this world with her soul. I swear to you, I only want to give your childe a chance at eternal happiness. Isn't that what you want for her too?"

Tony stared into James's eyes and knew everything he said was true. There was a time when James was like Tony, like Alex, cruel, hungry for the debauchery of night. He had grown, both in power and wisdom, and James understood Sadie in ways Tony was not ready to. To make up for all the horrible wrongs he perpetrated, there was only one way for him to make things even a little right for her.

Slowly, he laid Sadie back on the bed and leaned forward to press his lips to hers. He imagined that tiny part of her soul that was locked inside him reaching out to her, longing to be whole again. Doing this would return to Sadie what he had no right to take.

"Can I stay here tonight? I need to think about what comes after."

"You're welcome to stay, Tony."

Tony gave a curt nod and climbed into the bed beside her. "I'll do it," he promised. "Tomorrow night, I'll say goodbye."

"Very well. The witch won't be a threat to you or anyone after that. I know it doesn't feel like it, Tony, but you're making the best decision you can for her. You're being the sire you were meant to be."

Tony pulled her close and closed his eyes, waiting for the sun.

Chapter Twenty-Nine

Sadie opened her eyes and somehow knew exactly where she was. It was so strange. She knew she was in Vancouver, lying on a bed in a house that belonged to a vampire named James. Tony left her there because she was ill. But why did he leave her there?

She sat up slowly, clutching her stomach as a hunger pang, like the ones she experienced after her turn, rolled through her. When was the last time she fed? Sadie couldn't remember. As the pain subsided, she threw her legs over the side of the bed and made her way toward the door.

She stepped out into the hall wanting to find James, still unsure how she even knew him. The house was big, too big in her opinion, and it felt empty. There was a chill that settled over her despite the warmth in the air. Sadie moved down the stairs, her hand sliding along the polished banister as she kept eyes on her surroundings.

Sadie was frightened, but somehow still completely calm. She had no idea what any of it meant, but she kept moving forward with determination to find answers. She reached the end of the stairs, took a right, and entered the first door she came upon. Inside was a library that made Rick's look amateur. The walls were nearly twenty feet high, and each space was filled in with a book. A smile overtook her face. There were several ornate desks and a few velvet couches with a full bar sitting against the farthest wall. A slight noise behind her caused her to turn sharply, ready to flee or fight, but she felt peace wash over her when her gaze settled on James's face.

"I thought you might be hungry," he said, holding out a wine glass. Sadie could smell the blood and salivated. "It comes from a willing donor, I assure you," he added with a smile.

"How do you know they were willing?"

A voice behind her laughed and said, "Because it came from the hospital's blood supply, love."

She turned sharply and saw a man sitting on one of the black couches, a book in one hand and a coffee mug in the other. He smiled and then winked at her. She didn't know how she knew his name was John, but it flashed in her mind like a neon sign.

"We have a connection there," James said gently. "They brought it over earlier."

Sadie reached for the glass and downed it in two gulps. It was not satisfying but was a good start. She handed the glass back to James and wiped her mouth with the back of her hand. "Do you get your blood from them a lot?"

"Heavens no," John cackled. "Why would you order hamburger when you can have Kobe Steak?" He dropped the book he was reading onto the couch and lifted his mug to her in a toast.

"Get out of here," James said, unable to suppress his smile. "Let me talk to our guest."

John set his mug on the little antique table. He stood up and stretched his arms above his head with an exaggerated sigh. He was wearing a grey suit and tie, just like James. Sadie wondered if they were going somewhere. She looked down at her worn jeans and dirty sweater, feeling immediately out of place.

"See you around," John said as he passed her, bowing his head and looking at her with sharp hazel eyes. "Sister."

"Go," James said, and this time there was no hint of a smile.

After John was gone and the door closed, James pointed to one of the sofas. "Shall we have a seat? I'm sure there are a lot of questions swimming around in your head, and I am more than happy to answer them."

"Okay," she said, shifting her body awkwardly. "Is it okay if we talk out there?"

She pointed to the open double doors that led out to the gated patio. Sadie was feeling claustrophobic in that room, even if it was the size of the Victorian's parlor and foyer combined. She needed the fresh air to help her balance, to clear her mind as she struggled to understand all the scenarios buzzing inside her head.

"Certainly," James said. "I'll just have Martin bring you another drink."

He opened the library door and called out to an old man who appeared moments later with another glass of kindly donated blood. He handed it to Sadie then led her out to the patio where white glittering lights were strung across the iron gate, twinkling against the night like stars.

Sadie sat down in one of the iron-backed chairs that surrounded a tile-topped garden table. James sat next to her and reached into his jacket's inner pocket for a cigar. "Do you mind?" he asked. She shook her head no, and he lit it like an old man would, not the young twenty-something he appeared to be.

"How is it that I know who you are?" she asked, not even scrambling for an icebreaker. There wasn't a point anyway. She had a million questions, and somehow, she knew this English gentleman had all the answers. "We've never met, right?"

He blew a thick cloud of grey smoke into the air and shook his head. "No, we've never met. While you were sleeping, I implemented my thoughts, gave you the backstory of why you were waking up in a strange house with even stranger vampires. I thought it would soften the blow."

"It did," she said with gratitude. "How did you do it? No other vampire has been able to get in my head."

James smiled. "Eventually, with many centuries behind them, they would have at least found a way to share the past. It takes much time to learn the dark gifts. Lucky for our kind, time is abundant."

"How old are you?"

"Old," he chuckled, then added, "Very, very old."

"The man in the library, you're his sire, right?"

"Oh yes," he said with a tender smile. "John is mine. Nearly as old as I am, but not quite." He took another puff off his cigar and sat back in his chair. "He's always been a cheeky little devil. Maybe that was what drew me to him. There was something spritely about him always, even when he was living in my dungeons and cleaning my piss pot every night." He saw the confusion in Sadie's eyes. "I was a duke," he said. "And after my father died, I was in line for a throne. I had already partaken of the dark blood, and when it was time to pass the title to my brother and pretend to die, I knew I wanted to take John with me."

"Pretend to die?" she asked.

"I wasn't going to age, and I knew it. My sire was very old but ready to go into whatever waits for those like us. So, I learned everything from old scrolls and tall tales. My face wasn't changing, you see, it remained as youthful as it was when I took my father's title. I knew enough to know that we must move on in order to survive."

"Move on?"

"My darling girl, surely your sire told you that we can't stay in one spot forever or else our secret would eventually be known. Tell me, when did Rick open his pub?"

Sadie thought about it. "Maybe ten years ago. It was before I moved to Brave Beach."

"Rick," James said with a shake of his head. "We all know him. Not all of us like him, as his desire to mix among mortals is generally frowned upon. And yet, I have always admired him. The way he clings to the human world and wants so much to be a part of it and all the changes it endures. It won't be long before Rick moves on as well. Did you imagine Brave Beach would be your home forever?"

"I don't know what I thought about the future," Sadie told him. "I'm only just beginning to realize my world never has an end."

"Soon a year will feel like a minute, and later, many years from now, they will feel like seconds. Time will cease for you, Sadie. There will be no measurement of your years. You will simply exist, like the rain and the waves."

Sadie felt like she wanted to cry, and it took her a few moments to realize she felt that way because she was missing Tony. And although she could feel he was close, there seemed to be a distance between them that wasn't there before.

"Why did he bring me to you?"

"What do you remember about the night he left you with Oscar?" James asked, lifting his chin and letting his warm gaze settle over her completely.

"I don't remember anything," she said. It was like all her memories from that night had been wiped clean and she was a blank slate. "I only remember coming down the stairs and seeing Oscar sitting next to the fireplace."

"Do you want me to tell you? Tony will be here soon, and he'll tell you if that's what you want."

Sadie felt a surge of relief that Tony was coming back for her. But for some reason, she didn't want to hear the story from him. She wanted James to tell her. Was it because his voice was so calm, his eyes so gentle and kind? Or was it because a part of her was afraid Tony would never tell her the whole truth?

"Will you tell me?"

"It was a witch that ensnared Rick. She then got her claws into Tony and Alex. That's not to say they didn't go to her themselves. It was weakness and fear of what you gave them, Sadie. It wasn't a gift to them, a gift so many of us would do anything to have. It's important you know that they didn't know what you are, or what you gave them. This witch is crueler and more evil than any vampire I've ever known. Because we don't steal souls, Sadie. We set them free. That's not what this witch wanted."

"I have no idea who you're talking about. What witch?" Sadie set her glass on the table and rubbed at her temples. Nothing was making sense, and she desperately needed it to. She was breaking, crumbling like the rocks on the same cliff that took Mary Ann.

"While you were sleeping, I went and found this witch myself, to see what we were up against. There were things I didn't understand, like why your sister and your friend were haunting you with such cruel intentions. Why didn't they go on? Why hadn't all the souls moved on?"

"Keep talking. Why did they stay? Why are they all still here?"

"I looked inside the witch's mind while I watched through her window. Do you remember the night you went to Rick's house seeking advice? Your friend, Hayden, told you she saw vampires, and you went to him only to discover she was right all along."

"Of course I remember," Sadie said, though the truth was she nearly forgot that night until James brought it up. Her human memories were already fading.

"Then you remember the woman that was there. Angela was her name."

Sadie's eyes lit up with remembrance. "Yes. She had blonde hair, and she looked at me so strange."

"She knew what Rick was planning. And she felt something different about you. I don't think she knew then what it was, or what the dark blood would do to you. Once you were turned, she used her magic to draw your sister, your friend, and all the people your pack had taken, and brought them forward. It was her magic that stole their souls from the natural progression of this life to the next and made them so keen on destroying you."

"Why would she do that?"

"It was because she needed you. Whether it meant one of your pack took you to her or you gave up yourself, she wanted your blood. You see, you would have seen them Sadie, the souls I mean. But it would have been different if she hadn't worked her magic the way she did. You would have found one another, but only in passing. They can dive between our world and theirs, showing themselves when they want. But only to someone like you, darling. She stole their rightful, peaceful hereafter and dragged them into a waking hell."

Sadie sat forward in her seat and without thinking reached for James's hand and gripped it tight. "Do you know why I'm different? Why I'm not like them?"

A familiar voice spoke behind her. "Because you have your soul."

Sadie turned and ran at Tony, flinging her arms around his neck and crying into it. She hadn't even heard what he said, she was so overwhelmed with relief to see him. "Tony," she breathed against his ear. "You're here."

"I'll just leave the two of you alone," James said, rising from his seat and giving Tony a look of understanding. "When you are ready, you only need to call for me."

Tony gave a soft nod over Sadie's shoulder. When she pulled away from him, she was smiling, but the smile faded as she absorbed the look in his eyes.

"What is wrong?" she asked, her voice feather soft.

Tony took a breath. It was much harder than he imagined it would be. He had come to say goodbye, to release her to James. He knew that when he left that house on the hill, it would be the end of all the chaos that swarmed into his life when she did. The only way he knew how to explain what was coming was to start at the beginning and explain it all. When he finished telling her everything, Alex's deception and drinking from her, Tony being confronted by Mary Ann, ending with seeking help from Angela, his childe only stared at him with wide eyes. After several minutes, Tony couldn't stand the silence anymore.

"Say something, Sadie."

She turned her back on him, hand covering her mouth to stifle the sobs. "He drank from me," she said. "And they knew." Dylan, her friend, was there. He helped Alex hide his violation of her.

"They didn't know you," Tony said. "If Dylan could go back and change it, he would."

She turned to him. "And you? If you could go back to that night we met, would you kill me?"

"No," he said honestly. "I used to think I would, but not now. Not after everything."

Sadie's teary eyes focused on his face. "So, James is going to kill the witch that took my blood? The witch whose bed you've been in, and Alex... Well, she showed him, didn't she?"

"James is the only one strong enough to end her."

"And then what? We go back to the house, and you expect me to forgive Alex? Do you want me to forgive Dylan and Oscar, too?" She took a deep breath and said, "Am I supposed to forgive you?"

Tony dropped his eyes and shook his head. "No," he said softly. "How can you?"

Suddenly she was next to him, drawing him into her arms. "Because I'm yours," she breathed against his ear. "And you're mine. Forever."

Tony was washed with relief, but it lasted only a moment, and then he was holding her back to look in her eyes. "We can't do this anymore, Sadie. You're too special for me. You deserve better."

She laughed a little and shook her head. "No, I don't."

"Yes, you do. I wanted to be a good sire, Sadie. Once I knew you were mine it's all I wanted. I fucked everything up, and I can't change that. But I can make it right."

She stood there, the lights from the gate twinkling in her eyes as she watched him. Sadie wanted to understand him, and she wanted Tony to understand her. As she looked at him, she was reminded of that first moment she saw him, of how those sweet droopy eyes looked right through her and made her feel alive in ways no one ever had. It didn't matter, all those terrible things that happened between them before. All that mattered was James, and he was going to rid them of the witch, and they would have the chance to start over. She would learn to live with Alex, learn to forgive the vampire he couldn't help but be. Time would give her the tools needed to adapt to their life, and eventually, she would learn to be like them. Then it hit her, realization slapped her in the face. How had she not seen it before?

"You're here to let me go. Aren't you?"

Tony didn't answer. He held her gaze and tried not to lose the tears he could feel stinging his eyes. That little piece of Sadie's soul that slept inside him was stirring. He reached for her, but she snatched her hand away and Tony felt like she had staked him. He needed her to understand, to feel how hard it was for him to be standing there, knowing that it would be the last time.

"I thought James was going to tell you."

"Is that why I am here, Tony? So you can release me to him? To someone I don't even know."

"It's not like that. James is ancient, he knows things I don't. He can help you. He'll be good to you."

She took a step back. "If you want me gone, then do it, but leave me to myself, not to him."

"I can't, Sadie," he said as gently as he could. "If I do that, you'll stay here. You won't leave, and you have to leave. It's the only way I know you'll ever really live."

"Then to Rick," she pleaded. Her body shook, the soul she still clung to knew what it needed, and it was fighting the vampire who could only focus on what it wanted. "Release me to Rick."

"No," he said. "It has to be this way. I wish I could be better for you but look at what I've already done. Angela wants to kill you. Alex nearly drained you. And even though I know that, I also know I'll never leave him."

"I know that," she said. "I know what he means to you, what they mean to you, and I promise I'll accept that. I won't ever make you choose."

He kissed her hand that he was now holding. "I know you won't. That's the problem."

"Why are you doing this to me?"

"Because that part of you that I took inside myself when I tasted your blood, it made me realize something. I love you, Sadie. But I also know that when you're no longer in here," he said, touching his chest, "I'll lose that, because you and I are different. You'll never be like us no matter how hard you try. And I'm not so much of a monster that I would make you live forever ignoring who you are just because I know how much it will hurt to lose you."

"All this time I thought it was somehow going to work out. I had forgiven you and Rick for doing this to me. I thought that forgiveness would be enough."

"I wish it was," he said.

"I won't say goodbye to you now," she said firmly.

"Angela is on your tail, she's looking for you. James will do this for us, but you have to understand that after she's gone, he'll be your teacher, not me."

"All right," she said, surprising him. "But I'm not saying goodbye." She moved past him and straight to the patio doors.

"Sadie! Don't end it like this."

She paused in the open doorway and looked back at him. "I'm not," she promised. "I trusted you through everything. Now you trust me."

Tony could only watch as she disappeared inside the house. His mind was crowded with regret and sadness. He imagined the years she would now spend with James, somewhere far from the West Coast of the United States, and it tore him apart. He thought of his sire, of his brothers back in the house. They had always been there for him. They were alike, and even as he mourned Sadie's absence, he knew letting her go was the right choice to make. As he walked down the sloping hill away from James's house, he heard the shuffle of footsteps behind him. When he looked back, James was trotting after him.

"I tried," Tony said before James could speak. "I never actually got to say the words. Will it work if I just say them to you?"

"It would work," said James. "But it's not necessary. I'm leaving for Seattle now. I suggest you stay here. She's waiting for you upstairs."

"What does she want?"

"To have a final night with you," he said.

Tony looked up at the house and caught a glimpse of Sadie standing on the terrace looking down on him. When he looked at where James was standing, he was gone. Part of Tony wanted to fly back to Brave Beach, to seek the comfort of his pack. Instead, he started back up the hill toward the house, knowing this would be his last night as a sire. This was the last night he had to feel the love. When the sun set the next night, that love would disappear right along with it.

CHAPTER THIRTY

Tony flew to the balcony and waited there for several minutes before stepping into the bedroom to find Sadie standing beside the fireplace. She turned over her shoulder and met his eyes.

"We should have that first date now," she said.

"What are you talking about?"

"Our first date," she repeated, turning to face him completely. "The one Kevin interrupted that night. We never really did get to have it."

Tony dropped his eyes, not wanting to look at her and be reminded of what he had done, but before he knew it, he was looking at her again. "What do you want to do, Sadie?"

A smile pulled at the corner of her mouth, and she shrugged her shoulders. "I don't know. We can't really do what we would have done when I was human. What do vampires do, Tony?"

"I wish I could make you understand," he said, that part of her inside him pulling hard. "I'm trying to give you a second chance. You can have a good life with James, a life as close to human as you want. I know that's what you want, Sadie. You want to be that girl again. The one I destroyed."

"I don't know that girl anymore."

He reached out and pressed his palm against her chest, above the spot where the beat of her heart once called to him. "She's in there. And the rest of her is in me, in Alex." Saying his sire's name made his body tense. He hated the thought of what Alex had done. What he would have kept doing if Tony hadn't made this choice to let her go. "I'm giving her back to you."

Her eyes blazed. "And what about what I want? Does that even matter to you?"

"You think you want this," he told her, reaching for her arm to pull her close when she tried to walk away. "But you don't. You're not like us, and you know it. Being with my pack will kill you, Sadie."

"I'm already dead."

He shook his head hard. "No, you're not."

Elongated seconds of silence erupted around them. Tony was seeing her, really seeing her, for the first time. When she narrowed her eyes at him, full lips pouting down, it was like he was meeting someone he only ever dreamed about. She was angry at him, not because he was releasing her to James, but because he wasn't giving her a choice. He turned her without consent, and now he was abandoning her without it, too.

"You don't want James as a teacher?" he asked. She shook her head softly, her eyes glassy with tears. "You want to stay with me?" She surprised him when she shook her head again. "I don't understand, Sadie."

"I don't want to live forever," she said, her voice so soft it barely rose above the wind outside. "I don't want to kill people, Tony. Even the bad ones. Every kill leaves me broken. I want you to really let me go."

He took a step back from her, his body trembling under the weight of her words. "You want to die," he said, still not believing it was true.

"Yes." She clutched her hands under her chin. "I want to go on. You said I still have part of my soul, and that when you release me, I'll have it all. There's nothing for me to fear in death, but there is so much for me to fear in this life."

He could only stare at her. The girl he killed was dead, and the woman Sadie had become was living and pleading with him to make all the horrible things he'd done to her right again. "I don't know if I can."

"You're being selfish," she said sternly. "That's what death has turned you into. You don't want me to choose this, because you don't want to live forever with knowing I did. You're weak, Tony."

She saw the anger flash in his eyes, knew her words were poking the sleeping monster inside him and prodding it to the surface. His eyes began to scorch with the familiar golden glow, but so did hers. She was like him, in ways he didn't even know.

He made to turn his back on her, but she grabbed his arm, nails digging into his flesh. "No," she said, the tips of her fangs visible as she spoke. "Why should it be so easy for you? It was easy to take my life, but now, when it's not so easy to give it back, you try to run away. Well, I won't let you, Tony. You owe me."

He held her stare, felt the tears on his cheeks, and before he knew what was happening, he was clutching the back of her head and holding her lips to his. She clung to him, pulling him closer as their tongues met in that oh-so-familiar dance. When she pulled back, he could hear her words in his head. *Release me. Please.*

"Not yet," he begged.

If he released her now, her soul would be complete, and that part of her that had given him the ability to feel and love again, would disappear with her. He wanted to keep that feeling, the love, just a little bit longer. Just long enough for him to be hers one last time.

“Say it,” she said, her plea gut-wrenching. “Say it now, while you’re strong enough to mean it.”

His lips trembled as he tried to force the words. She put her hands on either side of his face and stared into his eyes. He understood. He loved her because she was real, and for a while, she had been his.

"I release you," his voice shaking as he said the words. She bore her gaze deeper inside him. "I release you," he said again, his voice stronger, more powerful. "I release you!"

They both felt it. The jolt inside him as her soul stirred and began to burrow through him to find its way back home to her. She pressed her lips to him and kissed him hard, drinking in his taste and imploring him to do the same. Tony still felt it. The love.

"You were everything," he said, his eyes on hers, watching as the amber faded into blue. “Nothing will ever be the same without you.”

She smiled softly. “I’ll always be with you, Tony. Remember, they’re just words. You’re releasing me, but I will never let go of you.”

His hands moved to the hem of her T-shirt, and she lifted her arms obediently so he could slip it over her head. Tony skimmed his fingers up her side, her cold skin feeling just a little warmer. He unbuttoned her jeans, drew the zipper slowly, and waited as she pushed them down her hips. Sadie smiled at him as she began to undress him, until the only thing standing between them was air.

Tony leaned her back onto the bed and pressed his body against hers. She found his hands just above her head and linked her fingers with his. He kissed her again, slowly at first and then harder.

"Stay with me," he whispered.

"I'm here right now," she told him.

Tony dropped his face into the crook of her neck and wondered for a moment if he shouldn't sink his fangs into her flesh, to steal back that part he had just given back. Then he felt her squeeze his hand tight. It was still there. The love.

It was a feeling that pulled Tony from his death sleep. A feeling so sharp and painful that he woke up screaming. He sat up with a jolt and looked across the room at the dancing flames in the fireplace. The room felt alien and cold, such a contrast to how it felt hours before. Tony reached beside him and panic set in as he realized the space next to him was empty.

"Sadie?"

He could still smell her. His eyes looked at the French doors leading to the balcony. They were closed and the curtains drawn, but he could see the early morning sun filtering through a crack between the drapes.

For a moment he could only sit there staring at the sliver of light that touched the carpet. "Sadie," he said, almost whispering her name. Then he said it again, a little louder, and again, louder still. Then he wasn't saying her name anymore. He was screaming it. "Sadie!" Tony pushed the covers off his body and hurried off the bed. He had only taken a couple of steps toward the light when a voice stopped him.

"No, Tony," James's voice came from the east corner of the room, his body hidden in shadows. "She is already gone."

Tony searched for James in the dark. "You knew," he accused, his voice breaking under the reality that she was really and truly gone. "You knew what was going to happen. How this was all going to end, didn't you?"

"Of course, I knew," said James gently. "She was never meant for this life, Tony. I know it, you know it, and so did she."

"You never intended to be her teacher. You wanted me to release her so she could die. How could you do that, James? She was mine! Sadie was the only thing that mattered anymore. And you took her from me."

“I did what she wanted. It wasn’t fair, Tony. The blood is a gift. It was never meant to be a life sentence for those that don’t want the darkness. Keeping her in our world was no different than the witch keeping the souls tethered to all of you. She is free now, and in the light where she always belonged.”

For a moment, all Tony could do was stare at James with tear-filled eyes. Sadie’s scent, her voice, and touch, it was all still so present. He shook his head and grabbed at his hair. "Why do I still feel it?" he groaned, then dropped to his knees with an agonizing howl. "Why do I still feel the love?"

James emerged from the shadows and knelt next to him. "Because even the damned can love, Tony. And now you know it."

Tony lifted his eyes to James and wished so deeply that he could stay there forever. That he would never have to go back to the house, even as he longed for his sire’s comfort. The awful feeling that jolted him awake was slowly fading, but the remnants of that hurt lingered. He wondered if it always would.

"Was she in pain?" he asked.

"It was quite quick," James promised. "She was ready."

"Angela?"

"She's gone." James reached into his suit jacket and pulled out an envelope. "Sadie left this for Rick."

Tony took the envelope from James's hand and ran his finger over the name written on it. He felt deeply for Rick then. Knew that right now the man who sired their line was crouching in the darkness and crying for the daughter he wanted so badly.

“And she left this for you,” said James. He opened his hand so that Tony could see the ankh pendant and gold chain he gave Sadie. The one that once belonged to the sister Alex took from her. He couldn’t help but wonder if they found each other in whatever place Sadie lived now. Tony hoped they had.

He looked at it then back at James. "How am I going to do it?" he asked softly. "How am I going to live forever without her?"

James brushed his hand over Tony's head and pulled him in so he could kiss his forehead. Then he dropped the necklace into Tony's open palm. "It will take time. You won't forget her, not even as centuries go by. Her memory, well, it lives inside you. She'll always be there. You were hers, and even death cannot erase that from the history books."

Tony could feel himself fading. The sun was rising higher in the sky and pulling him back to slumber. James was so old that it would be hours before he would have to retire to sleep. So, he let Tony fall into his arms and held him until he could hold him no longer.

Tony stood at the bottom of the hill and looked up at the house he called home. The house where Sadie was reborn. He could feel his brothers inside and knew they felt him, too. Seconds later Alex ran through the front door and down the hill until he skidded to a stop in front of his childe. They stared at one another until Alex could stand the silence no longer.

"I'm sorry," he muttered.

Tony looked away, swallowed back tears, and then shrugged his shoulders. "It wasn't meant to be."

"If I could go back and change things, I would," said Alex. "Do you believe me?"

Tony looked at him and decided truth was the only answer. "I don't know, Alex."

"You're my childe, and I did a terrible thing to you. I know I'm a bastard, I always will be. But I never wanted to hurt you, Tony."

"That I believe," Tony said. "I know what it feels like now. Because from the moment she turned, all I felt was love for her. The same love Rick has for you, and you have for us."

Alex flinched a little as Tony said the word 'love'. It was such a foreign concept to him now, a feeling he didn't believe he could possess.

Tony laughed a little under his breath. "You don't have to say it, Alex. I know the bastard you are won't let you. But we can love. We can love the creatures that we are and the ones we'll become."

"I felt it, you know. When she stepped into the sun, I felt it. She wasn't mine, but she was our blood." Alex stepped forward and placed his hand on Tony's shoulder. "I don't ever want to feel that again. Do you hear what I'm saying?"

Tony knew exactly what Alex was saying. He was saying, 'I love you.'

"Let's go," Alex said, nodding back toward the house. "Come see Oscar and Dylan. Then we'll go to the strip for dinner. It'll be like the old days."

"Not tonight, Alex."

"You have to eat."

Tony nodded his head. "And I will. But for now, I need to be alone."

"Why do I get the feeling that 'now' is going to be a very long time?"

"It won't be," Tony assured. "Just tonight."

"Whatever you need." Alex gave Tony's shoulder one last squeeze then made his way back to the house. Tony walked down the hill toward the beach below the cliffs. The moon was high and bright in the sky, dapples of shimmering moonlight danced on the water's surface. He was going to miss her, and Tony knew it would take years, maybe centuries, until he would be the vampire he was before Sadie came into his life.

Later, he would go into town alone and give Rick Sadie's letter. He knew that Alex feared how Rick would see him now that she was gone. Tony knew it might take time, but Rick would always cherish Alex, more than anything. That was a sire's love.

And as the days moved forward, he would ride the shadows with his brothers and feed off human blood like he always had. No, Sadie was not meant for this life, but Tony was born for it.

He stood there for a few more minutes and watched the waves roll in. Suddenly, a shiver moved through him. The call of someone connected to his blood. He turned around and looked up at the bluff. His whole body went stiff as he saw the figure standing on the point, bathed in moonlight and looking down on him with a smile.

"Sadie," he whispered.

A feeling of elation moved through him. She was just as beautiful as always, but there was something different about her now. The way she shimmered under the white glare of the moon, and the way he saw clouds right through her. He wanted to run to her, but his feet were frozen to the spot.

"Sadie!" He screamed her name, and she responded with only a smile.

The wind blew hair over his eyes, and he pushed it away quickly. When he looked back at the bluff she was gone. But it was still there, buried deep inside him.

The love.

THE END

RECOGNITION

This book would not have been possible if not for the following people.

Maria, who donated her own time and resources to making my dream come true.

Julie, Dani, and Caitlin, who always hyped me up and never let me give up.

My Sissy, who has always encouraged me to pursue this dream.

My children, Camron and Courtney who inspire me every day.

Sarah Coronado James, my amazing editor, who donated her time freely and

helped this book become what it is.

My extended family and friends. You sure know how to make a girl feel loved.

And that is beyond measure.

xoxo Stephanie

Made in the USA
Coppell, TX
05 March 2026

72985526R00229